KRAKENBLOOD

KRAKENBLOOD

MARC COLLINS

BLACK LIBRARY

A BLACK LIBRARY PUBLICATION

First published in 2025.
This edition published in Great Britain in 2026 by
Black Library, Games Workshop Ltd., Willow Road,
Nottingham, NG7 2WS, UK.

Represented by: Games Workshop Limited – Irish branch,
Unit 3, Lower Liffey Street, Dublin 1,
D01 K199, Ireland.

10 9 8 7 6 5 4 3 2 1

Produced by Games Workshop in Nottingham.
Cover illustration by Christopher Cant.

A CIP record for this book is available from the British Library.

ISBN 13: 978-1-83609-376-3

See Black Library on the internet at
blacklibrary.com

Find out more about Games Workshop
and the worlds of Warhammer at
warhammer.com

Printed and bound in the UK.

For Eve – light in the dark and fire in the cold.
And for Mark-Anthony – friend and brother, skjald and gothi.

For more than a hundred centuries the Emperor
has sat immobile on the Golden Throne of Earth.
He is the Master of Mankind. By the might of his
inexhaustible armies a million worlds stand
against the dark.

Yet, he is a rotting carcass, the Carrion Lord of
the Imperium held in life by marvels from the
Dark Age of Technology and the thousand souls
sacrificed each day so his may continue to burn.

To be a man in such times is to be one amongst
untold billions. It is to live in the cruelest and
most bloody regime imaginable. It is to suffer an
eternity of carnage and slaughter. It is to have cries
of anguish and sorrow drowned by the thirsting
laughter of dark gods.

This is a dark and terrible era where you will find
little comfort or hope. Forget the power of technology
and science. Forget the promise of progress and
advancement. Forget any notion of common
humanity or compassion.

There is no peace amongst the stars, for in the grim
darkness of the far future, there is only war.

Up from the ice, each casts their voice
To chase their fate, which guides all choice.
A warrior wild, his visage bold
His fate to burn against the cold.
But fire dies, all ends are feared
When set against the will of wyrd.

– From *The Saga of Ivar Krakenblood*, Wolf Priest of Fenris,
Seeker and Sought

PROLOGUE

All sagas are writ in blood.

Sunnifa finally understands this as she pushes herself up from the ice, rising from her own red snow. Her lifeblood stains her teeth in a snarl that was once a grin, faded now, gone forever like the promise of youth. She braces herself on her sword, driving the tip into the thick winter ice. Struggling to walk.

She almost slips.

Her feet threaten to slide out from under her, so slick is the ice with offal and entrail, all the leavings of battle. Fenris yawns around her, and the rising storm claws at the edges of the glacial sheet.

There are so many dead here that were she weaker, it might make her weep. Fenris abhors weakness. Especially now. Too many have gone to the Underverse or to the Halls of Russ. More still taken by the outsiders with their triple-barred 'I' sigils and machine stink.

She spits a bloody gobbet to one side and begins to limp through the field of the slain, pausing now and then in recognition. Wincing with the pain of loss. Friends and family lie dead around her. Sunnifa sees her cousin, Torgulf, cloven fully in twain. There are claw marks in the frost where he has tried to drag himself towards his own legs.

Her eyes flick up from the mortal detritus of war, drawn by movement through the gathering mist.

A boy staggers from the fug like a drunkard. There is blood on his mail and soaked into his leathers and furs. It runs from a gash in the side of his head too, staining his pale skin, covering the black ink of his tattoos.

They are of an age, Sunnifa reckons. Four or five great years old. Sixteen, if she thinks in the Terran count of the upplanders. Surely he must have felt young and eager as well, before. Flush with the fire of battle. Now he looks like a wight, dredged up from beneath the ice and given this shambling half-life once more.

He sees her and his eyes tighten with bitter hate. He lives. Not a revenant. Merely a man, staggering and reaching to his side. The boy raises a short spear and lobs it with what remains of his strength. It cuts the air with a low whistle, and Sunnifa sways to the side. He lurches onwards in the spear's wake, closing the distance. She matches him. Both of them move with stunted gait. Only desperate hate drives them. Muscles aching, streaked with blood and sweat despite the biting cold, they finally clash.

Sunnifa swings wide and the boy pushes in past her guard. He has pulled a dagger from his belt and drives it into her side. She feels something burst. Crimson sputum sprays from her lips. She pivots and drives the pommel of the sword into the side of his neck. He stumbles away, cursing.

Sunnifa seizes the opportunity and roars with all that remains of her strength, slamming the sword through leather and flesh. She pins him to the ice and slumps, using her weight to keep him there. He scrabbles and claws at her as he dies.

She will not be far behind him.

Sunnifa feels her chest heaving. Each breath is forced from her in a burbling rasp. Lung-struck. Land-drowning. Yet at the end she had distinguished herself. Her ancestors would be proud. She imagines soon she will hear the horns calling her to their side. To fight and feast with Russ and the Allfather.

Her eyes are closed when she hears it. Made soft by distance, yet growing louder and sharper. Sunnifa opens her eyes. She does not even have the air left in her to gasp.

A black shadow stands, silhouetted against the gathering storm. It looms like Morkai itself. The face that glowers down at her is a wolf's skull. The figure is armoured like a god. Wrought of night and ash.

'Be at peace, child of the frost,' it rasps with the voice of a machine. 'Your struggles are at an end. Let the cold take you. Know that you pass with honour.'

She tries to push herself back up and rage against the hulking Sky Warrior, but she cannot. Fenris has taken everything from her. She has given it all she has.

The wolf-skull helm draws closer, till she can see the gleaming lenses that pass for its eyes. Sunnifa did not expect Morkai to be kind, at the end.

When she dies, it is with her eyes open. Staring at the impossible figure.

CHAPTER ONE

BLOOD PRICE

Ivar Krakenblood's gauntleted fingers brush across the sword-maiden's face with exaggerated care and close her eyes for the last time.

'We should have been here,' he says finally. 'To shepherd at least a few of the near-slain from their first death.'

His mentor advances behind him. Ivar rises and turns, regarding Ulrik the Slayer with the wary awe that has never truly left him. The other warrior is a force of nature caged in flesh. In his every grim motion and pronouncement Ivar sees the distant echo of Leman Russ. The soul and spirit of the primarch lives in him.

The Wolf Helm of Russ is locked at Ulrik's belt. The ancient's face is weathered, his hair and beard faded to white, yet he radiates strength and determination. Ivar yearns to have even a fraction of that surety of purpose.

'We cannot be everywhere,' Ulrik says with a sigh. The wind whips about them, casting frost up onto the black and bronze of the Slayer's armour. He bends to examine the dead boy, tilting his head one way then the other. 'Weak,' he pronounces.

'It was not their time,' Ivar muses. 'Their wyrd led them only to death.'

'As ours leads us to our task,' Ulrik says, rising. 'Do you know why I have brought you here, Ivar?'

Ivar pauses. Within the confines of his helm he can hear the hammering of his own hearts. Blood rushes in his ears. He looks down again at the dead pair and remembers that, despite his myriad gifts, he was once as they were. Fragile. Brittle little toys in the hands of fate. Now he stands beyond their weakness. 'You wish to test me, Wolf High Priest.'

Ulrik chuckles at the formality, a dull rumble in tune with the winds. He stands ancient and indomitable. Fenris sings in his bones and bleeds from every pore. He and this world are one, perhaps more than any other living soul in the Chapter.

'I am always testing you, pup,' Ulrik says. Ivar tenses, though he knows it is no insult. 'I am old, Ivar. The oldest of us not yet given to the iron sleep. All who serve as we do… they shall be tested, and one day, when I am gone, that warrior will stand as my replacement.'

'Lord, I–' Ivar begins, but Ulrik raises one gauntleted hand.

'I will not leave this life without a fight, pup. You need not worry. I shall fight as I have always done. I will serve until the enemies of the Rout finally bring me down. That is all any of us can hope for.' He hesitates then. Ivar hears the barest hint of it creep into his master's voice. 'For any of us to continue in this life, there must always be a blood price. Our fates must be sanctified with death. Do you understand that, when you stand as Wolf Priest?'

'I understand,' Ivar says at last. At his core he knows the truth of it. *We are called to our purpose – tending the souls of the living and the legacy of the slain.* 'I know what is expected of me. I do not shirk from it. I simply…'

Ulrik snorts and turns from him. They are walking onwards now, up from the ice and onto the steep slopes of the land. 'Kraken blooded, kraken minded,' he interrupts. 'There is a hunger in you, pup. Relentless. It drives you on as sure as land thirst.'

'Perhaps it is duty,' Ivar says, too quickly. 'My wyrd.'

'Glory,' the Slayer says patiently, 'is not the same as duty. It is an ill thing to wish glory alone to be your destiny. Those who yearn for an end worthy of the sagas, shall never find the end they imagined. Those songs will be mournful in the singing.'

'I understand,' Ivar began.

'You do not,' Ulrik finished. 'But you will. Follow me, pup.'

Fenris claws at them. As they climb, the wind seeks to pitch them from the rocks and throw them beneath the hungry waves. Even through his helm Ivar can *taste* the sharp cold of the world and scent its salt.

There is something else on the growing gale. An animal reek, riven through with spilled blood and torn guts. It is the smell of predation, yet it is more than that. It stinks of gluttony and waste.

'What is the greatest strength of our world?' Ulrik asks, pausing to look back at Ivar.

The Wolf Priest hesitates and many answers whir within his mind. He bows his head.

The strength of Fenris is…

'Our people,' Ivar says at last. 'The flesh and blood of our world rose up to conquer the stars and slay the beasts where they nested. We challenged false gods and cast them from the heavens.'

'Very good,' Ulrik says, and nods ahead of them.

There is a wound in the world.

That is the only way Ivar can truly think of it. Not merely a cave but a festering cut into the body of Fenris. Icicles rim the entrance like fangs, alongside the grey stone of stalactites. The stone has been shaped by geologic pressure, by glacial action, and by the work of claws. It has been riven like meat.

The wrongness is a physical thing. It radiates from the aperture, and Ivar holds in the face of it. His armour growls as he moves towards it. Ulrik's hand grasps his pauldron.

'The strength of Fenris lies in its people, yes, and so it falls to us to protect them. The first trial you must undertake upon this new path is to shed blood for theirs. You have walked the path of priest and warrior for many years now, since the Spur's test. Now comes a truer blooding. The beasts are wild and mad in the wake of the sorcerers and their wiles. The sons of Magnus have left their heathen mark here, and it festers like old bloodrot. Even now Fenris is in upheaval.' He gestures into the looming darkness. 'There are trolls below. We will slay them in their lair and safeguard those who dwell nearby.'

Trolls. The thought radiates through his mind. Old kill-lessons blossom. Cants of battle and *skjald*'s wisdom on how they might be bested.

'The battle, before?' Ivar asks. 'Did this lead to that end?'

'They fear, and so they flee or they fight. Some wish for better land, further from the predation. Others would take advantage of a tribe already weakened. Cravens and carrion birds. Such should not be our way.'

Ivar's fist tightens and then unclenches. Within the iron and bone of the helm, his dark skin prickles with growing outrage. His old scars ache down his chest, the old burn of a kraken's wrath. He is as Fenris-marked as any other soul. He has seen the wild heart of their world, red with the blood of its inhabitants.

There is always a blood price upon Fenris.

Ivar looks to the skies and thinks of all those who have been taken by the rapacious hunger of the Allfather's watchers, doomed by the Cyclops' wrath. Somewhere beyond the skies, there are kin who yet suffer. Sometimes he dreams of distant screams that shake the foundations of the strongest land.

Some prices are too high, and some wounds never truly heal. Some slights can never be forgiven.

'Show me what I must do, lord,' Ivar says at last.

The descent is a strange and liminal thing. It does not feel as though it is part of the world – not as the passageways and vaults beneath the Aett are. There is no solidity here. All surety flees. The cave winds and sprawls, intestinal, like the innards of some vast beast.

Water drips in a relentless tattoo, matched to the slow pulse of Ivar's hearts. The air, even filtered through his helm, is rancid with spoiled meat. It is a place touched by the passage of Morkai, clotted with death's embrace, like a crater filled with brackish water.

The blood-scent draws them deeper, past great pillars of stone gouged by claws, under hanging mosses that crawl with unclean bioluminescence. Ivar does not need the pale illumination to see. His sight is surer than that. Even without the helm's systems, cradled by iron and bone, the darkness holds no secrets for him.

Something crunches beneath his boots.

Ivar looks down and sees the first of the bones. The remnants of the beasts' gluttony is everywhere, strewn without care or ceremony. Femurs, snapped open, their marrow gulped down, lie in ragged piles, littered with fragments. The top quarter of a skull leers up at Ivar, in mockery of his own visage.

'Hold,' Ulrik whispers over the vox. They are both helmed now. Each draws his weapon and they ignite in the cold gloom, shedding light and energy in a wave of purity. Each crozius is a sacred thing. Blessed in the sight of the Wolf Priests, anointed in accordance with the ways of Fenris. Allfather-blessed and spirit-sanctified. 'We are not alone, pup.'

'Where are they?' Ivar asks as the world growls around him with tectonic thunder. The surrounding passages sprawl, no longer serpentine but instead a rat's warren of tunnels and burrows. Something has hewn at the walls, expanding its den until it seethes like rot beneath Fenris' skin.

Ulrik is turning when the first of the brood slams into him.

The massive presence bowls the Slayer over into the darkness. Ivar pushes himself back, crozius raised in sudden defiance. The haft is wound with tendrils, rising up to brace the wolf's skull and bladed wings worked in adamantine and bronze. The light it casts illuminates the monster as it turns, as it lurches forwards out of the shadows, bellowing into his face.

Its maw is all peg teeth and fangs. Mismatched. Cobbled together as though made by the hand of a drunken craftsman god. Scaled shoulders hunch forwards and it roars again, drenching Ivar's helm in spittle and blood.

Ivar swings for the monster and it slides backwards, eyes narrowing with sudden irritation. They are predator and prey and neither entirely sure which is which. Ivar's voice growls from him with subdued fury. 'Come, monster, show me your mettle!'

It howls forward, goaded. Claws flash down and Ivar ducks out of the way. He moves to the right, behind a gleaming pillar of crystalline stone. The creature flails after him, arms swinging round like a club of flesh. The pillar chips and then shatters before the troll hurls its bulk through the cloud of debris. Ivar blocks and parries, drawing back where he can, weaving inwards where he must.

The bladed wings of the crozius, limned with killing light, gouge in at its flanks. Once. Twice. Three times. Ivar kicks it in the chest, as though might alone could topple it. The thing staggers back as ichor dribbles from its wounds.

There it is, he thinks. *There is the old legends come to life. Monster and beast. Eater of men. Slayer of kin.*

The wounds in its hoary blue-white hide are knitting back together. It grunts – with dulled pain or muted rage, Ivar cannot tell – and lumbers forward again. The monster mocks him. It drums its massive paws against the bone-laden floor and crushes them to powder. The cavern shakes again.

Ivar lunges at the troll, crozius raised in both hands, and swings. It strikes in the same moment, slamming its massive fists into the crackling head of the mace. It drives Ivar down and then seizes the weapon. The foetid stink of burning flesh oozes from it, and it trembles with something like mirth.

Like Ivar, it enjoys the kill. It takes some bestial pride in it.

'Fenrys hjolda!' The cry jolts both Ivar and the beast, forcing the monster to turn. Ulrik the Slayer barrels into it, out of the darkness, slamming it into the chamber's wall with a percussive boom.

He is not alone.

The monster's lesser kin follow at his heels. Weaker examples of the breed. Stunted and malformed vermin, scrabbling and snapping at Ulrik's back. He turns with contemptuous disdain and fires his plasma pistol one-handed, atomising the knot of wretched flesh. The troll-kin scream and squeal as the fire consumes them, a sudden sun-bright pulse of blue flame.

Ashes colour the air. For an instant they seem to hold their shape, screaming simulacra of slaughtered monsters, lit by the plasma light, and then they blow apart in the murder wind.

The monster turns for a moment, distracted by the pain of its murdered progeny, an animal keening forced from its distended lips. Ivar seizes the moment and swings upwards, gouging the troll's face across the right eye. It reels back, ichor gouting down its maimed face, squealing now. It wrenches its head around, and Ivar stares into that one remaining eye.

The eye burns with hate and then with more than that. The flesh splits. Fire blossoms out from the wound, coiling about the monster's face in a myriad of colours. It spreads like a creeping vine, winding through the meat of the beast. The scales ripple and change with a serpent's guile.

'*Maleficarum,*' Ivar breathes. The corruption of the Archenemy. Chaos' foul power. The mocking horror cast from the hands of the Cyclops' bastard sons.

The troll laughs, or seems to. Its shoulders shake and it lurches forwards again. It swings madly, fists grazing the walls, showering Ivar with shards of granite. Sparks fly from the contact and Ivar ducks under them, swinging for the troll's legs. The ichor flows sluggishly and the troll staggers. Ulrik meets it, gouging at the monster's back.

Flesh burns at the contact. Fluids cook off to steam. Still the thing changes. Skin and muscle shift and morph, running like wax, lashing from the bone like snakes. Venom glistens at the tip of bone needles, flexing like teeth in the meat.

Every part of it is screaming now.

The sound rings off the walls. Unholy. Unclean. The two warriors standing against it hear the mockery in the sound. The distant ringing of past battles. The muted menace of the sorcerers' last great infamy. Runes burn on its skin, shedding their dark light. The monster howls and thrashes. Each gouge and slash begets new atrocities, spreading and rising from its tormented form.

'Monster!' Ulrik bellows. Unholy mirth burbles from it once again.

'These wounds are forever. Your mongrel world shall never

heal.' It does not speak. Something speaks through it, goaded to sudden voice. *'We have left our mark upon you. Cut into your very fates. Doomed dogs! Damned by Prosperine hands!'*

'Speak. No. More!' Ulrik snarls.

Its head snaps around, single eye blazing with hate. It radiates loathing, till the walls glisten with its benighted illumination. Its jaws yawn wide. Wider. Too wide. Tendrils made of muscle and sinew vomit forth and seize Ulrik's raised weapon arm. The armour sizzles but does not buckle or melt.

It is master-crafted. More than that, it is sacred.

He swings his pistol up and fires. The monster's distended lower jaw explodes. The searing blast is so intense, so close, that for a moment it blinds even Ivar's auto-senses. A star being born and dying, all in one second.

Its howl degenerates into a brutal animal squeal of pain. Part of the ancient enmity is driven from it in a cleansing fire, purging the animus of the Cyclops. The once-troll flails back, claws scraping against the walls. It pushes itself off and slams forwards once more, into Ulrik. New limbs bleed from its torso, clawing and gouging at the warrior – trying in desperate animal futility to pry the Wolf Helm of Russ free.

The Slayer does not falter. He takes the blows as they rain down upon him. Ivar cannot stand idle, and so he swings at its broad back, tearing into undulating flesh. Faces made of ghost light and spite push outwards, laughing at his efforts even as cut after cut obliterates their visages.

A knot of mutating flesh and bone surges forward to coil around Ivar's mace hand. Gnawing at him like a jackal at a bone. Ivar grunts in pain and slashes down once more. The trap falls away in a rush of stinking fluids, scuttling into the shadows. The monster spits bile and shrill invective at them. A wave of sound and fury, seeking to unman them.

They are more than men. More than flesh or bone. In sacred symmetry the two move as one to sanctify the moment. Each crozius rises and falls. Each strike cleaves open flesh or reduces it to powder. They stave in its skull and crush the malicious eye to jelly. Ichor pours from it only to boil away as soon as the disruptor field touches it.

The creature finally unravels. Muscles uncoil and try desperately to wriggle away, only to be crushed beneath boots. It dissolves further beneath the onslaught. Battered down. Beaten. Ivar snarls as he hews into it, striking with such ferocity that even the stone beneath it is cut and broken.

They pause for a long moment, both watching the thing as it dies. Even its regenerative gifts are no match for them, not even woven through with a sorcerer's wiles.

'Now,' Ulrik breathes. 'Now you are blooded, pup. Ready for what comes next.'

'What comes next?' Ivar asks, his helm tilting as he watches the troll's carcass degrade and flow away like so much waste.

'This was but the first of your trials. A test of your mettle.' The old Slayer pauses, eyes lingering upon the dying monster. 'There is a fate for which you are well suited.'

CHAPTER TWO

TRIALS

They wait amidst the snow and ashes. Behind them the cave burns, its entrance collapsed by well-placed krak grenades. A tomb for the monstrous dead.

Ivar and Ulrik check each other for wounds, for taint, for weakness. The old Wolf Priest nods, content, and steps back. They sit down upon the rocks and stare at each other for a long time, as the winter winds sweep in.

They can wait a while. The Thunderhawk will not be inbound for some time. The summons has only just gone out. Their armour purrs as they settle and Ivar waits for his master's wisdom. Nothing the Slayer does is without reason. He has always known this to be so – ever since Ulrik chose him for the priesthood and cast others to their own fates.

'You come from a proud lineage,' Ulrik says. Ivar nods and bows his head.

'So I am told, lord.'

'The blood of heroes is in the veins of all the Rout, true enough, but now the Allfather presents an opportunity for you to honour your ancestors. What do you know of Gorm Krakenblood?'

Gorm. Ivar breathes a long breath. *Now there is a name with weight.*

'Gorm Krakenblood is a fine warrior. A Varagyr. There are generations between us, but we are of the same tribe and blood.' Ivar mulls for a moment. 'They say he was lost in service to the Chapter.'

'Aye, they say that,' Ulrik allows. Fenris speaks around them, in gale and wave. The crash and thrum of the world creeps in to infest every word Ulrik says. They all breathe together. Master, devotee, and world.

'Remove your helm,' Ulrik says, reaching up to pull his own free. The hiss of releasing hydraulics kisses the air. The warrior's face, with all its worn lines and scars, is heraldic. A testament to his strength as sure as the crags and mountains of Asaheim.

Ivar removes his helm and places it reverently upon the snow. It is rare that he bares his head in the presence of others, save moments such as this, amongst those of the priesthood. His dark skin is beaded with sweat, freezing into tiny ice crystals as he exhales. Black tribal braids, bound with copper rings, stir in the rising wind. They remain one of the few affectations that honour his birth tribe.

'Now we see each other. Eye to eye and soul to soul.' Ulrik nods and scoops up a handful of snow and frigid earth. He grinds it between gauntleted fingers until all is merely water and dust. 'These are times of upheaval, even now. Our world is not as it once was. Marked by the Sorcerer's fury, all certainties are knocked askew.'

Ivar nods. He has heard it himself. Whispered by kaerls and brothers alike. He closes his eyes and can picture it, dredged up from memory.

The skies burning with false fire as the discs and silver towers of the enemy swept across it. Daemons clawing at the heavens, then plunging like living daggers towards Fenris itself. A monstrous giant, crimson and winged, turning its burning eye towards him—

Ivar shakes away the thought and marks himself against maleficarum. The Cyclops is beyond flesh and its evil eye can be drawn by the slightest of sympathetic gestures. Ivar recognises his failing, even as a momentary lapse. 'I know the songs and stories,' Ivar says. 'The wrath of Magnus crashed down upon us like the sea upon the shore. The Thousand Sons wished to deliver their own wyrd upon us, and see Fenris reduced to dust and shards, like their own vanished home world.'

'You know our histories, all the sagas of old. You have studied the tales and heard them from the lips of ancients. When Magnus' whelps came here, they sought to humble us, and break us as Russ broke them.'

Russ. The very thought of him is electric. The Great Wolf that stalks between stars. Even now, beyond time, outwith the galaxy's confines, he fights. All sons of the Chapter know this in their hearts.

'At the core of all histories, all sagas, there is Russ,' Ivar says.

The wind whips. The earth trembles. There are names carved upon the heart of the world and to give them voice still makes the cold cradle of Fenris stir.

Allfather. Russ. Bjorn.

Great names and mighty deeds. Ivar wonders if one day he will match them. His fingers clench. He knows it is pride to dream such dreams.

'At the heart of all, there he stands,' Ulrik affirms. He raises a hand and strokes his grey beard. His augmetic eye clicks and whirs. Scars flex around it. Ulrik stands as battle-worn and indomitable as the world itself; timeless. 'Some have wondered what

Fenris would have been without Russ, yet I often think of what he would have been without Fenris. When the Lord of Winter and War first came to our world, he was raised by a she-wolf. Already the savagery of Mother Fenris was in him, World Spirit calling to primarch soul. We are shaped by our crucibles, be we godling or man.'

'And what does this have to do with–'

'Hush, pup. Listen a while and you may learn something, hmm?' The old Slayer rumbles with laughter. 'We all follow on from Russ' great legacy. Walking in his footsteps, tracing his marks upon the snow. Out, up, and into the stars. As your fore-bear did. Gorm Krakenblood journeyed forth from Fenris at the heels of our old foe. For they had stolen from us.'

'They took much and more from the hearth,' Ivar says and bows his head. *The future of Fenris, the strength of its people. Robbed away, stolen to the Uppland. Never to return home and be honoured by their people. Red snow, scattered to the stellar winds, becoming the ashes of the betrayed.*

'Aye, that they did, pup,' Ulrik says, genuine sadness colouring his voice. 'More than you will ever know. Gorm Krakenblood sought to repay them for their violations. He sought what they had taken. The *Vargrtiðhorn*.'

Ivar pauses and raises his eyes. Few outside the Wolf Priests and their mysteries know of the sacred Vargrtiðhorn. 'A totem of the Wolftime,' Ivar says at last. 'To be blown when the galaxy closes in about us, red in claw and fang, to tear down the very mountains of Asaheim.'

'The very same. Pried from its resting place and taken by the Archenemy. Borne away on the winds of Magnus' spite. Do you recognise the task I lay before you now?'

'I am ready, lord. For whatever faith you put in me.'

Ulrik stands and brushes the debris from his hands. 'You will lead a small undertaking of the Rout and seek what has become of Gorm Krakenblood. Bring him home.'

'And the Vargrtiðhorn?'

Ulrik is silent. His fingers drum against his armour and his body shakes with a sigh exaggerated by the plate's systems. 'If it is with him, then bear it back. If not? Then we shall seek it anew when the fates read true. Your destiny lies not in its pursuit, but in honouring your blood-kin. This shall be your test and trial.'

'But, my lord–'

'I have spoken,' Ulrik growls. He turns from Ivar, casting his eye across the ice plains. A new howl has joined the wind. Across the slate of the sky, a Thunderhawk cuts towards them.

'As you will,' Ivar says, teeth grinding together. 'How shall I chase this fate, then? The Inquisition are yet abroad. Watching for our slightest folly.'

Ulrik smiles. 'You will have aid in that regard, pup. Fate provides. The Allfather provides, from the oddest of quarters.'

CHAPTER THREE

DISTANT RELATIONS

When you first see it, from the Uppland, it is like the clouded eye of a murdered god. Then you find its beauty.

The old witch has said that to him many times on his journey, and now her presence has become as caustic as her metaphors.

Perhaps, Garald Helvintr muses, *you had to have been born here to appreciate whatever beauty they imagined.* It is hard for him to truly grasp the world before them. This Fenris. In a universe of savage wonders and hellish cradles, it ranks highly amongst them. War-ravaged and winter-scoured. Not like the worlds he has known in his time. Not like the life he was plucked from.

Sad birth stories are for singers and sagas. You will be better than that.

The voice haunts him, drawn up from the old crone's Underverse no doubt. Rokkvi, the man Garald had grown to call father, was just as ruled by superstition as the witch.

Garald pauses before the observation window, leaning against it, bracing his arm along the armaglass. He watches the small ship groupings as they circle the world, intent on its defence.

Or its persecution. The thought brings a guilty smile to his lips. It is a world that has suffered, that continues to suffer. Turning in its mighty arc, yet dogged by suspicion and ingrained hatred. There are more strangers now in Fenrisian space than there have been for a generation. He is oddly proud to number amongst them.

Garald takes a moment to admire himself in the glass. Dark hair set against pale skin, his eyes a summer-sea green. His attire is less tribal than some others of his dynasty or their servants, but he evinces the demeanour of a warrior prince. Armour plates glimmer in the pale light, black inlaid with brass. He carries an axe at his belt and a pistol at the opposite hip. Both are new, fresh-forged for his undertaking.

He feels, in this moment, utterly deserving of his position and the title he aspires to. Even if it comes from the magnanimity of another.

'We all owe our position to the queen,' he grumbles to himself and pushes off from the window, turning with a flourish as he regards the rest of the chamber. It is a sparse ship, a stripped-down chariot from which to conduct his affairs, not an implement of glory like the *Wyrmslayer Queen*. He has yet, as Bodil continually reminds him, to earn the privilege of a potent command.

It is called the *Swift Spear*, and yet it feels anything but. Every part of the ship is a subdued gallows grey, a worn iron that speaks of long service and low esteem. There is a rattle in its bones and a resignation in the growl of its engines. Still, it will suffice. Kingdoms, he knows, have been carved from less.

The chamber's door opens with a hiss of ailing hydraulics and he smiles coldly as it does. Very few amongst his crew have access to his private wings, but there are few who can trump *her* access.

The old crone has reached the point where she requires a cane to walk, usually. Now she walks unaided, still at a limping pace, but without the long ironwood stave to rely upon. It quirks Garald's smile into a genuine thing, despite himself. Even being near the home world seems to revitalise the witch.

'Now you see her,' Bodil says haltingly. 'What do you think, youngblood?'

'A world is a world is a world,' he sighs. 'There's only so much you can tell from orbit. She's a proud little orb, true enough. Stoutly defended. We have calls for our codes every nineteen seconds. From the Astartes and from the Inquisition. We have fifty-seven separate targeting locks. If any here so wished, they could scrape us from the void like *skitja* from a boot. Is that not so?'

'Perhaps you are not so much the boyish fool I might have feared.'

'I am nothing if not underestimated, *gothi*.'

'Misunderstood in your time, are you? Of course you would think that. All the young do, when they are fresh from the ice and full of hot blood.' She laughs, her voice like the croaking of a tiny bird. 'There may be hope for you yet, if you have the will for it.'

His jaw tightens and the smile sets again into a forced grimace. 'One day I'm sure I'll prove that to you and your mistress.' He pauses. 'Or to the regent, whom we all serve.'

He looks at her as she reacts. Garald notes the creasing around her eyes and lips, the wrinkles upon wrinkles. Her ice-blue eyes glitter in that worn face, her skin dancing with old scars and older tattoos. She wears her age like the world below them does. With pride and determination.

'The regent is far from here,' she scolds. 'Busy with his great wars, as demigods ought to be. We are simply mortal flesh, one day to be ash again, while our spirits rise to the halls of the All-father to fight at His side forever.'

Garald glances back at the moving ship-lights beyond the armaglass. 'The Emperor's watchers might bring you that moment sooner than you think.'

Bodil dogs his step with questions, *questions, questions*. Never silent, always whispering or counselling. Ever her mistress' voice, distant thoughts repeated back like a vox-mimic.

When will you make your overtures to the Sky Warriors? What is your plan? How will you make sure her will is done?

'I will do what is needful,' Garald says, again and again.

Alarums ring out through the corridors of the ship as he stalks from his own wing up through the superstructure, towards the bridge. Brazen as any other example of House Helvintr's ship-craft, it looms pugnaciously out at the void. A hunter's vantage from which to tame a spiteful universe.

And they are hunters. Seekers after the greatest of prey. A rogue trader dynasty that once commanded dominions of its own. Lost grandeur, now. Stolen by jealous monsters. Yet even now, their fortunes are ascendant once more. Buoyed up by the regent's favour.

Wayfarers. Voidsailors. Forgers of paths. Slayers of beasts.

Deck officers and attendants salute as he passes, raising their hands to their chests in the sign of the aquila. Others raise their fists over their heart in a warrior's greeting. It is easy for him to tell who is a regent's man, sent to fill gaps in the roster, and those who are that ever-dwindling supply of Helvintr retainers.

Too many have been drawn away with their queen. Only the dregs remain to him. Treated like a common cadet, made to prove himself again and again. Garald bangs his fist against the central command throne's back as he passes, drawing their attention, taming their fervour.

I will not be broken by shame. Not a tamed canid to toil and slave for their approval. I will set the pace of this. I will lead the way.

'Hold our course and reduce thrust to two-thirds primary,' he says, with bristling confidence. 'I want auspex confirmations of local defence positions, targeting vectors from all ships regardless of allegiance, and for the vox to remain nice and open.'

'Do not goad them!' Bodil hisses. 'This is the–'

'The wolf's lair, yes, I know, you've said.' Garald sighs. 'And if this house has taught me anything it is that you do not waltz in unprepared. I do not come back to your cold hearth to start a fight. Far from it.' He lets his fingers drum reassuringly against the iron throne, the ship's thrum singing through its bones to his. Like speaking to like.

Both of them underestimated and abused by harsh masters. Shaped by their own adversity. Scarred inside and out. Garald lets himself laugh as the ship trembles forwards. More sirens call around him. Lights flicker and shift. Carved eagles and wolves seem to come to life as the radiance catches upon them in a dance of gold and bronze.

This is the moment that speaks to him. The surety that comes with command. Let the witch and her queen doubt. He will prove himself, no matter what.

'Give me communion with the lead Inquisition vessel,' he says at last. Silence hangs heavy before the bridge begins to ring with calls of 'Aye, lord!'

A ring of skulls lowers from the centre of the bridge, rotating around a dais of inlaid silver. The skulls are old, tokens of the great powers that wait upon the world below. Each one is the skull of a Fenrisian wolf. Lenses glint where the eyes once rested, and slowly they begin to glow.

Light casts itself forth and slowly resolves itself into shapes. Fractals blossom and die as they smooth out, and a figure is carved into the air by captive radiance.

Garald is almost surprised by the severity of the woman

who materialises. Around her eyes and down her cheeks dance dark tattoos, tiny rotes of service and rolls of duty, flowing like tears. A choker is clasped about her throat, wrought from human fingerbones, grasping the carved sigil of her station. Of her ordo.

She regards him with eyes that have seen too much, condoned far more and condemned too many. Her lips quirk into something that resembles a smile, as though his presence is more amusement than irritant.

'There is something to be said for the presumption, I suppose,' she says eventually with a sigh.

'Boldness, I have been told, is a quality to be desired in this line,' Garald says. He returns the smile. 'I am Garald–'

'Latterly named Helvintr, of that increasingly tedious and tawdry lineage,' she interrupts. *'Cousin at some remove from the self-proclaimed jarl of the dynasty. A thrall-child, as I understand it. Adopted into a facet of the family considered practically an offshoot or cadet branch, and lately brought closer into the fold as the regent's pet burns through resource after resource?'*

We are known to her. That is unexpected. Garald curses himself. Only fools underestimate the Inquisition. He collects himself, forces a smile.

'You are, as I expected, incredibly well informed. I'm sure I'm flattered to be worthy of such regard.'

Her image flickers as she laughs, then steadies into that cold detachment. *'All who truck with the regent are our affair, just as all those who find their way to Fenris are worthy of my scrutiny. Your house has been making a name for itself.'* She raises a hand, toying in the air idly, as though Garald is beneath her notice. *'Quite the list of triumphs and little infamies.'*

'I'll be sure to pass that on, next time there's a family council.' He knows he is playing with fire and yet he cannot help but lean in, yearning to burn. 'You still haven't told me your name or your rank, mamzel.'

'You have the cockiness of the breed, I'll give you that. Know that you address Lord Inquisitor Gulrun, of the Ordo Astartes. Why have you come here, little privateer? This den of wolves is not for you. This Chapter keeps its own counsel.'

'I come here,' he says, 'knowing all this, and bearing the authority of my line – who have oaths to Fenris as of old. I am a stranger here, true enough, but I have every trust that the promises laid down in generations past will hold. The Helvintr have a place here, and so I have a place here. I come to offer relief and supplies, and to resupply in turn, at the benevolent will of the dynasty's leader.'

'You would not be so foolish as to lie to a sworn agent of the Inquisition, would you, boy?'

Garald bristles at the barb. 'I am many things, lord, and sometimes even a fool, but in this instance, my word is true. I have been sent here for resupply and reconsecration. To bring me into lockstep with the old ways, and to sanctify my undertaking for the hunts to come.' He glances to one side and raises his hand gently, signalling to one of his vox-officers. 'We have already sent our missives to the Wolves of Fenris. They will judge whether we have the right to walk its earth.'

Silvered nails click, painted in cold light. Each one glimmers like a blade edge, or the tip of a quill. Warrior queen, savant, judgement and justice all.

She reminds him of Katla. Furious power bound up with cold cunning. Both wielding oaths and loyalty as surely as weapons, yet suffering no trespass or outrage. That is what it means to be a lord. A leader. A queen.

A word and she could end him. A single gesture and they would all burn. The defence systems of Fenris would never even have the chance to react before the Inquisition loosed its wrath against the *Swift Spear*. He cannot play the fool forever. He cannot continue to tempt fate.

You cannot go against the will of wyrd.

The crone's voice again, though she does not speak. Another lesson dredged up from his memory. He looks to her and she meets his gaze. She allows the barest nod of approval. That, he supposes, means something. He sits a little straighter and turns back to the light of the hololith.

The inquisitor speaks to someone just out of sight, the feed muted, before she returns her own attention to him.

'Perhaps you are not so much the fool, then,' she says. All playfulness, such as it ever was, is gone. No longer a felid toying with prey. Now simply bound by the certainties of duty. Shaped and trapped by her own destinies. He curses silently to himself. *How easily I have let the superstitions creep into my thoughts.*

'You do me an honour, my lord,' Garald says with a slight incline of his head. 'I'm happy that, on this occasion, I haven't proven myself foolish.'

The hololith ripples with her sigh. Lord Inquisitor Gulrun reaches for a dataslate and regards it, lip curling in cold amusement. *'It would appear your hosts agree with you. You have clearance, such as it is.'* She shakes her head and then continues. *'I would offer you some advice, trader. Do not tarry long here. The hearth of Fenris only burns cold. Linger by it… and you will die, frozen and alone.'*

'I am told that is the fate laid down for many Helvintrs, and more sons of Fenris besides. I am not afraid.'

I am not afraid.

And Garald can almost believe that as the shuttle plunges through the turbulent atmosphere, bucking and howling like a living thing. Outside the Aquila lander's observation cupola, the storm clouds roil and rumble.

To gaze upon Fenris is to look malice in the face. Garald wonders how mankind ever colonised this world, why they would even try. He braces himself against the command throne, watching as lightning claws at them in luminous flashes. Talons set to tear them from the heavens. The clouds draw in, a storm wall of tarnished grey. Rain and ice slicks the dome, flowing down the curve like tears.

The old gothi is with him. She sits alongside half a dozen voidsmen. All wear the dour void-leathers of the Helvintr, all have the snarling wolf and spear upon their shoulders. It matters not whether they hail from Fenris, or from the regent's endless reserves, or some other feral hellhole Katla has raided. Each has a lasgun slung over their shoulder and a bladed weapon belted at their waist. A knife, short sword or cutlass.

'The world weeps for us,' Bodil whispers by his ear. 'A fine omen. Mother Fenris weeps for her returning children. We always come back to the hearth, and this time... Oh, such a hearth.'

Garald ignores her. Teeth gritted. Fingers now locked, white-knuckled, around the throne's back. He forces his eyes up, fixes them upon the roiling storm clouds and their wrath.

Death world.

He thinks the words without judgement. So many of the worlds of the Imperium are catalogued as such. Worlds where life struggles to survive, where the tithes are taken in flesh rather than resources. Soldiers for headhunter Militarum regiments, culled from planets where survival is but a slender hope. This world is different, though. Like so many others it serves at the whim of the Emperor's Angels. The Adeptus Astartes.

Garald has never met a Space Marine. He cannot even conceive of a culture shaped by these squalls and elevated to such position.

Suddenly all of Bodil's warnings and superstitions are all about him, tearing at his mind as surely as the storms are trying to wrench them from the heavens.

'Throne preserve us,' he breathes. 'Deliver us from the ravages of the tempest and the lightning.'

'Do not fear the storms!' Bodil cries. The old woman's voice fills the ship, buffeted by the wind's roar. The voidsmen pound their fists against their chests and cheer. Then the engines scream and they plunge out of the clouds, into the slate grey of Fenris' empty skies.

The ship tilts and he sees it. By the God-Emperor, he sees it.

The mountain is the fang of a god-wolf. Arcing up from the surface, so massive it stretches beyond the clouds, out of the atmosphere. He has seen voidships with less sheer grandeur. Crafted, sculpted, in a bygone age of wonders. A miracle upon a world of monsters. He has read treatises about the Fang, the *Aett* as Bodil insists on terming it, and yet none of that has prepared him for the sheer majesty of it.

He pauses in his considerations and turns to the old woman. Her face is a mask of beatific serenity. It is as though contentment has finally found her, an oncoming tide that has dispelled all trace of curmudgeon or scold.

'I thought the docking platforms were in the upper tiers,' he says, brow furrowing. 'Haven't we gone too low?'

'The lords of Fenris would have you land upon the plains, and make the ascent yourself.' She seems entirely too pleased with that situation for Garald's liking. 'Consider it a rite of passage.'

'I am a sworn member of House Helvintr and I–'

'Here none of that matters,' she says, the words sighing out of her. 'Here we are only guests at best, and prey at worst. You have not yet earned the privilege of docking above. You will walk from the snow like an aspirant, and beg for their favour. You have her seal and her bond. That will get you far enough.'

'And what of you?'

'What of me? This is my home. I am simply returning to pay homage.'

'They do me an insult.'

'They honour you, in their way. They give you the opportunity to learn. To rise. As all must. Every child of the dynasty destined for greatness? They come here. They rise. As their ancestors once rose, to serve and then to rule.'

The ship grumbles in sympathy and banks sharply; stabilisers flare and burn hard. Then it rights itself, and begins the slow rumble down to the surface. Sirens wail and lights flash, bathing the interior in white and crimson. The voidsmen are on their feet now. Two rows of three, ahead of him. An honour guard for one who has been repeatedly told that he lacks all worth and honour.

Garald feels his hands tighten into fists. The leather of his gloves creaks with the effort. He steels himself one last time as the ramp falls and the cold hits him.

It is a physical thing. A wall. A wave. The cold of Fenris is like nothing he has ever felt. Perhaps only the void is more chill, more hostile to life. The men march out, but he can see their step falter. Just for a second, their discipline breaks.

How could it not?

Garald looks up at the sheer vastness of the mountain, king of even the mighty peaks that surround it. They stand upon a blasted plain, laid bare to the elements, an altar of sacrifice from which the foe can behold their ruin. The mountain is eternal, this place says. Nothing and no one shall unseat it. In his very soul, Garald knows the truth of that. He wonders how many have tested their might against this place, only to falter.

I will not falter. I am not weak.

Garald straightens his back. Kindles some small amount of

steel in his spine. He walks down through the retinue, and his feet finally touch the soil of Fenris itself. Bodil seems to react differently. The death world invigorates the old woman. The chill air strengthens her bones and she stands taller. She takes in deep lungfuls of it.

'There is no finer thing than letting the free winds of your home embrace you,' she says. 'Not least after months of breathing recycled oxygen and drinking reworked piss as though it were true water.'

'And here I thought ship life suited you,' he muses.

'A ship will carry you from place to place in search of duty. It is not to be all. Even amidst the sea of stars, and the howling void, it is not a life. I sail at my jarl's behest because it is my *purpose*. To sail without purpose is to be lost, marooned, and dead.'

'I wonder if the ones with the Warrant think the same.'

'I know she is of the same mind. And these warriors here? They are the wolves that stalk between stars, and that is not idle flattery.'

The world rumbles. Far ahead of them a great gate, vast and set into the side of the mountain, begins to grind open. Garald moves forward, stumbling across the wasted plain, still not accustomed to the cold. It becomes everything, a swaddling shroud that will drag him down. Drown him.

His mind tastes words from his education into the Fenrisian mysteries. *Underverse. Wights. Morkai.*

He could dismiss them all, at a remove. Out upon a ship, they remained as a manageable superstition. Cloaked in a gothi's delusions and generations of Helvintr mummery. Here, though, it was everywhere. It was a world that breathed malice, soul-deep and ancient. A potent symbol of the supernal might of the Astartes.

Worlds such as these are where monsters are bested, bred, and tamed.

This is the *mountain* though. The apotheosis of peaks. The very sight of it is too much. He almost stumbles, hands flinching out to brace himself for an impact that never comes. Garald forces them to his side, hands locked into fists.

He marches forwards into the mountain's great shadow, towards the waiting gate, even as horns ring out in warning or greeting.

The climb is agonising.

Chapter-serfs, *kaerls* in the tongue of Fenris, guide him up through the innards of the mountain with a stunning sense of detachment. Garald cannot understand how they manage to navigate as though born to it, moving up stairways and corridors with practised ease.

All is grey. The walls, the floors, the armour and uniforms of the soldiery. The only light bleeds from dull lumens, as though any illumination is anathema to the warriors who dwell here.

As though even the cold comfort of the empty void would not be enough to sate the mountain.

The kaerls stop before a door, taking their place at either side of it. They nod to the rogue trader, the upplander, the *interloper*. The door snarls open and suddenly there is blinding sunlight once more.

It seems hours since Garald has last seen the outside. He steps forwards uncertainly, out onto a spur of iron and stone that reaches out from the mountain's surface. A docking platform. Around the edges of it stand statues. Hunched gargoyles of metal, perhaps…

Garald blinks. *No. Not statues.* One of them moves.

He freezes. It advances, even now. A hulking thing of black iron and bone. Garald's advance falters.

It looks like death. The end of all things brought forth to meet him. Immense. Even the whipping winds and snow flurries slow as it stalks forwards. Bodil is already kneeling. The arms-men follow suit, cowed by a level of martial superiority they could only dream of.

Time stands still.

One moment the figure is striding away, and the next it stands before him.

Black armoured, its face a leering beast skull, draped in furs. It towers over him and gestures with one armoured hand. In the other it holds an immense maul.

'Kneel,' it growls. Garald slumps down. All strength is gone. There is only submission to the palpable will, the undeniable power, of the warrior. 'You are the one called Helvintr?' it asks at last.

Garald forces a nod, eyes downcast.

'Do not fear me,' the giant says. 'I am Ulrik, called the Slayer. Wolf High Priest of the Vlka Fenryka. Child of Fenris and servant of the Great Wolf.'

'It…' Garald forces the words out and his eyes up. 'It is an honour, lord.'

'Enough of that,' Ulrik growls. 'Your use lies not in grovelling, but in what you can provide for us.'

'Anything, lord,' he babbles. 'I… live only to serve.'

Never in his mortal life has fear grasped him so. Hands wrapped around his throat, choking the life from him. The cold seizes his chest and he struggles to breathe. If he weeps in this moment then he knows the tears will freeze to his cheeks.

He cannot help the fear he shows, even though it humiliates him. There is no mirth from the crone. Bodil simply nods in understanding. This is common. This is human. There is no shame in it.

'You shall serve as a chariot of demigods. A sure vessel upon storm-tossed seas. You shall bear our men out into the void, and serve them upon their most sacred task. This is demanded by the Allfather of Man. For this, you and the jarl you serve shall be rewarded. We shall *entertain* her requests.' The great figure rumbles with laughter. He turns to regard Bodil. 'That is all we shall promise your mistress, daughter of the ice.'

'That is all she expects, my lord Slayer.' She glances askance at Garald. 'He may seem a mere youth, dredged up from the ice, but my queen has seen his promise. She bid him come back to the cradle of wolves and honour the hearth of Fenris. With friendship, fidelity, and service.'

The Slayer's gaze is one of judgement and assessment. Such a stare has doubtless consigned uncounted others to failure and death. Garald forces his eyes up and meets it. He pushes himself unsteadily to his feet.

'I am ready to serve.'

'Good,' the Slayer says and turns from him. 'Follow. Destiny awaits you within the halls of the Aett.'

CHAPTER FOUR

THE DREAMING DEAD

The darkness beneath the Aett is all-consuming, enough to unman all but the mightiest.

Ivar knows no fear. This is his domain, as surely as it belongs to Morkai. The cold pits of the Underfang sprawl and wind beneath the great mountain, yet this place holds a special significance.

Ivar Krakenblood kneels in the shadows below the world, in the Hall of the Revered Fallen, and dares not raise his eyes to witness the slumbering glory before him. Even now, he feels unworthy.

The figure before him is more than a man. More than a brother. He is a slumbering legend. A king from a bygone age, preserved in ceramite; his legacy carved in bronze upon the sarcophagus. The Fell-Handed sleeps, unaware of the veneration laid at his feet.

Ivar finally looks up. He sees everything, every detail parsed by his helm's auto-senses. The brazen carvings that adorn the chassis. The craftsmanship is flawless, etched with love and care in the times after Russ had left them, by the legend that was Blademaker.

The pilgrimage that brought the Wolf Priest down to this place began as soon as they landed. The Slayer had given him his orders, set forth his wyrd, and left him to gather his thoughts and his fatesworn.

Now he kneels before the Chapter's ancient hero and lets his own mind drift like the dreaming dead.

Ivar's thoughts coil about the Slayer's words and the mission he has imparted. The old warrior still looms large in his estimations. His mentor. His master. He has set a destiny before Ivar, and he will seize it with both hands.

I will not disappoint you, lord. I shall not fail the Chapter or my bloodline.

Gorm Krakenblood's legacy now rests with Ivar. With kin. Blood calling to blood, as it does throughout the Rout. As it did between Russ and the Allfather. They are all bound by ancient wyrds, passed down the generations, parent to child. In some the aptitudes of the gothi run thick where others bear the quick and hot blood of the warrior.

'You should not be here, Krakenblood,' a voice says finally from the darkness.

Ivar rises, turns and sees a bionic hand lift through the shadows, dispelling them entirely as glow-globes waken to sudden life. It seems almost a sin that the meagre illumination lives while the ancients yet slumber. But it is not Ivar's place to judge such things. It is the duty of the figure who stands before him, and those like him.

Brynjar Drakefang has changed much since they were both Blood Claws. The Iron Priesthood is less forgiving than the destiny carved out for Ivar. Where once he bore a winding tattoo of blue ink, a drake's dance that coiled about his eye, now that entire side of his face is smooth metal, marred only by a crimson augmetic eye and–

Ivar allows himself a smile. The tattoo is still there, only now incarnated as a plasma-etched scrimshaw upon the plate. Brynjar's half-face returns the smile, though his is muted.

'Yet here I am, Brynjar,' Ivar says. 'I seek only the guidance of our honoured dead. They merely sleep and I would drink in their dreams.'

'Like some ice gothi,' he says with a hydraulic shake of his head. 'You are not mind-gifted, you know this.' He pauses for a moment and scratches at his chin thoughtfully. 'Mind-touched, certainly. Dropped from too many cliffs as a child. Left too long in your first death, air-starved and keening. But not a speaker with the Underverse. The Slayer would have seen that, before ever he took you into the mysteries.'

'The Allfather speaks in dreams, gift or no,' Ivar says softly. 'That is fact, as true and sure as the bones of the Aett. Truth hard as stone or steel.'

Brynjar steps forward and things move in the shadows behind him. They stalk around the gloom at the chamber's edge or swing down out of the darkness with simian gracelessness. They are servitors, Ivar realises. They are clad in simple craftsmen's leathers, the kind that a smith at the forge would wear. Their faces are gone, replaced by iron wolf-skull masks. They are nailed into the flesh of their scalp, the metal barbs coated in dried blood.

They are, all six of them, cruel and feral things. Tools and blades flicker from their finger stumps, tasting the air, craving the surety of work upon flesh or steel. Crimson augmetics burning in mimicry of Brynjar's own, scrutinising Ivar and ensuring he poses no threat to the slumbering ancients. The iron skulls twist, clicking and purring.

'Your pets are no less eager, I see,' Ivar says.

Brynjar laughs. 'I've been keeping them occupied, but they

are starved for company. Few venture down here without good reason. That is why it surprises me to see you. You do not linger amongst the ironclad dead. When they are roused to war? Absolutely. The first to intone rites and honour them… but you do not tend to their dreams. Why are you here?'

Ivar holds his peace and then reaches up, removing his helm with a hiss of escaping pressure.

His long hair spills back, copper rings glistening in the light. There are ashes upon his cheeks, drawn up from offering fires. The fingers of kaerls have marked his dark, scarred skin with runes of aversion. Warding him against the death that he courts, tames, and fends off. Now they are simply brothers. Now, he is only Ivar.

'We have known each other a long time, Brynjar,' he says at last.

The Iron Priest nods at this. One of the forge hounds lopes to Brynjar's side, and his augmetic hand drops to absently stroke the iron skull. The servitor beast snaps its head up, scrutinising Ivar. Its eyes flicker.

'We have,' Brynjar agrees at last. 'Since that first trial of aptitude, and the Kraken's Spur.'

Ivar's guts roil at the memory of their ordeal upon the Spur.

Death surging up for them in a tide of teeth and tendril. The great king of the deep, unthroned, and set to punish them for their transgression. Brave Jolnyr, dark eyes flaring in a moment of defiance before the kraken claims him.

Brynjar had called it kaerl work. For serfs to do. Only Ivar had seen the test for what it was.

'Since then we have walked our separate paths, yet I have always thought of you as a brother of my wyrd.'

In their youth he might have expected Brynjar to scoff, but he does not. The flesh of his half-face curls into a smile. 'We have always been bound by that past, Ivar. It does not fade from us easily. We all bear our scars. Self-made and otherwise.' He gestures at the Wolf Priest's armour. 'You've seen battle?'

'A test, from the Slayer,' Ivar rumbles.

'Some things truly never change…' Brynjar snorts. 'You are ever the obedient acolyte. Even when you serve, you are heaped with trials.'

'Have a care, Drakefang,' he says, genuinely wearied. 'The Slayer has imparted much to me, down the decades. Wisdom, trust and responsibility.' The darkness looms around them, drowning even the monumental shadows of the sleeping dead. 'We both walk our paths. I think we always knew they would inevitably wind together once more.'

'Perhaps I just assumed you would end up here, Krakenblood. Bound to your own iron sleep and denied death, hmm?' He laughs. 'Skitja, don't look so grave.' Brynjar shakes his head. 'Ever so serious. Destiny should not break you so. You should not be humbled by your wyrd. What is it? You come here whispering of fate – tell me true what you fear.'

'Will you stand with me, brother? To whatever end comes? With all the weight of our history. Because of it, not despite it?'

'I give you my oath. Now, tell me what it is that haunts you.'

'My fate, and that of others,' Ivar says softly.

'You've held the lives of others in your hands. You've seen battle and tended to the offal that follows. You have watched brothers die.' He looks up at the slumbering majesty of the Fell-Handed. 'It is the honour and glory of the Chapter that, like our ancients, we fear nothing. Laugh in Morkai's face as we are carried down onto red snow. This childish fretting is beneath you.'

'I do not fear battle, nor its consequences,' Ivar growls. 'I only wish…' He trails off. He casts his eyes down, unable to look at

Brynjar or the sacred dead. 'I only wish to leave a legacy, etched into the galaxy's skin. A saga for the ages.'

'Vanity, then. Hubris.'

'Call it what you will. None of us were raised up from the ice for weak ends.'

'The Iron Priests,' Brynjar begins. 'Some think us detached from the concerns of others. Aloof, as the Iron Masters are. That we hold to our mountains and work the forges in obsessive isolation.'

'I remember you thought much the same, as a Blood Claw.'

'We were all fools as youngbloods.' Brynjar laughs. 'We grow, and we learn, and our assumptions change. Travelling to Mars often has that effect.'

'Does their logic-mummery focus the mind more than our spirits?'

Brynjar's mirth corrodes, but a little. 'Careful, brother.' His servo-arm whirs and clicks, the gear-toothed wolf's head grinding and snapping. 'The machine spirits here are restless, as are those within my armour.'

Braziers flutter in the sudden wind of air-recyc turbines. Drawing chill air from outside the Aett, bearing it down into the depths to swaddle the ancients in Fenris' balm. Always there is that sense of an unsettled world. Even in the strongest fortress, it finds him.

'Forgive me, brother. My troubles are not their troubles, nor should they be yours.'

'Ah, but now you *intrigue* me, Krakenblood!' His joy was back, sudden and fierce. The flesh side of his face was animated, pale skin creasing. 'You come here, out of balance, and seek to snare me in your madness. Bind me to a fate you seem to loathe and fear.'

'There will be the chance to salvage much from this enterprise. Technology and relics lost to the Chapter. An honour for any who would undertake it, but especially for one of the Iron Priesthood.'

'Bribery and flattery now?'

'Simply opportunity. We can do this duty together. As brothers. Like before.'

Brynjar is silent as he regards the Fell-Handed's sarcophagus. His augmetic hand reaches out, hesitates, and then clenches into a fist. He draws it back, turns, and moves to leave.

'When you stand with the Chapter's elders and take up this quest, I will be there. I will hear their plans, brother. I owe you that much, at least.'

And then he is gone, out into the shadows of the undercrofts, trailed by his thralls. In the darkness beneath the world, Ivar allows himself a smile.

CHAPTER FIVE

WOLF KING'S CALL

Like children, they make war upon the ice.

That is the way of Fenris, for such a world cannot breed weaklings. Even in their ascendancy the warriors of the pack merely play out the patterns of their youth. To fight and die on the ice and rock of Fenris. To sail her seas and lie upon red snow. That is the fate of all born to the Chapter.

They know that all too well. The wound of Fjolnir's passing remains, almost physical. Fjolnir. War-wise, mjod-soaked, battle-drunk. Friend, brother and leader. Taken too soon into the All-father's embrace. Killed by the kraken, upon the Spur – roused from its deep slumber by the Sorcerer's lingering blights and maladies. *Curse Magnus and his sons for their outrages. The blood shed in their attack, the aftershocks that wound us still...*

It is no meek maleficarum that can unseat the world. Nor can any warrior who submits to it be thought strong.

Jolfr swings around and his axe follows suit. It is new-forged, double-handed. A kingly weapon for any warrior, entirely at home in the hands of a warrior of the Rout.

Vili sways back and away, a grin plastered on his youthful face. His vigour, that keenness that suffuses all of newer blood, carries his roaring chainsword round once more. The weapons meet in a shower of sparks – unpowered blade to revving teeth – sending a shudder of pressure up Jolfr's arm. Growling, he throws himself forwards, driving his elbow into Vili's chest, battering the youth backwards.

'Well struck, old man!' Vili laughs. 'There might be hope for you, yet!'

'Pride will tear the legs out from under you as surely as any bolt or blade, stripling!' Jolfr grunts. He turns the haft of the axe in his hands, steadying himself before he lunges at Vili. A blow lands with the flat of his axe. Then another. Another. Age and experience drive back youthful enthusiasm, forcing the boy to his knees in a rain of mock blows.

Vili makes a good effort of it, while he can. He guns the chainsword, pushing its engine hard. The teeth snap and bite like the kraken, gnawing at Jolfr's axe like the sea tears at the shore. He can only parry in futility, desperately trying to turn aside the blows as they strike him down. Savage joy floods him, every muscle saturated in combat-lust and kill-need.

Their brothers watch the false battle with bemusement. They are, all of them, known in the annals of the Chapter as Wolf King's Call. Their name is sacred. A promise, etched into the rocks of the world. They shall answer his call, whenever it comes. They have served the Allfather and the Chapter long enough that they bear the rank of Grey Hunters. Tested like well-used swords. Across all the dominions of the Allfather's Imperium, they have marched to war, never ignoring duty's summons. They have turned aside no challenge. Even in loss, they have forged on. Fjolnir's passing is not a wound that will stop their service. It will only embolden them.

Hrungnir and Orwandil watch on. Every now and then they

shout cheers or jibes, encouraging or shaming in equal measure. Good-natured ire they hurl at Jolfr, while Vili receives their tempered praise. They are older warriors. Set in their ways. Each crag-faced and war-worn. Hrungnir's hair is dark, cut short and severe, where Orwandil's is wild and red. Grey is creeping in, the slow fade of a season's change.

'He'll make a fine warrior, if he lives,' Orwandil muses.

'If, aye,' Hrungnir agrees. 'Still too much of the child in him. He has all the eagerness that caught him his first death.'

'We were all young once, brother.'

'Some of us never have the chance to age,' Hrungnir grumbles. 'He will, though.'

'You think so?'

'Oh, I know so. Brash fighters like him always prosper. Even the Blackmane was young, once.'

'True enough. True enough.' Orwandil laughs and turns away from the melee. His fists clench and unclench, eager for his own turn.

They are reconsecrating themselves for the purpose ahead of them. Whatever that may be. To fight as sworn brothers beneath Fenris' slate skies... There is no greater privilege. It binds them together. Makes them more than they could ever be alone.

That is the strength of the pack.

Jolfr growls with dark mirth, swinging his axe around again. The flat of it catches Vili on the cheek, and the young pup whirls back. He spits blood.

'Always something to learn, boy. Always another challenge. We all eventually face down something that we cannot conquer.'

'Like Fjolnir did?'

'To fall to the kraken is no small fate. It is no idle death. That is worthy of a saga. Fenris' soul is hungry and one day we will all be devoured. One way or another.'

'I don't fear death!' Vili says suddenly. Jolfr grins and shakes his head. He draws back, baiting the youth.

'I know, child. I know. The young are fearless. You pups throw yourselves into whatever maelstrom burns brightest. Chasing your glorious ends. But the true victory lies in enduring the storms. Serving the Rout to the death and beyond.' Vili's whirring blade catches at Jolfr's pauldron, chewing paint from the metal. Both laugh.

The winds whip around them. Stones skitter about their boots and the snow catches, dragged up by sudden squalls. They pause and taste the air. Scenting the world's torment.

Jolfr turns and looks into the rising gale. For a moment, just a moment, the flurries part. A figure walks from the grey tumult, black against the howling sky.

'Sometimes,' Jolfr says. 'Sometimes, though, we do not get a choice.'

They recognise him, even at this distance. The mock war stops. The weapons fall silent, lowered in respectful awe. They know him by the carvings upon his black armour and by the skull helm he wears.

Ivar Krakenblood returns to them from out of the storm. He stalks into their midst like winter and war incarnate. Shadows stalk with him, cast by the lunatic winds, and for just a moment it is as though Jolfr can see Morkai pacing behind the Wolf Priest. The howling gale transmutes into the roar of the death wolf.

As one, the pack goes to its knees.

'Rise,' Ivar calls and lifts one empty hand. He is unarmed, and yet his benediction is wielded like a weapon. 'None need bow to me. Not here. Not now. We are as brothers. Bound by old grief and new promise.'

'You honour us,' Vili says. Brash, too eager. Jolfr shakes his head and lowers his gaze, trying to hide his smile. He suspects that beneath his helm Ivar is smiling too.

'Perhaps,' Ivar muses. 'That remains to be seen. All I ask is this. You have stood with me in grief as we commended your pack leader to the Allfather. I need you to stand with me again. A task is set before me and I would have the aid of ones bound to my wyrd.'

'Why should that be us?' Orwandil asks, scraping the snow from his leg plates with the song of metal upon metal. 'There are other, worthier packs, surely?'

'That may be so. Yet I stood with you last. I felt the kinship in your loss. The bond of the kraken's wrath.' Genuine sadness creeps into his voice. The understanding, soul-deep and raw, of a brother's death. A sorrow too many of the Rout share in these nights of blood and fire. He pauses, standing for a moment as the eye of the storm.

Jolfr bows his head. Fjolnir's passing still aches. The kraken's wrath took him from them, and the Krakenblood returned his gene-seed to the Chapter. There is a symmetry there that Jolfr finds comforting. As though it were writ in the wyrd that it should be so.

That they should all be *chosen* for this moment.

'Will you stand with me?'

They walk with him.

The pack and Ivar stride through the halls of the Aett as kaerls heave on massive chains to open doors at the approach of their masters. The serfs fall to their knees as the Astartes pass, never looking up or back as the giants advance into the great rough-hewn space of the meeting hall.

Banded in iron and driftwood, it resonates like a tribal fief. The entire structure is the culture of Fenris, elevated by the

Imperium's technology but never truly bound by it. Even now, after ten thousand years, they stand apart. Holding sacred the ways of Russ, straddling two worlds just as he did. Sons of Fenris and children of Terra both.

Lumen orbs glimmer in bronze-etched faces, the snarling visages of wolves glaring down from the walls alongside banners and pelts. Weapons are hung from leather straps or braced upon metal barbs. Not a single one of them is ceremonial. All have seen use and wait, ready to be wielded once more.

Ivar nods as he enters, gesturing for his brothers to stand to one side. There are others already in attendance. The Space Marines of Wolf King's Call stiffen as they realise who they share the room with. Ulrik the Slayer is there, indomitable and singular, waiting at the head of a feasting table like a totem. Two mortals stand at his side – an elder who bears the look of the frost's children, and a finely dressed male who seems utterly out of his element.

Another pack is already here, standing in a knot at the Slayer's back. By their markings and the etched deeds Ivar knows them. 'Hail,' he calls. 'My brothers of Bloodiron Wrath.'

They nod respectfully and part, revealing the kneeling figure of Brynjar Drakefang behind them. Just as Ivar has picked his champions, so too has the Iron Priest. They stink of ashes and oil, tainted by Brynjar's domain. Each wound in their armour has been patched with exceptional care, worn with pride. Unpainted.

They are veterans. Shaped by iron and cold glory. Wolf Guard. Every scar and honour has been earned in blood.

The pack's leader removes his helm and clamps it at his hip. The face beneath is as rough as the armour. Scars twist the left corner of his mouth into a permanent sneer. His grey hair is a regal sweep, broken only by the gleaming bolts driven into the right side of his head, bracing an old injury.

'You honour us with your presence, Ytri,' Jolfr says with a nod. The older warrior is of Fjolnir's generation. His reputation for combat is well earned, for he is widely regarded as a brutally efficient war-leader.

'When Drakefang reached out, we could not help but be interested,' Ytri intones with a laugh. He sweeps his arm around, indicating his men. 'It has been some time since we have been challenged, and all the Krakenblood's promises reek of desperate glory.'

'Enough,' Ulrik rumbles. 'You have been gathered here for a reason.' He reaches for a pouch belted at his hip and draws out a leather-bound bundle. He lays it down before them all and unrolls it, revealing the vellum within.

It is an astrocartographic map, and it is beautiful.

The craftsmanship is undeniable. Ivar leans forwards, bracing his knuckles against the table, taking in every intricate detail. He can see the pale orb of Fenris, detailed in ice blue and gold. Wolves carved from starlight rear up from it, forging a silver path across the sector. Out, beyond it. Towards the edges, where serpents twine and snap at their own tails.

The lumen light makes the map seem to burn. Everything is picked out in lines of fire. The Imperium's past meeting its future. It seems all too much like an omen. Ivar draws back. There is a fleeting second of melancholy as he looks at it.

'This is it?' Ivar asks. 'Gorm's last voyage?'

'To the best of the Chapter's understanding,' Ulrik says with a nod. 'The last known course. Charted and scryed. The Rune Priests have cast the bones over it. The skjalds have consulted the histories. He sailed forth into the mouth of the Underverse, to seek the Vargrtiðhorn. That we might endure the storms to come, until the Wolftime.' Ulrik taps the map with one armoured finger. 'This is the road you will travel. To whatever end.'

'And there is nothing else known?'

'Only that this was one of many courses that the Archenemy forged as they fled Fenris. One way or the other.'

'A thin thread,' Brynjar puts in.

Ulrik looks around, meeting Drakefang's gaze. He continues regardless, unheeding of the Slayer's ire.

'The narrowest of guesses. We chase the dead.'

The packs jeer him. Wolf King's Call beat their fists against their chests. Jolfr stalks forward with a snarl. Ivar and Ulrik hold their peace. Watchful and aloof. The noise resounds off the chamber walls, as though the lupine braziers were mocking them in turn.

'I am no coward. I fear nothing,' Brynjar growls. 'It is simply a poor hunt with so weak a scent.' He looks around the chamber and shakes his head. 'And what do we have to chase it with? A few packs and a handful of mortals?'

'They have their part to play,' Ulrik says. 'This is Garald Helvintr. Whelp of a rogue trader dynasty. His mistress gifts him to us, in exchange for old claims of her house. The same thing mortals always clamour over. Men. Resources. Fire from the heavens.' He rumbles with laughter. 'We are of a mind to indulge her, though only if this one serves admirably. He shall be your *stýrimaðr*.' The Slayer's gaze finds Garald and the man meets it blankly. Still in shock, overwhelmed by the transhuman dread that afflicts so many mortals.

To look upon one of the Sky Warriors is too much for many. To stand in the presence of a living legend, a being as totemic as the Slayer, would break most.

The old woman, though, she keeps her eyes fixed. Where the whelp sees without seeing, she allows herself to take in every detail. The fierceness of her blood shines through, no matter how reduced and weakened by age she might be.

'His heart is true,' she says at last. 'He is young, but we were all young once. All pups begin by snapping at the heels of their betters, but eventually they hunt with the pack just as readily.' She looks at Garald and smiles.

Ulrik nods and then gestures between his apprentice and the rogue trader's retinue. 'This is Ivar Krakenblood. Wolf Priest of Fenris. He will lead the detachment of warriors. You shall be at his service.'

'I will do all I can, lord,' Garald says and finally looks up. Ivar stares back. Crimson lenses burn in that wolf-skull mask. This time the man does not look away. They appraise each other. Demigod and mortal. Bound together now in sacred purpose.

Garald seizes the initiative and steps forwards, leaning over the map, drumming his fingers against it as he traces out paths and patterns. 'A riftward course… Well, by today's reckoning. It would likely have been different when it was first forged.' He strokes his chin and then adjusts one of his coat sleeves. 'I can sail this course for you, though…' He pauses. 'Though I do wonder why you need me. You have masterful voidsailors of your own.'

'Many eyes watch Fenris now,' Ulrik rumbles. 'The Allfather's Inquisition still wait for opportunity against us. They would damn us for sins that are not our own and failings they only imagine to be true. So we shall slip a hidden blade out from this world in search of our prize. We will have our vengeance and the watchers shall be none the wiser.' He pauses, tilting his head. 'They would not suspect that we would lower ourselves to using you.'

'Well, I…' Garald swallows and then forces a smile. 'I have to say that, demeaning as that may be, I am rather fond of a good round of subterfuge.' He bows and steps back from the table. Ivar can scent the man's brittle fear, poorly disguised. Garald's mind is clearly racing, drifting through potentialities. Sifting his options. 'The lady of the dynasty will be warmed to hear of your confidence in us.'

'It is what must be done,' Ivar says. 'A necessary deception for our undertaking. One that will see an old wound healed and an obligation dispensed with. We will bring what kaerls we can to supplement the undertaking and bolster your house. The transfer is already under way.'

'You're expecting a swift departure then?' Garald asks, fiddling with one of his many rings.

'As soon as possible. We have tarried long enough.' Ivar looks around the circle. 'All that remains is the approval of my brothers.'

'You have chosen well,' Ulrik says and nods to Wolf King's Call. He turns and regards Brynjar. 'And you have balanced your wyrd well.' He pauses and nods to the Iron Priest. 'It is good to see you again, Drakefang.'

'It is an honour to be here, lord Slayer,' Brynjar says, dipping his head. 'I will keep our brother honest in this undertaking. I shall keep him close to the ice and the strong land of home.'

'See that you do,' Ulrik growls. 'We are too few, new blood or not, to suffer more losses. You will all be welcomed back to the hearth when this business is done.' He pauses and reaches out for a subtle clutch of buttons, hidden at one end of the table. He presses one.

Light blossoms up from the surface, forming a hololithic image that sets the map glimmering once again. For a single, beautiful moment, both route and destination are bound together in starlight and blazing promise.

It is a ship. A strike cruiser, carved from blue light. Even in this rendition, Ivar can see where the details lie. The bronze carvings and rune marks. The etchings of protection, victory, and safe passage. He has seen similar etched by hand, by the Rune Priests of the Chapter. Their own gothis.

'This,' Ulrik says, a flicker of admiration creeping into his voice, 'is the *Spinebreaker*.'

'We shall find it. We shall find *him*,' Ivar says. 'And we shall bring them all home. Allfather willing.'

CHAPTER SIX

TO GUARD LIFE AND HEARTH

Far from hearth and home
Into the storm-tossed void, he must roam
Seeking the path long carved by kin.
To dead worlds where the veil lies thin.
With axe, with sword, with fangs bared.
No foe shall stand, no soul be spared.

The sea of stars is a harsh mistress. The sea of souls harsher still.

Both yearn to snuff out human life. All know this to be true. From the earliest days of humanity, from the moment they looked heavenward, it has only ever been a foe to man. Inimical. Hateful. Where once mankind feared the oceans, here was their apotheosis.

The sons of Fenris rise to the challenge with aplomb.

Ice sheets are born and die across the hull as the ship moves away from the World of Winter and War. None look back. The gothi and the warriors of the Rout mark themselves against maleficarum, swear oaths and chant prayers. Bells ring and drums sound, resonating through the iron skeleton of the ship.

All vessels have their song. The engines pound like drumbeats, like hammers upon the anvil as they kindle and burn. Then it becomes a thrumming bass rumble, a roar dredged up from the deep places of the world they force the vessel away from. Runes burn, bright and cold upon the skin of the ship, catching the starlight of the Wolf's Eye, binding it to them. This ship, this stranger, shall bear the touch of its adoptive home. Out and into the trembling void.

Away from Fenris, in search of duty. A fraternity of choice.

Whispers chase them. The vox-calls and queries that dog their steps. All are answered with courtesy and grace, even though they know few will believe them. Deniability is a weapon all of its own.

Few linger in the viewing galleries of the *Swift Spear*. There is little point. Garald and his shipmasters have their craft to be about. The packs are settling into makeshift quarters, too small for the glory of the Rout to be contained. Already they divide up entire decks with predatory relish. Carving out petty king-doms of training rooms.

Only Ivar remains, gazing out at the void. He returns to it, day after day, as they draw closer to the system's edge. Conflict rules his heart. The eternal struggle of watching home fade away even as the future beckons with fitful promise. He could watch this forever, he realises. He could stand and watch Fenris turn and the Wolf's Eye burn. Seasons could pass. Land rise and fall. Entire tribes be consigned to blood or fire.

There would be a purity in that. Justice. Some sense of purpose.

He and his men are children of a death world. Most examples of the human species would consider it a miracle if they lived, let alone prospered. Yet the Vlka Fenryka are the honoured dead.

They fell in battle, early and well. Children of death. Born to die, and born from dying. There is a beautiful and baleful symmetry there that haunts them.

That haunts him.

Ivar Krakenblood clings to the parchment that bears the course of his ancestor, gripping it till the vellum threatens to tear.

He could tear the world apart with his determination, his rage, with tooth and claw.

Instead he waits. Watches.

The system recedes, slowly. He marks time only by the forced diurnal cycles of the ship. He watches the fitful luminescence change, shift, and adapt. Catching on steel-grey walls etched with battle oaths and tallies of service. Undertakings beyond count adorn the walls, speaking to the proud duties it has endured in the name of house, dynasty and Imperium.

'Again and again we return to the sea. Above, below, and under.' Ivar sighs the words out. An old song. A lament of seafarer and starfarer alike.

Ivar cannot remember where he heard it first. As a child, perhaps, or upon his ascendancy. Muttered by the Rune Priests as the bones were cast and counted. Or spoken in solemnity by the Slayer himself.

The ship shudders. Bells toll. The sacred chants are being raised from hidden alcoves and echoing up from lower decks. Somewhere, Ivar knows, Brynjar is casting forth sacred incense and interrogating the vessel's mighty machine spirit. Drumming his iron hand against the skin of the engines, letting his servo-arm scratch out the orisons of sanctification along the bones of the ship.

Translation beckons. The course ahead will burn bright, lit by warp light. A blazing star to mark the way. Towards destiny. Towards glory.

'THE HIGH PRIEST'

The scholar sits alone and breathes out one long sigh of satisfaction.

His eyes are closed. His hands are braced upon a table of carved plex-glass, gently stroking their way across the psycho-reactive wafers that sit upon it. Each one is perfect. Hand-crafted not in imitation of the limited later Imperial Tarots, but of the more ancient and subversive iterations that flourished when Terra was young.

In an age before the Imperium, cards such as these had been prized. Not always, of course. History rarely possessed such careful symmetry. Instead they had passed from the hands of seers and scholars, from true visionaries down to a child's artifice that anyone – gifted or not – could proclaim themselves a master of.

He envies them that surety.

Onouris does not have to open his eyes to know that he is surrounded by placid, all-encompassing light. Somewhere, elsewhere, a bell begins to chime. Not a dolorous lament – far from it. Instead it is light and pleasant. Like a summons to supper.

It is a reminder of the shift change. Sure as monastic rite. As regular as the distant stars.

The reading will have to wait. There will be time later. There is all the time in the universe.

Onouris reaches for his staff and clasps it tight in one hand. He does not need it to walk the world, as one might assume.

He requires it to shape it.

He stretches as he rises, turning away from the table, from the glimmering cards that still flicker and dance upon it. A gesture and a wall made of glass, or perhaps ice, or perhaps the *idea* of cold, ripples and becomes liquid. He passes through it, out from the light of study and into the roiling discord of the outer mysteries. When his skin touches the wall, the no-longer-solid barrier is refreshingly hot, scalding his browned skin with the reassurance that he can still endure pain.

When the stuff of the outer mysteries touches him, he barely has time to scream.

It is a cauldron of the unreal, where thought becomes flesh, and want becomes deed. He can taste the suddenness of blood upon his tongue and the bitter ozone tang as other minds seek his own. Onouris forces himself forwards, step by bloody step, as his skin shreds and re-forms, as his soul is winnowed, as his mind joins in communion with a chorus so pure it must be divine.

Friend.

Brother.

Saviour.

Master.

Each title is a blessing and a scourge. He is burdened with those responsibilities that he must carry out of the study, into the whirling maelstrom of Chaos, towards the inner truths. His steadfastness in the face of adversity anchors the rest of them, till their minds thrum in a single rhythm.

Order flourishes in his path. Little gifts. Madness becomes fractals. They form patterns, dance in the air like the birth and death of individual crystals of ice, cast to the stellar winds. He tames the world. He drives the inchoate into reasonable shapes. Each rise and fall of his staff draws the screaming storm-light down and binds it into footholds.

The crystals flatten and spread, becoming perfect circles. Each one a disc, guiding him across the developing space. They rotate gently, their surfaces blossoming into patterns in languages long dead, drawn up from the warp's akashic tides. He smiles through the pain, letting it sink into his bones, resonating through him with the choir's chorus.

Finally, mercifully, the agony recedes. Torment bleeds away from him in a living wave of black fire, driving back the multifarious energies that boil and rage. He reaches out his empty hand and braces it against a wall, the solidity of it a sudden realisation.

It too begins to ripple, now. Unseated by his presence.

The rational becomes the ephemeral. It weeps and drains away, flowing around him. Embracing him like an old friend. Like a brother. Dust spills down from the opening aperture and enfolds him. Light follows it, drifting like starlight.

He sees now. He understands. Sigils flare at his feet and he steps forwards into the ritual circle. He can hear a distant howl – a clarion call from the deep void. Like old pain and the sound of wolves.

Hate flares up within his soul, singing in baleful resonance with the lupine fury. The world quivers around him, shuddering with a fervent *need*. A hunger that he cannot truly express or bind.

This, my brothers, is what vengeance tastes like upon the tongue.

He sees his brothers, already waiting in communion. In the

blazing air above them, their thoughts take form. A dance of whispering familiars.

+Now, we can begin.+

CHAPTER SEVEN

SHATTERED VOID

It is not an easy path from Fenris. The void teems with madness and wrath. Howling storms drive them from the warp as certain as any tempest upon the Worldsea.

In the high spaces of the bridge, the crew chant prayers to ward off ill omens. It matters not whether they are Terran, Fenrisian, or from elsewhere. They whisper the catechisms and sing. Garald leans forward from his throne, eyes closed, speaking words he learned by rote long ago.

'Deliver us from the ravages of the storm. From the hate of the unreal. Save us, God-Emperor. Spare us.'

He screws his eyes closed and prays with all his soul that it will be true.

'Narayis,' he says across the vox, without looking. 'Tell me what you see.'

Narayis Sadraval is enshrined somewhere far above even the bridge – in her eyrie, swaddled in iron and chained with silver. The binds are a necessary evil that she has long since made peace with, a sign of affection from her masters, in truth. Without them she might dash herself to the floor, hurled from the throne by the tremors and exertions of her duty. Warp guidance is a painful thing, when the storms rage and the abyss screams, and she knows her limits.

Sweat already streaks her pale skin. Her breath catches behind her teeth and she hisses. Attendants mill about her, smoothing out her robes, wiping her brow, pouring water into copper goblets.

She tries to keep the tremor from her flesh. To be as still and stalwart as the bones of the vessel.

Calm is what you seek in the storm, child. Be the eye that holds tranquillity and seek the light.

Her father's words. Old knowledge and recitations etched into her mind as surely as ink upon flesh. Graven into her Navigator's soul. A harsh but fair master, he had ruled their house for decades with judgement and guile. She remembers how he had been in his prime, before the inevitable decline. Sharing that same dark hair and aquiline nose.

He is long gone now, lost to time and the ravages of the bloodline. She thinks of him often, especially as the waves of unreality buffet the ship. Stabs of psychostigmatic pain scythe through her, her nerves catching fire with the directed animus of the sea of souls.

It wants us. It always wants us. We fight it, every step. Every moment of every leap. We are the calm, seeking the light.

Every breath trembles from her. She quivers with the subtle motions of the ship and strains up, adjusting her position upon the throne. The chains kiss skin and whisper against silk.

'All is within parameters,' she says softly. 'I see the way, lord. I see our path.'

* * *

On the lower decks Brynjar leads the enginseers in song and suffering.

Bells toll and hammers ring against decking and the vast engines of the drive compartments. Plasma leaps and electricity sparks with roused Motive Force. The pale blue light fills the chamber until all glimmers like the ice of the home world. Brynjar watches, his mortal features contorting with subdued joy. He finds it adequate in the sight of the Allfather-Omnissiah.

His thralls caper in the illumination. Crawling up amongst the ductwork or swinging down from gantries. They mill about his feet and sniff the air.

'Peace, children,' he whispers. 'No journey lasts forever. You will serve and hunt soon enough.' Soon he knows he must leave the enginarium and its holy mysteries. The scent of sacred machine oil and incense will still cling to him, a comforting shroud, and he will bear it with pride.

The lessons of Fenris' Iron Masters live in him. Burning through his core like volcanic magma. Not even Krakenblood can take that away from him.

He sighs, lost in thought.

The rituals of the Iron Priesthood have always been a comfort. A balm against the failures of the past. He clenches his cybernetic fist and lets the digits tense. It reminds him of the sacrifices he has made. He has given so much of himself to the Chapter, more than others would understand. By their efforts are the weapons of the brotherhood maintained. Strong as the foundations of the Aett. He brings his fist up and drums it over his primary heart.

Brynjar is more than flesh and iron. More than any old rivalry. He is a creature of duty. A warrior of the Rout. He serves the will of the Allfather and the legacy of Russ – as though it were fresh-spoken and not ten thousand years calcified into form.

He stalks onwards and out of the central enginarium, his pets at his heels. Enginseers and senior magi of the Mechanicus kneel as he passes, their iron fingers knotted into the sign of the cog. Servitors halt as they see him, squealing in confused and worshipful binharic.

'From the blood and ashes of the old, the new is born,' he intones. 'We suffer in the flame so that we might be strengthened. That is the wisdom of the mountain and the forge.'

<All glory to the forge, wherein the perfection of the Machine God is engendered and maintained,> the tech-priests cant in his wake. The Martian Creed can wear many faces. That is a lesson learned upon the red sands.

<Be at peace, warrior-son of the Omnissiah,> a binharic utterance huffs from the shadows. Albertus-Nu, Magos of the Enginarium, regards Brynjar with what might be bemusement behind his gleaming augmetic eyes. Too little flesh remains of his original form to make an accurate estimate of age, but experience bleeds from him. He unfolds his arms, twinned sets of them, the lesser pivoting inwards again to form the sacred cog of the Adeptus Mechanicus. The other pair rise in place of biological limbs, offered up to the Machine God.

<I know peace, magos,> Brynjar cants in response. He bows his head in homage to his fellow devotee. <There is no greater peace than in the heart of a mechanism.>

<As all who serve the Omnissiah's design aspire to. From lowest servitor to mightiest archmagos, we are all mere spokes in the wheel. Components in the machine of human perfection. Some are base, others caught between their states. Some are truly exalted. The work of His hand, shaped by the Motive Force.>

<You honour me, magos.>

<It is not an honour to have your abilities noted, son of Fenris

and Mars. It is simple observation of established fact. Praise be to the logical mind and the clarity it brings.>

Child of Fenris and Mars…

He remembers intimately the lessons of the others he met upon the Forge World Principal. Techmarines in waiting, of many Chapters, all learning and toiling beneath the augmetic eyes of the magi. There had been suffering then, but he had risen above it, triumphed over the weakness of the self and been rewarded with the surety of knowledge. Yet it is the certainty of Fenris that guides his steps. From up and off the ice, across the Kraken's Spur so long ago, into the stars.

He bows his head again to Albertus-Nu, watching as the magos' iron fingers knot with sacred rapture.

<If you will excuse me, magos. I have other duties that must be attended to.>

<Service is succour, remember that!> The cant follows at Brynjar's heels, barb and promise both.

And now he moves onwards, out of the enginarium, into the purity of the vessel's heart, to find his brother once again.

The packs have made their lair, billeting away from the crew decks in old storage vaults.

The lingering reek of produce is everywhere. Meats and spices of a hundred worlds, seeping into the metal, retained by the vagaries of ship-life and recyc-system. The enhanced senses of the Vlka Fenryka are no strangers to them.

Jolfr and Ytri stand across from each other in a cavernous storage space that still bears the acrid spice of promethium vapours within it. Face to face, armoured but unhelmed, they scrutinise each other. Servants of opposing masters. So alike and yet so dissimilar. Reflections of a broken mirror.

Bloodiron Wrath and Wolf King's Call are known to each

other, though they have never served in the same campaigns. Nor in the same Great Companies. Brynjar's bleak warriors bear the sigils of the Ironwolves. Ivar's chosen, by contrast, wear the Seawolves colours. One as unyielding as the land of Asaheim, the other as fierce as the Worldsea itself.

Jolfr appraises Ytri honestly. He knows the calibre of warrior he is by sight alone. The scars worn with pride upon flesh and armour. The utilitarian repair of both. A brute weapon, almost more in keeping with an Iron Hand than a son of Russ.

He can see the tense consideration in the rough-hewn warrior's eyes. His judgement is sharper. It is no surprise when he gives it voice.

'You look soft,' Ytri says dismissively. 'It's odd to see one as old as you who looks so weak.'

Jolfr snorts and steps forwards, face to face with Ytri. He stares down at the warrior's ruined face. 'We can test it, if you like. I've killed a hundred things that looked worse than you and had that same disdain.'

'Ah, but would it really be sporting? We've only just started to get to know each other.' Ytri barks with laughter. 'You'd end up looking like me, brother.'

They circle. Like hunting beasts finding the measure of each other, they glower and pace. Jolfr bears his fangs. Ytri merely grins.

'Oh come, Jolfr. Have a little faith, eh? We are all on the same side.'

'So you say,' Jolfr grunts. 'Our patrons seem… less than unified.'

'Brothers and their rivalries,' Ytri says and smirks. He raises his hands. 'None of us are truly free of them, are we?'

'I think you are bored and smell opportunity,' Jolfr snarls, turning away from the other pack leader. 'You think the priests stand in opposition, and you wish to make sport of it.'

'Perhaps not as stupid as you are soft.'

'Call me that again,' Jolfr says with a grin. 'See what happens.'

A door hisses open and the members of their packs begin to file in, taking their respective sides.

'We could settle this here,' Ytri muses, flexing his knuckles. Totems rattle against his armour as he moves. Then he pauses. They all stop, the promise of violence suddenly blunted. The bones against his armour jump again, drumming out their own insane tattoo. He is no longer moving. The ship shakes around them. 'Or perhaps not.' He pauses and licks the air. He smirks. 'Unexpected immaterial translation. Duty calls.'

Ytri sighs. He turns away from Jolfr and his men, moving back to his own side of the petty demesne. He scoops up his weapon and tosses it lightly into the air, catching it as it lands in his hand again. The old blade is notched. Unlike his armour or his face it has never been repaired. The power field is inactive. Jolfr's eyes trace every inch of it. The old oaths carved in runes. The promises of victory and death. The wards against wights and the Neverborn.

'Till later then,' he says placidly, and goes to leave.

'There will not be a *later*,' Jolfr grumbles. 'This farce is over.'

'My brother, there is *always* a later.'

CHAPTER EIGHT

A MURDERED WORLD

The world is dead.

The world should not be here. And it is dead.

Murdered by forces greater than Garald can conceive of, for he has never witnessed the holy spectacle of Exterminatus. The corpse-planets he has seen in his brief lifetime have all been long in their graves.

It seems almost impossibly fresh.

It seems as though it had been forged anew, here when they tore from the warp. Waiting. A promise wrought in stone. Impossibly placed, as though ripped from its natural orbit and nestled near the nameless system's Mandeville point. Extruding no gravity.

The world is silent. Still. Nothing speaks from its surface. No signals or signs. Barely even the crackle of background radiation. It is bereft of spirit and soul. Nothing speaks to him as it did when he looked upon Fenris or walked its surface. This place resonates only of old death and regret. Cities lie sprawled and broken, their vast edifices ruined by fire. The cyclopean stones are pitted and warped by heat, littering the great plains of obsidian glass.

A cruel bauble, cast aside by absent gods.

The world has burned and curdled. Oceans of sludgy matter sit quiescent and seemingly lifeless. Unnaturally still, as unmoving as the landmasses. It chills Garald to his core even to look upon it.

'Auspex,' he orders, reaching up with one hand to click at the air. Voices chorus their affirmations around him. 'I want full auspex sweeps. If there's anything down there – hostile or of value – I want to know about it.'

'Wyrms never make themselves apparent until they strike,' Bodil grumbles from his side. One pale, bony hand is draped over the edge of the throne, dangerously close to touching him. Garald wants to shrink from it, to slap it away, to be rid of her incessant critique.

Yet somehow that wisdom is a comfort now, as the black planet does not turn and no longer burns.

Throne, but how could I have missed that? There is no orbital rotation, he realises. The world waits. It sits and does not spin. Suspended in a single moment.

'Auspex readings are inconclusive, lord,' a crew member says. Garald looks to the woman, brow furrowing. He knows her name and yet… The monstrous image before him has robbed him of the memory of it. Stolen his voice. He is humbled before the face of uncreation. He blinks and collects himself. Breath hisses from him in a ragged gasp. Garald swallows and forces himself up from the throne, gazing out at the becalmed world.

'Thank you, Officer Velaq,' he says at last. Clarity returns in a cold wave, gripping him like a vice. 'Keep scanning. I want a complete hololithic accounting of this world by the time our guests gather. They will want to know the lie of the land. Maintain active pursuit of Imperial signum codes. If there's a ship here, Astartes or otherwise, I want to know about it.'

'It will be here,' Bodil's voice rattles from behind him. He hears the clatter of bone upon the metal decking and turns as she scoops up the rune-etched tiles. She scrutinises them, one after the other, tracking the myriad futures and binding them into place. She grins and flashes her ruined teeth. 'This place is a dead place. Morkai has scoured it with his claws and knocked it out from the universe's turning. Cold and corroded are the lairs of monsters, even when they serve as the graves of heroes.'

'You really think this is where their ship came to lie?' He pauses and considers it. His hand reaches out, as though to trace his fingers along a map that is not there. 'We've followed the map's course. This is what we find.'

'The enemies of man delight in trickery and mockery. This is no different. A flame, burned out, snuffed out, around a great light? A world not holy in its cold, as Fenris is, but withered and broken...'

'How are the other systems faring? Voids up?'

'Aye, lord! Kindling!' comes the call, fresh and eager. 'Ignition is well within parameters. Maybe even slightly above. The Iron Wolf below has certainly been spurring our own adepts on to greater heights.'

Garald scoffs, though he can't deny it. Morale is up. Efficiency has increased. The ship's systems no longer simply hum or purr. They growl. They roar. That was the sound it made as the ship cut like a blade through the warp, the shuddering scream as it was forcibly ejected, and it is the sound it makes now as the Geller field finally surrenders and the voids crackle to life.

'Bring us around,' he says. 'This place shouldn't be. We'll pin its reality into shape. We'll make sure there's another map for the Wolves to follow.'

Velaq clicks her tongue as she scrutinises the readouts. 'When we know anything, you'll be notified, my lord.' Information streams down every screen, nests of symbols slowly coalescing into a coherent dataset. Magi chant from their alcoves, praising the Omnissiah-Interpreter in His divine role as master of information synthesis. Bells toll and censers swing.

All as clarity slowly forms around them. Like a promise. Like a threat.

Ivar is the first to make his way to the bridge, each step weighing on him. Slow and ponderous, he feels every plate of his armour.

Somehow the transit was easier than being back in material reality. The Geller field shielded them all from the warp's toxic weight, and yet here in the materium, there is only the crushing pain of inevitability.

He has seen the black planet waiting beyond. Nameless and looming. Gleaming with a dark lustre that needs no motion to project its utter wrongness. The crew have been forbidden from looking at it unless absolutely necessary. Ivar closed the last of the great blast shields himself.

'Into the lair of beasts, all shadows and suffering,' he whispers.

For a moment he is back in the cave. Trapped amidst darkness and monsters. The claws of the trolls waiting to tear him apart. He blinks and then he is elsewhere once more. The Kraken's Spur towers above him, rain-slick and lightning-lit. He can smell old death on the air. Stronger than the artificial air of the ship. More bitter than the cold that saturates its iron bones.

It is a strange place for him, this ship. Of Fenris and yet foreign. He has served upon ships before, weathering their eccentricities. Always they were of the Rout. Proud vessels of war. Great barques that would bear their warriors to the very heart of conflict.

Not soft ships such as this.

The walls mock him with their banal comforts. Carved wood and stone. Art hangs from slender silver hooks and statues pose in alcoves, all gold and marble. Beckoning figures, some martial and others the tasteful renditions of saints. Where they do not bear swords or weighty graven tomes, they show open hands or cover their faces. Some are swathed in rich red fabric.

To his warrior's mind it seems wasteful. There should be no part of the vessel not dedicated to the prosecution of the All-father's wars. Yet this is a rogue trader's vessel, he knows, and no matter how closely the dynasty cleaves to the old ways of Fenris, they will always have differing priorities.

'Even such as these have purpose,' he says to himself. 'We cannot all be blades in His armoury.'

When he enters the bridge it is as a shadowy presence. He stalks in, as silent and domineering as Morkai himself. He is the first of his brotherhood to enter the space since translation. A few of the crew turn to look at him, immediately and visibly paling, before turning back to their stations with greater focus.

Garald does not look around. Ivar pauses behind the throne. He leans forward, knowing how he must appear to the others present. All black armour and bone. A spectre made flesh and clad in battle plate that speaks only of death and ruin. The staring rictus of a skull, eyes aglow and yearning.

Ivar fixes his eyes upon the waiting world. The corpse of a planet.

'Helvintr,' he growls.

The man starts and turns, rising and placing a hand against the throne's back. The old woman stands, half-crouched, at the trader's side. She nods respectfully to the Wolf Priest and bares her ruined teeth in a smile.

'What do we know?' Ivar asks. 'Where has the course led us?'

'It...' Garald trails off. 'It shouldn't be here. If I didn't know any better it would seem like something had scooped the whole planet up and left it here. Waiting.'

'A message,' Ivar muses. 'A warning.'

'Perhaps. It defies all expected physical parameters. Implying that–'

'That it is of the warp. *Maleficarum*,' Ivar finishes.

'Just so.'

'And there is no sign of the *Spinebreaker*?'

'Nothing yet, lord. The survey continues apace.' Garald shoots a nervous look to another of his crew. 'This could merely be a step along the way. A marker.'

'Our enemies have a weakness for symbolism. This is meant to captivate us. Not to distract or misdirect. They do not want to deceive us here. No… they have left this for us intentionally.'

The bridge space is a rectangular chamber, dominated by the central throne and dais. Around it, in various pits of complex machinery and amongst banks of whirring cogitators, the other members of the crew toil, eyes fixed upon their screens. Hands continually in motion. The air fills with the clack of runic keys and the thrum of data-engines.

The gilding is old here. A faded grandeur that lingers around them. The crew cannot see the bars of their cage. The limits imposed on them. Ivar sees it. It is his duty to judge the souls of his brothers and the mortals who serve them.

They have served and suffered, yes, but he knows that they are coddled.

Too little ice in their blood. Too few from the home world. He admires the old gothi's drive and determination. *She is the iron in this undertaking. The strong hand of guidance.* His eyes drift to the leather pouch bound at her waist. Her withered, bird-like fingers clutch at tiles of bone, and he traces the runes there.

Ivar feels again the weight of his wyrd. Destiny's talons close about him as surely as the old woman grips the tiles. Like the pressure of the strange world grasps the ship.

'We have something,' an officer murmurs. She brushes dark hair back from her brow and frowns. 'Resolving, but quicker than it should.'

'As though it wants to be seen at this exact moment,' Ivar sighs. 'You see?'

'Accuracy, Velaq. Give me specifics.' Garald leans forward, fingers drumming nervously.

Officer Velaq hammers at the keys of the runeboard, watching the data scroll and realign. She pushes one final button and a hololithic map blossoms at the fore of the bridge, obscuring the world itself with a flickering rendition. The cold blue light pulses with a half-obscured crimson stain. Ivar recognises it instantly.

A strike cruiser.

'Clarify the signum codes,' he growls. Velaq flinches, her head snapping round to look at him like a prey animal. 'Show me the ship's name.'

The air within the bridge grows tense. Close, despite the ever-present chill. All attention is focused upon Ivar. He feels their eyes upon him. He can count the short, sharp breaths each crew member takes. Hear the pounding of their hearts.

'The *Spinebreaker*, my lord,' she says.

The doors hiss open behind him. Ivar turns and cocks his head as Ytri and Jolfr walk in, one in front of the other. Their packs trail behind them, keeping an uneasy distance.

Last of all comes Brynjar. The Iron Priest wears his armour and helm. The servo-arm twitches and snaps, the brazen wolf's head mimicking the warrior's own impatience. He stands for a moment, silhouetted in the corridor's light, haloed in gold like a mural. Every detail of his armour is apparent to Ivar. Every sweep of blue and gold, bronze and iron.

He is vital where I remain shrouded, Ivar muses to himself.

No matter how much of his soul he has given to the Martian

Priesthood or how much of him has been replaced, there is a relentless human energy to Brynjar. As a youth it had manifested almost purely as arrogance; now, though, it has transmuted into a commanding presence.

The packs fan out around the edges of the bridge, establishing a perimeter. They stalk like the huscarls of ancient jarls, weapons raised and ready. Brynjar leads the pack leaders along the central walkway to join Ivar around the throne.

Garald has the wherewithal to move away from the command dais, bowing his head in silent acceptance as the true council gathers.

'We have our target,' Ivar says. 'The war grave of Gorm Kraken-blood.'

CHAPTER NINE

VOICES OF THE DAMNED

Listen.

In impossible places, the warp speaks. It whispers and cajoles. It promises and it lies. A thousand voices speak as one. A million souls cry out in pain. It is the mortis cry of dying worlds and the death screams of a ship's machine spirit. Blood boiling away in the burning light of dying stars. Flesh flash-frozen in the hungry void.

This is the price of war. The reward of eternal service. Ten thousand years of ceaseless conflict. Here, where the black planets wait, there is only the rhythm and song of apocalypse. It is sung in the high deserts as surely as upon the open ice.

It has ever been so. Before humanity crawled from the muck and cast their eyes to uncertain heavens, so the melody of the Great Ocean was there. Lapping at the shores of awareness and sensation. Those who could read such things were thought of as shamans, wise men, healers. Visionaries and oracles.

How the times have changed.

Now those of the great gift are maligned and hated, even by an Imperium that depends upon them. Psychic might is both the core and the skeleton of this failing empire. It is the fire in the bloodstream of an inhumane regime. It is the fire of self-destruction at the heart of a species gone mad.

Listen.

You can hear it even now. Waiting. Potential dwells in all things. It simply requires the correct moment for it to be realised and awakened. Like a bell, waiting to be tolled. Now the time is upon us. Now all is as it must be. Now the only truth that matters shall be realised.

Fate cannot be fought. Only weathered.

A thousand voices speak from a million throats. The world waits, quiet and dead, yet the song persists... Ten thousand years old and still vital. Restrung with the galaxy's breaking, tuned to the screams of so many loyal servants.

The song is always the same. It is vengeance. And now the web draws tight.

The world waits in silent horror and majesty, as though it intones some silent song.

From afar it is a curiosity. A warning. It is only as they draw nearer that the sheer unnatural scope of it becomes apparent. Plains of black glass, carved by geologic forces and timeless warfare. Ruined cities which had slumped like candles, anchored by networks of trenches. It is a moment carved in time.

The Thunderhawk hurtles planetward. It is one of the few allowances made to the undertaking by the Rout, and it bears the name *Blade of Ice*. The pale blue armour bears iron and silver runes upon it, beaten into the metal inside and out.

Ivar rests his head against them, letting his helm bang gently against the ship's skeleton. Brynjar led the rites before they boarded, honouring the ancient and potent machine spirit. Anointing the iron of the ship the same way they would a wooden vessel before it took to the Worldsea.

Their ways are ancient and yet eternal.

They are all braced within the Thunderhawk. The iron rungs of their support cradles cling to them, holding them in place as the ship judders.

There is, strangely, no true bite of atmospheric entry. No sudden burst of flame and resistance. Ivar closes his eyes inside his helm and braces once again. Counting down the moments. His fingers twitch around the handle of his crozius.

Something whispers at his ear, thrumming through the gunship like the notes of a song. Then it is gone. Forgotten.

When Ivar opens his eyes he looks to Wolf King's Call. The pack are clustered together, pinned in place. Waiting for the moment to strike. All are helmed and so he marks them by their armour. Jolfr is entirely still, poised. His axe is mounted beside him, ready and waiting for blood. The edge of it catches the crimson light within the Thunderhawk, rendering it into an executioner's grin.

Orwandil's head droops and he hums to himself. Muttering some old tribal song. He drums his free hand against his knee plates like a tavern skjald. Hrungnir, by contrast, mirrors Jolfr in silence. In prayer, Ivar surmises. He approves.

Vili, the youngest of the pack, is looking straight at Ivar – caught somewhere between awe and trepidation. Ivar almost laughs. There are always pups like him, in war. Inheritors to greatness, chasing after it with their teeth nipping at the heels of presumed legends. The boy's armour is yet fresh. He is yet to be truly blooded.

Bloodiron Wrath are the counterweight.

Brynjar's chosen are hardened killers. All the primal joy has been bled from them, till only a cruel coldness remains. There is Falr, festooned with knives, his gauntlets spiked like an ancient caestus. Akaz is a blunter instrument. Stocky, even in his full armour, he stands like a sentinel. A dependable warrior. Brynjar owes him his life, numerous times over. Then there is Gillingr. A consummate executioner. He leans upon his axe, the great blade a testament to a craftsman's skill and a warrior's bearing. Last is Odr. Even motionless and watching, he brims with killing vigour. He does not carry his weapons, yet every part of him seems a weapon. Prepared for the moment of war. Readied to have battle joined. As they all are.

Ytri bears it best. The warrior's helmet is carved in a snarling wolf's visage, its chipped fangs cradling the mouth-grille. Crimson lenses turn to look at Ivar before his voice crackles forth in a snarl. He braces himself upon the hilt of his sword.

'You think the ghosts you seek are down there?'

'Why shouldn't they be?' Ivar asks. 'The map speaks and we follow. The same as any seafarer.'

Ytri laughs and shakes his ruined head. 'I would have expected better of you, Wolf Priest. You trained in the mysteries for how long? Following along after the Slayer, feeding on his scraps, and you still haven't seized your own path. I almost feel sorry for you.'

'Hold your tongue,' Vili calls over the engine roar. 'Ivar deserves your respect.'

'Does he? I haven't seen any sign of that yet. He might have coddled your pack, but he's yet to prove anything to me. Respect is earned.'

'Enough.'

Brynjar's voice rebounds down the transport hold. He has stood in silence towards the front of the vehicle in quiet communion with the noble vessel's soul. Now he steps forward, his thralls bowed at his feet as though in homage. Each of the whining tech-beasts begins to growl, a low, guttural sound reverberating from their mutilated throats.

'Ivar is not some idle braggart, Ytri. You will give him the deference he deserves.'

'As you will,' he says quietly. Chastened.

'Now we shall see if they can behave, brother,' Brynjar says as he looks to Ivar. The Wolf Priest is silent, distracted. His head lolls again and bangs against the rune-etched steel. 'Brother?' Brynjar asks again.

Ivar blinks away the sudden rush of pain that throbs within his temples. His teeth grind together as he stifles a growl of pain. 'Can you hear that?' Ivar slurs.

'All I hear is the ship, brother,' Brynjar says. He begins to move forward, steadying himself along one of the internal hull plates. 'What is it? What do you hear?'

'I hear a voice. It speaks like the storm…' Ivar lurches forward. The ship lurches with him. Suddenly the sound is rising, screaming. Everywhere.

'Listen,' Ivar hisses, as the planet begins to speak at last.

The sky catches fire.

Where once there was barely an atmosphere, now it kindles into a wrathful inferno. Bale aurorae tear at the ship with talons made of light and insanity. The Thunderhawk struggles, a mote in the storm. Dust in the infinite wind. Gales bear it lower. It struggles with the sudden thrum of gravity, the inevitability of the broken world.

Above, below, all is screaming. The voice of the damned speaks in atrocity. Over and over. It overwhelms every system it touches: gunship, armour, all.

The black planet resonates, tolling with impossible spiritual agony till the fire and the wind drags the Thunderhawk earthwards. A wing clips the tip of a peak of rearing obsidian, shattering it to flinders. The craft wheels about, struggling to right itself, fire trailing from its right engine.

Alarums sound, adding their own atonal screeching to the cacophony. The blunt prow of the Thunderhawk tears through a desiccated tower, reducing the withered extrusion to dust and rubble. It struggles to rise once more.

The compartment's iron-wrought walls begin to glow. Light fills it, eclipsing even the flickering emergency lumens. The crimson radiance grows more intense before it sublimes, transmuting to a blazing white-hot. Plates spasm and warp.

'She cannot hold,' Brynjar says quickly. A nest of tiny mecha-dendrites whir from the weld between his armour and his artificial hand, interfacing with the ship's systems in a flurry of clicks and binharic chirruping. He moves with a fluid efficiency, each and every motion calibrated to an algorithm that Ivar cannot understand.

The divinity of damage control, Ivar thinks, through waves of pain. It is fading now. Receding. Whatever psychic attack sought to unman them has passed over, replaced by fire and fury. 'Make them land!' Ivar calls. 'Better to stand on solid ground and fight than to be dashed against the rocks like a fish!'

Brynjar nods. The vox crackles with confirmation from the pilots. Another tremor wracks the gunship before the sirens hitch as though in true alarm.

The gunship drops. Brynjar staggers and the others pitch forward in their cradles. Ivar's hand is locked tight about his weapon. He does not close his eyes. He observes everything. He can feel the rush of physics tugging at his entire body, even through the armour plating. His teeth strain in his gums as he forces his jaws closed in a grimace.

Then the thrusters fire.

Blade of Ice scores across the black glass landscape like its namesake. It tears through grasping extrusions, frond-fingers that would seek to bind them in place. They claw at the ship's hull, desperately longing. *Blade of Ice* answers in kind. The heavy bolters howl, scouring the plateau before them with fire and shrapnel. The hungry sky cannot touch them, not this close to the ruined ground. Beneath the onslaught, the protrusions die and are born anew. Gnawing at the air, even as they are shattered again. Over and over.

The landing struts crush yet more terrain to powder as the Thunderhawk settles. The assault ramp drops, casting up plumes of dust and ashes. One by one the warriors of the Rout stride out onto a world that hates them.

The dead world has waited. Patiently. A predator, luxuriating in its nest. There is already one victim, pinned and drained. Now more prey has come, and the world stirs anew. Light flickers and dances across the waking planet. Deep lambency blossoms from the core outwards. The mountains are crowned with flame now, coiling like witch-light down around them in mockery of volcanic motion.

Ivar tightens his grip around the handle of the crozius and thumbs the ignition rune. Caged lightning writhes across the surface of the weapon, casting the winged wolf's skull in a halo of light.

'Whatever comes against us, we defy it,' Ivar snarls. He thrusts the weapon forward. The others ready themselves. Chainsword teeth bite and churn. Bolters are readied. Brynjar's hammer and Jolfr's axe join Ivar's weapon in radiant wrath. Ytri readies his blade but does not let it kindle. Not yet.

'Though this Underverse place is outside of the Allfather's gaze, we shall endure it. Remember that you are sons of Fenris. You are brothers of the Rout. We have lasted these ten thousand years, though all the wiles of the Archenemy have been set against us. Even our brothers have turned upon us, and the Allfather's misled followers have swarmed to stymie us. No more! This day we prove our courage! We sanctify our hate!'

Fists pound breastplates. Gauntlets hammer against hilt and handle. Bolters clatter against chest or thigh plate.

'Fenrys hjolda!' they bellow in one voice. One howl.

CHAPTER TEN

SONS OF CHAOS

The world waits and the city dreams.

It has waited for geologic aeons, ever since it was carved out of place. Wrenched from space and time. Yet it is newborn and screaming. Temporal progression has no place here. It is an afterthought of atrocity, an artist's sketch wrought in black stone and wonder and horror.

It is the idea of a world. The presentiment of a place. It is, in many ways, a cold cradle just as Fenris is.

This world, like that world, has its sons.

As the light ripples through the fabric of the false world, filling the city spires with light and crowning the mountains, so the children of Chaos begin to stir.

They were mortal once. Some of them remember those times and they dash their heads bloody against the walls of their confinement. Others have forgotten. Most have been born in the darkness beneath the world, nursing their own secret creeds and congregations.

Too many eyes open in the shadows and trace the path of the light. Claws scrabble against rock, dragging themselves out of windowless cells, up through winding passages and broken stairways. Hoots and clicks fill the spaces beneath the world, breaking into howls and screams of sorrow, fear and hate.

Scaled hands find weapons. Furred fingers close around haft or handle. The few projectile weapons are lovingly caressed, treasured as tokens of long-vanished ancestors. Whole clades of madness have bred in the darkness at the world's heart, driven there by the cruel spear brought low upon it. A thing of metal and machine. A cold blade from the stars.

They hate it. Despite everything, no matter that it is the core of their world and their culture, they despise it. Some tug at the scraps of ruined uniform that still cling to their changed bodies, and let the loathing fill their souls. Hate is pure. It remains the same, no matter the changes.

The first to emerge, blinking, into the unholy light of the world, bears the name Kaitan. The others chant it as they follow him. He stands taller with their support, buoyed up on the closest thing one of his breed will ever have to love.

Kaitan's skull is a sweeping crest of bone, surmounted by spiralling horns. His beak clicks and gnashes. Drool bubbles over the smooth edges of it to spatter on the tunnel floor. It is rewarding to see something there other than blood. He hoots and rears up, thrusting a ragged blade into the air.

Spears rise behind him or clatter against shields. Enough control remains amongst the rabble to stop them from firing into the ceiling. Ammunition is rare and sacred. It must be saved for the hunt.

Dimly, Kaitan remembers what it was to be a man. He remembers duty and discipline. Perhaps even honour. Something in the core of him screams as the razor wire of his new reality carves him apart, displacing him from the memory of something ideal into the debased and twisted thing he is now.

He vomits. Tiny bones crunch underfoot as he steps through the mess. Soon, though. Soon they will eat well. Better and bigger prey awaits. They have not had such opportunity in a generation.

Kaitan forces his jaws into alignment, swallowing down bile and spit. The scaled flesh of his palms is clammy with old, rancid sweat. He turns to look at his men. His clan. His horde.

'Kill the Wolves!' he bellows. 'Kill them all!'

The bestial tide surges forward against them and they hold like rocks in the storm. Solid land where the rush of the ocean threatens to draw them down, deep into the world forge.

They are made of stronger stuff. They are iron and blood. The salt and the rage is in them, one and all. Ivar cares not whether they are true brother or stranger. All stand as one, enmity and rivalry forgotten.

This is what they were made for.

The bolters sound. Mass-reactive shells hurtle into the enemy ranks like cast spears. Bodies begin to burst apart in a rain of blood and bone. Horns splinter, shattering under the relentless barrage. Ivar does not fire. He waits. Lightning crackles about his mace and he stalks forward. The weapon feels righteous in his hands, blazing with unmatched purity.

The first true kill must be his. The wolf that bears the prey-beast down and snaps its neck. All his training, every moment of trial and ordeal, has been for this. To stand as the leader of an endeavour. A symbol.

The mace falls and shatters a misshapen skull, atomising a creature's head in a misting of blood vapour. A glittering cloud of iridescent fluid spatters his armour. Ivar snarls. *Of course it is some inhuman ichor – why would it have any sort of consistency or purity?* It crawls across the black plate, still animate in some hideously unnatural way.

Only by moving forward can he purge himself of the taint of its presence. Behind him he can hear the others as they move and fire. Some, the youngest and brashest amongst them, gun their chain weapons. All of it adds to the great symphony of war, resounding across the plains. Challenging the anthems of false gods.

More of them surge in, crowding about him. The din of bolter fire fades, disappears, replaced by the screech of chainsword teeth against bone and flesh. The sizzle-crack of active power weapons – axes, hammers and swords – cleaving into the foe. The song of their deaths echoes out.

Claws and makeshift blades scrape across the black plate of Ivar's armour. It is not enough. It will never be enough. They are the patter of rain against the mountains. He drives them back with his shoulder and swings his whole body around – hammering the mace through three bodies. The caving ribs and breaking spines resonate through the conversion field with a thrum and a flash. The first turns to dust at the waist, bearing the brunt of the strike's fury. The others are hewn roughly in half. Intestines spool out in a wet rush.

They swarm onwards. So many. Too many. Claws and blades and teeth give way to tendrils of sinewy flesh. Slapping wetly against his armour, oozing slime that makes even ceramite sizzle. Ivar growls and pushes them back, creating distance with sweeps of his weapon. He has the measure of them. So many of them are lesser beings, smaller minds. Others burn with captive power. His eyes trace it, from the glow that permeates their distended skulls, to the witch-light dancing along their crude weapons.

They scream like monstrous children, the sons of Chaos itself. Heterogeneously mutated and hideous. Fur covers some in a sapphire shroud, where others bear clusters of vibrant feathers. Snouts. Beaks. Horns like rams or protrusions of gleaming antlers. No two are alike. Each is a clade of atrocity unto itself.

Runes scroll down the vision of his eye-lenses as he tracks the progress of the others. Brynjar, Jolfr and Ytri are not far behind him, holding a line of solid defence and offence. He turns for but a moment and sees them. Each one is a living engine of destruction. Axes and blades rise and fall. The servo-arm on Brynjar's back snakes out and seizes one of the monstrous foe by the skull, crushing it to slurry. A gesture and the mechanised limb flicks the glistening fluids from its toothed maw.

Spears and arrows scar the sky, trailing auroric fire. When they hit they detonate like small star-births. Ivar rears back and curses. Riotous green flame clings to his armour, coiling up and around his limbs. It shivers and sub-divides, becoming chains of myriad coloured conflagration.

The enemy boils out of tunnels and yawning apertures in the black glass. They pull themselves up, clawing at the earth with cloying longing. They spill up over the edges of the trenches and tumble from the low walls of the city's outermost buildings.

No matter that they die in droves, there are always more.

'Look at them! Look at the dreg-beasts they send against us. Less than nothing! The spoor of monsters and the slaves of darkness! This is all their pretender gods can muster.' His fist lashes out and floors another one. 'This is not the enemy that laid low our brother. This is their basest offerings! It is what has bred in the darkness they left behind!'

Another rune flashes in his display. The crimson marker that designates the fallen ship. Past the trenches, through the ruin of the city, there it waits. There Gorm Krakenblood lies. 'Our prize is not far,' Ivar growls. 'Nothing they throw at us can hold us. You have faced worse upon the ice as mere children!'

* * *

Brynjar fights, and it is not merely the battle of flesh and blood before them.

Whenever he leaves Fenris and bears the burden of the Iron Isles to the stars, he is at war with himself. Logic forever fights against animal instinct. The teachings of Mars have bit deep, worming beneath his skin like the ancient and forbidden cavern cities of Fenris.

He swings the hammer around and destroys another beast-man utterly. The thunderclap of atomisation is a sacred song, even above the din and roar of battle.

Perhaps, he thinks, *that is the problem.*

Brynjar has always envied Ivar's purity of purpose. A singular drive that has led him to greatness. The path of the Iron Priest has brought Brynjar fulfilment, yet too often he wonders what might have been. If he had been stronger and more determined when they were both tested.

Perhaps then he would have been the Slayer's pupil, without the Martian Creed cut into his soul.

He turns his hammer over and brings it down, hammering another monster into the earth. The noctilith and obsidian cracks beneath the powered impact. Light crawls up from the wounds, winding into the air. He growls at the witch-scent that stains the world. The more blood they shed, the stronger it grows. The world feeds upon death, charging like a battery of spilled souls. It is, he realises, a machine in its own right. Not directed by gears and pistons but by a raw will. Set to turning, now that they walk upon it.

Almost as one, the packs leap into the trenches, driving the enemy back where they are not crushed underfoot. They are broad earthworks, giant-scale, the sort of trenches that would allow Warhound Titans to walk double file. Carved not for true war but for some elaborate effect. Ashes and blood coat the surfaces as the warriors of the Rout advance. The walls glitter. They burn with captive heat and light, making the inhuman blood hiss and gleam.

Lesser minds might see a cruel beauty here. Brynjar does not allow it to addle his mind. Such concerns are for skjalds. There are no songs sung here. No great sagas recounted so that they can be learned from. There is only the echo of old woes.

'You feel it, don't you?' Brynjar calls. Ivar turns to look at him, driving back another horned beast without thought or effort. 'This place has a weight. It pushes down upon the spirit.'

'Aye… Enough enmity to drown a world. No wonder Gorm's force became waylaid here. It is a trap made of their spite.'

'The only way is through it. Tarry and we only play into their hands.' Brynjar draws his Helfrost pistol and fires into the thronging mass. They scream in one voice, a condensed screech of agony as flesh is flash-frozen. They shatter, destroyed in a blast of purest cold, sloughing apart in a rain of frostbitten skin. A broken horn hits the ground once before it becomes a mere flurry of dust.

He looks back to Ivar, but the Wolf Priest is distracted. Ivar stands, his armoured form heaving. Brynjar can feel the rage that radiates out from him, even without checking his armour systems.

'Brother?' he asks. Brynjar's hand snaps out and grasps Ivar's pauldron. 'What is it? What do you see?'

'There are a few amongst their number…' He growls, gritting his teeth. 'Leaders. Kill them and we disrupt the horde.'

'The same as the Devourer's legions, eh?' Brynjar laughs.

'The world is the enemy's resonator. Near or far, they direct their will through it. The world's fire burns in the greatest of the foe. Take the fight directly to them. Blade to blade. Tooth and claw.'

'If that is the will of the Wolf Priest, then I shall gladly heed it.' Brynjar grins. 'Not that any of us need the excuse!'

'Jolfr! Ytri!' Ivar calls. The two pack leaders and their warriors draw nearer, forming a knot of iron defence. The younger warriors hold the line. Vili continues to cleave and hew with his chainsword, practically dripping in the jewel-like blood of the beasts. Orwandil headbutts a lesser monster, driving it back in a shower of shattered cranium. He steps back and swings out with a roaring chainaxe, bisecting the reeling thing. He stands over it and hacks down, roaring his hate as it dies. Hrungnir laughs as he fights. The digits of a power fist flex and crackle as he beats and bludgeons. The enemy's blood cooks to powder.

Brynjar notes the others, the grim members of Ytri's pack. Bloodiron Wrath speak amongst themselves in clicks and hisses of vox-traffic. They trust in their leader to speak for them and to direct them to where is needful. Their bond is strong as steel, their resolve as sure as the foundations of the Aett.

'I have marked a number of targets,' Ivar growls. Runes flash across Brynjar's vision, both across his visor display and his own cybernetic ocular. Each targeting rune is tailored to one of the leaders. Ivar. Brynjar. Jolfr. Ytri.

He finds his target by sight alone. A muscle-swollen brute, tusked, its heaving brow burning with psychic fire. Lightning cracks behind it, silhouetting it against the tormented sky for a moment as it turns to glare at him. He raises his hammer in acceptance of the challenge.

'Bring them death!' Brynjar growls.

Ivar lunges out of the defensive formation, lashing fiercely with the blade-winged mace. He carves his way through them, roaring into their faces.

The vox-amplified howl is a physical wave, and the beasts scatter before him. The cowards show their backs to him, vistas of bare skin, fur, feathers, and scraps of leather. He hacks at them, cleaving through flesh and bone as though they were paper. The power field flares and sizzles with the effort. He forces his way onwards. The lesser beasts scatter, only a few turning to flail in meek defiance.

'You think yourselves worthy?' Ivar bellows. 'So many and yet so weak!'

They bray back at him, stinking of musky fear. His fist slams out and breaks a beak. Blood slicks his gauntlet.

All their deaths achieve is the merest of delays. He knows that. He has no doubt that their leaders know that. The degenerate things have bred here in darkness for so long. Beasts begetting beasts. It sickens him to look at them and at the rags they wear.

Once, long ago, they were Imperial. Before the enemy's taint wormed its way beneath their skin. Sullying their lineage forever. When he slays them it is a release. A consecration. He is tending to their flesh and spirit, as surely as he would for any brother of the Chapter.

The debased are granted only the mercy of the blade. The honoured know the Wolf Priest's blessing. That is what the Slayer has always taught him. The lessons of years of service. It is the wisdom of the trolls' cave and the Kraken's Spur.

To lead with strength and to punish the enemies of humanity with fervent wrath. To look inwards as well as out.

He lashes out with his crozius–

And feels its swing arrested with a clatter that sends shockwaves up his arm, even through the powered armour.

Ivar blinks within his helm.

'There you are,' he growls. The horned chieftain growls back, its beaked jaws lolling open, trailing thick yellowed saliva.

'There… are…' it slurs back, mocking his words. 'I, Kaitan!' it screeches. Other monsters take up the chant.

'Kaitan! Kaitan! Kaitan!'

'Then you have come to die, Kaitan,' Ivar says.

Fire kindles along the monster's ragged blade. Kaitan snorts and pushes forward with all its prodigious inhuman strength. Ivar strains, forced back step by step. His boots struggle to find purchase upon the smooth noctilith of the ground.

Ivar throws himself forwards, lightning warring with fire. The competing fields spark and hiss, science against sorcery. Monster against champion. The eternal refrain of mankind. Even before they clawed their way to the heavens to face down the xenos-breeds, humanity faced down its own monsters upon the home world.

Now the wolves that once beat at the gates are the ones that defend them.

Ivar strikes again. Each movement, each blow, is a killing stroke. It burns with humanity's vengeance. With the Allfather's sacred wrath. The monster does not quail beneath them like its mongrel kin. Kaitan rises to the challenge. It snarls and snaps at him, till his face plate is coated in its vile spittle. The stink of it defies the filters in his helm. Sour. Sweet. The surge of it almost overwhelms him.

The obsidian blade glimmers with each strike, soul-light rippling through it. Every time their weapons collide it is as though laughter wafts from the monster's weapon. Mockery in every motion. The power field crackles with each hit, ringing like a thunderclap as the foe's blows rain down upon him. Ivar feels Kaitan's claws tear lines of fire down his breastplate, gouging at the winged skull. Talons dislodge from the straps and ties that hold them there. He staggers back.

Ivar turns the crozius and thrusts it forward in one brutal movement. It hammers into Kaitan's sternum, knocking it back in a burst of blood. It slavers, head spasming from side to side.

The psychic spell seems to break, and for a moment it stares as though confused about where it is. Its eyes roll. It snorts, clawed feet scraping at the trench floor. Its chest is a ruin. Blood leaks freely, dribbling into the air, drifting as though on lunatic winds. Everything about it defies logic.

The fight becomes a dreamlike dance, weaving through the lesser throngs of beastmen. Driving Kaitan back through the trenches, into the shadow of the city's highest spires. Kaitan's hide shudders with sudden colour. Feathers moult and bloom anew. Scales ripple into fur. It howls as it thrusts its head forward, charging him like some immense elk. He grabs at the beast's horns, even as one gouges into his armour. Ivar feels blood running within the plate. He can taste it against his teeth. In his ears the first shrills of damage alert sound.

Ivar drives the pommel of the sacred mace down upon the monster's head. It flails up at him, trying to ward off the blows with its sword or bare hands. He ignores it. He seizes it by the throat and pulls it up with each strike. Braining it.

Blood runs down the thing's cheeks like tears and it brays in pitiable mortal agony. All bluster is gone. Whatever dignity the monster might once have had is obliterated. Ivar snarls as he deals the death blows. Till his voice is in perfect rhythm with the wet, percussive impacts.

Ivar pants, despite his transhuman biology. Weariness finally finds him as he casts it down onto its own red snow. The least of battle leavings, presented for the carrion birds. Yet this place has no avians of any kind to feast upon the aftermath. Only the monstrous and deformed things that now flee from him.

All psychic grandeur broken. Driven away by the bleak might of Fenris.

Ivar turns the crozius and brings one of the bladed wings down upon the monster's throat, obliterating its upper torso in a burst of powdered blood and vaporised bone. He snarls as he wrenches the head free, holding it aloft for the lesser monsters to behold.

'Look upon me!' he roars after them. Ivar stalks forwards, killing with by-blows. Ending lives as readily as they try to run. 'I am the shadow of Morkai and you are nothing before me!'

They squeal and falter. Ivar treads through their dead, feeling the crunch and squelch of their corpses beneath his boots. He scrapes their blood and viscera into the earth, till the ground is coated in a glistening layer of mutant gore.

A few brave remnants throw themselves at him in desperation, to do little more than paw at his armour. Their blades break. Their guns fall, useless even if they had a chance to fire. He is fury given form. Wrath bleeds from him. Every motion is a killing movement.

Unheralded, he passes deeper into the shadows of the city and its umbral embrace.

CHAPTER ELEVEN

KINGDOMS OF DUST

The city is less than a memory. It is a dream given form.

The walls have extruded from the black earth, carved from obsidian and noctilith. It sings with their every step, flickering with their thoughts as it interprets fresh minds and new ideas.

Each one is like a wound to the ones who made it. A new cut in an old war. Ivar is certain of that. The Thousand Sons were who Gorm Krakenblood hunted, and this stinks of their toxic sentimentality. Their mourning for a dead past.

Many a time Ivar sat as a pup, listening to the old histories from the mouths of skjalds. Of the savage joys and sorrows visited upon the home of the Prosperine serpents. In this broken shadow of a city, he can see the mournful echoes of lost Tizca.

They have gathered now. Blood-soaked and war-wracked. By some miracle of the Allfather's grace they bear meagre wounds. Their armour is scraped and bloodied, yet none of them stands impaired. Ivar looks upon his brothers with pride and nods gently. Even now he feels the weight of this place, and yet he does not falter.

'We walk someone else's memories,' Ivar says. 'Burned out and dead, but that is how it feels.'

'You're a Rune Priest now?' Ytri calls. 'Truly there is no end to your talents, gothi.'

'Be silent,' Ivar snarls. 'All you do is prove yourself a brainless whelp. A weak and addled mind.' He gestures through the winding streets. 'You all see the rune marks as I do. The signum code of the ship lies beyond these districts. We fight our way through. We endure. We fulfil our duty.'

'As you say,' Ytri grumbles. He stabs his blade experimentally into the stone of the ground, squatting down to worry it against a groove.

'Is there any word from orbit?' Jolfr asks as he steps forward. He brushes ashes from his armour. The older warrior is wearied. He carries his wounds and burdens plainly for all to see. His axe hangs limply, held in one hand. They all breathe deeply and take advantage of the calm in the storm. They had sent the gunship back skyward, a messenger to bear their words if the message itself would not break the dome of the sky.

'No word,' Ivar says. 'The ship is silent.' He looks to Brynjar. 'Is there any hope of making contact?'

'Doubtful, without sturdier hardware,' the Iron Priest growls. 'Perhaps when we reach the wreck. If its spirit can be coaxed…'

'A slim hope, but a hope nonetheless,' Ivar says with a nod. 'The beasts have scattered. All that remains is to cross the city. Beyond that, our target awaits.'

'There will be darker things than mere beasts within its confines,' Vili says with a scowl. They all look to the youth, and he lowers his head. 'They wish to make sport of us. Whatever directs their malice will be within.'

'Then we violate no palaces and trespass no temples,' Ivar says. 'The swiftest path to war and victory.' He thrusts the crackling mace ahead of him. One single motion. One way. 'We do not falter. We do not break. No interruptions or distractions. We bring swift ends to the enemies of man. Nothing less.'

'We are with you,' Brynjar affirms. 'Till the death.'

'There is more of a plan than simply running in a straight line, yes?' Jolfr puts in. Ivar looks at him, judging whether or not he jests. The old warrior shrugs.

'This place is made of lies,' Ivar says. 'We fight it with certainty. With purpose. We forge our own fate and impose it upon this dead city. That is my plan.'

'As much sense as can be expected from a place of madness,' Jolfr says.

'We have been brought here for a reason,' Ivar says. He moves forwards, leaning out from the corner of one of the mismatched buildings, their cyclopean stones turned tumbledown and ramshackle. The edges of the city are dying. Withered and drained districts, struggling to maintain their coherency.

Blue flame kindles at the heart of the dead metropolis. It rises like a pillar from ancient myth, questing for the heavens to meld with the unnatural fires that scour the sky.

For a moment it flares bright enough to overwhelm their visor displays till the arcane mechanisms click and refocus. Ivar raises his crozius again and sweeps it through the air.

'Keep trying to contact the ship in orbit. I want constant vigilance. Let nothing distract you. Wights have their ways. They will deceive you and drag you down into their Underverse.'

Ytri laughs. 'Let the bastards try.'

The city ripples with captive light.

Memories and dreams dance within its depths. Projected upon the glassaic surfaces of dead pyramids, colonising the ancient columns like creeping lichen. Ivar tries not to acknowledge the whispering ghosts or the phantom afterimages. To focus too long upon it is to court madness.

Echoes and flames are all that dwell in the confines of the murdered city. Dust and ashes cover everything, a fine grey pall that could have been laid down in the distant past or merely a day ago.

They trudge through it regardless. Brynjar and Ivar lead the way, forging onwards into the broad boulevards of the corpse-place. Not even insects thrive here, yet something buzzes at the edge of perception. Laughter drifts on the wind. The brothers turn at each hissed burst of mirth, every last utterance of mockery. Weapons raised. Alert and ever vigilant.

There is bravery in that. Mankind has always striven to face down the unknown and tame it. The Imperium is built upon such courage. Fenris, though, will never be tamed. Not by the hand of man or the will of false and hateful gods.

Ivar carries that wildness with him, and he defies the fates with it.

The whispered laughter becomes snarled threats. Condemnations. Accusations of weakness and cowardice in the face of the enemy. None answer it. The temptations of the infernal cannot find purchase upon them. There is nothing here for them to exploit. Fenris has reaved them clean of doubt and fear, as surely as the balms and workings of the Allfather's genesmiths.

Their violence is swift and surgical. Statues are broken. Obelisks toppled. The Wolves strike cleanly at the apparatus of the enemy. Anything that seems as though it could bear ritual significance is obliterated. The lines of pictoglyphs that cover almost every surface are annihilated by whirring chain-teeth, by the broad head of Ivar's mace and Brynjar's hammer, or with the pommels of other weapons.

They cut a scar into the dead city. If they can, they will make it bleed.

All that pours from it is light. Flashes and pulses of eldritch energy. Souls being born, or released, or dying, all at once. Blue transmuting to purple, blossoming and breaking apart into fractals of a million colours. As though the stone itself were trembling apart, ready to burst.

The ground shudders and convulses. Ivar throws himself forwards, into the jaws of the roiling metropolis. The stones of the earth reverberate, chattering like teeth, clattering together in gums of rock and noctilith. The city recoils. An unliving thing desperate to shake the parasites from its back. The lesser fauna have fled, hiding within its shadows, returning to their burrows in the world's tormented skin.

The light stops. It pauses in one moment of total darkness. Only the burning sky illuminates the warriors' progress. The shadows loom, deep, long and heavy. They shake with the motion of the world, the tectonic rage kindled in its dark heart.

Then the luminescence surges up and outwards. The walls catch fire. Ashes swirl up from the ground on impossible winds before they burst like tiny supernovas. The light re-forms and refracts as the fire spreads between them. Weaving into shapes. Lithe bodies formed of living flame, bleeding into reality. Resolving into the truth of what they are.

'Daemons,' Ivar snarls.

Each one is a monstrous being of seething flesh. Eyeless faces scream with their yawning mouths. Flames gout from every aperture, wielded as a living weapon, snapping like whips. Diving things like deep-sea predators, spined skin flaring with impossible hues, throw themselves down against the warriors. Imps caper from the shadows, giggling as they hurl knots of multi-coloured fire.

Ivar raises his bolt pistol and fires. His brothers unleash their weapons, joining together in a singular barrage.

Mass-reactive shells slam into the mass of the enemy and burst them apart in lurid gouts of blazing blood. It pours down upon the Space Wolves as though the sky is weeping. It sizzles as it hits ceramite. The fluid almost leaps from the plate, vibrating against the metal with oddly predatory motion. It undulates like the tide, clawing its way up Ivar's arm with tiny claws of kindled hate.

He sweeps it off him, relishing the tiny, shrill screaming as it is cast down to the dust and trampled underfoot.

They forge on. A bulwark of ceramite and plasteel amidst a sea of roiling, shifting flesh. They fire unceasingly, maintaining a clear field between the writhing monsters and themselves. They fire and reload until the ammo runs dry, and then once again they draw their weapons in glorious wrath.

The power weapons cleave through the riot of monsters, splitting apart faces which are already warped by the mad brush of an insane artist. Nests of eyes blink and weep. Tongues loll from gaping mouths, rimmed with glittering shark's teeth wrought from obsidian and old bones. They hurl themselves forwards to gnaw at the warriors' armour and flesh, laughing and screaming as they plunge downwards. Fins and tails snap against them, buffeting Ivar with a storm's fury.

Ivar howls back his defiance against them. His teeth grit inside his helm as he lashes out. Each strike is a thunderbolt, the blows of an angered demigod. The rain of unclean blood patters against his armour in a relentless tattoo, till it seems as though it has always been raging about him. As though it will drown him in spite and bitter longing.

He feels the weight in his limbs, biting into him with acid pressure. Pain follows it, a rush of agony even his rage cannot quell.

Ivar stumbles.

Hands grip him, pulling him up. Jolfr and Brynjar are at his side. He nods to them, lowering his head in momentary respect. 'My brothers,' he breathes. Ivar's voice is cracking with strain. His throat is hoarse from roaring. His lungs heave with every breath.

'We have you,' Brynjar says.

'One path. One purpose,' Jolfr growls.

As one the packs move onwards, through the storm of scintillating flesh. Around them the buildings loom like drunkards, high terraces extending out and over the winding streets. Like vast manta rays the daemons sweep down upon them, spines spreading, trailing streamers in unholy conflagration.

Ivar leads them onwards, pausing only to sweep his weapon at the heavens. Daemons burst apart in showers of molten blood, in gobbets of shimmering flesh, before they fade away – back to the warp, and the hells that they were spawned from.

Together they pass under a sweeping archway, its surface etched with desert beasts and mortuary trappings. They pass into an ornamental under-path, the walls alive with carved oaths of remembrance. The roar of the burning sky fades. The chittering and screeching of the enemy abates.

They stop for a moment. Each warrior begins, methodically, to scrape their armour clean and tend to their weapons. Whatever respite can be clawed back must be savoured. All know this. The rites and necessities of war are second nature to them, even here in extremis.

'Bastards,' Ytri rumbles as he raises his war-etched blade to his eyes. 'All the trickery of the warp and the filth that follows with it.' The other members of Bloodiron Wrath nod their approval.

Ivar is silent. He turns from them and looks to Brynjar. 'And still no word from orbit?'

'Nothing, brother,' he sighs. 'I have cast forth on many frequencies.

Each one is little more than screaming to the winds. If they hear us, then we cannot hear their responses. All that is left is to trust in the Allfather's mercy.'

'You have the right of it,' Falr hisses. His armour rattles as he leans closer, totems and blades rebounding from the plate. He carries his own blades, raised in aversion. The warrior's lean sharpness is predatory in the sudden gloom. 'They're throwing everything they can against us. The whole world is a weapon to stop us from reaching the ship.'

CHAPTER TWELVE

UPPLAND AND UNDERVERSE

'I don't want excuses, I want Throne-damned answers!'

Garald is up and out of his throne. He paces and shouts. When he does not get an answer that he likes, he rants and he raves. Desperation has made him sharp and irritable, a side that the crew have seldom seen from him.

All boyish foppery is gone, now. Stripped away by the sights before them, by the pressure of command. Rokkvi Helvintr had always elaborated upon the virtue of such weight – how suffering was good for the soul, and shaped heroes out of noble sacrifice.

'Warp take your obsession with hardship,' Garald mutters under his breath.

Everyone shares his crawling anxiety. Every last member of the bridge crew is on edge. Velaq is hunched over her console, desperately trying to calibrate the auspex to penetrate the spreading stain of unnatural clouds. Another officer – Tomen, he is sure – is broadcasting over and over into the vox.

'Lord Ivar. Lord Brynjar. Members of Wolf King's Call and Bloodiron Wrath,' he intones. 'Please respond.'

There is no answer. The dead world does not speak. Not in words. All that blights the vox is the unceasing storm-howl.

There has been no contact since *Blade of Ice* limped back to the heavens, clawing its way skyward in frantic desperation. Bringing with it the confirmation that all had arrived planetside, but far from the target location.

Now all that could be done was to track the growing tumult upon the surface. Away from the bitter outskirts, through the city's heart, towards the downed and silent ship. All while the *Spear's* systems click and whisper. The tech-priests in their ritual wisdom have retreated into the alcoves and hidden places of the ship, the better to commune with the spirits of switch and sensor.

Nothing will come of it. Very little can.

What can we do? Garald's mind races. He drives his fist into a wall plate and curses, rearing back at the pain and frustration. Silence falls. Everyone turns to look at him. He swears again.

You cannot ever lose the crew. Lose their trust, their respect, and you will end your days nailed to the hull. It has happened before. It will happen again. There is no more mercy in the Uppland than there is in the Underverse…

More recrimination dressed up as insight. His father had always excelled at that. Hard times, he had been convinced, always served to build character. For him the life of a rogue trader was always caveated with the understanding that it should not be an easy life. That toil served the God-Emperor's designs and had to be embraced close, like a lover.

Wasteful decadence had been anathema to him.

The *Swift Spear* was never intended to be Garald's ship. It is, in every respect, a poor throne to rule from. Yet this is what he has been left with, a burden disguised as a gift. *If I had a better vessel, then there would be no struggle here… We would be able to find the Wolves.*

It is a fool's grasp of the situation, and he knows it. There is nothing natural about any of this. Only the crackle and spit of the warp's fury as it intrudes again into the open vox-link. The dead world mocks him. It has taken his most precious cargo and holds it prisoner, behind bars of cloud and flame.

All while the localised warp phenomenon grows more restless.

'If we fire, we'd be firing blind,' he says aloud. He ignores the scrutiny of the crew, their fearful shifting gazes at his loss of control. Perhaps it is time to dispense with a little decorum… 'We would have no conception of where the packs are. No certainty of undoing these cursed storms.'

'They are the enemy's works, doubtless,' croons Bodil. She has ensconced herself beside the command throne, sitting cross-legged in the pooling fabric of her robes, casting her bones. 'The Archenemy of all life may cast up tumults to assail the very bones of the earth. Especially where they have control. They are nature, here. They are the weather and will that shape this planet. Not like the spirits and gods that attend to Fenris. There is no purity here. This is not a clean world. Merely a shadow.'

'Shadows don't usually do the killing,' Garald says. Calm returns to him in a slow wave, cresting over him. He steadies his breathing and lets his mind settle. He absently shakes his hand, trying to dispel the pain. 'I usually find it's things in the shadows that do it.'

'And our patrons will have to deal with those as well, no doubt,' the old woman says as she stands. Bodil groans with the effort. Her aged frame sags and strains with every movement. Old pain radiates out from her marrow like dying embers, stirred by the fire's last breath.

'Still no signals from them?' he asks again.

Tomen shakes his head in answer.

'We have no other options. Unless…' Garald opens the vox-link to the eyrie. 'Narayis?'

'*Lord,*' the Navigator whispers back. He can hear the pain that stains her voice, the sheer effort of concentration as the warp intrudes upon her sight and senses. Yet the strength in each syllable never falters. '*What is required of me, Lord Helvintr?*'

Throne love her, but she is nothing if not diligent.

'Your sight, can it defy these storms? Aid the auspex in giving us more precise coordinates for the packs?'

There is a long silence. Garald hears the intake of breath, the grinding of teeth. '*It can be done. It will take time.*'

'So be it. Make it happen.' He kills the link.

'Patience is not a weakness,' Bodil says, dusting herself off as she hobbles over to stand beside him. 'It is a hunter's skill. A *Helvintr* skill. Sharpen it and it will sustain you.'

'Cold comfort when we can't do anything until we have clarity. We could deploy the house troops, some of the rough and ready crew we claimed in the exchange…' His mind drifts to the men and women billeted below. Warriors, waiting for their chance to struggle and die. Content to serve their Allfather in whatever form that took, even as a flesh tithe to appease the mistress of the dynasty. That had been part of the pact. A cargo to be conserved. Not wasted.

'Not yet,' Bodil affirms. 'They will have their part to play, before the end. It is not now. Now, we wait. When the time comes we will do our duty. If that is what our wyrd wills.'

'I wish I had your faith in destiny,' Garald admits.

'If you have faith in the Allfather then you believe in wyrd. He crafts it and weaves it through the lives of men.' She smiles her withered smile. 'He is many things to countless souls. King and architect. Cartomancer and creator. Trust in Him.'

'I will,' Garald says quietly. 'I believe.'

* * *

Ytri has nothing left to him but bleak belief and faith in fury.

He snarls and pants within his beast-faced helm, wrestling with the need to do violence. The hulking warrior is half a bare-sark, reduced to impulse and instinct. Ytri shakes himself and checks his blade again. The etched words burn alongside the vicious notches in the weapon. He relishes the wounds of the past. They are what allow him to keep his keenness.

Like the blade, he has lost none of his edge.

The tunnels do not suit him. They are beneath him. The domain of worms and weaklings. Ytri has never hidden in his life. Not this one or the one he left upon the ice. He has always been bold, perhaps even brash.

Now the wolf within strains against its prison of flesh and bone. His choler rises unchecked. Ytri can barely hold his rage back. It is the same damnable anger that drives him upon the field of war and in the practice cages, through every brutal duel with his brothers.

Those who have fought him, or with him, call him the Iron Bastard and he relishes the title. Every strike against him is remembered. Every wound is filled in with crude skill, yet exceptional care.

Ytri wants to be seen and known. Judged only by his deeds. A projection of rugged strength and efficiency. Here he feels stymied. The old memories surge back – of the great cavern cities beneath the skin of Fenris, where all are forbidden to tread.

He has fought underground before, yet here there is an air of oppressive malice that he cannot stomach.

'I will bleed every one of them for this,' he snaps. 'Let them come. They can tear their little planet apart to get to us. I'll spit blood and teeth back in their faces. Beat them to death with the stones of their own wretched crypts.'

His gaze snaps to Ivar and Brynjar, currently locked in an

uneasy struggle, torn between courses. Like feuding captains whose minor rivalries will drown the entire ship.

Akaz rumbles with amusement and steps closer, till they are almost helm to helm. Unlike Ytri, he keeps his armour near pristine. It growls with his every step. As eager as Ytri is. Hungry to kill. 'All in good time, brother. Once they are done squabbling over direction.'

'We should have brought a gothi,' Ytri says. 'One of the mind-gifted would cut through these petty sorceries like a knife.'

'We have enough storms abounding as it stands,' Akaz says. Rough mirth haunts every word. The humour reeks of the gallows. Cast under the same pall as everything else upon and within this cursed earth. 'Chased into tunnels like rats.'

'We're not the vermin here,' Ytri growls. 'We should not be running or hiding.'

'It will not last,' Akaz offers, but the older warrior turns from him. He steps forwards and lets his anger speak at last.

'Why are we skulking here?' Ytri calls.

Ivar looks around. The Wolf Priest has been squatting, checking the ground for tracks. He rises and stands at his full height. The darkness of the tunnels fades as he approaches, dispelled by the sparking crozius that he holds, still lit.

Alcoves line the blackness of the walls, containing sarcophagi and preserved human remains. All of them are carved from the same black material, mimicries of a place. Around the history etched into the fabric of the world lie countless bones. Horned skulls. Clawed fingerbones. The detritus of generations of beasts that have bred and died in the darkness here. Consecrating the world in death, madness, and perverse evolution. Every part of Ytri yearns to smash them apart. Pulverise every last example of their culture.

That is what we are for. The wolves that stalk between stars. The death of the mutant, the heretic, and the xenos.

'I had no idea,' Ivar says, 'that you were so weak.'

Ytri freezes. He is robbed of speech. Ivar tilts his head and the skull mask sees to the very heart of him. Ytri knows he might as well be naked upon the open plain, the elements raking him down to nothing but flensed meat.

'What did you say?' he snarls. His own blade comes up, blazing white-hot.

Ivar does not even flinch. Ytri is beneath his notice. Below even his contempt.

'I said that you are weak,' Ivar repeats. He circles the other warrior. The rest gather round, weighing the situation. Not assessing the odds. Not even choosing sides. They simply watch. Wait.

Awaiting the lesson.

'You have given away your strength,' Ivar says. 'Look at you. Pacing like a beast, ruled by your choler. You shame yourself.' He reaches out and slams his palm against Ytri's chestplate. 'I have trusted you because of your reputation. Brynjar vouches for you. Bloodiron Wrath have a fine reputation as killers.' He reaches up and grips Ytri's shoulder. He pulls him in close till the vox-snarl is right against his ear. 'You are what you are because of your control. Not despite it. Do you understand? Tell me you understand.'

'I...' Ytri bows his head. He grits his teeth. 'Forgive me, lord.'

'There is nothing to forgive,' Ivar says. 'This place is insanity. They want this. To reduce us to slavering beasts. This place is the prison of their delusions. That we are monsters come to dash their world upon the rocks, and they are noble heroes.' He swings around and the crozius impacts the wall. Lightning ripples across the noctilith, writhing through the cracks. The walls pulse with a caged storm, screaming as the raw force dissipates, like a howl.

'We are better than that,' Ivar shouts. 'You are all stronger than the enemy thinks and fears. You are the Wolves of Fenris! No enemy stands against us. No fortress defies us. Russ and the Allfather did not shape us for idle duties. No!'

One by one they drum their fists against their armour. Rattling them against chestplates or slamming one gauntlet into an open palm.

Ivar swings his crozius around and hammers at one of the walls, where the cracks strain and spread. Again and again, slamming his weapon against the fabric of it until it ruptures, bursting outwards in a rain of fragments.

The others cheer as they crowd about it. Beyond they can see the looming profile of the ship, sprawled in the ashes of the world.

'Our goal is within sight. The enemy cannot stop us. They throw body after body at us. Slaves of flesh and blood. Never-born from behind reality's skin. None can stop us. It is as though they are afraid to even try and halt our advance!'

'Let them try!' Jolfr bellows. Wolf King's Call echo him. Vili punches the air and cheers.

The air in the confines of the tunnels grows fiercely close and hot. Light still spasms within the walls, spreading like a forest fire. The structure, the world, tastes their rage and yet recoils from their dedication. Tectonic pains wrack the caverns. More of the walls distort and fall away, letting the unclean light pour in.

'Truly this is some Hel,' Falr mutters. 'Or the gullet of some great beast that wishes to choke us down.'

'What are beasts to us?' Ivar laughs. 'We are sons of the World of Winter and War! In the far south, my tribe decorate their ships with the hides and bones of vanquished monsters! Each of you has cut your mark into our home world. You have risen up to conquer in the Allfather's name. Russ himself would be proud of you, my brothers!'

Falr nods. He draws his blades. 'And we will take trophies enough to pile before the Aett, as a sign of our might!'

'The enemy have built a false fortress. This night we tear it down!' Ivar bellows. He is moving now, sprinting, every iota of transhuman strength focused forwards. Ytri hears the others as they begin to run. Both packs move with him, their leaders forging ahead alongside Brynjar.

Their howls resound off the winding passageways and crypts, till the whole world sings with the wrath of Wolves.

CHAPTER THIRTEEN

RAMPARTS OF THE PROFANE

Together they stand upon the withered terrace and gaze at what has become of the *Spinebreaker*.

None can doubt or deny that it was a proud ship. The craftsmanship upon its hull was once impeccable – speaking of the finest shipwrights available to the Chapter and the Adeptus Mechanicus. The hull bears its colours proudly, even now. The pale blue is like the last ice of a great winter, the sea shining through with cold clarity and promise.

The strength of its soul, the pure dedication to its old purpose, makes the despoliation all the harsher.

Banners of flayed skin hang from the ship's walls or are pinned upon crude poles atop it. Cairns of bones stretch across the entirety of the ship, inlaid by countless feet and hooves. When things move upon those ramparts of the profane, they disgorge minor avalanches of the dead. A never-ending patter of constant atrocity.

Each of them stares at the dead ship. Assessing it for weaknesses. Judging what has become of it. Plotting the swiftest route to the heart of it.

'We arrive too late, as we thought,' Brynjar sighs. 'She has held firm against the worst of the corruption, but the marks of the enemy are upon her.' He gestures along the side of the ship. 'She hit the ground hard. I doubt she'll ever fly again. Even a full recovery crew would struggle. We do not have the manpower or the technical ability to make her voidworthy once more.'

'A pity,' Ivar grumbles. 'Her might would have made a fine asset.' He pauses. His mind races with his own tactical considerations. Within his helm his eyes flick along the ship's beached length.

'We split into two assault groups. Brynjar and Bloodiron Wrath will strike for the secondary enginarium. You will establish what system control you can. If you can summon aid from orbit, then do so. Any number of household troops. As much as they can spare. Regardless, I want you to prime the reactors for the rites of self-annihilation.'

'Allfather's teeth,' Brynjar curses. 'You cannot ask that of me, Ivar.'

'It must be done. We burn them from this world. We wound them. Bring the sky down upon them. If blowing the reactors does not undo their working and break the storm, then nothing will.' He pauses. 'More than that, we owe it to the Chapter's dead.'

'Such a loss, though…' Brynjar trails off. He growls in frustration. The haft of his hammer slips through his fingers, the ferrule ringing as it strikes the ground.

'Were there any other way, I would choose it, my brother.'

The ship waits. Beautiful, even in its ruin. Defiant, even in defeat. Ivar forces himself to look at it. He absorbs every detail. Not simply, he admits to himself, for the tactical necessity. He commits it to memory. He honours it, even as he condemns it to death.

'The judgement falls to me,' Ivar says. 'The execution must be yours. Only you understand the mysteries. And if you cannot, then I will have the trader destroy it from orbit. Better that it die than serve as a lair for these savage monsters.'

'I understand,' Brynjar says at last.

'Wisdom, indeed,' Jolfr says and bows his head. 'I am with you, Priest. To the end. We all stand with you. No matter their numbers.'

'And we will guard the Iron Priest,' Ytri says. 'Give me something to bury my sword in, and I'll make sure he gets his chance to burn the world to ashes.'

'Circumstance brought us together. Now we will show the enemy the price they pay.' He collects himself and steps to the edge of the terrace. The drop is sheer. High enough to kill any mortal man cast from it.

Once it might have held a winding garden, growing up the great edifice and tended by armies of horticultural labourers. Now it is a coalface of ambition. Dead and forgotten, the flowers and vines reduced to stunted crystalline growths. They shimmer in the light of the burning sky.

From the cliff's base, there is hardly any distance at all to the ship's quiescent corpse. He blink-marks the points of entry, the surest strikes to their targets. Ivar nods to himself.

Be as bold as Russ himself. Strike with certainty and fury, yet never forget that you are the master of both. Your strength lies in control.

'What of you?'

The voice snaps Ivar from his reverie and he turns from the cliff. Ytri steps forward. Ivar curses silently within his helm. The other warrior looms towards him, letting his blade hang loose so its deactivated tip scrapes against the stones.

'You send us for the mind and heart of the ship, but what is your goal?'

'I answer the Slayer's order,' Ivar says. 'I will return Gorm Krakenblood to the Chapter. In whatever form that may take.'

They leap from the cliff.

Lesser men could not survive the fall. They would be dashed apart, rent asunder as surely as any sailor thrown from their boat upon the Worldsea. Death rears up, wearing one of its many faces.

They do not meet its gaze. Morkai holds no power over them.

Ivar hits the ground, hands slamming into the black stone, before he pushes himself up and breaks into a run. High above the daemons twine and writhe, casting their light upon the advancing warriors. The flashes of illumination dispel the coiling shadows, catching on the great battlements of the grounded ship.

The sky rumbles with false thunder, and it is echoed by the roar of the beasts who have colonised the once-noble ship. They stream from it like vermin, like lice from a corpse. Feathered or furred, their faces terminating in slavering beaks or blunt snouts, the debased remains of the crew hurl themselves outwards from their nest.

Claws scrabble at the tortured earth. Ridges, tall as warriors in Terminator plate, rise around the ship, cast up by its impact. The force of its landing has remade the world, like the sweep of a god's chisel. The enemy pour over them. Banner poles snap as they struggle to use them as anchors. Rough blades and axes slip from clawed hands. One creature falls, its face striking the ground so hard that teeth fountain from its bleeding mouth.

Still they come. Trampling their own dead, even as others pause to feast on the corpses. Snapping jaws close around meat, tugging it away in ragged strands of muscle. Bones crunch between fanged maws as the marrow is slurped out and swallowed down.

The lowest. Bottom-feeding things. Scrabbling and clawing at the ground, at the corpses. Wild eyes flash in the planet's hell-light, darting with madness, hunger, and fear.

The monsters love their world and will defend it to the last drop of blood. The monsters despise their world and what it has made of them. They wish to live and die in equal measure. All is rendered flux for them, in the eye of a storm of change.

Flesh shreds and flows, feathers blossom and burst into flame. The air boils and shudders with madness given form, colours swarming without name. They would steal the minds of lesser men and turn the strongest citadels to water or mist.

The sons of Fenris hold. They stand firm against the onslaught. The rocks against the sea. The tide claws and scrapes at them, trying to drag them below.

Ivar snarls and shakes free a clawed hand. A blade of pitted flint gouges at his armour, breaking into flinders. So many and yet so weak. Impotent gnats, biting at the flanks of a predator king.

Not men, nor truly beasts. Beneath both.

'This is what they send against us!' Ivar howls above the tumult. His men cheer at his words, their own blows falling faster. Brynjar smashes one of them into the ground with his hammer. Axes and swords cleave at the enemy, till all is a storm of glittering blood. 'Weakness begets weakness! Our foe is enfeebled!' His crozius bisects one with its bladed wings. An axe blade, worn down almost to a nub, clatters at his neck, trying to break the seals there.

Smart little monsters. Determined beasts. Nothing more. Feral children, abandoned and hateful. Shaped by their cruel and cold cradle.

Ivar grins behind his helm. He laughs and the vox-amplified glee is a stuttering, hateful thing. In his hearts he knows that his men have been made strong by their own upbringing. Fenris sings in every one of them. It howls in fury and dominance.

It shames the lesser beasts.

That is why they break so easily. Though the Wolves take wounds, feel the sympathetic pain as armour is scored or violated, they push on, through the waves of the enemy. Flesh so weakling and ephemeral that it may as well not exist. A goatish, split-faced thing hurls itself up, screaming and laughing with too many voices, tongues lolling from its beaked maw.

Ivar uses his fist then. He slams it into the thing's face until bone cracks. Black blood leaks from its eightfold eyes. Ivar smells it, even in the helm, and rage fills his own veins. His teeth grit, fangs against fangs. The snarl builds in his throat, and he voices it in a static-laced howl.

His brothers, his pack, howl with him.

'The gunship is being repaired and rearmed, primed for any future sorties,' Garald sighs. 'That's a start, at the least. I want all relevant tactical data from it patched to our main auspex and relayed to Narayis. We'll overlay the terrain with our previous scans and determine their most likely tactical egress.'

'Aye, lord!' the crew chorus. Garald ignores them. He steeples his fingers and leans forward from his throne. His mind races. Blood pounds in his temples with the rhythm of his frantically beating heart.

Hololithic images war before him, aligning and shuddering as they grind together like glaciers. Past and present at war. Bodil mutters of ill omens, but he pays her no heed. His pale features narrow. Garald grits his teeth and raises one hand, tracing patterns in the air as he reconciles sight and thought.

'We have no knowledge of the numbers they face, or if there is any resistance at all. The enemy, such as it is, could be all sorceries and falsehoods…' He growls and stands, stalking around the throne.

The darkness of the bridge is like a living thing, writhing about him, disturbed only by the flickering of cogitator banks and the clatter of rune-keys. The ship's engines drone, the hum resonating up and through the ship like a fever-tremor.

Above them the lights flicker. The white lumens and the red both crackle, threatening to die. The engine's burr hitches, becoming a whine. The longer they stay here, he knows, the greater the risk that they will all be swept away in the maelstrom. The lurid colours beyond the viewing port dull the meek lights of the bridge. Garald knows the ship could die just as easily.

Be bold, my son. Even in the face of death.

He is colonised by old wisdom, infiltrated as surely as hull plates by void barnacles. Lessons etched into him with words like shipwright's marks by blade and hammer. *Now comes the test. Where the ship meets the void, and all is decided in that bleak instant.*

The image finally resolves, alloyed together in the air before him. He can see the glimmering marks that Narayis has writ upon it, coils of crimson light appended with the sigils of the Navis Nobilite.

He rises. Garald does not seem a warrior, then. Not a bold adventurer ready to put worlds to the torch with one hand while filling holds with prizes with the other. He seems a meek steward, gazing at the kingdom he administers as it drowns in quicksand.

'Boldness,' he mutters to himself. He reaches out, fingers faltering just shy of the hovering image… and then closes his hand into a fist. 'What levies do we have?'

'A few hundred household guard, princeling,' Bodil says. 'And the tithe of flesh besides.'

'Ready them,' Garald says at last. 'I won't sit idle in the stars doing nothing while they fight and die beneath the flames. Your people are winter and war, fire and ice. Let them prove it.'

* * *

'They say you are a skjald!' one of the men shouts. Kaedra turns, her eyebrow raised.

He is frost-born and oath-sworn, all muscle and bravado with an edge of low cunning that might pass as humour. Along his arms, spears are inscribed in ritual scarification, vertically, mirroring the path of his bones. Blond hair spills down his shoulders, out from under the steel and leather helm. He smiles, flashing missing teeth.

He is a weapon in every way that matters, and so he is sincere in his question. The strangeness is not that she should be here, that she should be ready to fight. She is a woman of Fenris, after all.

What surprises him is that she is also a saga-keeper.

'I have that honour,' she says, and smiles.

Kaedra is dark-haired, lean and pale. A daughter of Fenris, seven great years behind her, she too is armed and armoured. The rough leathers of home have been augmented by the flak-and-steel of the Helvintrs. She carries a hand axe at her hip and a lasgun upon her back. Some tell her, have always told her, that her tongue is another weapon at her disposal. Cutting, to a fault. As sharp as her storyteller's mind. 'I carry our tales to the Uppland, now, even as I carve new ones into the stars.'

'Better that you carve them into the enemy!' The big man laughs. She laughs with him.

'What is your name, kinsman?'

'Lyf,' he says, chest pushing out. The harnesses bite against his bulk. Lyf pats the sword in its scabbard, belted at his hip. Old, strong iron. Pitted like a barrow leaving, yet still vital. Still a killing edge. 'You'll sing the songs of me if I fall? Tell the sagas if I live to fight again?'

'Depends,' she says, rolling her shoulders. 'You have to make sure the deeds match the boasts.'

The bulk lander shakes and heaves, like any ship of the World-sea might. She does not know the ship's name, and there are none here who would know it. An unforgivable sin on her part, she concedes. *I will learn it, in time. All things can be known…* Kaedra frowns. *Though, not all things should be.*

'Hold your nerve,' Lyf chuckles. 'The bold have no fear of death, and the dead have no fear of anything. We will find land, one way or another. Fenrisians always do.'

'Even in the Underverse there is land,' she says, her head bobbing with the motion of the ship. 'Weak land that will never nourish, but land regardless.'

Another jolt. The ship plunges. Somewhere, further back, someone begins to howl in anticipation. The sound grates off her ears, resounding oddly in the confines of the vessel. Then it is gone, drowned out by the scream of fire against steel.

'There it is,' Kaedra whispers. 'The last dive.'

They cut their way through a wall of fire and spite, a coiling storm of madness. The walls begin to glow, awash with lambency in colours that should not exist. Rippling waves of it dance along the metalwork, casting all in their weirdling light.

'Ill omens,' Lyf says, at last. His eyes are darting like a frightened prey beast.

'The worse omen would be if it were ripping us apart, kinsman. You sail with the ship you have.'

The engines begin to roar. Stabilisers fire and it bucks like an ox. The fall arrests itself. They are, all of them, heaved up from their seats and slammed back down. Sudden pain blossoms through Kaedra, deep enough that she feels the bite of it in muscle and bone.

'Skitja!' she curses aloud.

The alarums drown her out as they begin their wailing. Machines should not sound like this, so close to the grief of women at the shore as they tear at their furs, cursing the gods and spirits.

She ignores them. All of them lock their respirator helms into place. Marked with bronze and iron, silver, bone and leather. Carved and inked and scrimshawed. They make the troops into wolves. In the confines of the helms the bells are quieted to a dull, aching ringing.

It tolls on and on, till the hatches thunder down. Harnesses snap up and away with a serpent's hiss, and the warriors move almost as one. The Helvintr troops take the lead in their grey-and-brown flak marked with the spears and wolf's head of the dynasty. The Fenrisian levies follow. Kaedra loses sight of Lyf, though she can still hear his boisterous cries, melding into the greater wall of noise.

They are cheering, howling, roaring their eagerness and their hate.

And the broken, deadened world beyond screams back at them.

CHAPTER FOURTEEN

TO THE HEART

The enemy's movements change in an instant, sudden as the seas.

The mass of beasts pauses, even as they are hewn apart. Limbs and heads fly free in welters of blood, yet the monsters show only confusion. Ivar stops to watch them, his entire body heaving, blood burning with the strain.

They are soaked in mutant gore, all of them. Red covers the pale blue, like the setting of a sun, or the swirling of blood in the pale waters of the sea. Unclean algae, lapping at ice. Ivar reaches up with one hand and smears the blood down his skull helm. He snarls again and moves forwards.

The monsters bray as one and then turn, frighted. A herd suddenly aware of impending disaster. Ivar scowls beneath his mask.

'So easily broken, are they?'

There is a roar then. Not from beast or man, but from machine. Ivar whirls about again and glares up at the heavens. Columns of fire trail from the blazing skies. At first he thinks it an omen, a starfall, but the shapes that resolve from within the tumult are not wrought of meteoric iron.

'Allfather's mercy…' Ivar breathes.

Tearing from the skies like comets, the bulk landers slam into the black earth, heaving up great waves of ash and stone shards. For a moment, all is dust. It settles over everything, rendering Astartes and beasts alike greyscale. The ramps hit the ground a second later and a ragged cheer goes up. Soldiers flood out, mismatched and boisterous. As wilful and bold as any raiding party.

The throng of mutants turn one way and then the other. Hooves stamp at the ground as they throw their heads back and screech.

'Forwards!' Ivar bellows. His warriors obey. As one they push onwards, hacking their way through the multitudes. Blood pools beneath their feet as they carve their crimson furrow through the enemy. The ship is so close now.

The ship troops are pouring in from the flank. Forming up into shield walls. Lasguns and autoguns begin to spit their deathly refrain. Others are throwing spears, or readying swords and axes.

The dance of man and monster begins once more.

Brynjar is at his side, his hammer thrust upwards to split the sky as readily as the ships do. Jolfr and Ytri marshal their warriors, falling in behind the priests.

They fire as one. Bolt pistols. Bolters. All committing in a single wall of fire and sound. Driving the horde back, step by faltering step, blow by bursting blow. They return to bladework after. Swords and axes fall. Hammer and mace join them.

By the time they finally reach one of the great entrance hatches, half-embedded in the noctilith, it yawns like a cave mouth. Ivar starts back. For a moment he is back upon Fenris, standing in the darkness of the cave mouth, smelling the charnel reek of the debased trolls.

The ship bears that same tainted stink. It clings to the iron of its hull and the steel of its grating. Caught as meat catches upon the spit. The great vessel, the *Spinebreaker*, lies silent, dark and dead, bearing its wounds the way a vast statue does – laid low and vandalised by savages. Just as Fenris has buried and mutilated its cavern cities. A broken past presaging a dead future.

Ivar raises the crozius, letting the purity of its light reach into the clinging shadows. The frosty illumination catches upon rune marks. Silver glitters amidst the black metal. The beauty and strength of the old ship is gone, subsumed beneath ruin and neglect. A questing fungal growth covers the vessel's interior, coiling up its walls, dripping from the rafters.

It stinks of dead flesh and cancerous ambition.

Ivar does not flinch from it. He holds the crozius higher until the blazing power field finds some of the moist strands, burning them to ashes. The entire organism shudders, recoils, and squeals in infrasonic agony.

One by one they pass into the heart of the enemy and, if the Allfather favours them, towards the end of their quest.

'It has seen better days,' Brynjar mutters darkly.

The ship is immense, a world unto itself. Part of Ivar, the deep-buried child who died his first death upon red snow, recoils from the sheer scale of it. The warrior he has become understands it, though.

The vessel's standard template construct layout is known to him. Not merely because he has checked and rechecked the technical schemata, but because it has been etched into his soul. The bone-deep communion born of the hypnogogic engines beneath the Aett. As a Blood Claw, he once knew that pain – the burning weight of knowledge, drowning him in its salt. Now, as a Wolf Priest, he has guided the young through the tumult and the fire.

Ivar struggles still, trying in vain to shepherd pack after pack of Wolves. To lead.

'Even the greatest of fortresses can be laid low,' Ivar replies. 'We forget that, and we join them in the rubble.'

Brynjar tilts his head. 'We have made it this far. That is a blessing in itself. If the spirits are good, then we can liberate communications from whatever taint has taken root here.'

'It's a foul place,' Jolfr grunts. 'These monsters have torn away whatever purity it once held. A tomb for a dead quest.'

'They'll join it then,' Ytri says. He hunches forward, scraping the gore-muck and dust from his armour with the edge of his sword. 'I'll bury them beneath the walls of this ship. The corridors can ring with the piss-weak prayers to their false gods.' He snarls, the words rasping through the vox. 'I'll kill them all. Every bastard one of them.'

'One way or another,' Ivar agrees. He looks to the other warriors. Battered, yet unbroken, their resolve alloyed in the crucible of the enemy. Now comes the true test of their steel. 'Brynjar, take your men and secure the enginarium. We need whatever power you can muster for communications. Tame the spirits. Break them if you must. I promise you, by the end of this, we will have freed them from their torment.'

'Aye, brother,' Brynjar says. Ivar can see how the tainted weight of this place settles upon him, like the stones of a cairn. The Iron Priest seems to sag, as though he were not made of iron, spite and absolute determination. 'I would do it even if you did not order it. They have made a mockery of this proud vessel. I would rather send it to the Underverse than allow it to be a nest for their filth.' He pauses. Just as Ivar has done, he is mapping the ship's structure in his mind. 'And what of you, brother?'

'I will bring Gorm back to the Chapter,' Ivar swears. 'No matter if a thousand stand between me and my destiny.'

* * *

The ship has no soul.

The machine spirits are quiescent, if not dead. The great vessel does not heave with recycled air. Its corridors are not lung-flesh, no forest of filters and respirators thrums within its corpse. No lightning dances in its marrow. No animus fills its iron skin.

The ship is dead, and like the dead it crawls with vermin.

Ivar is no stranger to death. Fenris bludgeons such lessons into its sons in their youth. Cradle to grave, it is a world of absolute mortality. Not for them the balms and unctions that preserve Imperial governors and cardinals for generations beyond count. Only the strong live to their maturity. The weak, the sick, the broken die their early, ignoble deaths. Devoured by the world.

The corridors yawn like empty arteries, devoid of any vitality. The spark has gone. Ivar feels the absence as though it were a void in his own soul. There is only the chill quiet, as sure as dishonour. As inevitable as the end of all things.

'What have they done to her?' Jolfr breathes at his back. Ivar turns. He had almost forgotten that the warriors of Wolf King's Call still stand with him. The shadows have rendered them as mere echoes. Wights, drawn up from the frozen dark. No light illuminates the rune marks upon their plate. Nor the proud symbol of the Chapter. Here they could be brothers of any number of their cousin bloodlines, their honour and glory stolen by the enemy's desecration of the ship.

'They have killed her, body and spirit,' Ivar says. Sadness wreathes every word. 'We will avenge her in victory.'

They say nothing. Ivar looks at their helmed heads, at the bronze marks around the eye-slits and upon their graven cheeks. Wolf King's Call carry their grief in silence, hidden behind the false faces.

'We will have vengeance,' Ivar growls. Now they nod. Their voices come, slow and steady, measured. The kill-urge is rising, but it does not overwhelm them.

'Aye, lord.'

'For the glory of the Rout!'

'They will be repaid in blood!'

The lessons of Russ echo from their lips, resounding off the walls. For a moment the dull, rusted steel seems to live again. It rings like the halls of the Aett, upon the world that bore them all.

The ship, dead though it may be, remembers the wisdom of Fenris as well.

The interior spaces have grown wild, despoiled by the passage of seeming generations of monsters. Every surface is coated in their spoor, scarred by claw marks. They have engraved ruin into its very heart.

Ivar knows his own pain is insignificant compared to what Brynjar must be feeling at the sight. Even now, driving his men onwards towards the enginarium decks, the Iron Priest must see the ancient machine's pain and be wounded in turn by it.

He cannot allow himself such latitude.

There is only the struggle now. Ivar clings to the certainty that no foe can fell him. No curse can blight him. No foe will keep him from home or hearth.

If I cannot remain whole for them, how can I safeguard their legacy?

He turns and regards the warriors who stand with him. Jolfr is blood-smeared, shoulders heaving with the effort of recent combat. Vili is beside him and the youngblood seems even more the worse for wear. There is a tremble to his armoured form. He struggles to lift one of his arms.

Ivar walks to him and places a hand on his shoulder. His scrutiny pins the young warrior in place as he checks and rechecks. The Fang of Morkai clicks hungrily at Ivar's wrist, responding to his subconscious intent. *Muscle fatigue. Minor damage.* The strain of fighting so many and for so long has worn upon the young warrior.

Ivar knows the signs. He has treated thousands of wounds in his time. The tics and spasms of an ailing body read as easily as the runes.

'You should have mentioned this earlier,' the Wolf Priest sighs.

'There was no time. We were in the fray of it!' Vili blusters emptily. Ivar snorts. The youth is a braggart and a brawler, like any son of the ice. Ivar's grip stills him and forces his helmeted gaze round.

The Wolf Priest keeps looking at him as his hands work. He lifts his right hand off Vili's shoulder and plucks a leather-bound vial from his belt. He raises it and presses it to one of the Fang's needles. It hisses and gurgles as it fills. Then it moves, whip-quick, plunging between plates and into Vili's system. He grunts and staggers back as though backhanded.

'There is always time,' Ivar says softly. 'I will not lose any more than I must. Not here, not now, on the edge of triumph.'

Vili is silent. He looks down, a hunter who has faltered in pursuit of his prey – knowing it could spell death for a tribe. Ivar draws back. The silence rushes in between them, not in judgement, nor in pity.

'If we wish to win then we must be stronger than the enemy. Smarter than their canniest wiles. Yet we will inevitably fail in that, youngblood.' Ivar shakes his head. 'We must rise higher than our pain.'

Vili flexes his arm again. Ivar hears the low intake of breath through the vox. He raises the arm, stretches it out. He nods, and Ivar returns it with mute approval.

'Where do we begin, then?' the young warrior asks at last. Sometimes Ivar forgets how recently he has risen up from the Blood Claws.

'If he is not at the bridge, then we seek some clue as to where Gorm rests. Doubtless if he has fallen, he will be where the fighting was thickest.'

'And if not?' Jolfr stalks around. Ivar looks the older warrior up and down, assessing him in spirit just as he has judged Vili in body. 'There are miles of ship to search. Crawling with the enemy. They have made a warren of this great vessel.' He growls, making the vox burr.

'If not,' Ivar says, 'then we will fight and die where we stand. In the company of heroes.'

Brynjar braces his iron hand against the bulkhead and grunts in disapproval.

It is as though he can feel the great spirit's pain by its absence. Not for the *Spinebreaker* the gritted teeth and muted cries. Instead it slumbers, though in rest or under barrow he cannot yet tell.

Restore motive thunder to its corpse. Wake the dead and shatter the mountains of the enemy. Bring fire and death as though the season of upheaval were upon us. You do not ask for much, my brother.

He shares the ache of the mutilated machine. His armour trembles involuntarily with every step. Runes and glyphs flicker and die along his augmented sight. There is only static and confusion. No noospheric symphony resonates through the vessel. No cogitators hum with sacred rhythm.

Ytri taps the tip of his sword against the wall beside Brynjar's hand. The Iron Priest turns to look at the ragged killer. Ytri shrugs, a languid, rolling motion. Then taps again.

'It isn't going anywhere then?' he muses.

'You always were a bastard, Ytri,' Brynjar growls. 'No respect for tradition.'

'Next you'll be telling me I lack for honour.'

'Oh, never that. You hold to your oaths. It remains one of your redeeming qualities.' He pauses. 'Few though they may be.'

Ytri draws the blade back. The din of battle has drifted down, even this far into the *Spinebreaker*'s innards. He meets Brynjar's gaze and holds it. Ytri is gore-slick and wound in entrails. Slivers of crawling flesh still adhere to his armour, worming at the seals and cracks. He brushes them off with one clawed gauntlet, almost as an afterthought.

They walk on, the other members of Bloodiron Wrath trailing behind, their weapons raised and ready.

Falr drums a spiked gauntlet against one of the metal walls. 'Hard to believe anything could kill a ship so completely,' he muses.

Brynjar looks around. Falr is so often a closed soul, dedicated only to the arts of the killer. The blades jangle against his armour as he moves, tilting his head as he inspects the ship. 'I do not think the savages could have torn it from the heavens alone.'

'Such things are not for us to know,' Brynjar replies sadly. 'All we can do is honour what has gone before. Victory or death.'

It is too quiet here, in the heart of the ship. Swathed in perpetual silent gloom. They do not kindle helm-lumens. That would draw too much attention. Instead they trust in their augmented vision, the gifts both technological and gene-granted.

Chains dangle like serpents, swaying lightly. Brynjar lets his eyes scan the iron sky as they emerge out into the enginarium proper. Above him, writ in silver, steel and sanctity, is a vast mural. It is beautiful. Etched with all the logical devotion of the Mechanicus and the savage skill of Fenris.

It is a stylised rendition of the Wolf that Stalks Between Stars, the old Legion rendered into a beast rampant. Binds trail from its jaws, limbs and claws – fluttering trails of lapis, rendered gossamer-thin by scale. Stars die between the wolf's jaws. Constellations are rent apart by the flailing talons.

Brynjar has never seen anything so beautiful. He feels his hearts contract, aching at the machine-worked perfection. Some ancient craftsman may as well have seen his split soul and divided loyalties, knowing that one day Brynjar Drakefang would stand beneath it in silent awe.

'Never saw you appreciate art before,' Ytri grumbles.

Brynjar looks around, his armour echoing his own sigh. 'Great works done in the name of the Allfather-Omnissiah must be savoured, my friend. He is the Smith-of-the-Heavens and set the skies burning with stars before ever we were raised up. This is an omen.' He pauses. 'And a good one, at that.'

Ytri tilts his head and gestures with his blade, up into the alcoves that rest just below the immense mural. 'Not all good omens, though, are they?'

Brynjar looks up. His helm clicks and his bionic eye whirs, enhancing the image.

Bodies hang there. Strung from chains and caged in makeshift gibbets, suspended by their necks or with their limbs entwined. Pinned and displayed, like the work of some butcher bird or the leavings of an immense arachnid.

Unlike the writhing and mutating flesh of the enemy, the red-robed figures are nests of desiccated skin and rusted metal. Brynjar can see the places where the rust has branched off, becoming whorls of insane abstraction. It reminds him of budding fungus. Of coral, coaxed and grown in a blood-dimmed tide.

'We have work to do,' Brynjar says.

It stretches ahead of them, vast and empty, a steel sepulchre.

Time and malice have reduced the ship from a proud bulwark to a ruin. Carved as though it were a rune-etched marker set over the grave of a hero.

Nothing here is inviolate. Time reduces all things to dust.

The least of the monsters have fled from their lairs, scenting blood and fresh meat. Entwined with the hammer of the common soldiery outside the ship, while the subtle scalpel finds its way past the ribs of iron and adamantine.

Ivar Krakenblood knows this in his marrow. The ship, too, remembers. Instinct. Tactic. Memory. All coil within the hearts of man and machine.

Yet beasts remember too. Deep within the core of their abused flesh and tortured psyches, they remember. Limbic responses blossom and flare in the cold dark of their minds. Bubbling up like rising magma, kindling like vast engines.

The keener predators have waited in their lairs. Knowing their enemies would seek to violate them. All too aware that the prize they covet lies within. Mouths split open in infinite flesh, yawning and flecked with blood and spittle.

Hunt. Feed.

The yearning has never left them. It has only slumbered. Claws scrape against the decking and tendrils flail, leaving trails of slime in their wake. They stir and rise. Flexing like the predator kings of the deep. Stretching upwards with perilous hunger.

Like kraken.

CHAPTER FIFTEEN

DARKNESS AND LIGHT

They ascend through the corpse of a murdered god.

Ivar curses under his breath. Brynjar would have more poetry for the moment. The teachings of Mars never robbed him of his soul, only invigorated it. This is his domain, just as the apothecarion remains Ivar's.

Tarnish spreads over every surface, a crawling verdigris insinuating itself into every crack and crevice. Patterns glimmer amidst the ruin, trying to catch Ivar's eye. He knows if he pays them any heed then they will try to ensnare him. They shift and realign, dogging his steps.

Whispering begins to fill the airless confines of the ship. A thousand mouths. Countless voices. All raised in dark worship and false prophecy. Crooning of the doom of mankind. The fall of Fenris and Terra. Vengeance rising up from a sea of dust and ashes.

'Ignore them,' Ivar says over the vox. Stern and even, his voice eclipses the chorus of lies. The others nod. Jolfr pushes up and past his brothers, gesturing behind him almost idly as he does.

'Vili, Orwandil. Make sure nothing surprises us.'

The two bow lightly and turn. Walking slowly backwards, their weapons are trained on the whispering gloom. Ivar looks back with them and then turns away. Jolfr follows him, shoulder to shoulder now. There is still enough room for two mortals to walk on either side of them.

'Hard to believe this thing was ever void-worthy,' Jolfr says.

'Aye,' Ivar mutters. 'Once it sailed the stars in the Allfather's name and now it languishes in the dust of a dead world. Pinned like bait by the serpents who assail us.'

'We could still be on the boy's ship, in orbit.' Jolfr shrugs. 'The enemy do not present us with any true challenge. This is a trap. A pit of vipers for us to be drowned in. They cannot truly best us, not in skill of arms alone.'

'The same as always. Weaklings and bastards fight with cowards' weapons. Just as they did on Fenris.'

'I heard it said that you fought one of their monsters at the hearth, at the Slayer's side.' Awe creeps into Jolfr's tone. 'It must have been a fine thing to watch him kill, and share in the glory.'

Glory.

Ivar smiles behind the grinning skull. 'It was…'

Words fail him. To watch the Slayer in combat, the volcanic fury of his wrath, the killing fire of plasma and crozius… Seeing the enemy wilt before him. Bearing the privilege of sharing in the kill. As part of a privileged brotherhood. As a member of a pack.

'A singular honour,' Ivar finishes. He pauses. 'Oh, Throne of the Allfather…'

They pass as one into what was once the bridge.

Most of it is gone, subsumed in the vast and rancid mass that rises from the deck. Great limbs of bone scrape at the ceiling, their ivory boughs hung with flensed skin and undulating flesh.

The living and the dead alike form its bulk. Bodies writhe around the trunk, coiling like snakes. The fur, scales and feathers of the beastmen – generations of them – flare, bright and shifting amidst the dark, bulbous flesh. Ochre bleeds in crimson, transmutes into amethyst, burns again into emerald. Colours that should not be – that have never been – blossom and die.

The old, dead flesh has not been allowed to moulder. Instead it twists and screams in unlife, a howling chrysalis from which the future is born, over and over again. Rags hang on pinions of bone, the remnants of uniforms and armour.

It is a mockery beast. Nothing else that Ivar has beheld, no threat from the unholy arsenals of Chaos, compares to this. It is the Tree of Life and Death, rendered in falsehood, carved from atrocity.

The flesh-bark splits wetly. Great and swollen eyes blink in the crevices, bloodshot and staring. Bloody rheum dribbles from them like sap, thick and golden where it isn't stained black and red. Jagged rents spiral out from the eyes and yawn wide. Teeth gnash in black gums, surrounding the vast chasms of deeper, near-infinite darkness. Things squirm in the shadows.

'*Children,*' the umbra breathes. Air rushes upwards in a pulse of corrupt exhalation. Something flexes beneath their feet, making the decking undulate and shake. *'You have come home. New. New flesh. Wolves in the halls. Dogs at the gates. Once more.'*

'I have not come to speak with abominations,' Ivar growls. 'I have come to bring a brother home.'

'Home. Home. Home,' the monstrous construct echoes. Each foetid breath forces new poison into the empty air alongside yet more spurts of rancid bile and black blood.

The pack moves out and around the central dais, circling the squirming mass of flesh and bone. Witchfire kindles in the vaults of the ceiling, burning like unclean lanterns in the gourd-growths that hang from the iron ribs.

Skulls.

Nestled together in bunches, each one aglow with witch-light. Distended and warped by the touch of maleficarum.

Ivar's skin burns within his armour, prickling with phantom heat, seared with false fire. The unholy tree is a locus of arcane power, reshaping the world around them by psychic might alone. So many minds, shaped and perverted. Twisted into this resonant obelisk as a monument to some past greatness.

He tastes it again. The rancid witchery that infested the trolls and guided the bestial hordes. A singular mind, stretching out across eternity. Speaking in the voice of wights and all the ululations of the Underverse.

Ivar raises his pistol.

The eyes set in the corpse tree flex wide. The mouths ape them, flapping open and closed as the entire monstrous edifice begins to shudder. It is laughing, Ivar realises. Inhuman joy flutters through it, till its flesh is squirming in a nest of serpents and tendrils.

Pseudopods unfold themselves, barbed and leaking iridescent venom.

'I name you falsehood and desecration,' Ivar growls. The others spread out around the chamber, blades and bolters ready. Runes flash in Ivar's eye-lenses, denoting the exact location of each warrior. Vili, holding back despite his eagerness, cleaving closely to Jolfr. The old Wolf stalks around the gaping bridge space, moving to the left. Orwandil and Hrungnir close from the right.

'False. False. False.'

The monster's quivering intensifies, like an arrhythmic heart. It spasms with tortured knowledge, motivated only by torment and deepest hate.

Emotions bleed from it in a wave. The walls contort, the plasteel trembling and straining. Panels buckle and break. Yet more of the coiling tendrils force their way free.

Ivar sights. Not at the bulk of the thing, but higher. Up into the boughs of the beast, where the skull-lanterns shake and burn.

He fires, even as the first barbs plunge for the hearts of his kin.

Brynjar prays.

His voice rises like the cries of a tribal gothi as he calls the Rout to task. It thunders in an echo of artillery, riven through with the volcanic bombast that rules both the Island of the Iron Masters and distant, crimson-shrouded Mars.

In this place, amidst the ruin of the once-great ship, he is at home. Both sides of his soul howl in praise: of great Fenris and her station amidst the roiling cosmos; of Russ, who tamed her people and bound them to the Allfather.

Who gave us ships such as these, with which to claw the Uppland from our enemies.

His voice is flesh and machine. Vox-utterance and binharic war and wind together as he conducts the galvanic choir. Brynjar's ornate armour burns with kindled Motive Force, casting forth its purifying light.

The others toil with him. Above. Below. He guides them with precision, rendering their flesh and armour, their minds and souls, into cogs in one great mechanism.

By the effort of countless hands are the Great Works accomplished. With fire and steel are miracles crafted.

'Toll, my brothers. Toll the bells. Anoint this engine in the Machine God's sight!'

There are none left who truly understand the mysteries of the machine. Brynjar casts his eyes up to where the dead hang, defiled and silent. Oil and blood streaks their soiled crimson robes. If there were more time then he would climb up himself and return them to the deck, repatriate their implants to the Machine God. Instead he must give them to the cleansing flame.

Damn you, Ivar. For making me do this.

He takes no pleasure in what is to come. To kill a ship is a blasphemous thing, even for a warrior such as himself. Even for one who has consigned the vessels of humanity's enemies to extinction.

Duty. That is what guides him. Brynjar's iron hand clenches and unclenches at his side. His other holds tight to his hammer. Drumming the ferrule against the decking, in time with his chants and exhortations.

'In the machine there is purpose! In the grand design of the Allfather-Omnissiah there is wisdom!'

Light kindles within the great plasma reservoirs. The reactor thrums, struggling and sputtering. Lumens crackle to life, lending their own feeble illumination to the radiance of newborn suns that the reactors are creating.

Above them the corpses of the tech-priests and enginseers begin to sway. Slowly at first. Moving as if stirred by some sudden breeze. Brynjar looks up, his enhanced sight drinking in the subtle motions of the bodies. Yet it is not an impossible wind that moves them.

There are things moving on the ceiling, from the ceiling, *through* the ceiling. They unfold and squirm like serpents. Like the tentacles of some thing dredged up from the deep places beneath the ice, or the roots of some impossible tree.

Unnatural life on a dead world, digging its way through the iron bones of the dead ship. A parasite king, nestled in the heart of sanctity. Drawn by the light it would destroy. Light and darkness, locked together in that primal struggle. The same one that has raged since men first tamed fire and swung torches out from their caves into the primordial shadow.

Brynjar does not fear the dark nor the things that dwell within it. He is forged of fire and iron. Shaped by the World of Winter and War. Drawn back to the cradle-system of mankind, to stand upon one of its sacred worlds. He learned there to tame the flame. To shape it into weapons.

No wyrm can stand against him.

It tries. By the Throne, it tries.

Writhing roots burst from the metal ceiling, forcing their way along the iron girders, coiling down the support struts. They subdivide with relentless intensity, fingers of flesh scrabbling across the steel, splitting into webs of capillaries.

One of Brynjar's thralls looks up, its head snapping taut. A growl builds, low in its throat. Bloody drool trickles from the iron maw of its mask. It turns from its labours, mechadendrite tendrils slipping away from the cogitator engine it was tending to. Claws extend in their place.

It snarls and lunges forwards at one of the advancing tendrils. Thicker protrusions are creeping down the walls, the trickle becoming a flood. Its talons scour down the web of flesh and bone. Blood spills in a rush, spraying across the thrall's iron face and bare limbs. It thrashes back, smoke hissing from the contact. Boils flare up, urgent and red. The animal growls become a keening wail.

On Brynjar's eye-lenses, one of the runes begins to pulse urgently.

'From out of the deeps there come monsters. In the dark they breed, and by Chaos are they empowered,' he intones. He reaches forward, his free hand a blur as he manipulates the control panels before him. Runic keys clatter. Brynjar pulls hard at levers all the while intoning his sacred prayers.

'Priest!' Ytri calls.

Brynjar ignores him, lost to the pulse and rhythm of the machine. His rage is the fire of the reactor's heart. At the iron of his wrist, Brynjar's own connectors slither free. They find the input jacks. He feels the pain of interface, the glorious agony of connection with so ancient and venerable a spirit.

<Be at peace, holy machine. You are born of the wrath of Fenris, just as we are. Rouse yourself against corruption. Sing with the rapture of your fury! Raise your voice in sacred communion!>

He can taste the choler of its spirit. The machine soul bellows up from the tormented core of the ship, as though it can sense the rot that spreads through it. Toxic seeds planted in the unwilling soil of the once noble *Spinebreaker*.

Furnaces echo the machine spirit's anger. Flames surge upwards, scraping at the iron sky. The metal glows crimson at their passage, refracting light and reflecting heat. Under such scalding intensity even the boldest of the fleshy growths shudders back.

Something like fear colours the air in a hiss of foul musk.

'Priest!' Ytri shouts again. 'Let me cut this bastard thing from the ship!'

'The season of fire comes again!' Brynjar bellows with laughter. 'With flame and steel shall we reward all maleficarum!'

Falr laughs as he swings himself up amidst the mess of gantries and beams, moving with a primal eagerness that makes the blades and totems rattle and dance. The others move too, divided in attention yet bound together in purpose.

Brynjar barely has to direct them. He cannot find the focus, even if he wanted to. There is only the joy of communion. The burning touch of mortal soul to mechanised godhood.

Understanding floods him in a rush, a torrent of information that would drown lesser minds. It is as though his armour, his flesh, his very being are aflame. Burning with the captive lightning of the spirit's vast soul.

Nothing I have learned has prepared me for this. This is the truth no magos or Iron Master can impart. These vessels remember what so many have forgotten.

His hand moves faster. His voice matches it. Every word is forced from between clenched teeth. The organic side of his face is locked in rictus, matching the augmetic approximation. Brynjar feels phantom pain lance across the metal plate, burning in the furrows carved in mimicry of the long-vanished drake dance. It burns so hot that he fears it blazes blue once again.

'Skitja,' he hisses. His concentration breaks for but a moment. A moment is enough.

The tendrils surge down with renewed vigour. One seizes the gantry onto which Falr has only just landed. His blades are in his hands a second later, hewing with an arborist's urgency. Budding pseudopods flail away in a rain of glittering blood, arcs of it dying away as soon as it is shed. It becomes motes of shimmering pollen, hallucinogenic rains of spores, flakes of gold and precious stone.

When the monster bleeds it is everything and nothing, so much a slave to flux that it can hold no true shape now that it is roused. It contorts again. Eyes reach out on stems, then peel open and apart. Tiny mouths snap and whisper in their place. Lurid red drips from their needle teeth as they contort in hideous laughter.

Then they move. Too fast, snapping at Falr's plate. He staggers back and then throws himself forwards, blades up. Bite matches bite. He snips the heads from stalks, left and right, even as the roots of the thing knot themselves through the grating at his feet.

It sluices apart in a rain of muscle fibres, reshaping and unwinding, coiling around a new central aperture. More teeth glisten there, sudden and sharp. The strands of muscle and sinew, ligament and cartilage snap outwards in a wet, vomiting motion and envelop Brynjar's brother.

Falr screams his hate into the thing's unface. He fights it, every step of the way. His knives flash, tearing away limblets and tendrils. He bellows his rage at it, even when the blades fall from his fingers. Falr uses his fists instead, as though he can bludgeon it into submission with his hands alone. Brawn struggling now where blades failed to stop the oncoming storm of mutation.

Brynjar knows Falr's record. He has recounted it himself. Etched oaths and memories into the man's armour. Now he can only watch as the corpse tree pins Falr in place, winding about him, squeezing until the carved words buckle and crack. Blood trickles sluggishly down the plate.

Another tentacle coils up, flexing its corpse sinews. It snaps taut and hurtles forward, locking around Falr's helmet and neck. Fingers slither from its mass, tugging at the seals, pawing incessantly. A susurrus of whispered laughter flutters into the air, disgorged from a hundred mouths.

The others begin to fire. Explosions rock the monstrous thing, detonating around and within it. Ichor jets from its sundered flesh, the wounds screaming and vomiting unclean blood.

Tendrils burst apart, releasing Falr suddenly. With nothing to support him, he falls.

Brynjar's prayers shift as he watches, helpless. His chants become a single drawn out roar of rage.

CHAPTER SIXTEEN

A CROWN OF FIRE

The ship rouses like an old drunk, trembling from sleep to wakefulness.

Lights flare along its immense length, sending mad shadows out across the sprawling battlefield, illuminating the glorious slain.

Dozens have fallen, taken by blade or claw. Some bear mortal wounds that felled them where they stood. Others took glancing blows which rent their suits apart. A slow and sad death.

The Wolf Priests have counselled them that land-drowning is a danger of the Uppland. The black waters of eternity can overwhelm a mortal as easily as the icy seawater of home.

Kaedra spits her defiance at the enemy. Rage burns in her heart at the sight of so many dead. Mangled and ruined, despoiled by the enemy. She can see one of the beaked monsters squatting on a kinsman's chest, taking great heaving bites from his cold flesh. Blood trickles down its snapping maw, freezing against bone, keratin and feathers.

She can only watch with horrified awe as it feeds. Its very existence defies logic and sense.

What cursed lives do these beasts live that they can ignore the killing, airless cold?

Horns sound from somewhere far behind her, roaring into the darkness from the rousing ship. A corpse no longer, it does not move. Instead there is sound and fury. Then the tumult fades and there is a lesser utterance, yet to her ears far more profound. Every syllable is coloured with pain and rage.

'I speak with the voice of the ship. I speak to all who cleave to their oaths. Above and below. Hear me. Heed the words of Brynjar Drakefang. Iron Priest of Fenris. Master of the Spinebreaker's *anger. I speak with the ship's voice. I see with its countless eyes. I commend that data to the ether, as the Allfather-Omnissiah would will. I cast it forth that those above might see with my sight.*

'Send fire from the heavens. Punish the enemies of the Rout.'

'Finally,' Garald says, letting out a breath. He throws himself up from the throne so violently he almost staggers and falls. Below, others echo his joy. Cheers and prayers rise from the officers' nooks and the crew pits.

Somewhere, one of the tech-priests begins to cant in holy binharic song. It breaks through the weighty silence that has gripped the bridge. Servo-skulls drift from side to side, awaiting orders that are still unvoiced.

The vox crackle has barely faded away. Brynjar's words still hang in the bridge's air and linger in the minds of the crew. He looks to Velaq at her auspex station.

'Have we confirmed the veracity of the data transfer?'

'Aye, lord. It is the Wolves. Older signifier codes on the vox-castings, but the auspex readings are holding true. We have confirmation of allied positions relative to the wreck.' She pauses, brow furrowed. 'And enemy positions.'

'So much for a dead world…' Garald mutters. 'What are the enemy dispositions? The numbers, if you have them.'

'Thousands, lord,' she says. Her words are a breathy rush, swelling to fill the great space of the bridge.

'All the more to bring Morkai's last bite to,' Bodil purrs. The silence has galled her, he knows. She has been pacing the bridge for the last few hours, casting her aspersions and chanting her prayers at the crew.

Lionising the brave souls of Fenris who have given themselves to the Uppland to defend the Allfather's honour. Or encouraging those of other lineages, other worlds, to stand as firm and steadfast as the blood of Fenris, which burns in the hearts of all warriors of worth.

'If it's death you want to bring them then I will heartily provide.' Garald's words make her head snap around, and she grins her broken-toothed smile.

'Perhaps there is some true wolf in you after all,' she says.

Garald forces a smile of his own. They will never let him forget that he does not hail from that roiling world of fire and ice. That he was not raised up from the glacial wastes and never fought or bled in some tribal dance of violence.

A thrall-child. An offering son. Taken in some raid or another and judged worthy enough to be considered as an ersatz heir. Rokkvi Helvintr, a lesser scion of that line and house, would have died without inheritor had circumstances not intervened as they had. Leaving Garald as a cadet son to a cadet house. Trusted with lesser tasks and duties until necessity had forced another indignity.

Had I known where that path would lead me, I would never have set out upon it. I would have fought it every step of the way.

Too late now to wish for a different present, let alone a peaceful future.

He reaches down and pats the head of his axe, taking a moment to revel in its iron permanence. A shiver passes through him.

Garald ignores the crone's words and gestures. 'Now we have a line of fire. Punish the enemy. Hew these storms apart. Bring death to the enemies of humanity. For Terra. For Fenris. For the lords who fight below.'

The skulls detonate in a rush of fragments and screaming soul-light.

That gets its attention. The entire bulk of the monster pivots, swinging round and driving its spears down against him. For a moment the others are forgotten, a faint awareness at the edges of its gestalt mind.

Ivar's crozius meets the first barbs of bone, carving them apart in a shower of sparks and shards.

He grins. At last, a challenge. The enemy's rotten core laid bare, a seam of rot spreading through the ship, mocking them with every transformative breath. It hisses its cruel alchemy into the congealing air.

The spears of osseous matter shatter against his armour or the edge of his weapon. Each fragment writhes away from his plate, wriggling like startled fish. Tiny mouths flap open along their lengths, gurgling and whispering. Ivar's helm systems struggle to block them out. They claw at the audio inloads, trying to over-load them with a rush of insane heretic babble.

Some vomit forth old codes. Last wishes and dying decla-rations spew from others. The old crew's hopes and dreams recycled into a never-ending litany of pain and torment.

'Do not listen to them!' Ivar calls.

'Easy for you to say!' Jolfr shouts back. The great double-handed axe slices through questing tendrils of flesh and bone, each one edged with human canines. The teeth spin away in clouds of shredded enamel as Jolfr barges through the thing's limbs. 'The thing is hard as ironwood!'

'Just pretend you are cutting firewood,' Vili laughs. Ivar envies him the bravado of youth, fleeting though it might be.

'Focus!' Ivar calls.

Hrungnir and Orwandil weave their way back, closing with their fellows. Their bolters sound in a near-constant rush. Flame and shrapnel bites at the air. The monster screams in its million voices. Thick blood oozes down its flanks, never more than a sluggish trickle.

Every part of it is so honed as a weapon and an insult… It does not know how to die.

Hrungnir's cry breaks Ivar from his thoughts. The warrior bellows his fury as one of the flailing spears finds its mark. It impales him, slamming through his armour high on the chest-plate, next to his right pauldron. Lesser barbs extrude their way from the bony surface, anchoring themselves in his flesh. Hrungnir snarls, beating at the spur with the butt of his bolter. Orwandil spins about and fires. The shells catch the bone-spear at the middle of its span. Hrungnir cries out again as metal, bone and fire rake across his armour. He staggers back and his hand shoots up to grasp at the protruding spear.

'Void take them,' Hrungnir grunts. 'Allfather curse them to the lowest reaches of the Underverse!'

Ivar rushes to his side. His hands seize the barb, and he snaps it with a flick of his wrist. He reaches for his belt and pulls up a vial of unguent, smearing it across the wound. It hisses on contact, boiling off into the air and leaving only a clinging silver residue. Ivar's hand moves up, tilting Hrungnir's head, forcing him to meet his gaze. The other warrior nods.

'I'm fine, priest. Stop wasting time when we can kill it!'

Ivar turns back towards the totemic monstrosity. Severed limbs squirm away from it with wormish thrashing, leaving slimy trails of blood. Bolt rounds burst within its flesh, stretching its bulk in cystic contortions.

The decking strains and cracks. Great rents spiral out at Ivar's feet. He looks down and snarls, pushing Hrungnir away so hard that his brother hits the wall with a thunderous clatter.

The ship shakes.

At first Ivar thinks it is simply the beast's agony that rocks it. Then he feels the tremor and hears the roar, even through miles of armour plating and corridors.

He knows the sound well. It is the howl of fire from above. Of orbital bombardment.

Perhaps it is not the wounds we give you that set you panicked, eh? You know death is near. One way or another. And like any parasite, you claw your way free.

Its eyes snap around as though tasting his thoughts. More tendrils unfurl from the central mass, flailing with perverted muscles, clawing at the air with borrowed bone. It knows him. Whatever passes for fear coils in its myriad hearts, pulsing its corrupted blood through trembling veins. It spasms like a snake and the decking splits, heaving wide.

Ivar looks down and then leaps. He throws himself forwards, arms outstretched, his crozius gripped in both hands. He turns it as he flies through the air, and one disruptor-fielded wing cleaves into the side of the monster.

It screams. All its voices become one voice. A strangled note of absolute agony.

Ivar heaves, every iota of his strength channelled into the blow. He levers his weight against the thing's bulk and *pulls*.

He drags the weapon down its flank. Every undulation, every buck, drives him deeper. Into the darkness lit only by the boiling blood. It spatters against walls and upon his armour. It crawls and screams, still hissing from the weapon's passage. The crozius is embedded so deeply in the flesh that he almost cannot see its own illumination.

Still he holds on, and still he falls. Above he can hear the resounding symphony of destruction as every bolter commits itself.

The monster bleeds spikes of bone to throw him off. Ivar denies it. He remembers the long-ago bite of the kraken, barbs tearing at his flesh with avaricious suckers. Mighty beyond ken, able to tear apart even the stoutest of ships.

He is armoured better now. He wears the black plate of his priesthood with pride. With honour. Within its shell nothing can truly harm him. He has died once and been reborn. The Chapter has raised him up. Made him mighty. Nigh immortal.

Like a legend from the sagas, I walk with heroes.

He pulls one hand back and begins to punch at the wall of unliving and undying flesh. Bludgeoning it until his knuckles ache even through the armour. He snarls as he drags the crozius through skin and muscle, breaking bone until yet more unclean blood stains his armour.

Ivar claws at the monster as it tears at him. Locked in the oldest and most hateful struggle, he cleaves his way down it. The way the legends say Russ did to the very flesh of Fenris.

The tendrils coil themselves into a knot of bone and drive themselves forwards, hammering Ivar at the centre of his chest and hurling him back. He hits the ground and rolls through filth, still clinging to his crozius. His head snaps up and he growls, low in the throat.

'Is that all you have, beast?'

It rumbles, recognising the challenge. Yet more maws open in its flesh, tongues lolling from between barbed teeth. Poisoned drool and blood dribbles from the apertures, hitting the decking with a hiss.

Ivar looks around, regaining his bearings. And he stops.

For one of his calling, his new surroundings are hideously familiar. Compared to the rest of the ship this section is fully powered – not the weak and lingering light that now struggles through the machine's veins. It has been sealed off. Ensured. Protected.

The white walls are smeared with grime and blood, patinaed with the creeping growths of the monstrous thing. It oozes and flows, liquid flesh lapping at Ivar's greaves, slithering into solidity, coiling about its prize.

It is almost as though the construct-thing has fed upon the Motive Force here. In the ship's apothecarion.

Here in this sacred place the odious thing winds its way around a central prize. Capillary vines cling to it, pulsing urgently, desperate to worm their way inside. A pale azure light radiates outwards, near obscured by the swarming roots.

A *stasis chamber*.

Medicae-grade, even swathed and swaddled in the reassuring presence of Fenrisian mysticism. The stasis-light shimmers through runic apertures, burning like captured starlight. It is that alone which keeps the beast at bay. Perhaps the last vestiges of the ship's original power remain here, twined about a prize that the Archenemy yearns to claim.

The sides of the casket, where they show through, are sullied enamel and rusted iron. Gnawed at, worn down by the relentless motion of tendrils. Pitted with cracks and crusted with bloody residue.

His eyes scan the chamber. Colonised relentlessly by the corpse tree's growth, the room is all but unrecognisable. Medicae implements are scattered amidst the detritus, lying cold and still alongside discarded ribcages.

Ivar lets his crozius drop to his side. He raises his pistol and smiles within his skull helm.

'Like the drakes in old stories, you guard what is most precious. Is that right? Like the Tree of Life and Death, and the wyrms that bite at the roots.'

It gurgles in response. Row after row of rheumy eyes open down its central mass, weeping bloody tears as another mouth tears itself into being.

'All your dreams are poison. They always lead you here. Again and again. To this moment. In the dark and the dust and the ashes. Ten thousand years you have dug your graves and lined them with your valiant dead. No more. No more. Behold your barque, laid low. Your champions, slain.'

Ivar ignores the prattle of the monster even as the trunk distends and the skin stretches and tears. A skull pushes outwards, jaw rattling in a silent scream. It twists, snapping around without a spine, suspended amidst hanging sinews and taut muscles.

The forehead warps, struggling up into new points. Dividing, subdividing, becoming a nest of antlers. Its jaws snap shut with a clacking rattle. Locking into place, beginning to run like wax and flowing into a jagged beak.

'You are all the same,' Ivar says with a weary shake of his head. 'You talk too much.'

He pulls the trigger.

Ivar fires past the skull. He fires past the monstrous growth and the prize it encircles. His aim is true. There is no failing to recognise or correct.

His bolt pistol bucks in his hand and the shell hurtles forwards, propellant ablaze. It sears past the beast, trailed by the thing's odious laughter.

The shell impacts. It detonates.

The monster screams. Revelation envelops it in a blossoming awareness. Ivar's shell strikes amidst a ramshackle pile of canisters, nested about the base of a pillar of tubing.

Ivar knows this ship as intimately as though he had served upon it. He has laboured within chambers such as this, within entire decks given over to tending to the wounds of brothers. Like a gothi in a house of healing, he has honed his craft. Were it not violated, he could pick out where every tool would lie. He knows its systems and its eccentricities.

The shell ruptures the canisters and pipes alike. They burst apart. Igniting, the flame roars to engulf the monstrous amalgam. Hyper-oxygenated gas surges up like a geyser, burning blue-white in its intensity, enveloping the monster in a rush of purity and punishment.

Ivar stands silhouetted in the hell-light of annihilation. Shrouded in the screams of the dying monster.

A second later the first sirens begin to sound like the heralds of apocalypse.

CHAPTER SEVENTEEN

FINAL FLIGHTS

Kaedra grins as she slays another beast.

It is harder than her days on the ice, but it brings the same joy. So little difference between slaying rival tribesmen and slaying monsters upon the surface of a corpse world. Already she has lived so much more than any of her kin could even dream of.

Iridescent blood coats her armour. Leather, iron mail and void-cladding are transmuted into a glittering mosaic of ruin. Death and madness spirals about her, weaving through the empty air. If she focused, if she truly looked, perhaps she would notice the patterns that shudder through the airless blackness. She does not look. Not even when they embed themselves upon the black stone of the world and unfold their meaning.

Such things are nothing more than hollow maleficarum. No gothi of her home would bless her if she paid those signs any heed.

Ignorance is as much a weapon as her axe or lasgun. A barb to be driven deep into the eye and brain of the enemy. A foe that cannot confound you, never bind you in its deceits, it will be unable to conquer you.

Fenris is not an easy conquest. Time and again that has been proven. Nor are its people. She fights as they have always fought. To the death, consequences be damned.

It is an honour to die. What better fate than to make your red snow, somewhere out amongst the stars, doing the Allfather's will?

She relishes the chance.

Kaedra has lived a life knowing she would never ascend, that the Sky Warriors would never choose her for eternal service. All that remained to her was to fight. She would prove herself by whatever means.

'Skjald!' a voice calls through the rumble of battle. 'Skjald! You're still alive!'

Lyf has found her, somehow. She grins at him through the carved face plate of her helm. 'Aye! Despite the best efforts of the little beasts.'

He cleaves into one with his blade, returning her grin. The mewling thing claws at him, gouging at his breastplate in its death throes. Lyf flinches back, kicking the corpse away. It spasms on the black earth until it finally lies still.

'Allfather's balls, but they die hard,' he grunts.

'Takes more to kill us than it does to kill them!' Kaedra jokes back. Squads of grey-clad armsmen push in beside the knot of Fenrisians, laying down suppressing fire. Las and bullets lash out. Feathered things tumble away, smashing to the ground in rains of fluids and torn flesh.

Like a boil being lanced.

Feedback screeches through their helmets. Everyone falters for a moment; even the disciplined ship troops stop firing. The sound resolves at last and becomes a voice, resonating with the alarums blaring behind the words.

'This is Brynjar. Fall back. Hold the line about the landers. We are coming. They must be ready to leave as soon as we arrive. The

ship is being commended to the fires of Fenris. It will burn. Every-thing will burn.'

'Fall back!' Kaedra cries. Lyf nods and takes up the shout. All of them begin to pull back, firing as they retreat. Even in flight they litter the ground with the enemy dead, every step dogged by shrill cries of animal pain.

The echoes catch in the empty air, resounding where they shouldn't. They dance and change, twisting on the non-existent breeze. As though the mere passage of them brings some tainted air with them.

By the time they reach the makeshift firing lines, Kaedra could swear that it has become laughter.

'Brother. If you can hear this, then you must get out. There is precious little time. Falr is dead. We must return his legacy to orbit. Ivar, if you can hear me, then respond. I have control of the vox-arrays now, and am relaying all communications to the rogue trader's ship, but we must...'

Ivar stares at the stasis casket.

Words cannot reach him. He can hear Brynjar's urgent calls and those of his brothers above. Yet he kneels, fascinated, his hands working almost without realising their craft. Folds of charred flesh peel away, crisping apart as he wipes them clear of the viewing aperture. The blue light washes over him, and for the first time in so long, he feels peace.

It is not the thrashing hues of the seas of his home, riven through with salt grey and ice white. It is a purer radiance. Flaw-less, despite the years it has languished. No work of the enemy has violated it. Not truly.

'We are coming, brother!' Jolfr calls. He scrambles down, hand over hand, lowering himself using empty eye sockets as hand-holds, past fluted and blackened bone. Ivar glances upwards and then returns to his work. He presses runic switches, his eyes alight with reflected confirmation sigils.

'It is… beautiful,' Ivar whispers to himself. Genuine awe creeps into his voice. Jolfr hits the ground with a wet, crunching impact and strides over to the Wolf Priest's side.

'What is?' Jolfr asks, his voice a whispered rumble. Ivar gestures up from where he labours. Jolfr follows his gaze. He steps back. 'By the Allfather…'

A warrior lies within the casket, limned with cold light. It catches on his dark skin and the ringed braids of his hair and beard. It glitters upon his armour, the ice blue of the Chapter. There is a name upon the armour, etched in honour upon the breastplate, picked out in bronze and iron.

Krakenblood.

Preserved only by the casket's mechanisms, he seems merely asleep rather than dead. Lying as though in rest or in state. He is unarmed. His arms are crossed over his waist, gripping a roll of leather and parchment.

'Our prize,' Ivar says softly. 'From the heart of the enemy and the clutches of its horrors. This is what we have sought. A fallen brother, and the knowledge he guarded to the end.'

'And you can get him out?'

'I can. The disengagement is taking time, but he will be returned to us.'

He pauses and presses another switch. There is a terminal exhalation, a halting hydraulic wheeze as the casket grinds open and the light dims. Hoarfrost blossoms on the edges of the casket, creeping along the metal. Revealed at last, the corpse is coated in crystals of ice. Some cling to his cheeks, like forgotten tears.

Around them, the other brothers of Wolf King's Call finally hit the decking. They close in like the wolves that they emulate. A pack, drawing near to their prey.

'Skitja,' Vili mutters. 'This is him? The dead hero?'

'Aye, pup,' Jolfr replies. 'Now you see how badly they wanted to keep him from us?'

'We three will carry him,' Ivar says. 'That is our duty.' He nods to Jolfr and Vili. Both warriors step back, almost surprised by the casual honour done to them. 'The rest of you will see us safely to the ships.'

'Aye, brother.' Hrungnir nods. He winces at the gesture, his wound still fresh. 'We shall guard him like a fallen chieftain. Even if we have to join him in death.'

The three lift him.

They heft him up onto their shoulders, in honour. Ivar's hand drops, clinging to the handle of his crozius. The corpse's weight, even divided between three, almost floors him. Legacy presses down upon him as surely as the armoured bulk. Threatening to crush him, body and soul.

They carry him.

Ivar thinks of when he first met these warriors, the sons of Fenris who bear the pack-name of Wolf King's Call. They bore their own Varagyr, Fjolnir, into the sanctity of Ivar's apothecarion, wracked by their grief.

Here, now, there is only duty.

They bear two fallen heroes out from the ship-grave.

Ivar and Brynjar lead them out, from the depths of the ship, past withering growths and dying flowers of flesh. They tread the corpses of the enemy into the decking till their boots are slick with old rot and fresh blood.

Even here the effects of that central pyre have radiated out, like the motive lifeblood of the ship spills out from the reactor.

As they pass through the outer bulkheads of the ship, they behold the hell that has become of the world. Fire licks the skies, burning in every hue of colour. An unimaginable riot, surging upwards to eclipse the stars. The storm is dying. Above and about them the unnatural currents blow out, tied too deeply to the font of the enemy's power. Death begetting death, where once both coiled with unnatural life.

'Forwards,' Ivar whispers softly. 'Bear them home.'

Gorm's wounds are old and cold, sealed and silent. Falr's still run with fresh blood, dribbling down to stain the armour of his brothers.

Every step hurts. The commingled pain of victory and loss.

There is always a cost. We pay it in blood and agony.

For a moment the enemy are scattered and confused. Ivar sees them, fallen to their knees, braying and wailing without a thought to guide them. Some are weeping blood. Shaking themselves and screaming. Eyes find them, few at first, but then focus ripples through the horde. Roaring themselves raw, they throw themselves up from the dust in heedless waves. Cruel cunning is dashed upon the rocks of animal rage. Something primal, almost noble in its simple purity.

His warriors crush them as they pass, by-blows reducing skulls to fragments. Boots stave in chests, weapons and fists snap spines. Still they come. Clawing and slavering, claws battering against armour, weapons breaking with the force of their swings. Ivar's fist dashes another to the ground.

Behind the waiting drop-ships another spear of orbital fire tears into the world's skin. It shudders beneath their feet, rippling with captive Chaos. Light and energy trembles below the ground, reaching into the depths towards the false planet's dead core.

Faces push up against the black stone underfoot. Screaming, howling their eternal torment and displeasure. They burst into crawling runes and fractal patterns, tearing themselves apart so they can become whispers.

'Forwards,' Ivar says again. 'The only way is through.'

The cordon is holding, barely. By the Allfather, it seems almost a miracle. Fenrisians fight alongside armsmen. Hacking. Slashing. Lashing out with searing crimson las bolts and autogun rounds. The dead and the wounded lie behind the soldiers, braced against the ships or sheltered within. Blood-streaked, pallid, or the ashen grey of the slain, they have been dragged into safety by comrades and kin. Ivar sees the trails of blood and viscera, bold across the rock, as though the bodies had been smeared by some immense hand.

'I wish we had shields,' Jolfr whispers. 'When we brought Fjolnir to you, it was upon shields.'

'Ice honour,' Ivar says with a nod. 'An old courtesy. You do not fail Gorm now. What matters is that you stand with him. You carry him, with the same love as you bore your own Varagyr.'

Jolfr is quiet before he nods.

Ivar looks to Brynjar as they draw even. The Iron Priest is inscrutable behind his helm, but the tension radiates from him. Brynjar and Bloodiron Wrath all bristle in their grief. Ytri mutters to himself. He pauses and lashes out, venting his choler upon the broken monsters until he is coated anew in mortal detritus.

Ivar looks down at one of the soldiers. The man freezes, caught in the glare of the wolf skull's attentions.

'My lord…' he says, falling to his knees.

'Take us up,' Ivar growls. He turns to the others at the line. 'All of you! Back to the ships! This world will burn with the Allfather's judgement.' He pauses. 'And a wolf's vengeance.'

'THE CANDLE'

Onouris breaks from the trance with a hiss of pain and deep longing.

He dreamed of darkness where here there is only light. So bright now that it hurts his eyes even when they are closed. His armour is no shield from the relentless radiance. They have made sure of it. The light, like the pain, is a reminder.

He cannot forget the lessons of the past. He wears them upon his soul like the ashes and dust upon his plate. They have etched themselves into his flesh and spirit.

'Brother,' Qar says.

Onouris turns to look at his brother, smiling gently. For a moment he can pretend that the agony cannot touch him. He must be strong, if the rites are to be observed.

'You worry too much,' Onouris says. His voice has been reduced to a dry whisper by his devotions to the art. His fingers ache from being pressed so tightly to the relic. His mind throbs from the pressure of its scream. 'All is as it should be. The signs remain in alignment.'

'You sound so sure, and yet their ways are built upon false signs and deceptions.' Qar reaches out, his fingers swimming in the light as though through deep and brilliant water. Onouris' hand is faster. He seizes his brother by the wrist and holds him in place.

'We are used to lies, my brother. We have been raised on them our entire lives. Choked them down, day after day. There is nothing else for us.'

'Here there is,' Qar says quietly. 'Here we sift truth from out of the mouth of delusions.'

'As you say.' Onouris sighs. 'I wish no quarrel, brother. Not now. The mirror fractures as readily as we look upon it. Dreams and realities are unmade by less. All we have is our fraternity.'

All we have is brotherhood.

The thought alone makes the turbulent immaterium shudder around them, like the convulsing heart of a star. Heat joins the light. Onouris takes a deep breath and *focuses* his mind. The warp stills. He gestures, and they are elsewhere, elsewhen.

'More memory palaces, Onouris?' Qar laughs bitterly.

They stand now in a chamber of smooth white stone, bathed in late afternoon sunlight. Qar steps through the aperture in the east wall, out and onto the waiting terrace. He takes a lungful of air that Onouris knows tastes of spice and salt. The barest hint of smoke lingers on the breeze.

It is beautiful and perfect, and it will not last. It cannot. Not until all their works are finally completed. Only then can he allow dreams to become reality.

'It will suffice, for a time,' he says. 'We were happy here, were we not?'

'It was home,' Qar says emptily. 'Until it wasn't.'

'Now we have a new home,' Onouris soothes. 'And a brighter purpose. We hoard treasures here that others can only imagine. Anchors of human history. Tools of our magnum opus.'

Onouris sits at the table that dominates the room. Black wood and ivory are interwoven beautifully, inlaid with lapis. He places his hands upon it, feeling the gentle pulse of the false world. The undercurrent of fear, caught in the marrow of the place. A storm waiting to break.

He reaches out and one of the sacred cards flickers into being, dancing from finger to finger. He holds it cautiously, as though it might burn him. He stays poised, like a gambler about to push his advantage. He has yet to look at it.

'Do you ever think of how things once were?' Qar asks quietly.

Onouris' attention snaps up and round. His brother is rendered a silhouette by the midday sun. A statue in black and crimson, as stalwart and unmoving as a temple idol. An echo of simpler times. It forces another sad smile to Onouris' lips.

'I think of nothing else,' Onouris admits. 'Between our labours here, I walk old memories. I remember them all. The Throne-world. The home world. Everywhere we have walked, fought, and bled together.'

He places the card down.

'Everywhere I look, brother, I see the ghosts of our past.'

CHAPTER EIGHTEEN

WIGHTGRAVE

Blood and loss, for hope and life
The dead are never free from strife.
To sit at the Allfather's right hand,
Lamented from their final stand.
Paths reclaimed, while heroes fell
When spirits scream, entombed in Hel.

The black planet burns behind them. Less than it was. Less than a memory. They have anointed it in fire and blood. A fitting offering for the works of the enemy, though the loss of the *Spinebreaker* remains like a wound.

Ivar watches it die. He forces himself to reckon with the act, Brynjar's silence haunting him at his side, keener in his judgement.

It was not his order. It was not his choice. He would have rather seen it moulder as a tomb, a monument. As though one defilement were better than another.

The pain of it haunts them all.

Some gather to mourn and to offer up their respects to the great soul of the dead ship. Others tend to their wounds, trying vainly to scrub away the insults of the corpse planet. The Helvintr boy idles far back, timid in the face of the Wolves and their grief. The packs bear it worst of all. Ytri and Jolfr lead their men into the depths of the vessel, to their makeshift quarters. Resentment curdles in them.

'This is our prize,' Ivar says at last.

He lays the map out with reverence. Fingers brush along it, tracing the edges of the parchment, smoothing it out upon its leather bindings. 'The last secret that Gorm guarded to his grave. This is his hoard. What he yearned to protect for his brothers.'

The barrack halls remain spartan, their utility all that matters. The central table is a rough-hewn slab of plain, unornamented steel. Around them their weapons have been arrayed, balanced against the walls like offerings to a chieftain.

The map catches the light, glimmering beneath the lumen-strips above.

Brynjar leans in and scrutinises the map. His servo-arm swings around, clicking as it lowers over his shoulder. It snatches a tiny fragment from the edges and brings it up to Brynjar's artificial eye.

The crimson orb flickers and glows. Binharic burbles from the Iron Priest before he sighs.

'Authentic,' he confirms. 'Chronological accuracy established, and the source reads as Imperial standard.' A line of red light flickers out from the augmetic, scanning the document further. 'It bears his seal.'

'This was the path he walked,' Ivar says reverently. 'His last great hunt.' His finger moves across the map. 'There. That is where we found him.' He gestures at a segment marked Morkai's

Lair. A black and roiling world, ringed by spectral wolves – great shadow-furred monsters seeking to devour all who venture near.

'And where does the path lead?' Brynjar asks.

'Onwards to the bitter end,' Ivar laughs. Mania has crept into his words and his motions. The others look askance. Brynjar meets Ytri's eyes and shakes his head before Ivar continues, 'There is a warp anomaly nearby. The map terms it as the Forge of Outrages. And beyond that? The False Sun, burning with old light and shame. That is where the Vargrtiðhorn lies.'

To see it writ upon parchment sets Ivar's hearts beating. Asserting the hope upon reality. Making it a truth. Twinning it with his own capricious wyrd.

This could be my destiny. My legend.

'Fine tidings then to return to the hearth,' Brynjar says.

Ivar is silent. He looks away from Brynjar, focused upon the map.

'Brother,' Brynjar says again. 'We are returning to Fenris, are we not?'

'We have an opportunity before us,' Ivar says at last.

There is uproar. Instant and fierce. Brynjar seizes him by the gorget and pulls him forwards. Ivar's hand flies up, grasping the Iron Priest by the wrist.

'Do not do this, brother,' Ivar says.

Brynjar laughs bitterly. 'You have lost your senses, brother. You have let awe and glory-thirst addle you. If you think this will bring you the legacy you seek then you are mad and nothing more. You will be no brother of mine.'

'You would judge me, brother? We both fought for rank and position. Blood was shed and we suffered together. We lost and we mourned. Even if they were only brothers of the moment. A pack of convenience.'

'Do not invoke their names to defend your overreach!' Brynjar snaps. 'Falr is dead now too. Would you have him die for nothing?'

'I would ask you the same.'

Brynjar's fist snaps up, poised to strike. Ivar stares it down. He does not flinch. Ivar almost laughs.

'What will this achieve, brother? We could brawl, like children by a firepit. Or we can talk. We can *reason*. The priests of Mars pride themselves on their logic. Were you absent when they hammered that lesson into your skull?'

'Do not speak of what you do not understand!' Brynjar snaps.

'I understand well enough,' Ivar shouts. His arm snaps out, sweeping around the chamber. All his brothers have gathered around him. The mortal crew congregate as well. Garald Helvintr stands nearby, watching with cautious awe. The gothi stands at his side, fingers moving in a constant dance.

Weighing fates. Judging futures.

'We have an opportunity,' Ivar says. 'A chance to finish what Gorm started. His saga stands unfinished. His duty yet undone.'

'*His saga,*' Brynjar says. 'Not yours. His. He is your blood but you are not him. His fate is only your fate if you make it so. Have I misjudged you, Krakenblood? Are you some death-seeker now?'

'I do not seek it, but nor do I fear it,' Ivar says.

Brynjar nods, almost softly. 'That I do believe, brother.'

'Russ take your belief,' Ytri snarls. 'He means to lead us into the jaws of the enemy.' He spits to one side. 'We had a mission. The Slayer himself laid it down. The champions of the Chapter gave us our task, and you curse their trust!'

'Two packs,' Jolfr puts in. 'A handful of mortals.' He glances over at the rogue trader. 'Capable mortals though they may be. It is not the stuff that victory is made of.'

'Wars have been won with less,' Ivar protests. 'There have been worlds laid low with but a handful of Space Marines. And none of those were of the Vlka Fenryka.' He slams his fists against the tactical table. 'Where is your ambition, brothers? Where is your pride!'

'It lies in not dying with you, you mangy bastard,' Ytri grumbles.

Ivar's skull mask tilts. 'You would defy me?'

'By Falr's corpse, you are damned right I do.' He swaggers forwards to Brynjar's side. Both are still scarred and ruined from the relentless melee below, armour clawed and pitted where it has been worked at by acids and stranger fluids.

The others are silent. Even Jolfr's protests have died in his throat. The old warrior looks at Ivar with his lined eyes, his mouth set in grim neutrality. When he looks away, that is the cut that Ivar feels deeper.

'There is no glory here,' Ytri snarls. The others turn to look at him. Even Jolfr pauses, before he looks away in a final shame. The iron walls of the ship have never felt more like a cell. A cage. 'And we march straight on into the mouth of hell, do we not?' He points at Ivar. 'You will kill us all with your damned pride.'

'Be silent,' Jolfr snaps. 'He is proud, aye, but he knows the path we must walk. This has been a humbling. Yet I trust him to see us through the storms.'

'You doubt me,' Ivar says. 'Perhaps you all do. You think this some fool's crusade. The folly of a desperate warrior, clawing at glory.' He laughs. They are all watching him now, faces set hard. 'I have been entrusted with this mission by the Slayer himself. I have walked in his shadow and learned at his feet. If that is not enough for you, then challenge me. Tear the mission from my claws. I promise you I am not some aged beast to be slain by the first pretender who tries.' He steps forwards. 'If you challenge me, Ytri, I promise you it will not end well for you.'

The pack leader looks at him with cold loathing and then turns away, stalking from the chamber with his warriors at his heels.

Ivar looks to Brynjar. The Iron Priest's half-face remains impassive. Brynjar taps the ferrule of his great hammer against the decking. 'You are making a mistake, brother,' he says resignedly.

'Only the Chapter, Russ and the Allfather may judge me. If need be I will answer to them, aye, but it will be with the Vargrtiðhorn as a sign of my triumph and my faith.'

Wolf King's Call turns from him.

As one, each member marches off, away from Ivar and out into the ship. Only the mortals remain. Each one with downcast eyes, pale from shock, as though gods have gone to war about them.

The rogue trader, to his credit, keeps his composure better than most, forcing his eyes up to meet Ivar's gaze. They are both trembling, Ivar realises. One with barely constrained rage and the other with fearful awe.

'What is our course?' Garald asks at last. His hand has gone to his axe, a meek gesture of reassurance. As though that could give him *courage*. Make him a *warrior*.

Ivar almost laughs, yet it catches in his throat. Bitter and joyless. He stands before the crew alone, more isolated than he has ever felt. Even silent and solitary toil in the deeps of the Aett cannot compare.

I have striven amongst the dead and the dark and never known pain such as this.

'Our course is to follow this map,' Ivar says. 'I will make its information available to your Navigator and your bridge crew. The original will remain with me.'

He traces his fingers along the original. The Forge of Outrages is a mangled scrawl of iron black and riotous purples, bleeding away into crimson and ochre. His gauntleted digits move across it, across the pale tan of the parchment, to linger on the golden whorls of the False Sun.

Silver runes glitter beneath his touch, like warding sigils.

'My lord, it might be better–' Garald looks up again and immediately stops speaking. Even helmed, masked in bone and iron and spite, he can tell when Ivar's displeasure runs thick.

He moves off, his functionaries at his side. Only the gothi, Bodil, lingers to observe Ivar, before she too hobbles away.

And he is alone, again. With only his thoughts and old ghosts for company.

In the ship's makeshift apothecarion, Ivar continues to hold his vigil. He thinks not only of the flesh but of the spirit as he tends to Gorm Krakenblood's corpse.

He has borne his second death well, Ivar thinks. The stasis field has done its work to an exceptional degree, considering the circumstances. He tests the limbs, lifting them experimentally. It is still as though the warrior has only just passed.

Ivar spares a glance for Falr's body, lying in its own cold berth. The warrior died poorly. Mutilated by the monster below, mangled from a fall. Ivar's helm lenses click as he analyses and interprets the wounds.

They carried them from the corpse world with all the respect due to them, bearing them up from death and shame. Ivar nods to himself. There is a sacred honour in that. Now he readies to honour the warrior once more.

The Fang of Morkai clicks and whirs. The blades rattle with a hungry eagerness. Ivar stills them as he works at Gorm's armour, removing it plate by plate. Exposing the warrior's scar-riven torso. Old wounds, almost beyond count, decorate the grizzled expanse of Gorm's chest. Ivar judges them by eye. A blade wound from an ork's cleaver along his right side. The marks of aeldari shurikens along one arm and shoulder. Burns line his torso, where some flame or acid has kissed.

Ivar wishes he had paid more attention to Gorm's record. The litany of combat written upon his skin is testament enough, but the context…

'It would be worthy of the sagas,' he whispers. 'The Saga of Gorm Krakenblood, Varagyr of Fenris. How the skjalds would sing it.' Ivar raises his hand and begins to make the first incision. He feels the resistance of flesh and bone as the blades bite. 'And beyond his?' Ivar pauses in his labours, laughing dryly. 'Why not the Saga of Ivar Krakenblood, Seeker after Fate? Wolf Priest and Warrior.'

He works at the body, bracing his hand against the cold flesh. His fingers trace the old wounds even as he wrings new promise from the corpse. Ivar sighs. He steadies himself.

'Thus does your legacy rejoin the Chapter. Back to the cold of Fenris. Back to the hearth.'

The ship rings with sudden noise, stirring the cold air. The white walls of the apothecarion flex for a moment as the lumens flicker. Ivar allows himself a moment to look up from his work, absently reaching for the stasis casket. 'It is fitting that some part of you returns to stasis, I think, kinsman. You waited so long to be brought back. Now your strength will find some other arm. Some youngblood fresh from the wars of his tribe. A Krakenblood, perhaps. Or one of the other creeds beyond count.'

The corpse keeps its silence. Ivar almost laughs at the thought of it answering. It is a rare conjunction of fate that he is afforded the chance to tend to the remains of his own lineage, and the dead do not speak.

What would a forebear say to me? How would he judge my record? What would he make of my choices?

He cannot say. Even the thought itself sets his mind to roiling.

This is the path his wyrd has set for him. In defiance of all reason. Ivar glances to the side of the corpse. The worn parchment has been spread out, pinned down by smooth black stones at the corners. The map is not a beautiful thing. Not like the Slayer's gift. There is no grace or artistry to it. A relic of desperation, etched in an uncertain hand.

'Whatever secrets you divined are now mine,' he says to the corpse. Ivar's hand reaches out to touch the map and he hesitates. He looks down at the blood dappling his fingers. Ivar draws back. He cannot, will not, soil it. Not even with the blood of heroes.

The ship shudders again. The engines hum somewhere far behind him, straining against the yearning of the daemonic world. The warp is already howling around them. Perhaps this time the Geller fields will not preserve them. The laughter of the infernal already dogs their heels.

He returns his attentions to the matter at hand.

With care he lifts the progenoid from Gorm's chest and places it reverently into the waiting stasis casket. He pauses and whispers a prayer. For a moment the apothecarion's cold is the chill of winter winds atop the high mountains, and they are both home. He closes his eyes within his helm and bows his head.

'You should not be here,' Ivar says at last.

'I have the freedom of the ship, my lord. I go where I please. Where it pleases the Allfather that I should go…'

The old woman, the gothi Bodil, limps into the medicae vaults and grins her crooked grin. Gingerly she lowers herself onto a metal stool, looking up at him as he works. He can feel her appreciation, that crawling sense of mortal wonder. It is an awe that exposure often robs the kaerls and serfs of.

For the gothi this is close to religious rapture.

They are kin, he knows. Not merely in their shared home

world but because they tend to the souls of their charges. He glances at her. 'Why have you come here?'

'Do I disturb you?'

'Nothing disturbs me. Not any more.'

'For they shall know no fear,' she quotes. She nods approvingly. 'It is more than that, though. Isn't it?'

'You see much, for a mortal.'

'I've had a long time to practise.' She laughs, pats a pouch at her waist. 'And besides, I am not without my aids.'

'You read the fates, then?'

'You have seen me do so before, lord. Do not pretend that you are above such things! The Sky Warriors must always be mindful of the Allfather's guidance, whether it comes from casting bones or dealing cards.'

'And what do your scryings tell you about my fate?' Ivar leans forwards, turning from the corpse. Now she has his interest, and she knows it. An old trick – ever the domain of tricksters and deceivers – yet wielded, in her case, without agenda.

In a galaxy of scrabbling pretenders and would-be tyrants, she is content to serve. There is some comfort in that.

Bodil fusses. She pulls the pouch from where it hangs and empties it unceremoniously onto an empty table. Bone rattles against metal. Bodil huffs with concentration as she pivots round, hunched over, picking at the tiles, moving to a rhythm only she knows. She clicks her tongue as she works, peering over the runes like a mother avian tending her brood.

Her brow furrows.

'What do you see?' Ivar asks quietly.

She looks up. Suddenly she can sense his irritation. The tension in his stance. Slick with blood, fingers coated in old life. He stands between life and death. Beyond them. That shall be his blessing and his curse.

'You are the blade that cuts past from present, and both from future.' She hesitates. 'You seek that which is greater than yourself. Chasing eternity. You want your name writ upon the bones of Fenris. A saga for the ages.'

'I seek only to do my duty.'

'Ah, but do you? You could have turned back. Perhaps you even should have. Instead you forge on. Leading this ship into the dark. Chasing shadows.'

'Ghosts,' he muses. Ivar looks at the corpse before him. 'We chase ghosts.'

'The dead are not easily courted,' Bodil says at last. 'You pass from light to shadow, from the frostfire of Fenris into the darkness that waits beneath reality's skin. Pride is a blade, my lord, but it cannot be wielded without cost.'

'Speak plainly, gothi,' Ivar says.

'Chase the horn yourself and you will lose everything, Ivar Krakenblood. You will have your saga, but there will be a price.'

Ivar looks from her. 'Then let it be paid.'

CHAPTER NINETEEN

ECHOES

She does not walk the ship. Not now. She cannot.

Narayis Sadraval sits, enthroned, bound to her station by chains of silver and cold iron. They have been sanctified by Ecclesiarchy priests, the better to repel the evil eye of the Archenemy. They shine like the wards cut into the walls of her eyrie.

Her hair is a brown tangle smoothed back from her bare forehead, where ritual tattoos flow and curl. Mathematically precise coils wind about her warp eye. The inksmiths of Navigator House Sadraval are masters of their craft – knowing that flesh, like steel, is a resource that must be sanctified.

Navigator House Belisarius tends to the needs of the Wolves. Perhaps this makes us cousins. I wonder how much this undertaking has raised the worth of my bloodline.

Incense rises in lazy tongues of grey, coagulating around her in gently spiced clouds. She breathes deeply and then allows herself to laugh at the conceited thought.

This close to the Rift there can be no half-measures. So she trusts in her attendants and her juniors. She mutters the prayers and mantras of her house. Balms against an unsteady soul.

Her eyes are locked open. She sees with all three of them. Pinning the infinite in place. Tracing their way through the madness of the empyrean. She does not fear the sea of souls. Over time she has learned that it must be respected. Fought. Held at arm's length. But always treated with fearful awe.

It is not the enemy. Ignorance is the enemy. Complacency is death.

Her father's words drift up from the sea of memory. Gone now, these last years. First to the heights of their estate and then to the crypts. She did not see him, before the end, but she can picture him as he would have been. Shrunken and bloated in equal measure. Webbed and weeping. A babbling and delusional thing, dissociated from the material universe.

She tries to close her eyes. There are no tears, not yet. Automatic systems will mist her face to prevent ocular dehydration before long. She has no need to cry.

'I am stronger than this,' she whispers to herself. 'My will guides the ship. I follow the course. I am the light. I am one with the light…'

She finds it again. A pulse of gold in the midst of madness. The Astronomican's radiance steels her nerve. Narayis feels the warmth spreading through her. The God-Emperor's own blessing.

Others have sought it for so long, in so many different ways. It is only the Navis Nobilite who truly understand His will. She truly believes that. As much as the more rugged devotees of the dynasty she has been bartered to couch it in more rustically spiritual terms, she knows that she possesses a greater purity.

Narayis…

There is something in the darkness.

Her eyes flick around the chamber, chasing shadows. She can see nothing but she heard it, a whisper both alien and familiar.

It comes again in a rush of mocking laughter. Closer now. Almost at her ear. If she looked away from her duty then she is almost certain she would see them. Poised by the side of the throne, clawed hands reaching for her. The smell of old rot is all around, suffocating the recycled air and the faint scent of flowers and spices that her chambers usually retain.

You always were weak, child. Too fragile to bear this burden. It is not your fault. It is in your blood.

The lumens flicker. Her mortal eyes dart downwards, then flinch closed. She can feel her warp eye straining, desperate to maintain its function. Struggling with the rampant immaterium that surrounds her.

This is what you have trained for, Narayis, she thinks to herself. *This is what you were made for.*

The Geller fields oscillate beyond the ship's hull, sharing her woes. One moment of weakness is all it takes. So she must be as strong as they are.

No. Stronger.

The ship convulses as it dives through a squall, cleaving into a knot of turbulence it might otherwise have avoided. She feels pain lancing through her. Bone deep. Cutting at her soul even as the chains bite against her skin. Before her throne the shadows have congealed. Darkness has flowed, slithered, out from under the failing lights. Like spilled ink on a child's parchment, it spreads. Reaching out for her.

Something steps out from the dark. Robes scrape the decking, tarnished and moth-eaten. Soiled with old stains, they drag and catch upon the metal. Fish-pale skin peeks out from the cuffs of them. Gnarled flesh clenches and unclenches, like the drowned dead of some oceanic world.

Laughter bubbles up from within it as it sees her. It pins Narayis Sadraval in place like a specimen, holding her attention as effortlessly as it did in life.

You cannot be here.

The thought consumes everything else. The impossibility of the figure dominates the chamber, as surely as the stretched and leering form before her. Conjured from memory and nightmare, dredged from the pain of her training. Her failings. Her punishments.

The thing's lips peel back in a rotted grin, teeth hideously mismatched. Some are blunt pegs, more befitting of a cattle-beast while others have transmuted into fangs. Stubby canines sit alongside slim needles. Webbed fingers flex where they haven't fully melded together.

He is all the madness of their species given form. Everything she fears. That one day she will degenerate and thrash, gilled and hidden, in some oubliette. Denied the stars forever. No longer able to gaze at the unbridled eternities that wait beyond atmosphere and materium.

He was her instructor once. Malim Vertax. A cruel man who understood intimately that Navigators must be shaped with their lessons beaten into them like metal.

'Stubborn child,' the dream, the memory, the ghost, hisses. No longer merely in her head. He leans down, face to face with her, blackened gums drawn back as he smiles and laughs. *'You were always my favourite. Not because you were the best of them, but because you were the least. False weight against which your brothers and sisters, even cousins, could be measured. Traded away to a bastard house of pretenders and miscreants. The least and lesser…'*

Narayis struggles. Her body betrays her and she spasms involuntarily, filled with primal fear. She pushes upwards till the chains cut off her circulation. She can feel the pain, and worse than that, the spreading absence of pain. Her heart hammers in her chest, a drumbeat set to an insane rhythm.

'No,' she whispers. To him. To herself. 'No. This isn't real. You aren't here.'

His hands find her shoulders and pin her back against the throne. Systems begin to chorus around her, screaming in their binharic voices. The lumens cease their flickering and begin to pulse. Urgent emergency crimson floods the chamber. She cannot break from the warp. She cannot do anything. She can feel her consciousness slipping away, deeper into herself.

Narayis screams within the prison of her own mind. She throws herself at the walls being raised around her soul. There is pain, as real as any mortal agony. Her body shudders with wracking sobs. She can see the stark prison being crafted around her. Walled in. Bricked up within the eyrie of her absolute dread. Bound in nightmare.

'*Oh, child,*' the ghoul-thing sighs indulgently. '*We are real enough to kill each and every one of you. First, though, we shall have sport. As is a noble's prerogative.*'

Cold creeps into the ship's corridors, and Garald draws his coat tighter about his body.

Even the leather does not blunt the chill and so he pauses to consider the implications. It feels almost terminal, like the onset of shipdeath. Garald can think of nothing worse than to be trapped within these confines as it dies, walled inside a tomb of ice and steel. Left to drift upon the stellar winds, a warning to haunt surer sailors.

Part of him knows that will never be his fate. Where so many others of the Helvintr Dynasty dream of a glorious end, drenched in blood with spear in hand – no doubt clinging to the hide of some void horror – he has always known that he will die a soft death. Far from pain and fear.

Because you are not one of us, my son.

The voice whispers out of memory and he shudders at the very idea of it. The man Garald called father was… Garald sighs. Rokkvi had been a terror, true enough. Garald's life had been a storm of disappointment and failed grandeur from the moment he had been claimed into the dynasty. A thrall-child. A useful prop and implement for a man so fixated on appearances, so determined to prove himself despite his low standing amidst the family. Ever with longing eyes cast towards the throne and the flagship.

To be a mere cadet branch of a rogue trader house is an insult unto itself. To be derided as *lesser* as a matter of course. His father could never make peace with that, as Garald has. Garald has carved out his place, no matter what the gothi might think. There is a pride in that, a contentment with his abilities that no one can steal away from him.

A tremor passes through the ship. A fleeting palsy. Somewhere distant, a siren begins to shrill. The aches and pains of a vessel pushed to its limits, driven relentlessly by the ambitions of its masters.

The Wolves will not idle. They cannot abide it. Their unabating need will not allow it.

Garald has never met beings such as the Wolves of Fenris. When he looks upon them he knows, in his heart, the primal fear of man-as-prey. The terror that has always haunted humanity. From the plains of their origin, up through the forests and mountains, till they were masters of city and sky. *We never stop being hunted.*

Grim surety floods him, sharp as adrenaline.

He pauses and lets his hand drop to the axe belted at his hip. Another hand-me-down trinket from an uncaring lineage. One that he has practised with, though. He has grown accomplished, in his own way, with each hour spent in the practice cages or amongst his sworn huscarls.

Enough to be reassured by its presence. It is the steel in his arm, and he stands a little taller with it in his grip. And yet…

Coward. You always were a coward.

Garald snaps around at the voice and draws the weapon. He holds the axe out before him like a ward, his hand trembling. He cuts at the empty air, flailing for the enemy he fully anticipates will be standing before him, grim-faced and mocking.

There is nothing. No one.

Only the cold and the dark. The ship feels suddenly alien. A foreign land he has never walked before. The decking no longer sits right beneath his feet. A tremor passes through him and he cannot tell if it is his body responding, or the ship shaking around him.

The shadows wait. They mock and they laugh. Garald stands, blade held before him, forcing his eyes to remain open.

When it steps from the darkness to embrace him, he is still not ready.

In the bowels of the enginarium, Brynjar Drakefang looks up.

The vagaries of a ship's operation might be lost on the others, but he has long since grown attuned to the subtle changes of a machine's soul. Tending to the Dreadnoughts in the darkness beneath the Aett has imparted secrets beyond count. He has trained in the ancient and esoteric systems of Astartes wargear, honouring the proud spirits of the weapons and armour.

Such is his duty in the name of Russ and the sight of the Allfather.

Not for the sake of honour or glory. Only to ensure that the great engine of creation yet turns. Brynjar is yoked to his duty, bound with chains as strong as iron and as enduring as the roots of the world. He has made his promises. Sacrificed his hand within the roiling magma of Fenris.

Brynjar is no neophyte to be awed by signs and wonders. That is why, when the rhythm of the ship shifts an octave, he notices and pauses in his labours.

Something has changed in the depths of the vessel. He rises from the cogitator array he has diligently been attending to and turns. He reaches out, and his grip finds the haft of his hammer.

Behind him, something has begun to drip.

A scent rises to fill the chamber. Salt spray and blood, tinged with the acidic tang of something feral and primordial. The darkness writhes like questing tendrils and the lashing of the sea. A figure walks from it. Armour scraped till the paint no longer clings to it, the blue long since obliterated. Spilled life has matted upon the plate. Flesh peeks through, pale where it is not bruised and cut by sucker and claw.

It is Jolnyr. Jolnyr, who looks at him with once-dark eyes turned clouded and corpse-like. Every part of his being bears the wounds that ended him: the kraken's wrath driven down upon him, smashing his body into the rock of the Spur. So long ago.

The impossible figure looks upon him without love. Only judgement dwells in the eyes of the dead man. When it begins to speak, each word is forced from silt-filled lungs and a drowned throat.

'You have forgotten me, brother,' the false Jolnyr slurs. The words resonate oddly, bouncing off the high steel of the ceilings. *'Have you risen so far that you can ignore the memory of those crushed beneath your ascent? Has the Wolf Priest?'*

'Be silent, daemon,' Brynjar snarls. He kindles the hammer and lightning crackles around its head. 'You have no place here.'

'Daemon, am I?' Jolnyr laughs. He stalks around Brynjar, pacing with predatory glee.

'Some warp delusion. A madness lingering within the Geller field. You are a figment. Nothing.'

'You wound me, Brynjar,' False Jolnyr says with another laugh. He gestures down at his ruined form. Old wounds weep anew with every movement. *'Not as much as the kraken did...'*

'You will not mock his death,' Brynjar growls. 'He died serving the Chapter. He died–'

'Doing kaerl work. Isn't that what you said?'

'I was wrong. I recognised my failing and was sure to correct it. As is expected of me. That is how I have survived. How I have thrived in service of the Rout.'

Lightning dances between vast pylons, arcs of skittering Motive Force, casting them both in a pale blue numinosity. Brynjar's eyes narrow. The light passes through the false brother. Something flickers beneath his skin.

Brynjar's half-face bares its teeth as he steps forwards, weapon raised to dispel the phantasm.

The gothi is gone now. Ivar waits alone, eyes closed, within the apothecarion's chill environs. He reaches up and removes his helm, feeling the air kiss his skin as he pulls the wolf-skull visage free with a gasp of released hydraulic pressure.

He places it to one side and double-checks the stasis vault's seals. The sigils flicker their reassuring green. Content that Gorm's legacy is secure he goes to leave. Ivar runs a hand through his braided hair, brushing sweat from the copper rings that hold it in place.

The air stirs, and the subtle motion makes Ivar pause. He turns, expecting that someone will have entered the chamber to seek aid or counsel.

There is no one there. The door remains sealed. The chamber remains empty. None disturb his work.

Perhaps the crew know better now. They have grown used to the presence of the demigods, with all the fear and awe they bring.

'Ours is a lonely path,' Ivar mutters. 'Chasing destiny like prey through the snows.'

'And you have such quarry in your sights,' says a voice from behind him. As cold as the confines of the ship. It breathes with the dust of the charnel-house world they have so recently fled. The chuckle that follows is a rough thing. *'Such a fate.'*

Ivar turns. In truth he is almost unsurprised by what he beholds.

Gorm Krakenblood sits up upon the examination table, his dark skin bloodlessly pale. His hair hangs lank and his joints move oddly, gnarled as they are by rigor mortis. His body resounds with moans and clicks, as though some insectoid thing has taken up residence beneath his skin.

'What are you then?' Ivar asks. 'Some bonethief thing? A monster of the warp or the spawn of xenos? What wears a brother's skin and speaks of destiny?' Ivar's hand snaps out and seizes a long dissecting blade from a waiting tray.

Denied the weapon of his office, he must turn all things into weapons.

'Are you so afraid that you have to conjure phantasms to explain away the inevitable?' It laughs, a gurgling, gravel-choked sound. Ivar's blade snaps around and cuts at the empty air.

'There is no inevitability to you, trickster,' Ivar snaps. 'You are nothing. As much an echo as your dead little world. You taunt and you mock, because you have no bite to you. I doubt my blade would even find purchase. Come a little closer, let us test it.'

'I am your sins, brother. Can you not look me in the eye?' The Gorm-thing laughs from the shadows. It has moved. Slithered

from the bench to the corner of the room, as though the light itself could take it apart.

Ivar looks at it. Fear does not take him. 'I can. I am.' He steps forwards and then leaps over the table, swinging the blade down. 'There is nothing honest in you. Only lies and bitter hate!'

He tastes ashes. Liquid blackness bubbles from the thing's flesh, coiling around the blade. Holding it in place.

'*Such venom, brother!*' it says, still laughing. '*All I wish to do is talk. You came so far for purpose. Direction. Let me instruct you.*'

'The dead do not speak,' Ivar says. 'They do not pass on their judgements. They walk at the Allfather's right hand. They feast at His table. Else they go into the Underverse.' He draws his hand back and slams it forwards, to erase the mockery's face forever.

It comes apart in a rush of smoke and skeletal impressions, passing through him like the cold touch of Morkai. It seethes back into form, barely holding Gorm's shape. Its eyes and teeth burn, leaving after-image impressions of its toxic mirth.

'*Nothing else remains to us, eh?*' It rattles with amusement. Ivar can hear the sound of bones breaking beneath its skin, like a serpent with them caught in its gullet. The lumen light makes the mockery shimmer, flickering like bad pict-footage. '*Only service or suffering.*'

'Only duty,' Ivar says as he stalks forwards once more, flicking the diseased non-blood from the blade. He hears the decking sizzle with its impact.

'*You do not truly believe that, do you, Ivar?*'

'I know it to be true. I am a weapon in the Allfather's armoury. I endure only to serve. I tend to my brothers, body and soul, because it is my duty. Just as you…' Ivar catches himself. 'Just as he ranged forth in service of the Rout.'

The rancid laughter bubbles up again from unflexing lungs. It is as though, so fresh from the non-death of stasis, the whole carcass has begun to calcify. Caught between states. Not rotting or corroding, but transmuting as the ancient alchymists of Terra would have claimed it.

Becoming flux. Less and more than he has been.

'Ranged far and wide. Fought and bled. Died for the dream of a silent grandsire. Here is my reward – picked over like carrion by a mere pup. An insult to my bloodline.'

'I honour my lineage,' Ivar begins.

*'Oh do you? Ivar Krakenblood, marked of salt and storm. Raised up and given position, feeding upon the scraps that the Slayer throws to you. But who are you **truly**?'* It laughs again. *'I know you, brother. I know your soul. You have chosen this path, not for the honour of blood or the vengeance of the Rout. No… You crave glory, Ivar. You yearn for your name to live forever. Even if it kills you.'*

Ivar's fingers clench into fists.

Gorm snarls and leaps from the table, landing before him. Plates are peeled back, revealing the wounded meat beneath. Ivar feels the ache in his own flesh, the kraken's wounds obscured by armour. Old scars, bearing fresh pain.

Another bond they share.

'You do not know me,' Ivar says.

'I do not have to,' Gorm says, grinning. *'We all share this pride. It is what drives us to the grave. Here I lie, entombed in glory. Cold and dead. Holding my burden close.'* Dead fingers reach out to stroke the map. For one terrible moment Ivar fears that rot will crawl across its surface, obliterating the stellar path.

He hurls himself forwards, blade snapping out, cleaving at air and ephemera. The figure sneers and slides back, fangs bared at Ivar, as though interrupted mid-meal.

The map remains pure. Ivar releases the breath he was holding and steps forwards, face to face with Gorm. 'I know you are not

Gorm Krakenblood. You walk in his likeness and speak as he might have spoken. You are not his soul dredged up from the Underverse in torment. You are less than nothing. You speak and I will not listen. I will not be moved.'

'Then you will die, Ivar Krakenblood. Alone and unmourned, here amongst the cruel stars. You will bear your shame like a curse. A brand. All Fenris will revile you. Killer of ships. Ender of dreams. Chaser of wyrd.' Gorm's face splits into another smile. *'Consorter with daemons.'* It circles the central mortuarium bench, watching him with gleaming eyes, like a felid finally tiring of toying with its food. Fingerbones snap and lengthen, stretching themselves into claws.

Ivar's blade does not tremble. At his other wrist he feels the Fang's hungry blades realigning. 'I do not fear judgement any more than I fear you.'

'And that, kinsman,' the Gorm-thing hisses as it throws itself at him, jaws stretching wide, *'is your first mistake!'*

CHAPTER TWENTY

THE HUNGER OF THE DEAD

There is no sustenance in the Underverse.

For the dead and the daemonic there is no true respite, no rest, no refreshment.

As a child upon the ice, every son of Fenris learned that. For when maleficarum spoke in its forked voice, when you warded yourself with the eye and the horn, it was always with a primal and crawling hunger.

That yearning was the reason that corpses would wash up on the shore, stirred from the deep places. Carrion things that were not even fit for trophy taking. Wights waited, ready to drag the unsuspecting down. Men and women reduced to ghouls. Gnawing at the bones of the world, yearning to bring their revenant poison to the realm of the living once more.

Brynjar's hammer sweeps down, slamming into the decking with a burst of unleashed energy. The metal vaporises, rising about him in a hissing cloud of particulate steel. Brynjar whirls round, snarling. His half-face is a mask of rage as he stalks about the enginarium, his cybernetic eye clicking as it scans for his prey.

'Jolnyr was many things,' Brynjar calls. 'He was never a craven.'

'*No, I wasn't,*' sighs a voice from the high shadows. Brynjar's gaze snaps up.

The thing wearing Jolnyr's face paces along one of the gantries, leaning over the edge. It seems more drawn, the skin too tight around its skull. The hair hangs, lank and dead, drenched in seawater and blood.

'*When you die and sit at the Allfather's right hand, between the feasting and the fighting, you gain a clarity you never had in life…*' The mockery chuckles, speaking words that Jolnyr – young and brash, doomed to die – would never have the mind to hold, let alone utter. '*Do you know what I see, brother? A galaxy broken and divided. Drowning in fire and death. You are struggling against the inevitable. You sit at the shore, trying to drain the sea with your drinking horn, and lamenting when the tide does not lower. That is madness. Every last one of us is nothing but a suture in the galaxy's hide. We cannot stem all wounds.*' It pauses and laughs again. '*You could not even protect Fenris.*'

'Lies!' Brynjar shouts.

'*Are they? Did the Thousand Sons of the Sorcerer not descend upon you and impale Fenris with their silver spires? Sanction and outrage followed, and our people were allowed to be made sport of by the Allfather's watchful crows.*'

'They are not your peop–'

'*And yet you would ask us all to cleave to such an end. Embrace it close, let it die in our arms. Not even I had that luxury.*' The laughter becomes a drowned gurgle. Fresh blood trickles down its chin. '*I died, my duty unfulfilled. A footnote to the glory of others. An afterthought. How many of you stopped and mourned for your fallen brother? I was forgotten as soon as I was broken apart under the kraken's tendrils. Not for Jolnyr to rise and become a Priest or a champion. No hero's end. Only the darkness of the Underverse amongst the unworthy dead.'*

Brynjar snarls as he stalks towards it. He pursues the lie-thing as other warriors in other wars might hunt the illusions of the drukhari. Like chasing phantoms.

You are not Jolnyr. You are not him.

'I will not believe that was his fate. He died fighting against the world's rage, standing proud against the king of Fenris' seas. On sacred ground he fell, with salt and blood upon him. You can diminish his sacrifice all you want, but you will not shame him with falsehoods. He sits at the right hand of the Allfather.' Brynjar's hammer scores the air, smashing a support console to shards of metal and circuitry. 'An honour you will never know. Because you are nothing.'

'*Perhaps.*' It tilts its head thoughtfully. '*Perhaps both are true. Or neither. It is so hard to follow, sometimes. The little paradises and perditions that souls and minds conjure. All of us moulded by our wants. I had... such dreams, once.*'

'You do not dream. Daemons are beyond such things.'

'*I'm proud of you,*' it says with a sad smile. '*You have grown wise. Tempered. The boy who stood and blustered before Ivar would not make these grand speeches and defiances.*'

'Be silent.'

'*You will be honoured, come the end. When all struggle is over. All the games at last concluded.*'

'This is no game,' Brynjar growls. His armour feels heavy now, the hammer like dead weight in his hands.

The false Jolnyr sighs. '*That is all this has ever been.*'

Garald recoils, so violently that his back slams against the steel wall of the corridor. His hands tremble, drumming against the metal, unsteady as his heartbeat.

'Are you not pleased to see me?' his father asks, head tilting to one side, lolling as though its neck were broken. Garald remembers a marionette he owned as a child, a simple thing of steel wire and painted wood. This rendition of Rokkvi shares its jerky motions. His face is carved with the same sick smile that once adorned the puppet. *And yet I dare not look for the hand that moves this one.*

'Pleased…?' Garald forces the word out. The old man is exactly as he remembers him. The long grey braids and beard, framing a face made birdlike by time and torment. Summer-green eyes that have seen too many winters. Clouded, now. Dead. Skin greyed and sallow. Sickly and sweat-sheened.

It seems at once ghoulish and vital. Alive and dead in equal measure. Sometimes it moves too quickly, a blur of sudden motion, writhing in some unknowable torment. Other times it lumbers and staggers, a drunkard's slowness, the struggle against the cold and cloying water of the deep sea.

It leaves wet footprints, and then they boil off. Evaporated in an instant. Ice rimes the walls and then vanishes in a puff of madness. At the corners of his sight Garald can see the swaying shapes of deep-water vegetation and hear the long, drawn-out squeal of claw and tendril against steel.

This is a ship of fools and terror. We shall not see the end. No captain. No crew. Just a wight vessel, cutting through the Underverse, hungry and alone.

'You always were a slow student. You've done well, despite that. It is…' The thing pauses and Rokkvi's face contorts as it seeks the correct utterance. It struggles with the very act of emotion. **'Good** *to see you,'* it purrs. *'I am very proud.'*

Garald pushes himself up. He stands as straight as he is able and sets his features grimly. He faces it down. *It is, after all, nothing more than fear. An illusion. It cannot hurt you. It cannot kill you.*

It is so close now, too close. Pressing in at him so the corridor feels as narrow as a coffin. Almost face to face.

'I cannot say the same,' he finally admits. The words are forced out from a near-paralysed throat. 'I have never truly missed you.'

Things laugh in the shadows behind Rokkvi, moments before the thing itself chortles. Soon it is hacking with mirth, shaking, and the projected silhouette stutters with it. Changing shape. Flitting between new and terrible forms.

Garald's hand slips down and unhooks the holster of his pistol. He takes hold of the grip and then feels it. Cold fingers snap taut around his wrist. Pain surges up his arm, his nerves on fire. It is as though he has plunged it into an icy sea. Fronded, bladed, tentacled things kiss and bite.

'Come, child. There is nothing to fear. This is inevitable. Look at the galaxy. Stare into the Rift's heart and tell me there is hope. You nibble at the edges of opportunity, like the parasites we have always been. You build petty fiefdoms of industry and trade. Playing at being heir to the huntress' throne. That will never be you. The grave is your only inheritance.'

Sick, watery bile dribbles from the corpse-thing's lips. A black tongue laps at the discharge. Its eyes, too, are black. All pupil. Not the eyes of a man but an infernal predator. The skin stretches.

Perhaps it overestimated my affection for the man. Or maybe it knew that he was nothing but a canker in my past. A burden I had to bear.

The illusion is failing now. The rot wriggles up from beneath the tearing skin. The smile spreads and splits, rows of jagged teeth ripping their way through the mockery. Strings of ragged meat cling to the distending bone and fangs.

And you were always weak. The voice rumbles, forced upon the universe, imprinted into existence. The words burn in his mind. Garald thinks he might vomit. He could scream. *Never good enough. Not for any of them. A wayward child, chasing glory that was never meant for you. You have always been such a disappointment. A guttering little soul in the dark.*

His hand snaps up and he begins to fire. It is already in motion, a slick, bleeding shadow that screeches and laughs. The monster oozes away, the bullet holes the only memorial to its passing.

Garald spins about. The corridor seems to contract around him. The steel presses at his back, sweat smearing it as his skin brushes along the rivets. He tastes iron and copper. Garald's teeth grind. Static dances between them. *Witchery.*

The arts of psyker and the ravages of the daemon are foreign to him, yet he knows in his soul that this is what it is. Loose in his ship.

He does not know where he is. *Oh, Throne of Earth.*

The ship embraces madness around him, stealing thought and recognition. Garald feels his legs give way beneath him. He could surrender, here and now. Sink back into the cold and the dark.

Give in. Like you always do. Like the weak child you are.

The voice in his head that is not his own speaks.

'I am not weak,' he says. Each word is forced through his teeth. His pulse steadies.

Of course not. The brave little soldier. Never the paragon, for you could never claim to be an exemplar, could you?

'Enough,' Garald snaps.

Ah! Now there is some little fire! It laughs again, a grating, hateful sound that echoes in his skull like knives. *Not enough, though. Too little. Too late. You're too small a thing to waste time on illusions.*

Garald fires again. 'Come on, you bastard! Fight me!'

Sinewy corpse arms snap outwards from the shadows behind

him. The laughter is no longer in his head. It is at his ear, its breath a cold rush of cancerous rot.

'As you wish.'

'I have walked with kings and shed blood upon the ice!' the Gorm-thing says, claws bleeding fire as they tear at the air.

Ivar draws back, clattering against the apothecarion's shelves, knocking bottles to the floor in a rain of breaking glass. He grits his teeth, his voice struggling to remain calm. 'You have served no jarls. Walked no ice. Slain no foes. You are nothing, less than nothing.'

'And yet we talk?' Gorm rumbles with laughter. Its scarred skin tremors. Greying braids shake. Grey eyes stare lifelessly at Ivar, every tilt of the head assessing. **'You think me a wight, dredged up to hold you to your oaths and shame you.'**

'I think you the lingering trickery of an enemy.' Ivar puts himself between the falsehood and Falr's body, ensuring no corruption will despoil him. 'And I have my duty to perform.'

'A hero's reward, isn't it? Destined for the vaults beneath the mountain. Bound in shadow. Warded in cold iron.'

'Where you and Morkai can never harm it,' Ivar affirms. 'Safe from the ravages of maleficarum.' Ivar steps forwards and lashes out with blade and Fang. Gorm recoils, black blood steaming from its face. Its mouth creases into a snarl, fangs lengthening.

'You speak that word as though it should shame me. Your own kin.'

'Would that you were,' Ivar growls and sneers as the thing's ruptured flesh reknits. He shakes his head. 'I could ask him what drove him into the sea of stars, if not duty. I could ask why he risked so much and suffered in the attempt.'

'I can still answer those questions, pup,' it hisses. **'You need not suffer in your ignorance.'**

Suffer. The word echoes in Ivar's mind.

'Ah, but it is a blessing, that. Have you forgotten? A mind too small to doubt, but not too small as not to know.'

Ivar closes his eyes. The physical war cannot be won. He understands that now.

'You parrot fables from the hearth,' he grumbles. Gorm's form seems to flicker, doubt rippling through the illusionary figure. Beneath its guise, Ivar sees the coiling thing of unflesh, tendrils sniffing at the air with a fungal elegance. Eyeless, mouthless, it regards him for that perfect second of clarity. Scents dredged from the deeps of memory spiral out from it. Salt and copper. Life and death so intimately entwined that he cannot tell where one ends and another begins.

He knows it. He marks it.

'Just as you can create nothing of your own,' Ivar says, 'you scratch at the past and hold up the slivers of remembrance as though they were profound knowledge. No better than a cairn robber, or one of the madmen who plumb the depths of the old dead cities beneath Fenris' skin.' He laughs. It spasms again, writhing with impotent hatred.

'Ah, there you are,' Ivar says. 'You don't like being ignored, do you? Stripped of your power. Your influence. Not able to leech thought and feeling like the bottom-feeding parasite you truly are.'

Do not mock me. The thing's thought-voice is an ache across his mind. A thunderbolt of migraine-bright agony. *Only death awaits you, in your defiance. Enough.*

'You cultivate fear like a farmer,' Ivar says with another laugh. 'Fattening up your herd. Forcing us to play your games. As though we were simpletons to be manipulated.'

That is all you are for. You think yourselves so superior. The little executioners, destiny cast to the wind. What are you, in the end?

The illusion shatters.

The Gorm-thing dissolves away, splintering into facets and fragments. Screaming faces, laughing mockeries, a riot of falsehoods. Each one hovers in the air for a moment then flies apart.

Ivar's hand is already moving. Up into the midst of the madness. The Fang of Morkai purrs hungrily and he drives it into where the thing's throat had been.

A screech fills the apothecarion till the walls shake. Bottles of viscous fluid tumble and burst, staining the floor in ochre and crimson. It spatters at Ivar's armour and runs like rivers along the flooring. He smiles as he holds his hand in place, letting the blades, drills and needles drink their fill.

Black blood fountains from what passes for its face as Ivar carves into it. Gouging out new wounds in the fish-pale skin, tearing false eyes into the eyeless flesh.

The daemon-thing screams and writhes as Ivar pushes it back, slamming it against the wall so hard that tiles crack. The creature's limbs come apart into crawling pseudopods, wrapping about his arm, striving with all its Neverborn strength to drive him back.

Yet the Fang is a part of him. Bound as tight as duty.

Its hateful ichor smokes as it strikes his armour. Ivar does not move. He does not let himself. Every iota of transhuman strength is focused on pinning it in place, like an anatomical specimen. Something washed up upon the shore and reeking of the caustic deep. A lightless creature meant only to suffer and die rather than blight the Allfather's universe.

'Die,' Ivar hisses through clenched teeth. 'You who would dishonour our glorious dead.'

He died a craven fool. He died screaming. The last of his huscarls bound him to his cold sleep, because they could not accept their own failure.

Witch-light crackles along the metal surfaces. The corpse-berths tremble, resonating with captured illumination. The lumens pulse in time with Ivar's hearts and the breathy rattle of the monstrous imposter fills the apothecarion.

It is like lightning being earthed. Everything burns, sun-bright and urgent, hot and fierce, till the sweat stings upon his skin. Ivar growls, low in his throat, feeling the hateful kiss of the tendrils as they plunge for his face, snapping at his forehead. Finding purchase.

The light dies, agony flares, and there is only darkness for him.

CHAPTER TWENTY-ONE

DREAMS AND DEATH

When he awakens he is without his plate.

Ivar stands upon a vast plateau of ice and rock, stretching off forever on a scale that Fenris could only dream of. His armour is gone, his crozius forgotten. He stands in rough ring mail and leather, studded with claws and fangs, a fur hung about his neck.

It feels too large. Smothering. Ivar struggles against it, as though it were some vast beast trying to drag him down–

Drowning, drowning, death and dreams beneath the cold ice. Is it not a wonder to submit, to relax, to surrender? So many fallen brothers wait below. Jolnyr is with us. Falr and Gorm. All the others. If you simply lie back and accept...

–into the depths with its wet and sucking embrace. A flurry of cephalopodic motion at the corner of his eye draws his attention, and then it is gone. Forgotten.

This could be home, he thinks. *Perhaps it is home.*

He does not recognise the place, but then he is young...

Ivar Krakenblood looks down at his own reflection, a boy of barely three great years, sharp and dark against the salt-grime of the ice. He barely recognises the face. Fresh and youthful, yet already touched by battle.

He can feel something warm running down his side in a dull trickle. A gap in his defences where the cold can creep in. Ivar blinks and his teeth grind together.

Before his ascension, before the trials and surgeries, before he had been made…

Made what?

Different. Changed. Honoured?

Memory is a confusion, a storm-tossed sea that tolerates no interlopers. Past, present, future, all reduced to mere suggestions. Even the pain knows no true direction, no source and no destination.

The winds howl around him. Above him the storm breaks, and the clouds tremor with thunderheads. Blue-white lightning arcs to the ground, cleaving mountains and breaking ice. The world trembles with tectonic force and somewhere he hears the distant rumble of volcanoes spewing forth their choler.

This world is a trap. A bauble out of time. Left to rot and run wild. It was a failed experiment. Just as you are.

'No,' Ivar says, almost to himself. 'I do not die here.'

But you did. You do.

Fog stains the ice in a sudden rush of vapour, as though an airburst has just scraped away the top of the frozen water beneath him. He blinks it away and staggers forwards, swaying as he does.

Figures rush through the mists, weapons raised almost as high as their voices. Spears and arrows garrotte the skies, some trailing harsh lines of smoke and fire.

He remembers this battle. Somewhere in the core of his soul, he remembers. Ivar had been a child then, a true son of Fenris and the Krakenblood tribe. Even here in the south, there had been ice and cold. They were reaving further north, then. He sees a man charge past him, trailing a cloak of kraken's leather, hooks and barbs rattling as it clips stone.

'Krakenblood!' the crowd chant. 'Krakenblood!'

The cloaked warrior turns and gestures at Ivar, looking back only to thrust his weapon towards the enemy advancing across the plain.

He expects to see a kinsman. Some echo of his past. Instead the figure bleeds away, stolen like smoke, as the vision changes. The warrior swells with power, armed and armoured as a demigod. The crowd screams.

'Ulrik! Ulrik! Ulrik!'

Another tribe. A warband more than an army. Two sides of the same coin, caught in the savage struggles beneath the eyes of waiting demigods. Ivar begins to run, pursuing the Slayer as he plunges heedless into the fray. Disrupting the ritual, changing how it should be. Detachment forgotten.

'Wait,' Ivar calls. 'Wait!'

How many times have I stood in his shadow? Chasing him like a pup? Some prodigal, banished from the hearth, seeking his place? Am I still the boy upon the Kraken's Spur, desperate for the chance to ascend?

The mortal warriors and the choosers of the slain ignore him, passing through the fog like ghosts. Lost to memory. He watches the armoured figure as he plunges into the gloom, blade first. Warriors and kinsmen chant his name.

Ivar should be running with them, he knows. He should stand as a member of the pack. Fighting and dying beneath the storm-addled skies.

This is where you die for the first time. A fitting grave.

It hurts to think, to remember. Ivar's skull aches and even the act of remembering the past feels like casting his mind forwards into some impossible future. Where he falls in battle only to be raised up by the Allfather's Sky Warriors.

To learn at the Slayer's side. To stand as Vlka Fenryka and wage the Allfather's wars across the sky's span.

Not for you. Give up. Give in. Feel the cold in your bones. Let this miserable rock finally claim you as it should have when you were born.

'No.'

Ivar begins to run.

He plunges into the unfolding maelstrom of battle, through it. Faces he barely remembers from a childhood that no longer matters pass him in a blur. Every trap and trick of the enemy glances from his armour.

Not mail and leather. Plate etched from night. Sacred black against the limitless expanse of grey and white.

The other warriors freeze in place. Every neck snaps taut, heads raised as they begin to scream at the sky. They tremble and spasm as the sound is dragged from them, forced up and out and into the world like air from drowning lungs.

You cannot fight fate. This is your wyrd. To die here, unremembered and unmourned. More meat for the dogs of your home world to pick over. An ignoble death. A wight's end. Dead in battle or fallen in the trials. You. Should. Simply. **End.**

'I am a son of Fenris!' Ivar calls to the empty air. 'No force in this galaxy can change that. I did not falter then. I did not die. I will not do so here, under the blade of some figment. A lie-thing that kills with words and deceits.'

His fellows, his enemies and his kin, have grown pale. Kelp coils about their limbs, weighing them down like chains. Scuttling things with too many legs and writhing worms crawl through myriad wounds. The bite of an axe, the cut of a sword, the tearing teeth of some ravenous beast. The darkness swaddles the Slayer like a shroud, glistening like oil, running with new blood and crusted with the old.

The wights do not tear at him. Not one of them moves. They

stand like trembling statues as the breath pours from them to join the fog, hissing from their splayed lips. Then water follows, first in a trickle then a torrent, then a tide. The lungs of the drowned, emptying in sea salt, blood and mucus.

The ice begins to crack beneath their feet and then heaves up. Ivar barely keeps his balance, staggering back. His boots lock him in place, gouging the ice even as it shatters ahead of him. Breaking apart into great planes, shimmering in the air like fractals, forming patterns that he should not know. He forces his mind to ignore them, even as they burn their way onto his retinas. Tears stain his eyes within his helm. Ivar's breathing is a taut rhythm, measured and human.

He watches it rise.

The screaming figures vanish beneath its bulk, swept away in the torrential arc of its body. Water fountains into the air and crashes down upon Ivar like a final rain. The storm that will drown the world billows around him, trying its damnedest to knock him down amongst the damned and the dead.

He sees a flicker of the Slayer's master-crafted armour, black against the shattered ice, then gone. Subsumed into the greater and writhing whole.

It is a king of beasts. The kraken rises to eclipse the sky, bellowing in animal rage. Its skin burns with bioluminescence, dredged up from the deep places of the world, aglow with symbols. The air curdles with whispers. They bleed from the monster and take form upon the air. Dancing webs of sigils and signs, nests of constructs and glyphs. Phantom feathers blaze about the kraken, like a phoenix taken to wing.

It is the cancer that spawned within the dead *Spinebreaker*. The poison seeping from the living wound the corrupted trolls had gouged into Fenris. Everything Ivar has struggled against as a keeper of the Chapter's soul and a healer of its flesh.

Do you know what strength is? The true Slayer's voice speaks from out of memory, carried on the wind, bound up in this figmented place. *Strength is standing firm in the face of maleficarum. To bear its fire and the scars it brings, even if it kills you.*

Ivar stands firm even as tentacles as vast as bulk landers claw at the stars.

It splays itself out like some immense tree, burning at the end of all things. Behind it the firmament cracks, unclean light oozing from the wounds in reality. The Sorcerer's vengeance come again.

Ivar forces himself forwards. Step by grudging step, he pushes his armoured bulk onwards. Ice and bones crunch beneath his tread.

The agony is a balm. It washes through him in a cleansing tide. It affirms his purpose with every step. Laughter forces itself from between his gritted teeth, blood thundering in his skull.

The world shakes. Ivar ignores it. Behind him, around him, the snow-capped peaks erupt in fire. Magma boils up, scoring the air with trailing pyroclastic wrath. It begins to rain ashes.

The planet howls around them.

Wolves howl with it.

Singular purpose sings through the world, resonating with the potency of its soul. Every last voice – wolf, demigod and mortal – is raised in one note. They roar together. One world, one people, bound together in a single moment.

'For the glory of Russ!' Ivar bellows.

'Russ! Russ! Russ!' The word echoes about him, like a shield.

It is in the ice and fire. The very fabric of the world is alive with its syllables. The name that binds them, one and all, to Fenris and to the Imperium. The first of their blood and the greatest exemplar of their world.

'Russ! Russ! Russ!'

The word is the strength in Ivar's arm. His muscles burn, not with weakness or fatigue, but with that same potency.

I walk with legends…

The thought propels him forwards. The sky is aflame, burning, falling, crashing down upon the vast dream kraken. Not in an apocalyptic end, but in a righteous judgement.

He looks up. The heavens tremble. Stars shake in their places and fall, trailing fiery tears, plunging into the earth like spears.

Each one of them rings with Russ' sacred name.

Garald staggers through the ship, through hallways that have become a madhouse.

Crew members have collapsed, weeping, to their knees. Some claw at their faces, tear at their hair. He sees a gunnery ensign slamming his head, over and over, into the side of a bulkhead, till blood and vitreous humour trickle down it like perverse tears.

Everywhere there is horror. Everything reduced to a crimson smear of cackling insanity. The laughter is everywhere behind it. In a thousand voices, from out of so many warped pasts, it laughs. All meaning is obliterated beneath its power and presence.

He limps onwards. Blood runs from his own head wound. Claw marks throb dully in his throat, staunched by a torn scrap of uniform. He presses his hand to it and it comes away red and brown, stained with his gently fleeting life.

Give in. Just give in. It will be so much easier. They cannot save you. They are lost to their own pain. Their loss will destroy them, just as it will you.

It could have killed him. It should have killed him. Garald spits a gobbet of bloody spittle and pushes open another door, forcing it with his shoulder. There was a moment, a fleeting instant, where the thing lost control. Distracted by some distant struggle. The ship had shaken with a warp tremor and it had sounded…

Like howling.

Every step is agony. It lets him suffer to sweeten the meal. Soon it will come, in the form of the dead or devoid of its cloaks, coiling around him with its tendrils and spite. In its own time, moving to some ineffable design.

I will not be a victim. No more. I will prove my worth.

This high within the great vessel the signs of ruin begin to abate. The wards are stronger and the defences keener. Garald's footfalls disturb piles of shells, scattering them like fallen leaves, glittering in the half-light.

There are no bodies. No blood. The servitor-directed turrets bled their ammunition away for nothing, shooting at ghosts. Garald wonders if it was some illusion that deceived their lobotomised minds, or if the thing was simply too fast. Too cunning.

'God-Emperor,' Garald whispers. He feels pain high in his chest and leans against the wall, catching his breath. 'You who reign upon Terra. If I have been lax in my prayers, that we should suffer so…' He winces, pushes himself off the wall with one blood-slick hand, and staggers on again.

The door looms ahead of him. Silver inlaid with iron. Winged figures, kneeling, their foreheads covered by their praying hands, are etched upon it, set high so their mortal eyes can look down upon the supplicants who gather before the sanctum.

Garald braces himself against the keypad laid next to the door, his fingers a bloody blur as he enters his access code and lets the needles of the gene-lock bite deep. It hisses open with a whisper of sepulchral air.

'No, no, no, no…' Someone whimpers from the darkness as Garald moves into the sanctum. The voice dissolves into sobs, wet and wracking.

Narayis is sprawled in her throne, slumped and trembling. Garald pushes closer to her, cautiously, making sure that her Navigator's eye is not exposed.

She cannot see. Narayis thrashes and mewls, clawing at the air. Her wrists are scraped bloody by the chains as she has strained against them. The blood covers the arms of the throne and her fingers have scratched at the metal, working mad patterns into her own spilled life.

'Do not send me to the eyrie, Vertax. It's not my time. I am whole. I am untainted. Please! I can be better!'

'Narayis,' Garald says, reaching out. His hand waits, trembling in the air before her.

'It's so dark,' she whispers. There are red tears running from her human eyes and the closed third eye in her forehead. Light flickers behind the Navigator's warp eye, straining against the eyelid. 'It blinds and binds and it hurts. The pain. The dark...'

'Navigator Sadraval!' he snaps.

She tenses and a keening whine slips from between her lips. 'L-lord?'

'You are a daughter of a noble house. You have served my own family line for many years. You are stronger than this.'

'The darkness is everywhere. About. Below. Above.'

Garald looks up.

'Oh, sacred Throne.'

The darkness recoils at his words, as though hurt by that simple oath of purity. It dribbles down the walls from the perch where it congeals. It slithers wetly in the shadow, made of the shadow. A thing of choate night.

'You are stronger,' he says. 'Narayis. You are stronger than it is.'

'I can't.'

'You can! I only need one thing from you. I need you to *look*.'

Fresh tears run down her cheeks. 'Then you must not,' she whispers.

Garald turns away as the thing made of darkness plunges towards the prone Navigator. He holds his hand out and back, his pistol up and ready.

Narayis Sadraval looks up and her warp eye snaps open. Unlight pulses, refracting off the gilded and sigil-worked walls. She screams, and the darkness screams with her as the power of her immaterial sight cuts through the gloom.

Brynjar pants with effort as he stalks the thing across the overhead gantries.

It still wears Jolnyr's face. Fixed like a pict or the graven visage of a ceremonial statue. It smiles relentlessly, even as it sways and shifts from place to place. It no longer uses its mouth to speak. The words simply materialise, burned into Brynjar's mind.

He will damn you. You know this already. He walks someone else's path. A false wyrd.

'Enough from you,' Brynjar says. 'The dead do not speak. You have no voice here, daemon.'

Betraying the brother you failed to save, for the brother who will be your doom! Such a paragon of the Fenrisian way!

'No more,' Brynjar growls. His hammer scores through the air, trailing lightning in an arc of after-image.

You know he leads you astray. A wayward son. Your doubts from the Spur were well founded, brother! Look at me!

Blood erupts from every pore, coating the Jolnyr-thing's armour in sanguine red. Every last wound dealt to him in their trial, the initiation upon the Kraken's Spur, expresses itself upon its flesh. The deformed and warped skull tilts up, gurning toothlessly at Brynjar, brain matter staining its shoulders.

This will be the fate of all your brothers. Ground beneath the weight of his ambition.

'That is the difference between you and I,' Brynjar says, and laughs. 'I have faith in my brothers.'

He swings the hammer down, its head crackling, the disruption field burning live.

The daemon's hands fly up, gripping it. The stink of cooking flesh surrounds them both as it laughs. Hands lengthening into claws, closing around the killing light. Smoke wafts from the conjunction, coiling upwards into the air as it seeks to devour the light.

There will be no mercy. Only the laughter of the gods.

Light blossoms through its mutilated flesh, purple and blue, white and pink. The blood boils away from the armoured form as it flows, shifting to a new configuration. There is a flash of blue and gold as the image of Jolnyr comes apart.

For a moment it looks confused. The daemon's mouth yawns wide, far beyond the capability of a mortal face, and it begins to scream.

Ivar laughs.

The kraken's hateful tendrils crowd in and the crozius in his hands reduces each to clouds of atomised flesh and seething warp-matter.

The monstrous thing is cloaked in lightning, boiling off its hide, motes of energy bleeding into the ether. Cohesion flees it in a tide, like seawater pulsing outwards from its skin.

You cannot fight fate. Not even by seizing another. You are damned, Ivar Krakenblood. As doomed as your forebear.

Flame kindles in its eyes as it writhes upwards, screaming to the heavens.

Ivar plunges into the gap, bringing the crozius up and over his head and slamming it down into the centre of the blazing eye.

As the world erupts in fire.

* * *

There is light where there was once darkness.

It trembles through the ship's bones like the passing of a storm. Witchfire is born and dies along the iron of the decking, strung along the spinal battlements, channelled through the great thoroughfares of the ship.

Upon the bridge men and women finally slump at their stations or pull themselves to their feet, no longer in the thrall of their own terrible ghosts. On the lower decks, where the Astartes secret themselves away, the packs finally break free of the labyrinth their quarters had become. Panting, weapons raised, the corridors once again familiar.

The engines sing their holy song, thrumming with blessed rhythm, to the binharic delight of the tech-priests. Incense once again circulates through the vents around the reactors, as iron fingers smear unguents in their ritual patterns.

Peace returns in its comforting pall.

CHAPTER TWENTY-TWO

WOUNDS

They meet in uneasy silence.

Ivar bears his few scars with pride, etched upon his plate. The blood of the enemy lies alongside his own. He has helmed himself once more. They may see his pain, but not his shame. The others have suffered more. Brynjar bears the marks of the daemon that have been seared upon his flesh, just as they have been worked upon his armour. Burns that will be long in the healing, where it sought to lay him low. Bound in falsehoods, challenged by hollow lies.

Brynjar leans upon his hammer, eyes downcast. His augmetic eye pulses weakly, clicking in occasional diagnostic rhythm.

They stand at opposite sides of the chamber, a great wooden table between them. At Ivar's side stand the members of Wolf King's Call, while the remaining warriors of Bloodiron Wrath flank Brynjar. There are new scars upon Ytri's flesh and armour, gouged there by immaterial hands, not yet sealed or tended. The others glower at Ivar, streaked in their own blood and the gory remnants of maddened crew.

Garald sits at the head of the table, acknowledging neither of them, one hand toying with the rings of the other. His own injuries have been dressed and attended. He bears them with silent shame, rather than martial pride.

'Your Navigator,' Ivar says at last. 'She is well?'

'As well as can be expected,' Garald mutters. 'She says we cannot break from the warp yet. Whatever bore down upon her, it stirred the currents of the immaterium. Cross the threshold now and she reckons it would snap the ship clean in half. It's not a mighty vessel, as you well know.' He laughs bitterly. 'When the danger is passed, she will bring us out. God-Emperor willing.'

'We have all suffered,' Ivar says. 'There have been many losses amongst your crew.'

'They knew the price that might be expected of them. All void-sailors do. We throw ourselves into the abyss, headlong, and never know when we'll feel a world beneath our feet again.'

'The same as any sailor,' Ivar affirms. 'How many dead?'

Garald scratches at the nape of his neck and then sighs. 'Hundreds, perhaps thousands. We are still in the process of counting. Logisticians and discipline-masters have been dispatched to the lower decks. We have weathered worse, lord.'

'Most do not choose to sail into a storm,' Brynjar says. He looks up, meeting and holding Ivar's gaze. 'This could have been avoided.'

'If it is our fate to face the tempest–'

'But it is not *our* fate!' Brynjar snaps. He swings his arm out, gesturing at Ivar. He steps forwards and the other pack move with him. Ytri's sword comes up. The scarred warrior lets his mouth twist into another wound in his face.

'This is not my doing,' Ivar says. He steps forwards to meet the Iron Priest but holds one hand back, stilling his own pack's mounting wrath. 'If anything, this is vindication.'

'Vindication?' Brynjar laughs. 'These deaths are yours to bear. The blood is on your hands, Ivar. We should turn back, before it is too late.'

'We have our course.'

'Allfather damn your course!' Brynjar growls. 'Gorm Krakenblood set and sailed that course. Look where it led him! He lies, cold and dead, beneath our feet! Falr joined him. For what? Your pride? Your damnable need for glory?'

'These are my trials to bear. My decisions to make. The Slayer chose me for this purpose. He set my hand to the task.' Ivar spreads his arms. His black armour shines in the lights of the meeting hall. 'If you disagree, then I stand ready for your challenge, brother.'

The others bristle. They can hear Ivar's grin in his words.

'You were not enough to best me when we were judged, Drakefang. You would not prevail now.' Ivar pauses. 'Trust me, brother. I wish no enmity with you. If this path is false then I shall recognise my failing and correct it. I shall throw myself at the mercy of the Chapter, even if the Great Wolf himself must judge me.'

The Iron Priest is silent and then turns from Ivar with a snort. He looks back only once. 'You are bold to the point of madness, brother. Anyone else I would have thought a maniac. You will be the death of us, Ivar.'

'If I am right, brother, then our names shall never die. We shall be feasted and remembered until the Wolftime.'

Brynjar screams in rage as his hammer smashes another training servitor to scrap, battering what remains away with a brutal sideswipe.

They are not Astartes grade. Poor craftsmanship even for mortal training needs. Brynjar's expert eye assesses them relentlessly, noting the wear and tear. The microsecond delays which speak of lax ritual repair. The Iron Priest almost pities the rogue trader his inherited tools. Shoddily constructed and ill-maintained.

He kicks the remains of the servitor one last time and then turns away. 'Another!' he calls. Arming serfs move in the shadows, preparing another servitor for the slaughter. Each one studiously avoids looking at the hulking warrior.

'How many is that now?'

Brynjar looks around. Ytri stalks from the shadows of the chamber, arms folded as he leans against a metal support pillar. Beside his head Brynjar can just make out the winding etchings of victory tallies and comradely taunts.

'Three,' Brynjar says quietly.

'Ah, the little wolf prince may not take that too kindly,' Ytri says with a shrug. 'All that choler has to go somewhere, though.'

'He tests me, as he has always tested me!' Brynjar snarls. 'That damnable superiority.'

'I can see why the Slayer likes him,' Ytri says. 'Most men would follow Krakenblood into war and death, sagas on their lips and fire in their hearts.'

'Not you, though?'

'We already have.' Ytri laughs. 'And he leads well enough. It's where he's leading us that gives me pause.'

'As it does me,' Brynjar sighs. He squeezes the haft of the hammer and the disruptor field disengages with a snap. 'We watch and we wait. If he oversteps, if he damns us with his petty glory-seeking, then we will force him to turn back.'

Ytri raises an eyebrow and shakes his head. 'You think he can succeed, don't you?'

'Let us simply say that I am prepared for my doubts to be unfounded.'

* * *

'What did you see?'

Kaedra's head has been banging idly against the wall of the barrack hall, soothing her aches with fresh jolts of agony. Every moment that her bloodied hair and scalp hits the steel, each time she feels it sing like razors through her skull, she grasps a moment of fleeting peace.

'What?' she asks. Kaedra opens her eyes and turns her head incrementally, enough to see Lyf. Squatting like a toad, his eyes wide. There is blood on his face too, drying to brown against his frost-pale skin.

'What did you see? When the death madness swept the ship?'

The death madness. The ghost plague. The last dream.

So many names for the flutter of immaterial spite that enveloped them. Kaedra tries to laugh but it catches in her throat. She coughs instead, heaving herself forwards and up, trying to kill it in its cradle. Lyf reaches for her, but she bats his hand away and presses herself back against the cold of the wall.

The soldiers, warriors and crew still gathered in these halls all avoid the bunks. Sleep is not a thing to be desired after the time of caustic dreams. Kaedra swallows hard, takes a shuddering breath, and then looks at Lyf again.

'When I was a girl, there was a fever. Someone said a bad star had fallen. That the tribe had earned Fenris' ire.' She laughs. 'We had no idea what true suffering was, then, but we did suffer.'

He nods. Watching her. Waiting for her to continue.

'I had a brother. The sickness took him. We had to watch him retch and bleed, shit himself to death. A foul end, for anyone, let alone someone you love. We burned him. Gave him back to the air and the earth. He is what I saw. In the grip of his sickness. Half-burned and drowning on dry land. He wore so many faces of death, and he laughed. *It* laughed,' she says, catching herself. 'It was maleficarum, and I could not fight it or run from it.'

'That is not weakness,' Lyf says sharply. 'It is said that even the lords struggled against the madness. If the Sky Warriors cannot conquer it easily, what hope do any of us poor bastards have?'

That makes her laugh. 'Same as we ever had. Little and less. Never mattered if it was the Sky Warriors we followed to war or the trader prince we serve now. We were always bound for red snow.' She pauses, collects herself, and braces her hands on her knees. Leather and void plate creak with her motions. 'What did you see?'

'Friend,' Lyf says with an uneasy shrug. 'Close as kin we were. Died in some stupid squabble I barely remember. We were just boys…' His words trail off into a sigh. 'Cleaved right through the skull. No hope for him. No salvation from the skies. He took two with him. Tough. I liked him. I think I must have killed another three, right after? Trying to get to him.'

'And that was who you saw?'

'Some wight mockery of him, aye.'

That had been the truth from every set of lips. The dead dredged up from painful memory. The lost, the mourned, and the hated. Regrets. Doubts. Those who should have been saved or those who gratefully passed from this world.

Shame, sorrow and fear haunt them as surely as the false dead.

'The Underverse is full of tricks,' she says. 'And we have come through them. Bloodied, but unbroken.'

'For now,' he grumbles. He draws a knife and taps the point of it against the deck, sighing as he idly scrapes patterns into the metal. 'We're lucky to be alive.'

'Just as we were every day back home,' she says. She leans her head back and lets it gently bang against the wall again, in time with Lyf's tapping. 'And then, as now, the only way is onwards.'

'Together,' he says, nodding.

'Together, all of us.'

'THE SHATTERED WORLD'

Pain burns sudden and sharp against his mind.

Around Onouris the dead scream, writhing in their torment as readily as they do around the adoptive home world. Light and fire cradle him. His robes burn away, reduced to fluttering ashes as a deeper reality reasserts itself.

He is clad once again as he should be. Not in the trappings of a scholar, but in the armour of a true warrior. Each plate is master-worked, inlaid with lapis and sapphire. Bone sigils shimmer faintly amidst gold. He feels whole again. Renewed, despite his injuries.

'You are wounded,' Qar says. His brother moves with considered care, navigating the renewed calumny that whips about Onouris. It shimmers like mercury and burns with sulphurous light, blending and shifting with every movement of his form. Slowly he forces his clarity outwards and reshapes the world.

The madness fades.

Everywhere he looks there are pristine wooden tables, heaving with scrolls and ancient texts. He has crafted a place that does not truly exist. An ur-library, redolent with examples of all learning. It is Leng and it is the Library of Ptolemy. There are aspects that are carved wholesale from some of the finest athenaeums upon Prospero – timeworn things that heave with the dust of ages, that remind him of his childhood, and the great glass temples dedicated to knowledge.

There are texts here that have never been read aloud, that have never taken form as ink upon page. It is a place of dreams and nightmares. Akashic. Liminal.

Onouris sighs. 'Perfect.' On the table before them sit plain glasses of rich wine. He intuits the vintage, assessing its quality with more than mortal senses. It too is an improbable realisation.

Yet here, in the eye of probability, anything is possible.

He looks up, past the waiting refreshment, and frowns.

Their prize, the core of their working, sits. Wreathed in pale and unclean radiance, spoiled moonlight upon winter ice. He reaches out to touch it, fingers drifting in the air above it. Static lambency sparks upwards, crackling between his digits. His armour purrs with every movement, channelling his psychic focus through its systems. He is one with it, more than any other warrior of the Legions or their mediocre successors.

'Perfect, is it?' Qar scoffs. The other warrior moves with a lithe grace, almost gliding from place to place. He stops to pluck a book from a shelf, flicking at it idly. He chuckles lightly to himself. 'A pretty verse. "History is a blade. All most men can do is note which way it cuts." A lesson we have learned well.'

Onouris' head tilts. 'And what is the origin?'

'*The Lays of Ancient Terra and the Songs of Old Night*. No record of who composed it. Not even in your prescient little volumes.' He closes it with a heavy thud and slides it back onto the shelf. 'That is our burden, I suppose. So much knowledge at our fingertips and still so little wisdom.'

'You underestimate our resolve, brother.' Onouris gestures for him to sit before taking his own seat. The chairs match the table and the shelves, the wood so deep and dark that it drinks in almost all light.

It completes the symmetry of a place rendered unreal by the workings of mind and soul.

Qar sits uneasily. He seems out of place within these figmented places, and yet they are essential for the working. Reality is cold and dead. The warp untrammelled is a pestilential undertaking. Here, between the two, weaving them together, shaping the cloth of fate... That is how they will triumph.

Onouris has been here longer than he can remember, sifting truth from insanity. Chasing echoes of lost kings and dead worlds. He has nestled his head amidst the roots of great trees, even as he hears the dogs snapping their jaws, in search of it.

And yet when he looks up, he realises he was never where he thought he was. All ends are denied him. All destinies are distant. He has never sat in the shadow of the tree, nor smelled the gentle waft of its fruit.

Dreams within dreams. Illusions even for those who served the throne of delusion itself. Devotion is no true shield, not from the master they follow.

'We keep our vigil. We hold to the task,' Onouris says. He sounds for all the world as though he is trying to convince himself more than Qar. 'The scryings only grow more accurate as we progress. The universe is in flux now. It has been convulsing since the Rift first cut the galaxy's throat. That rising tide is what shall bear us to our goal.'

'Oh ye of so much faith,' Qar says. He reaches down to the pouch at his hip and draws out his own set of psy-reactive wafers. Each one begins to smoulder as he places them down upon the tabletop. Smoke rises in thin wisps as they burn their way into the wood, searing away the fiction that Onouris has painstakingly crafted around them.

Qar smiles. 'Let us think of the future, not dwell in the past.' The walls flicker, then vibrate, then burst apart in shimmering fractals. The light refracts, becoming a seething mass of contradictory patterns.

'Must you kill every dream?' Onouris asks.

Ashes fall like snow around them.

It is the curse of this age that the future looks so much like the past. Burning in the fires of eternal and unceasing war.

Everything is drowned in smoke and rubble. The library is a ruin of charred wood and dead knowledge. Every surety turned to nothing more than whispers and dust. There are desperate oaths etched into the walls by blade tips and writing quills. The final personal cries of a dying city.

Forgive me.

Save me.

If you find this, know that I loved you.

Onouris closes his eyes and turns away. When he opens them he forces himself to look down at the evolving spread. The symbols have grown so bright that they are searing themselves onto the wood of the table. They burn his eyes. Onouris can still see them when he closes his eyes, white against the darkness. His retinas ache.

He sees a cage of cruel iron, rimed with fire. He beholds the hierophant of woes as he holds court, and the wolf bound in fetters of glimmering gossamer. The beast struggles, but it cannot free itself. All it does is drive the wire that chains it deeper into its fur and flesh. Blood stains its sides, sluggishly trickling down the monster's neck.

'And is this past or future?' Onouris asks, uncertain.

Qar rumbles with his bitter laughter. 'My brother. This is only ever inevitable.'

CHAPTER TWENTY-THREE

THE INFERNAL SMITHIES

They burn beneath the world's cold skin
Molten iron, aglow with sin.
Shaped by hands of daemons bold
Sworn to pacts and oaths of old.
The doom of men, and ship, and soul
Where darkling jaws consume you whole.

No ghosts weigh the ship down. The unclean spirits have ceased their whispering, in man or machine. It plunges like a dagger through the madness of the tides. Cleaving like the Fenrisian ice-breakers of old. The *Swift Spear* wears its name well as it defies the ruinous warp. Waves of colours without name buffet down upon them, squalls formed of hate and spite.

In her eyrie, Narayis forces her sight forwards. Blood still stains her cheeks. She will not clean it away. Time and again she has rebuked the attendants who have tried. Narayis wears her suffering like armour. The Space Wolves can keep their powered plate and the rogue trader can maintain his finery.

She will garb herself in pain.

Her warp eye burns with absolute focus, rimed in witch-light. Soul and sight blaze as she parses their course. The viewing apertures crawl with runes and wards. The fresh chains are taut at her wrists.

Narayis thanks the God-Emperor for His mercy. Without this gilded cage and His guidance, she fears what would have become of her. Sworn to lesser men and weaker ships.

'I am of the Navis Nobilite,' she whispers to herself. Effort strains her voice, stretching it out into a rough growl. 'I will not falter. I cannot break.'

Her warp-sight grasps the Astronomican's radiance once more.

Throne of Earth… *Save me from false signals.*

It should not be this difficult. Even this close to the Rift. She has trained for circumstances such as these. Aberrant warp phenomenon, mass real space-immaterium overlap. Any Navigator of worth has learned the skills required to manage such a situation until they are as intrinsic as breathing. Instinct and art, commingling at the apogee of her gift. The walls vibrate. The decking shivers.

Narayis' eyes move, matching the motions of her questing warp eye. Her fingers tighten against the arms of her throne. The metal is rough from decades, perhaps centuries, of wear at the hands of its occupants. She is merely the last of many.

Legacy.

The words of falsehood can cut like knives of truth. She feels the wounds like the tightness of the chains against her skin. The knowledge that it was a false phantom will not save her. It cannot.

There is an expectation now.

She can feel the pressure roiling in her gut. She wants to vomit. Perhaps that would provide the release she needs. Narayis thumbs a key upon the throne's arm. 'Water,' she croaks. 'Please. Water.'

The door slides open and an attendant waddles into the room, her purple robes trailing behind her, moving with exaggerated care. Her eyes are perpetually downcast, focused upon the ground. The servant is veiled, her eyes hidden between wafts of silk. Even if the girl wanted to look up, in some burst of madness, she would not be able to behold her mistress with her warp eye bared.

Too many dead are a burden that neither house nor dynasty can afford.

Such is the price of war, not the misfortune of service.

The girl places a simple metal cup by Narayis' right hand and then scampers back. 'May this bring you peace, my lady,' she murmurs.

'Thank you, child,' she says, nodding. Her voice is hoarse from her agonies. Everything aches. She raises the cup to her lips and drinks deeply. A placid calm spreads through her, salving her throat as she realigns her sight.

Focus. Breathe. Embrace the flow of it. Do not fight the tides, for they will dash you to atoms. Instead, defy them. Use their strength against them. Be the clarity that cuts. Embrace the Blade of Hope.

Old mantras bubble up to fill her mind. Narayis remembers the wizened old tutors, staggering from chamber to chamber, opining on 'the correct applications of empyreal sight' or 'the duties expected of one of the high scions of a noble house'.

They had been hateful old mystics, like Vertax. Ever ready to rap knuckles or strike the spine with their rune-inlaid batons. She remembers the old bruises, always hidden so that they would never be seen when she was on display. Pain had been the currency of education, a tithe to eke out the gift and strengthen her determination to succeed.

Navigator houses bred such desperate scheming, like sewers breed scum.

Narayis remembers the years of being pitted against her siblings, vying for the merest crumb of love and attention.

Perhaps the ghoul-thing was right. Perhaps I was always the least of them.

Doubt will kill them faster than storms. She knows this. Narayis is better than this, Throne damn and take them. She could never be accused of being idly trained. Her family had spared no expense, on any of its operational representatives. Even now her chains are of the finest silver, cold and reassuring against her skin. She flexes again, cleaving to the light.

She has it. Purpose floods her.

Something pulses through the ship. A ripple of psy-reactive force and electromagnetic distortion that roils the warp around them so deftly that the ship is almost crushed. Tendrils of incandescent force lash and coil about the vessel's Geller field until it screams. The sound is a burr of static agony, white-hot and yearning.

Everything begins to blur. The runes upon the viewport and upon the walls of her chamber start to smoke. They bleed trails and tears of molten iron and silver.

They are, she realises, one of the only reasons she is still alive.

The ship tremors and struggles like a burden beast trying to shake free from its labours. There is no control. Only the machine spirit's vast and transcendent rage as it is bound, caged, here where it should be at its most free.

'Be still,' she begs. 'Focus. Follow my guidance. We can break from this. One purpose. One vision. Together.'

The ship brays in binharic suffering, a keening song of outrage. It convulses. Lumens flicker and die. When the emergency lighting kicks in it paints everything in shades of scarlet. Narayis screams with the *Swift Spear*. Sympathetic pain ripples through her nerves as she strains up and then crashes back against the throne. She can smell burning flesh.

It is her own.

The shaking intensifies. She feels something hot at her wrist as she is thrown forwards, hard enough for the chains to cut her flesh, as darkness finally takes her.

Outside, beyond, great questing armatures seize the ship in their coldly logical embrace.

CHAPTER TWENTY-FOUR

FORGE OF HEL

It waits.

Perhaps it has always waited. Ten thousand years of agony and ecstasy, sprawled in the warp, unfurled like a perverse flower or the motion of some immense and grotesque arachnid. It is spider and web, predator and trap.

Minds driven mad by absolute knowledge conceived of it and brought it into being. It is an abominable work of genius. Every facet of it has been carved and intricately assembled. Everything is an aspect of the machine, writ large and made manifest. Spikes and spires as immense as hab-blocks stud its surface, crawling with unclean runes.

The enormous arms of the station-structure close about the ship, puncturing its Geller field with contemptuous ease. Waves of tormented space-time burst away from its pinned form, even as the drills and clamps bite deep.

Vessel configurations such as the *Swift Spear* are familiar to the masters of the forge. Yet more detritus cast up from the sea of souls, to be fed upon by the scavenger-kings who wait beyond.

Fanes burn along the length and breadth of the station, honouring the Omnissiah-Chaotica, the Eightfold Smith. A thousand hammers beat out their relentless tattoo as souls are rendered down into raw materials for the eternal industry. Docking umbilicals slither into place, moving with unnatural life as bolts bite and lock.

Things lope from their vaults, led by figures that hover or advance upon mechanical limbs. Black robes trail along the floors, catching on spurs of bone more extruded than implanted. Servitors lumber ahead of their masters, swinging censers amidst clouds of blood-mist. They advance through the wide avenues of Creation and Destruction, under the turning constellations of gears and the immense plasma reactors which feed the temple's glory.

The slave clades part and one of the magi strides forward into the umbilical, its stubby body held in a lanky exo-frame of coiling mechadendrites and bladed struts. Pacing like an avian horror, the magos waves one hand and speaks in a blurt of poison binharic.

<Answer to the true Master of Machines. Submit to the authority of the True Mechanicum.>

The doors of the *Swift Spear* resist. Valiantly the sanctified systems struggle against the scrapcode intrusion. Aboard, the enginseers and adepts of the Adeptus Mechanicus screech their defiance even as their minds smoulder and burn out with the defilement. One of them falls, cybernetic eyes burning, his melting face dribbling like unclean tallow onto the decking below.

For a moment the ship holds. It struggles to endure in the face of the enemy's corruption. Systems crackle and spark. Weapons seize and fail to fire. Munitions fall from their cradles, crushing entire loading crews.

A million tiny accidents haunt the ship, enfolded in the

writing sorcerous protection of the forge-fane, conjured at the hands of its master.

<Be at peace, children of falsehood!> the magos blurts. Its stilt-like legs push it up, as though preening for their attention. <You have been lost and now you are found. You find yourself at the mercy of the Architect of Sorrows, the illustrious Magos Nyrandvari. Be honoured and amazed that a scion of once-holy Mars has deigned to lower themself to an audience with you.>

Nyrandvari nods, and its cybernetic soldiery move.

The skitarii, if they even deserve the name, are hideous. Each one is a work of divine madness. Armoured plates cover what remains of their flesh, hammered into the meat of them with nails of black iron. None of the implants that they have been blessed with are fully functional. Each one jerks with random nerve-firings. Some vent steam and smoke from crude ventilation ports along their chests and spines. Their robes and cloaks are soaked in blood and ink, casting them halfway between ancient red and holy black.

They wear their ignorance as a shroud. A sacrament.

The doors grind open.

Across the span of the ship, other boarding teams, led by lesser magi, are beginning their own breaching protocols. Only Nyrandvari performs the dark miracle by sheer force of will and ability. Not for it the brutal undertaking of controlled breaching explosives or heavy skitarii with their implanted heavy bolters or plasma cannons. Nor the single-minded strength of gun-servitors.

When it speaks with the voice of the Machine God Unbound, Magos Nyrandvari requires only the force of its workings.

The first skitarii begin to march as the primary access hatch disengages. Two by two, they push forwards into the ship. One pauses, head tilting in sudden curiosity.

The skitarius' head detonates in a shower of brain meat and

smouldering circuitry. Its partner dies a second later, cored through in a shower of shattered metal. The ranks behind are already raising their weapons, seeking targets. More shells fly from the darkness. One strikes a skitarius at the hip, tearing the right leg out from under it.

Absolvor bolt pistol, the analytical portion of Nyrandvari's mind chirrups. Sensors taste the air, parsing the fyceline reek. Its eye-lenses adjust and it pitches forwards, its engineered length contorting to provide it with a better vantage. Personal voids flare around its support cradle as it coos and chitters to itself. *Fenris pattern. Mark IV. Curious.*

A true answer surges forth a moment later.

A warrior in black hurtles through the aperture, slamming into the midst of the skitarii like a tectonic event. The great mace he holds swings about, slamming one of the cyborgs into the wall. Tiny blades, each one mere microns thick, gash its back, even through the armour. The twitching machine-man leaks blood and oil, before the mace falls again and obliterates its entire torso.

He is already snapping round, his free hand thrusting out and grasping another soldier by the skull. Even the steel of its cerebral dome cracks like an egg under the sheer pressure of the assault, before the crozius shatters both of its legs.

He is a rush of black and bone. Monstrous and yet beautiful, as so many of the great works are.

The Astartes are a wondrous thing, for even in their ruin and degradation they impart a simple truth: the galaxy will be conquered at the tip of the needle before the edge of the sword.

Nyrandvari chortles to itself in a lilting chorus. Its hands come together in demented applause, with all the eagerness of a child. Its cybernetic eyes realign with a clicking whir. It leans forwards until the sensor-vanes and antennae which crowd the life-support apparatus in which it nestles can flex and taste the air. Passive and active sensors sweep over the warrior, even in its butchery. A mere thought and Nyrandvari gene-samples the environment.

<Astartes. Sixth Legion stock. Degraded by a factor of…> Analytic engines vibrate around its distended skull. Beneath the rebreather sutured into its jaw, what remains of its lips twist into a grin. <Perhaps I should have been informed by the heathen trappings you wear so proudly. Though amongst the Legiones Astartes your psycho-religious divergences were always of great interest to the Mechanicum.>

The warrior turns, as though seeing the magos for the first time. Nyrandvari spreads its arms, presenting itself in challenge. <It was always an amusement to us that you were our brothers in insight, yet wrapped so very deeply in your own ignorances. Other examples of cross-cultural cohesion were always present. Yet it was only in the Seventeenth that true kinship was attained.> It pauses in consideration. The wolf-helmed warrior advances, heedless of the knowledge it offers him. Others would already be running or deploying operational countermeasures, voiding excreta or purging fear-musk.

Nyrandvari is not other magi. It has its pride to consider.

<Ten thousand years I have endured here, little lapdog. It takes more than a gene-forged simpleton to threaten all I have built. Let Sarum and Samech preen upon the mortal stage. Even Xana has its place in the truth of the Great Work. Temples can be brought to ruin and forges can grow cold… Yet here I stand. Endure. Thrive even, by the standards of your stumbling drunkard of an Imperium.>

'Be silent,' the Space Wolf snarls. 'The least of the dead and the damned do not speak. Not in the tongues of men or machines.' He fires.

Bolt rounds strike and burst, limning the magos in fire and shrapnel. Fields ripple around it, dancing with unnatural void-light.

<How will you stop me, gene-progeny of the Sixth? Will you smash everything to pieces with that wonderful little toy? I will add it to my collection, soon enough. The others of your mongrel breed? I shall vivisect them for sport. You I will preserve, so that you may watch and learn from a true master of the flesh-craft. Genetics are merely the blueprints, laid out upon the table of the gods. All flesh is a simple engine of meat and muscle and electrical impulse.>

The Wolf is moving, even now. Throwing himself forwards, raising his wonderful weapon. The wings are burning, aglow like the Anathema's hateful aquila.

A nest of writhing tendrils winds up one side of the armature cradle, forming themselves into a replacement limb. They spasm and flex like a kraken. An orb glimmers in the centre, extruded from somewhere within the magos' robes. The mechadendrites slither over it, interfacing. The device clicks and opens, resets and alters its patterns. Red light bleeds from the interior as it manipulates the thing.

The tentacles of black iron spasm and hurl the orb forwards, propelled in a rush of kinetic force and poisonous illumination. It strikes the warrior's chestplate like the tolling of an enormous bell, and he cannot even scream as his armour systems seize. All the weight of it suddenly forces itself down upon him. The generator sputters, wheezes, and fails entirely.

Nyrandvari stalks forwards, looming over the disabled Space Wolf, tilting one way and the other, as a magos biologis might ponder over a particularly interesting insect specimen.

<You cannot fight me, little wolf. This is my domain. My fief complete. You are not the first to intrude upon my studies,

merely the latest detritus to wash onto the shore. I will pick you clean, mark my words. I will eke out your pain into a sonata. I shall play it for my own amusement. I will core out your flesh to strengthen my troops and I shall render your armour down to materiel.>

It gurgles with flesh-laughter, letting the binharic communion lapse into wet snuffling joy. The more robust of Nyrandvari's soldiers step forward, weapons raised as they surround the hobbled Space Wolf.

The others tread over him and past him, flowing into the vessel's arteries like a wave of infection.

Brynjar screams at them as they invade the sacred spaces of the vessel.

He spits his hate in the faces of every last debased echo of Martian perfection. He fights as they try to restrain him, driving them back with fist and hammer. There is nothing left in them that speaks of purity. Rust has colonised their plates, warring alongside random osseous growths and swollen flesh.

They chant in a repetitive hiss of scrapcode. A mantra ingrained upon their very souls by the relentless action of hyper-memetics and cerebral remodelling. They are vessels more than they are warriors. Mere pawns and puppets of whatever power rules in this place.

He drives his fist into the chest of one of them, knocking it through a railing and into the darkness of the lower enginarium. It screams all the way down, still chanting its doggerel till it impacts wetly.

Blood and oil pour from it, spreading outwards like splayed wings.

Brynjar fights on. He swings his hammer around and cracks the neck of a heavily armoured line-breaker, cleaving the top half of its storm shield off. It tumbles back in a rain of shrapnel, splinters ricocheting away into the shadows, trailing sparks. Servitors fight around him, loyalist and traitor both, their lumbering subroutines reducing them to echoes of past glories. Like ships of the line trading their blows in pugilistic fervour. Heavy weapons scream across the space of the enginarium, till the walls glow and catch fire.

'Bastards!' Brynjar howls at them. He leaps from one of the primary support gantries and slams another corrupted skitarius into the decking, stamping on its head until his boot is soaked in blood, brain matter, and other less identifiable leavings.

They think they can challenge me here? In my place of strength? With the glory of the Machine God about me? Let them try!

The lessons of Mars return to him in waves. The rites of destruction and salvation. The appropriate application of martial violence in service of the Cult Mechanicus. The secrets of tending to Dreadnought and tank.

To serve as he does is to be blessed in the sight of the Allfather-Omnissiah: the Master of Fenris and the Lord of the Imperium. All things to all men. Across whatever tribe or creed they swear to, there is but one Emperor.

He is a child of three worlds. Fenris, Terra, and Mars have all cut their holy mark into his soul. They have freed him from the flesh.

That is the power and the glory that he channels now.

His terrible children strike from the shadows, an ersatz pack pressed into service as the enemy ebbs and surges. The iron-wrought servitor-things that call Brynjar master hiss and spit as they attack, claws raking across plates. Hooking into gaps, dragging them down to be gnawed at with their steel jaws.

Brynjar dodges another strike then whirls about, hammer crumpling a corrupted warrior. A heavy weapons unit lumbers forwards to replace it, capacitors screeching as it braces itself to fire. A bolt of plasma scores across his armour. Brynjar's helm shrills with alarms as he throws himself to one side. Pain rampages up his arm. He can feel, with every sense remaining to him, the agony of flesh and machine. Plates seize and melt.

Behind him an explosion rocks the enginarium as a power conduit detonates. Plasma run-off and unleashed electricity surge about it. Steam fountains up from a ruptured coolant feed. Brynjar hooks the heavy gun-unit around the back of the neck with his hammer's head and yanks it hard. It hurtles past him, impaling itself on the piping. Evaporating blood fills the air around them with the stink of broiling meat.

'Is this all that you have?' Brynjar spits.

The masters of the mad coterie stalk amongst their soldiery, black-robed and whispering. Corroded augmetics gleam beneath their hoods, burning with subtle warp fire. They are everything Brynjar despises. The corrupt, so weak that they have drunk down poison to call it sanctity.

They have spat upon the oaths I made, of red snow and red sand.

Censers swing from the priests' arms, disgorging writhing smoke, burning the air with sulphurous fumes. Corruption bubbles from them like a physical thing. At their passage the iron floors rust and systems misfire.

Scrapcode tears at Brynjar. His vision crazes. Pain surges from his armour to his nerves, setting his black carapace ablaze. All becomes agony. A web of it spreading through him, eclipsing all other thoughts.

Rage pulses with every beat of his hearts. It drives him on. He swings again, narrowly missing one of the vat-muscled killers. The head of the hammer tears through a nest of cables, erupting with sparks. It annihilates them utterly.

Brynjar sways, battle-drunk, before the first net hits him.

He flinches back, hand already moving to pull it free. The strands bite like razors, clawing into his armour. He feels phantom pain flowing through his augmetic fingers.

<Flee!> he calls, speaking on holy frequencies, canting to his disciples. The skitarii burble with laughter as they hear it. Shots chase the servitors as they caper into the darkness. One snaps taut, back broken by a single shot. One of the skitarii stalks closer to it, firing another rad round into its quivering skull.

It is only when current begins to pour through the netting that Brynjar finally allows himself to scream.

CHAPTER TWENTY-FIVE

BLACK IRON GODS

Ivar awakens to silence and pain.

Chains bind his wrists, tight enough to draw blood. He can feel it, flowing and clotting, around his bare skin.

Bare…

He is naked. Completely denuded of armour and protection. The air in the chamber is warm, a sweltering heat drawn up by some infernal bellows in the depths below. Scarlet light radiates up from beneath the grated floor.

His dark skin prickles. Sweat slicks him. Ivar struggles, yet the bonds hold him tight. All movement accomplishes is the resonance of fresh pain. Rattling through him, caged by flesh and bone.

'Where…?' he slurs.

'Where indeed?' a voice answers. Ivar looks round and growls.

The stunted magos-thing that called itself Nyrandvari totters forwards. The obscene exoskeleton grips it tight, bonded to it by implant and coaxed pseudo-organic growth. The light from below only makes the monstrous thing seem more ghoulish.

The puckered flesh is fish-pale, the pallor of the drowned. It seems half-formed, more crafted than natural.

Ivar wonders if it still wears the flesh it was born to, before the smiths of Mars and the warp took it to pieces and reforged it. Or if it was, instead, some clone. Vat-grown and engineered.

'It is good that you are awake,' it croons. Its flesh voice grates. Each syllable cuts. Ivar's head snaps from side to side, trying to block out the hateful stimulus. It buries itself in his mind, his soul, until he feels tainted by every utterance. 'It is important that you are conscious, before we begin.'

'Begin…' Ivar shakes himself again. 'Begin what?'

'It has been some time since I have had the pleasure of one of your breed, here in my humble abode.' Nyrandvari titters softly to itself, like a doll from a child's nightmare. Its hairless head leans forwards as its cybernetic eyes realign and expand. It raises one stubby arm, and the armature extends. Blades and needles click and clatter as they extrude.

For one hideous moment, Ivar is reminded of Morkai's Fang and the sacred motion of the blades. A holy thing mocked and perverted. He grits his teeth and meets the monster's gaze.

'I will kill you, you mongrel thing. I will tear you from that petty throne and cast you down from this Hell Forge, to let you burn in the fires of your false gods.'

'From anyone else that would simply be a tiresome boast. You are my prisoner. Indeed, my property.' It burbles as it reaches out and rubs its tiny questing digits together. The blades hang in the air, poised and unmoving. 'The arrogance of the Sixth Legion gene stock remains unbowed, even after ten thousand years of societal regression, cultural collapse, and operational atrophy.'

'You would judge us?'

'You are a slave who has embraced his bonds. So eager for lash and shackle that you may as well have grafted them to your hide. I stand as lord and master of my domain. I have carved out my place in the firmament. I have shaped it from metal and flesh. Such is the glory bestowed in service to the Omnissiah-Chaotica.' It pauses, gurgling as it reintegrates itself with the support cradle.

The blades begin to flex again, mimicking its own avaricious movements. 'Such an arrogant breed,' it continues. Ivar struggles anew. The chains seem to bite deeper with every movement. The sound of the thing's voice sets his teeth on edge. Even the dull ache in his wrists is better than suffering its attentions. 'In time you will understand, Sixth. You will learn your place in the True Machine God's designs. The Great Work cannot be understood with a mind untouched by madness. That is what my hidebound fellows could never truly grasp.'

'You are insane.'

'Madness is the ultimate in subjective appreciation. Is it insanity to pluck the murderous spawn of a thousand worlds, mere children, and shape them into weapons? Some would call the monumental hubris of attempting to unify the galaxy with flawed implements as the delusions of an addled mind! And yet, your Emperor set his sights upon the stars, and reached out to claim them.' It gurgles with childish bemusement. 'To take a galaxy that already had its masters. The bones of your empire are Martian, through and through. Without the forge worlds, there would be no Imperium. Without Mars, there would be no Great Crusade. He forgot that at his peril, do not doubt. The pretender. The thief!'

The chamber's light flares in sympathetic agitation. Ivar blinks at the sudden light.

They are one. Magos and machine. This forge is his, utterly, just as he belongs to it. Chained together in their undying hatred.

'He is the Master of Mankind. The Allfather. King of gods, spirits and men.'

'I almost pity you, child.' Its tiny body shakes as it sighs. 'To cling so fervently to outright lies. Countless others of your brood have embraced the truth. They saw his deceits and rose against them. Some still do, even in these nights of ending. Be it single brothers or entire Chapters. They all come to us in the end. The wisdom of the True Mechanicum cannot be gainsaid. We were there at the beginning, after all. We beheld Mars as it burned with unchained knowledge. The wisdom of ages, not bound in vaults or sealed away by petty diktats.'

'Desecration,' Ivar retorts. Blood bubbles at the corners of his mouth.

'The old order must always give way to the new. The weak surrender to the strong. That is the law of life, laid down at the very birth of thinking meat.'

'No loyalty. No… honour.'

'You overestimate the worth of that currency,' it coos. Indulgent. A parent imparting a lesson to a particularly unruly child. 'Half the galaxy aflame, and still you sift the ashes for *honour. Duty. Glory.*'

'We have to fight for something. Live and die for that which is greater than ourselves. You have given up your soul. It is no wonder that you do not understand,' Ivar slurs.

'Ah, but had I been born on a toxic heap of rocks and snow, then I would know true contentment? Is that it? You think your grey wasteland is superior to the forge world on which I was incepted? Fenris is a dust mote in the eyes of the true godhead. It is nothing, as much as the sorcerers might try to make it so.'

'And yet, they fail. Time and again. No vengeance. All their wrath and fury for nothing.'

'All things end in time, little wolf,' Nyrandvari says. 'Even the mountains of Fenris will not endure forever. They will be torn down. Entropy is as unforgiving as glaciers. One day all your works will be dust. Your boasts and songs will be forgotten. Only the immaterium is eternal. Burning behind reality's veil in its infinite requiem.' It grows still and quiet, all frenetic trembling and undulating ceasing. 'If only you understood. It is within all of you to be taught, after all.'

'I will never yield to your false gods and unclean spirits,' Ivar growls. He forces a blood-slicked smile. 'The Rout has its reputation, after all.'

'A well-founded but far from flawless one,' the magos chitters, waving one clawed manipulator. 'There is precedence in all the bloodlines of the False Omnissiah's *loyal* sons.'

'You insult us and profane so many others,' Ivar growls. 'All because your own fidelity proved its weight false.'

'You cannot betray a lie.' The magos chuckles. 'And it was all lies. Even before he dragged humanity up by its neck and set it to building his empire. Before he stole Martian fire from the true Machine God. He was only ever false.' Its arms rearrange themselves, folding and unfolding, digits coiling outwards into claws of black iron. Lightning flickers between them as it raises one hand towards its face.

A moment of absolute stillness engulfs them both. It toys with primordial forces between its fingers, as though it were a child contemplating a new toy. The light washes over them both, and Ivar feels his skin crawl. Prickling hot and then cold, stirring with the thing's conjured power.

'It is almost a shame that you are so incapable of understanding,' Nyrandvari sighs. It sags infinitesimally. A tiny loss of control. 'There will be time later, for your illumination. We are nothing if not seekers of wisdom. The quest for knowledge will not end until all information is bound, reordered, and liberated from the confines flesh has made for it. Free, as it was upon Mars so long ago.'

Nyrandvari shakes its head sadly. 'And they called it a Death of Innocence. Nothing could be further from the truth. Innocence is worthless. A deceit we all embrace. Each and every soul in this galaxy is drenched in sin. Generations beyond count. Species without number or name. All have erred and all wear their failings. Such is the will of the warp.' It pauses again. 'Such is destiny, fate. *Wyrd* as your barbarian kind might have it.'

Ivar snarls at that. He strains forwards and the chains cut into him again. Blood dapples his face. The light catches it, crimson on dark skin, and makes the droplets seem to burn for one moment.

'So easily provoked, like all good guard dogs,' Nyrandvari chortles. A number of other sounds emit from it, a blurted rush of code-forms and debased binharic. 'Do I not do your precious fief the respect it is due? You must forgive me. There was never much time for me to grow to love your stunted gene-breed.'

'Then why am I here? Why do I still live? If you would kill me, false magos, then do it. Do not prattle on. Just kill me.'

Nyrandvari is silent. The magos' stunted head tilts. Calculations flicker across its eye-lenses. It gestures again and the armature rig contorts, hunching its central body up and forwards. New limbs extrude from the back plate, unfolding with an unwieldy spidery movement.

It reorients itself. The limbs bend in impossible ways, reshaping themselves till blood and oil patter the floor to hiss and ignite under the withering heat.

It makes itself a symbol. Hateful and warped. A twisted mockery of all that has come before, and all it has forsaken. It makes itself into the sign of an eight-pointed cog.

Not a cog. A star…

Mechadendrite cables slither free from the tip of one bladed limb, sniffing at the air. Nyrandvari takes a clattering step forward and leans over, trailing the barbed interface needles down Ivar's chest. They skitter across the broad expanse of skin, pausing to linger over the curvature of his fused ribcage. They pry at the connection nodes upon his torso, clicking as they begin to commune with his black carapace.

'I can only apologise,' Nyrandvari says. 'This will be extremely painful for you.' It pauses, then lets the needles plunge home. 'But most illuminating for me.'

Ivar cannot answer as the first howls of agony are torn from him.

CHAPTER TWENTY-SIX

PERDITIO EX MACHINA

Brynjar wakes screaming.

A raw bellow of rage tears itself from his throat out and into the chamber he finds himself in. The walls are the grey of the ship, the air barely recycled oxygen, tainted with blood and the stink of unclean oil.

He tries to shake himself, struggling against his own armour. It barely responds. Every motion is rendered an effort. He can hear the rattle as the plate grinds, riven through with errors and scrapcode repetitions.

I am a son of Fenris and a scion of Mars. I have endured worse than this.

He is linked to his armour more intimately than any of his brothers. His augmetics click and whir as they process the inload, barely coping with the rancid flood of data. Toxic information burns in barely legible symbols as they stream through his cybernetics, intent on worming their way into his soul.

.'The poison of cowards,' he whispers. Within the confines of his helm, his flesh voice brings moments of reprieve. He can focus on every breath, not be overwhelmed by the enemy's wiles. Even the idea of canting in binharic hurts, itself a deeper sacrilege done against him.

'Allfather-Omnissiah, bless me that I might do your will. Give me your strength. Let me rise like the hot heart of Fenris. Let my wrath be my Motive Force. I will be your destruction upon the false prophets of the enemy. Let me be your fire, lord.'

Each word is warded in purifying thought. His every utterance is matched by another cognitive engram unfolding. In his prayers he honours the machine spirits of his armour and his own augmented flesh.

Brynjar's prayers burn inside him, in sacred unity with the machine.

He can still see. His armour's systems allow him that small mercy.

He understands why when the first of the figures begin to circle him. Black-robed and whispering, they look up at him from beneath their hoods, each face a nest of writhing mechadendrites, squirming like worms. Their hands are knotted together before them, in constant motion, shifting through iterations of eight-barbed cogs.

<You serve the False Omnissiah,> one of them cants at last. They all move in the same instant, heads tilting as they regard him with augmetic lenses set deep in the crawling mechanisms of their faces.

'To the unclean I bring purity. No maleficarum shall find purchase here. By the rites of Mars and the Iron Masters, purge me of weakness. Free me from doubt. Deliver me from the frailty of the flesh.'

<It cannot hear you, your empty godhead. Glory to the Omnissiah-Chaotica, lord of the New Mechanicum. Shepherd of the lost sons of sacred Mars.>

Brynjar struggles to lunge forward, to throw himself at the

enemy. He cannot move. His armour still refuses to respond. Systems lock and grind. The magi of the Dark Mechanicum chitter with bemusement.

The servo-arm at his shoulder lilts one way and then the other. The cog-teeth of the Iron Wolf try to move, but cannot answer. He closes his eye, hidden within the helm.

'The Allfather moves in all things, as sure as the stars in the heavens,' he intones. 'He moves Fenris. He moves me. Lord, be the strength in my arm. Jarl-of-Jarls, grant me the will to conquer my enemies.'

<You will be dissected,> one says idly. <Your wargear is of interesting manufacture. Your gene-craft is novel. We will fetch the knives and, at the master's instruction, we can begin.> Its lenses sparkle with malign interest. <We are looking forward to the procedure. It should prove most illuminating.>

As they move, the lumens above begin to flicker, tormented by the very presence of the unholy. Each motion reveals a new atrocity. The intricate scarification of flesh and machine replacements, the gurgling tubes of green and purple liquid riven through with bloody whorls. They twitch like veterans on too many combat stimms, every movement without grace.

Every action an affront.

Lesser constructs caper after them, bounding from place to place with a depraved eagerness. Tiny, grubby metal hands paw at any examples of technology they can find. He can only watch as two of them slowly heft his thunder hammer, cooing as they shuffle away and out of sight.

<It will be easier if you do not fight. To resist is to die, but were you to accept the truth of the New Mechanicum… What wonders we could make of you.>

His every last thought is coloured through with rage, bleeding into his armour, warring with the contradictory feedback of the scrapcode. As though he could burn himself clean with hate alone. Brynjar strains every muscle.

The armour judders forwards, hunching over until it is face to face with the lead adept. The coiled malice of its face reaches out, tendrils brushing against his face plate as though savouring his defiance.

<You are strong. This is good. It will allow for a more protracted demonstration of Astartes physiology. You should be proud. From your unmaking, new understanding shall be gleaned. You shall aid in our own quest for knowledge, stunted though your appreciation may be.>

Pain surges through him with every beat of his hearts. His blood burns, alive with the caustic fire carried by feedback into his nerves. He can feel the ripples of agony through his black carapace, resonating out into the meat of his muscles.

The weakness of the flesh.

The lessons of Mars are hammer blows upon his mind and soul. He remembers the sanctity of service upon red sands, the looming figures of the magi who would instruct him, greater and more holy than these weak pretenders before him.

Remember that the Motive Force is present in all things, the primary animus of man and machine. There is glory in unity. Just as you are bound to your armour, so you are bound in all things to the Omnissiah.

Old equations unspool within his mind, blossoming out through his implants and his armour. He feels his fingers move, ceramite and flesh in concert. The merest flicker.

Machine spirits chorus through him. Spurred by his faith. Moving as though animated by the Omnissiah's will itself.

The monsters busy themselves in idle atrocity. They roam the chamber, digging their sharpened talons into cogitator banks and machinery, prying cogs and pistons from the walls to turn them over in their unclean hands. The ritualised desecration is so intrinsic to them that it consumes all other focus.

Finally, Brynjar feels his artificial hand clench into a fist.

The magi turn as one, lenses flickering with confusion as the grinding burr of his armour resounds through the chamber. Brynjar rises like a monster from the sea, rearing up with deliberate malice.

His fist falls like thunder, shattering the iron skull of the first of them. Metallic worms spill out, writhing away, seeking the shadows, even as Brynjar strides forwards to crush them and their host beneath his boots.

The remaining three begin to screech in their tormented binharic, scrapcode howling from them as they crowd in around him, almost as an immune system might respond to a foreign body. Lightning kindles about their claws, bright and sharp in the gloom.

Brynjar knows no fear. Rage fills him, fuels him. All pain and doubt flee beneath its shadow, burned away in the undying purity of it. Singing with the faith of Fenris, the Imperium and Mars.

Talons rake his armour, setting the servos burring once more. The monstrous hereteks gouge his plate till it splits and bleeds, trying to drive him back. To restrain him once more.

They struggle in futility.

Brynjar's spine hits the wall and he pushes off it hard. The servo-arm twists, pivoting away from his shoulder. It locks around the throat of the nearest magos, hefting it into the air. Tightening.

It screams impotently, limbs battering against his armour, trying desperately to close around the servo-arm. It yanks down hard, trying to find its footing again. Brynjar snarls, and with a thought, the arm snaps its neck. It drops in a flutter of black robes and oil.

The last two back away, as though it will save them. Already they have deluded themselves into thinking that they are the masters here. Fatted on weak vessels and easy prey. Despite their alterations they remain pitiably mortal at their core.

They know the fear that accompanies being hunted.

Brynjar's mind traces noospheric pathways as he advances upon them. Those systems at least remain maintained. He senses other consciousnesses within the network, though they are dulled and enfeebled. He cannot hear the tech-priests of the ship – their voices do not join the chorus.

<Come to me,> he cants as he strides forwards, casting his will into the noosphere even as he readies his body.

Every part of him is sharpened into a weapon as he throws himself at them.

He moves slowly towards the door of the chamber, covered in blood and oil.

It has been locked but the artifice is crude. Not even fused shut, merely code-sealed. The corruption of the enemy writhes in it. Were circumstances ideal, he would be armed. Brynjar would smash it to flinders if his hammer was in his hands. As before, he has only his fists here. Only his wit and his long-nurtured skills.

He will not sicken his soul with the works of the Archenemy.

He reaches out and smaller interface wires slither from his mechanical wrist. Pausing, sniffing the air like a serpent's tongue, they hesitate a moment. Perhaps the noble spirits of his cybernetics can sense the techno-heresy that waits within.

'Forgive me for what must be done in the name of the Allfather-Omnissiah. Preserve soul and spirit from mechanical maleficarum.'

The contact is a lightning shock of tainted communion. Gears grind as they resist him. They have made the ship itself fight him as a body fights an infection. As though *he* were some interloper.

As though I do not belong. He snarls away the thought. A son of Fenris and a disciple of Mars cannot be a stranger upon a ship. He takes to it as easily as the voidborn. Bound within the sacred chrysalis of iron and plasma, reshaped and remade by worlds of fire and forge.

Pernicious datagheists linger, oozing their way towards his armour's systems. He purges them with ruthless engrams, sharpening his thoughts into weapons. The enemy has already underestimated his resolve, thinking him a savage.

That will be their undoing, he knows. He will carve their folly into their iron bones and break their fane around them. The profanity of the Dark Mechanicum's very existence is a seeping wound upon the galaxy. It is more than duty which now guides Brynjar's hand.

It is a sacred oath.

The lock clicks and the door whirs open, hissing softly as it finally surrenders. He steps out into the corridor and looks around, gaining his bearings. Still near the enginarium. Brynjar squats down and presses his hand to the decking, closing his remaining flesh eye.

No motion. We slumber. Yet to be roused. They've stilled the vessel's heart.

He hears scraping around him and turns, fists raised, servo-arm seeking prey.

It is not the enemy.

They have obeyed his previous instructions. They fled and waited. Now, one by one, they emerge from hiding. One squeezes itself out of a ventilation shaft, iron bones realigning and cracking as it contorts itself. Like vermin forcing their way through grating. The iron wolf skull stares up at him, turning quizzically, a low growl building in its mutilated throat.

Brynjar loves them, in his way. He has crafted them by hand. Tended to them as though they were children or favoured pets. Each is a testament to his devotion. To his artistry.

One by one his thralls gather, chittering with data-cant. Every mechanical part of them burrs eagerly, their implants primed for violence and service. They are servants of the Chapter, devotees of Russ as the destroyer – the fiery blade of execution that punishes the unworthy – just as surely as they are implements of creation.

They all stand, crimson emergency light reflecting from their armour and implants. They claw at the decking with animal urgency, talons and implements retracting and extending, gouging marks into the metalwork.

'Serve the Allfather-Omnissiah's will.' He looks at them, speaking and emitting the words in glorious unison. 'Find the others. Liberate them if you can. The ship has been taken. Inconvenience our enemy wherever possible. Kill the heretics. Turn the systems of this noble machine against them. Am I understood?'

They sniff the air like the pack they are, heads raised in a silent howl. He tastes it against his mind, blurted on noospheric eddies.

<Go,> Brynjar cants again. Stronger now, a harsh goad against their minds. Flesh and cybernetics tense in response. Brain meat pulses, mechanisms thrum. They slaver, growl, and then turn on their heels – fleeing into the waiting corridors of the ship.

Brynjar wills his helm display to respond. The runes that represent his brothers appear. A handful within the ship, which he transmits to his thralls. There is one beyond that draws his eye.

'Skitja,' he mutters. 'You do not make it easy for me, do you, brother?'

'Bastards!' Ytri snarls, throwing himself against the door again.

The metal dents but does not buckle. They are being held, he realises, in an old bilge hold. The walls are encrusted with long-dried effluent, but the chamber's integrity is beyond question.

The enemy had been swift and cunning, tricksters made of

iron and barbed with lies. Swarming through the corridors like biting insects, their stings laden with corrupt Motive Force. Burning within nerve and armour.

And when they had awoken, it was in the pit that surrounds them. A further insult from the damned. Designed to hold back immense pressure. Reinforced. Enough even to blunt the rage of a Space Marine, it had been an apt choice.

He steps back and then slams his fist against it once more. He watches the locks strain. 'If I had my sword, I would hack it apart, and I wouldn't stop until I had turned every last one of those tin soldiers into scrap!'

'We'll all share in that hunt,' Jolfr growls. 'These makeshift cells cannot hold us long. They will be expecting us to break free. Who knows what they have waiting for us.'

'You think I *fear* them?' Ytri laughs. He draws his fist back again and then brings it up over his primary heart. 'Our oaths are to stalk these monsters to their lairs and drown them in their blood.'

The others wait. Watching. Poised and ready for violence. A word would unleash them.

'Where do you think the Priests have ended up?' Vili asks.

Akaz scoffs. 'Dead, mostly likely. Hung out like trophies for the sport of the traitors.' He looks to Ytri. 'When we are free, we should avenge them. A thousand dead for every one of ours. Just as we will avenge Falr.'

'Even if we have to beat them to death with our bare hands,' Jolfr says, nodding. He places a hand on Ytri's shoulder, no doubt feeling the tension that vibrates through him. 'We have had our differences, brother. I know this. We have let our pride blind us. There's choler in our hearts, aye. Enough to fill an ocean. Torn between our masters and their own rivalry. That ends now. We must be of one purpose.'

'One purpose, eh?'

'We fought together on that dead world. Carved our way through the tomb they made of that ship. Dragged our legacy up from the dust. That is not nothing, brother. When we are back on Fenris' soil, I will gladly reckon with you. In the training halls or upon the ice, with spears to mark our battleground. Here and now? We must be of one will.'

Ytri nods approvingly. 'And make the bastards suffer.'

'So they feel it even in what passes for their souls. A wound so great that the hell-constructs they build next will suffer from it. Till the next Season of Fire settles upon them. Storm and tumult, for every last one of them.'

This makes Ytri laugh. He shakes his head and then walks to Jolfr. He seizes the other warrior by the forearm. 'I thought you coddled. Weak. So wounded from the loss of your brother that you became so very desperate to serve the Wolf Priest. I was wrong, brother. I recognise my failing and once we are free I shall be sure to correct it. Be that in the pits or the feasting halls.'

'As it should be.' Jolfr returns the embrace. He meets Ytri's gaze, seemingly noting the genuine sincerity in the scarred visage. 'There is nothing to forgive, brother.'

Ytri turns back to the door. He gestures for the others to join him.

'Now,' he grunts. 'Let's see how many of these bastards we can take with us.'

'Never seen a little lord this close,' Lyf whispers.

Kaedra snorts as she stalks from one end of the chamber to the other. When she first began her pacing, the wounded and lax had begun to complain. A few sharp kicks had dispelled their gripes, or had banished them away from her path.

She looks over, following Lyf's nod.

The rogue trader. Garald Helvintr himself. She laughs bitterly and turns away. 'Would be better if he had some trick to get us out of here.' She looks around. 'It's all the flesh crew. The meat. None of the iron-touched. No priests.'

'Aye, I'd noticed that,' Lyf says. He scratches at his chin. 'The trader seems to be keeping the crew calm, at the least.'

'Even the least of jarls have their uses. Let the man be a symbol, if that's what he's good for.' She drums her knuckles against the wall. 'We'll find a way, or we'll carve one.'

'That's the way of Fenris,' Lyf laughs. 'It's just a wall. A mountain. A machine. It can be broken. Land comes and goes. Only we endure.'

'Don't get ideas,' Kaedra says with a smile. 'They'll start calling you a skjald as well.'

'Still never heard any of your verse! Maybe you'll find the time before we all die in glorious battle, eh? Recite one before you craft me my own, eh?'

'You're too stupid and ugly to die, Lyf,' she grumbles.

'I've been told that before,' he says. 'Sounds better from a skjald's lips somehow.'

'You have my word, Lyf. Before the end, I'll make sure that your deeds live forever.' She pauses, tilting her head as though weighing the thought. 'Assuming we manage to get out of here alive.'

Lyf is about to answer when a commotion arises by the sealed doors of the chamber.

Garald has moved from the group he was attending to, hurrying to the door. Even from where she stands Kaedra can see the internal keypad beside the frame, its shell prised off. Men and women with no training in the iron mysteries had tried and failed to override the locks.

Now there are noises, echoing from the other side of the door. A low scraping sound, building to an insistent rattle of metal on metal. Garald raises his hand, pressing it against the door, before he starts backwards.

Mechanisms click and spark. Slowly, the door begins to grind open.

'By the Allfather,' Kaedra whispers.

The grinning iron skull of a wolf stares at them. It tilts its head quizzically and then slinks backwards, creating space for the crew to move forward. Slowly, in ones and twos, led by Garald, they advance out of the makeshift cell.

'One of the Iron Priest's creatures,' Garald muses. He turns and gestures. 'Those of you who are warriors or armsmen, we will find whatever arms we can muster. Safeguard the crew. We will take back what stations we can. Weapons and motive control are priority. Am I understood?'

'Aye, lord!' they call with one voice. Kaedra shouts with them. One crew. One will. One body.

'We will take our ship back from these monsters. Whatever the cost may be.'

CHAPTER TWENTY-SEVEN

FROM THE FLESH OF WOLVES

Ivar slumps in his restraints. Blood trickles from his eyes, from his ears. He can taste copper in his throat and can feel tiny rivers of his own life dribbling from his interface ports. It runs down his chest, to drip and dapple upon the floor.

Ivar looks up, blinking away the crimson haze. Nyrandvari leans back, rocking on the heels of its iron feet. It looks decidedly pleased with itself. Removed from the armatures, its flesh arms clap together in glee.

'Oh but you are a wonder, aren't you?' it burbles. 'Even by the standards of your breed. Astartes are Astartes, but you? Sixth Legion gene stock, in the...' It waves one of its hands. 'What is it they are known as? *Primaris.* Yes. Of the Primaris pattern. Further alterations to the False Omnissiah's old ideal. Remarkable.'

'Come... closer, monster. I will show you just how impressive we can be.'

'Beautiful Fenrisian defiance. Some things are truly never diminished with age. Too many of your kin have withered over time.' It begins to pace. The lights within the chamber flicker with its movements, pulsing in time with its meandering thoughts. Gases vent up in sulphurous sighs, reeking of infernal industry. The great machine continues to move around them. Realigning. Chambers shift and change, remade and unmade.

Chaotic clockwork whirs. The floors ring with the motions of skitarii and misshapen servitors as they adapt to their place in this immense design. Set in motion by will alone. The magos' iron determination.

'I admire your fire,' Nyrandvari continues. 'It will be a pleasure to make you the first of my vivisections.'

Ivar pushes forwards again, fangs bared in a snarl of defiance. Blood flies, making the tattered black robes glisten red for a fleeting moment.

Nyrandvari ignores it. 'Then your fellows. The mortals I shall convert into servitors, or render down to flesh gruel. Whatever is most efficient come the hour.' It fits itself back into the waiting armatures and the ends wriggle, metallic tendrils slithering forth like the questing tentacles of anemones. 'The demands of my undertakings are quite intensive, you understand. Especially when such wilful savages harm my precious endeavours.'

It raises a hand and wiggles it. Hololithic projectors whir to life, casting the room in deeper crimson as it forms an image before Ivar's face. Tithes and tallies begin to stream down the air before him.

A litany of murdered ships, intercepted fleets, despoiled colony vessels. Lists of body parts, organs, materiel and ship components. Everything rendered down into numbers, the cold consideration that had once defined the Mechanicum of old.

Turned to madness. Run to excess.

'Fine harvests,' it coos. 'Since the time of the Rift, the wars of mortals and gods have given us much to dwell upon. This is a breaking place. We bring the joys of holy dissolution to the mechanisms of heathens and aliens. All the better to feed the Long War.'

'Just a parasite. No better than the scum that clings to a void whale's flank.'

The hand that weaves through the air pauses. Lightning crackles between the tendrils. It lunges forward, driving the limb into Ivar's side. He bellows in pain and rage, sweat and blood flying as he struggles against his bonds.

'Careful,' it hisses. 'I am master here. I have made this place. Wrought in glory and iron majesty. It was *my* work. An opus machina to rival any of the hidebound sycophants of Mars.'

'No honour... in treachery,' Ivar slurs.

'I do admire the fury of the wolf that I see in you. So intrinsic to your culture, and embedded in your unique biology. Loyalty at any cost is a noble aspiration, certainly, but I parted ways with such conceits long ago.' It turns from him, pacing from side to side, as though dictating to a symposium. 'It is a difficult habit to keep when undermined by lies. False gods and promises do not inspire true loyalty, or love.'

'Perhaps you were not worthy of His loyalty.'

Nyrandvari chuckles to itself. 'Perhaps. A thing such as he was always bound to spurn those who worshipped him in ignorance. He was not a grateful godhead, as all false gods prove to be.'

'You have embraced the same falsehood. I can smell it on you. The canker of the warp. The taint of maleficarum.'

'If I were to take you apart, bit by bit, I wonder if I could tame that remarkable gift of yours.' The magos turns away and silences a sudden alarm with a wave of one extended limb. 'You pride yourself on being a seeker after truth. A hunter of corruption. When your kind...' It pauses. 'When those who would *become* your kind first came to be. Chaplains.' It laughs again. 'Another insult from your absent god. Worshipped when it suited him, venerated when it was required, even when we were scorned for our faith. As the robes of religion are stolen and draped around the shoulders of hollow reason.'

'Ever the victim,' Ivar spits. Blood trickles from his mouth again even as his shoulders rattle with laughter. 'Truly, I'm surprised none of your acolytes have cut your throat yet, to put you out of your misery.'

It stalks back over to him and contracts its limb. It folds open at the elbow, disgorging another nest of barbed wires. Squirming over his bare chest, they embed themselves in the flesh. Tiny drills whine, an ultrasonic hiss that makes his ears ache. Even his senses, enhanced as they are, cannot adapt.

'You are a savage,' Nyrandvari hisses. 'A heathen. A barbarian. You are the implement that tears down walls and burns libraries to cinders.'

Ivar laughs. 'Gladly.'

The pain builds. It screams through him as it incises flesh, tearing at bone. He tastes his own marrow on the furnace air. His eyes roll. Sanguine tears roll down his cheeks again.

'But I will teach you,' Nyrandvari whispers. 'If it takes a thousand years, I will educate you. By the end you will be either a compliant pet... Or you will be spare materials for the great works to come.'

Brynjar moves through the ship with his wrath unbound, his armoured boots hammering against the decking. He takes corners recklessly, throwing himself heedless into the increasing patrols of the enemy.

Monstrous scavengers stalk the corridors, trailing their oversized hooks and cutters behind them in grotesque procession. Brynjar kills them where he finds them, smashing through their ranks, no matter the cost.

There are so many, within. Defilers all. His flesh aches with the myriad wounds the enemy deals, cuts and barbs driven into his armour. He tastes blood, even now.

The enemy must think themselves mighty indeed to have seized such a prize. A vessel of a rogue trader's house would be a fine haul – laden with mercantile goods, armaments, perhaps even archeotech. To find one on a sacred hunt, brimming with warrior flesh and with examples of the Vlka Fenryka... For any traitor that would be a gift from their foul gods.

I will choke them on what they call victory.

He moves onwards, mapping his course as he does. The ship's schemata flicker across his artificial vision, guiding him through its innards. Door systems jam and stutter. The lumens above pulse between blinding white and arterial crimson. In places the walls are already weeping with corrosion. Rust spirals through systems with an implacable relentlessness, verdigris trails wherever the feet of the Archenemy have fallen.

<SYSTEM ERROR! REPENT IN THE NAME OF THE OMNISSIAH! SYSTEM ERR–%%^*%^^*>

The ship's soul is screaming. Bound within failing iron, yoked to an infernal machine, it suffers, venting its agony in binharic waves, in noospheric tremors. The *Swift Spear* ails, falters.

You will not die, noble machine. Fenris' wrath will sing within you once more.

In the enginarium around him, in the central fanes below, the enemy are trying to take the great edifices apart. Squads of slave-servitors and the hateful iron silhouettes of skitarii move around the vast space. Tearing at the mechanisms, rending apart cogitators, throwing sacred components aside to moulder in junk heaps.

The empty space is filled with chanting, alive with the blasphemy of the enemy. Brynjar needs but a second to gain his bearings. They have not yet truly defiled it. Surface mutilations that will render only minor impediment to function. It will likely be spared for some deeper despoliation. Instead, they have butchered the adepts and menials who tended to it. A handful at most. No one, he notes, of rank.

A binharic scream resounds suddenly, as though in response to his confusion.

Brynjar's head snaps round and he rushes to his left. Up a winding spiral of iron steps, into a forest of cogitators and thermal modulation vanes. Amber light rises around him, shimmering with heat haze and the plumes of steam. He rounds the corner of one of the larger vanes, its surface flashing with warning runes, and sees the enemy silhouetted against the illumination.

Three corrupted skitarii stand with their backs to him, gazing up at their handiwork. Bound to the red-hot ironwork like a sacrificial victim or a condemned prisoner, the priest of Mars writhes from the heat and current. Feedback loops of exhausted and tormented binary weep from him. His robes are torn, what little flesh remains slicked with blood and oil.

His head lolls weakly, light flickering dully in his augmetic eyes as he tries to cant a prayer. To force a balm through the absolute agony that defines his existence.

Brynjar growls. The sound makes the torturers turn, their iron jaws clattering with primordial hunger. There are two lesser monsters, twitching ruined creatures, each a mismatched assemblage of artificial limbs and organs. Something that might once have been flesh sits enshrined where their heads should be, their skin stretched and pinned like anatomical specimens.

He throws himself forwards, bringing both of his hands together to seize the first creature's head and constrict. Bearing it backwards with his momentum. Slamming it towards the iron barricades.

Its face comes apart in a welter of scrap and gore, wrenched asunder even before it hits the wall. The other raises its rad weapon, primed to fire. The ancient Geiger-click of the gun ratchets up, green light building within the confines of the chamber.

Brynjar's servo-arm hurtles forwards, grasping the weapon in iron teeth and *squeezing* till it breaks. It vents strange gases and high-dose rads, forcing the thing to stagger back, before Brynjar's fist destroys its iron skull in a rain of brain meat and plasteks.

The last has waited for him, poised in some obscene analytic loop. The alpha is an honoured horror. Iron spikes reach up from its gorget, entwining around its mutilated skull like a crown. There is no visible humanity left. Brynjar wonders if fragments of it nestle within the metal cocoon, awaiting their grim metamorphosis.

He does not have the chance to ponder it long.

Every movement of the hulking alpha is an insult, a motive blasphemy upon the Allfather-Omnissiah's universe.

Brynjar allows himself a grin.

<I wondered if there would be any challenge amongst your scrap-kin.>

It blurts its own challenge, hooved feet scraping at the floor as it lurches forwards. Brynjar sidesteps it, driving the back of his fist into the side of its head. He pulls it back, crying out with the sudden pain of electro-discharge. It turns to him, armoured form smoking as it channels the corrupted Motive Force through itself. Electoos flicker and writhe beneath its skin as it throws wide its arms and roars with all the force of a Titan's war-horn.

Brynjar growls and lunges forwards. Its bladed hand flies up between them, disrupting the rhythm of the Iron Priest's assault. Like an aberrance in code. A murmur in the steel heart of a machine.

The ruin of perfection, shaped into a weapon. Primed to gouge out all that is sacred.

Brynjar steps back and the alpha follows him. It rolls its shoulders as it moves, drinking in the light of the coolant vanes.

Brynjar feints left, and again it matches the movement. He lets his servo-arm drive forwards, snapping closed around the joint of the warrior's bladed limb. Its augmetics flex wide as Brynjar squeezes.

He reaches down and yanks the blade-arm up through its skull. Matter detonates, becomes dust as lightning meets lightning in a mutually assured destructive release. It bursts apart, screaming in corrupted binary as Brynjar stomps down what remains, crushing it to nothing.

He turns back, rushing to the ailing magos, as the alpha's signal finally dies.

Nyrandvari draws back suddenly, tendrils whipping away like a frightened serpent. The magos chitters in a sudden rush of perplexed scrapcode, turning from Ivar and pacing furiously.

Lights flicker in its eyes, communing with distant systems, interrogating mutilated subordinates. It raises its arms and begins to bray in some binharic tantrum. When it turns back to regard the Wolf Priest, its artificial gaze resonates with terribly human hatred.

'Motes in the storm. Gnats!' it screeches. 'Grit in the mechanisms. They must think themselves so very clever. Your brothers and thralls and acolytes!'

Ivar laughs weakly. 'Treachery is always repaid with death.'

'Yes,' Nyrandvari agrees. It closes one stunted hand into a fist. The great clattering motion around them pauses. Reorients. Ivar hears the whine of vast servos, the crunching of gears. The world around him contorts and contracts. The room unfolds, becomes something else. He hears pistons engage, and the platform begins to rise, up through the Hell Forge, bathing him in unholy light.

'Let me show you the rewards of your petty defiance, my specimen,' the magos hisses. 'It will be the last thing you see before I take your eyes from you.'

CHAPTER TWENTY-EIGHT

MERE ANARCHY

They have nailed the magos deep into the iron of his own workings.

It takes time for Brynjar to pull them free, to lower the mutilated tech-priest to the ground. He is no healer, not like Ivar is, but he does his part. Tending to a being who is more mechanical than flesh.

Albertus-Nu, magos of Mars, acolyte of the Mysteries of the Sacred Engine, looks up at the Iron Priest with dulled augmetics. It is oil, coolant and hydraulic fluid that cover him more than it is blood.

<Your coming was a blessing from the Omnissiah,> the old priest cants. <Ordained by the Machine God. A thousand thanks be upon you, brother of the cog.>

<You honour me, magos,> Brynjar responds. Even here amidst the glories of the engine fane, the very act of canting hurts. The Archenemy's hateful presence curdles in the air, making each thought and breath ache like knives. <One of our own has been taken,> Brynjar says. <I must defy the enemy, take the fight to

the heart of their corrupt machine. I must be the implement that breaks the wheel of their falsehood.>

<I fear I will be of little practical utility in this endeavour. I am limited by structural compromise.> He looks up, past Brynjar, regarding the etched majesty of the enginarium that looms around them. <I would be of more use here, trying to rouse the ship's noble spirit.>

<You are not iron alone,> Brynjar pulses. <Flesh will serve just as ably. My thralls are nearby, seeking to free others. It falls to you to marshal the crew of the engine decks. Drive back the invader. We need weapons control and drive function.>

<I will perform to my optimal ability.> He rises unsteadily to his feet, augmetics straining as he does. He braces himself with his arms, even as a smaller pair emerge from beneath his robe, knotted together in an oddly biological display of concern.

<That is all we can ask of you, magos. It is what the Allfather-Omnissiah demands.>

They are fighting.

For the first time Garald feels the surety of purpose that the Space Wolves must feel, the iron determination that defines his adoptive home world. Walking its surface was not enough. The piecemeal inheritance of his dynasty never truly meshed. Now he understands. In the company of these warriors, he finally comprehends what it means to fight and die for the cause.

'For the Imperium!' he roars. 'For the Emperor! For Fenris!'

Other voices take up the call, be they from Fenris or not.

They have all armed themselves as best they are able. Fire-arms from the initial confused invasion, scooped up from cold repose upon the decking, liberated from piles of blood and viscera. Others have raided armouries along the way, looting caches put aside for armsmen at defensive intersections.

Almost all have located some blade or other. Axe. Sword. Dagger. Even makeshift bludgeoning tools. It matters not to them if the enemy are armed. They would not care if they were outnumbered a hundred to one.

All that matters is the struggle.

Like a tribal warband they surge through the corridors. Songs erupt unbidden from their lips. Old naval shanties. Work songs in honour of eternal toil and glorious service. Chants and calls from the ice. Feral certainties spat anew into the Uppland.

They advance like a rabble, the rushing of a motley tide. Each of them clad in their uniforms, or in armour. Metal plates. Leather. Furs. Flak. Battering their weapons against their chests or upon shields.

'Fire!' Garald calls. He almost surprises himself with the outburst. Turning his own axe over and over in one hand, he raises his pistol. The weapon bucks in his hand, but the shot goes wide.

It does not matter. It is not alone.

Everyone else commits to the fight. Bullets and las fire burst around the enemy, driving the iron devils of the Dark Mechanicum back. Shrapnel sparks from their warped bodies as tainted oil gouts into the air.

Armsmen hang back, firing from the rear lines as the Fenrisian shieldbreakers throw themselves into the fray. Spittle froths from their lips, hair whips, and the blades rise and fall.

The skitarii retreat in rapid lockstep. Despite their nature as the hollow artifice of Chaos, they work with a surprising unity.

They are few. Garald wonders if it is the hubris of the enemy, or perhaps some fear contracts their iron hearts which has so thinned their numbers. He wonders if they are even capable of fear. He knows that the Adeptus Astartes are immune to it. No dread can hold them. Because the Emperor has exalted them. These things, though, are reduced. Perhaps there is too little meat in their minds for terror to touch. Inured to it by the horror of their very existence.

Now it will end. I will see it ended.

He fires again. Bullets ricochet from the armoured warriors. Spikes careen from their plate. They hold, like rocks against the howling of the sea.

A round catches one of the skitarii under its skull-bonded helm, blowing out the side of its head. Jaw and cheek burst apart, shattering into a cloud of bone and blood. Garald pushes forwards, joining his fire with the others'. The first shot tears through a skitarius' shoulder in a spatter of oil. The next is a cruel gut-shot. The cyborg doubles over and he seizes the initiative, driving his axe into the back of its lowered head.

'Helvintr! Fenris! Imperium!' they call. Garald cheers with them. His heart is pounding. His skull aches with the rush of adrenaline. Death crowds in and he cannot tell whether it is here for him or the foe.

There is only the rush of combat. The singular thrill and shock of it. He sees a warrior woman, wild and laughing, as she swings an axe for another of the skitarii. It turns the blow aside, jostling her back while its allies begin to fire.

Beams of searing unlight ripple through the corridor, their very passing turning the gilding of the walls into tarnished, running slurry. One of them strikes a heavyset warrior and bursts him apart in a rain of smoking fluid. He unwinds messily, intestines looping down in a wet puddle.

They have been toying with us, Garald realises at last. *Throne of Terra…*

'Fight!' he screams. 'Fight and die for your Emperor and your ship!'

They clog the corridor with bodies. The skitarii stand and form their line, three across, shoulder to shoulder. Sighting, raising their obscene weapons. They fire again, even as the crew surge forward and through the blockade. Garald watches another man die screaming, torn apart into a cloud of dust. An after-image hangs in the air, a glowing wound in the shape of a flailing and screaming human being.

He can taste human ash in his mouth. Garald's teeth ache with the unholy channelling of the warp, a clinging static pain. His head throbs and thrums like the pounding of a drum. Like thunder in the veins of the ship.

They press on.

The enemy knows they are here, but Garald is no stranger to the ship. He knows its secret ways. Brynjar's lumbering servitor-things guide them, bounding along the corridors, squeezing themselves through apertures, seeking the ideal path.

Every compartment they find, they force open, adding the strength of the crew to their growing pack.

In a crew of thousands, they can muster the strength to resist. To fight. To die, if they must. Blood to feed the relentless machine of war and suffering. All in pursuit of their goal. Of a prize that will turn the tide.

To free the Wolves from whatever bondage holds them.

As though I could. Some hero from a fable. And yet I must try.

Perhaps some part of him had always thought that legends were pressed, fully formed, from a distant Imperial mould. Not painstakingly carved with the artisanship of the God-Emperor.

Worlds such as Fenris are not simply forges for warrior kings. They are glorious crucibles of pain and iron resolve. Suffering wielded like hammer and blade, to shape strength and pare away weakness.

To become a weapon.

And they are all weapons now.

Grenades hurtle into the ranks of the skitarii and burst apart like fruit, fountaining components both biological and mechanical into the air. Tearing them apart, buying the crew a moment of blessed reprieve.

'Forwards! For the lords of Fenris! For House Helvintr! For the Emperor!'

For mortals it is no easy thing to kill bare-handed, not in the face of the monsters that the galaxy sets against them.

The Wolves of Fenris know no such weakness. Every part of them is sharpened into a weapon, flensed down to the killing core.

They fight with their armoured fists, with their boots. They stave in skulls with their hands alone, drive their own helmed faces into the enemy's. Blood and oil stain them; gobbets of withered flesh cling to them like stubborn fungus. Red and black and ash upon the blue-grey of their plate.

Odr and Vili stand shoulder to shoulder, defending the rear, lashing out with simple and brutal enthusiasm. Odr's is pure rage that the enemy would even dare to challenge him, where Vili brims with youthful vigour. To prove himself the equal of the warriors he walks with.

'You fight well!' Odr allows, calling over the din of falling fists. He drives his knuckles through the face plate of a screaming skitarius, breaking its vox-grille. More unclean fluids coat his fingers, clogging in the mechanisms, writhing as though trying to still his wrath forever.

'I have had good teachers!' Vili laughs. Odr almost envies him the joy that sings in the warrior's heart, devoted to the pleasure of the murder-make. 'And Bloodiron Wrath set a fine example!'

'A pity there is not better sport for you!' Odr grunts. He drives thumb and forefinger through the ocular implants of another monster, flicking shards of plex-glass from his fingers. 'Half-men and false men. The leavings of forge and healer. Barely enough blood in them left to make red snow.'

Vili backhands another with a laugh, slamming its head into one of the walls. It recoils, chittering mindlessly. It swings at him with implanted sword blades, barely turned aside by the sweep of Vili's arm.

He winces in pain, feeling the burning lines etched through armour and flesh. He flinches back, bringing his other arm round in another attack.

Odr is quicker. His foot lashes out, cracking the slashing automaton's breastplate and hurling it backwards.

'Move faster!' Odr snarls, turning his head to bellow at his brothers.

'We need our weapons,' Jolfr grumbles. 'We cannot go on like this forever.'

'Can we not?' Ytri laughs between blows. 'I enjoy it! It reminds me of a simpler time. Upon the ice.'

'You do not remember your first death and the days before!' Jolfr replies.

'Perhaps not, but we have all seen it. We forget, at our peril, the men we are raised up from. To be born of Fenris is to be as much a weapon as my sword or your axe.'

'I will feel better when my axe is in my hands again,' Jolfr growls. 'Before these mongrels defile them.'

'Aye, I cannot imagine that Brynjar fares better than we do. These things will offend him to his core.'

'Then I hope he reaps his own bloody tally!'

'I have no fear of that. He is a baresark, that one. Once the iron erodes but a little, the beast is free of its cage. He has kindled such rage in his heart, like a reactor burning hot.'

Within his helm, Jolfr scowls. Every skirmish, every little victory, has been gained by snapping at the enemy's heels. Chasing their detachments through the ship's innards. Up from the bilge tanks, towards the barracks chambers where their stolen weapons lie. Jolfr has lost count of how many have died in the attempt to slow them down. All of them bear the scars of the defiance. Gouges and cuts mar their armour, scores and burns from the esoteric weapons of the enemy.

Carried with pride.

The enemy's wounds are worn like a curse. They fall back in twos and threes, some limping, a few crawling along the decking, dragging themselves by their iron fingers.

The Wolves surge forwards with the unity of the pack. One will guiding them, howling with one voice. Ytri and Jolfr close upon the foe like fangs, tearing into their ranks and forcing them apart.

Blows fall upon their armour, clawing at them, tearing at seals. Working at joints. Desperation pitted against determination. The two warriors throw themselves headlong through the gap they have created, crashing into the barrack hall. Still moving, hurling the enemy aside, they pivot and grasp for their weapons.

The weapons crackle to life in the same instant, their wielders finally complete once more as they turn to meet the enemy's steel with steel.

'Fenrys hjolda!' they scream, as their brothers push in around them.

The choir rings with countless voices, but they do not speak.

Their song is not spoken. It extrudes outwards in a multi-spectrum rush of binharic communion, of noospheric defiance. It is the joy of service. The realisation that their purpose was decided long ago. Shaped by the great designs of the Omnissiah. Prepared for a singular and glorious destiny.

Albertus-Nu's wandering course has led him through the

warrens of the underdecks, a slow and limping exploration as he forces his limbs to respond to motive commands. Each new chamber he unlocks disgorges yet more of his crew: menials, minor enginseers, functionaries of every stripe.

Now they join him. Canting and praying, kneeling before the votive dais as he allows the sensoria to extend to their full span. The old magos leans forward, hunching like an invalid as the lights rise behind him, silhouetting him in blue-white radiance.

<Know that you serve the Omnissiah incarnate. Machine God be praised for the dutiful adherence of flesh and steel.>

'Machine God be praised!'

<Embrace the glory of His sight. Know the potency and purity of devotion to that iron will! Is this not your ship?>

'This is our ship!'

<Then rise, children of the Machine, servants of the Omnissiah. Rise from your pits, from your alcoves, from your shrines! Rise and take this ship back for your own! This is its beating heart! This is the singing core of the *Swift Spear*! Behold the bounty of the Omnissiah, laid out before you! Would you surrender it to the enemy?>

'No!'

<Would you let them defile your holy places and tear down your fanes? See your weapons turned to unholy purpose?>

'Never!'

Albertus-Nu is one with the enginarium, bound to the great spirit of the machine. He feels the static dancing from his steel bones, radiating up and through him in waves of purifying force. <Take back your vessel!>

They rise in a tide of iron and defiance, wrath and fury kindled till they burn white-hot and terrible.

Servitors lumber from their berths, crackling with electrostatic force so intense that their eyes burn out, melting in their sockets at the ruinous power unleashed through them. The labourers yoked to the great engine pits come with them, their tools transmuted into weapons. Pipes. Wrenches. Work-blades and chisels. All turned towards the purpose of defence and defiance.

The enemy are few. We are many. The enemy are weak. We are strong.

They are guided by one will. Albertus-Nu's sermons still ring in their ears, carried upon the vox, the noosphere, the binharic currents that saturate the ship and give it purpose. A balm against corruption. They move like antibodies through an ailing body, fighting infection, driving back the unclean.

Chaos cannot thrive amidst unleashed order. It perishes, crushed down and rendered powerless. They know they unleash something different. Each of them understands. Albertus-Nu *makes* them understand.

Every hand turned against the enemy in directed anarchy, in the unbridled insanity of absolute determination. Everything transformed into a weapon. Till the enemy bleeds and dies. Till all that remains is ashes and dust.

Brynjar hears but does not heed.

He moves through the madness of the ship with his own singular purpose. Alone, devoid of brothers or aid. Following the signal that dominates his attention. The rune pulsing white-hot against his vision.

Ivar.

He wonders sometimes at the bond that unifies them. The blood spilled so long ago upon the Kraken's Spur no longer matters. Long since turned to powder, returned to the sea. Drowned and burned and bludgeoned by time and tide. The death that claimed Jolnyr has grown so many faces. As many as the deaths that stalk them here.

Between attack and defence lies opportunity. He means to seize it.

Vox-prompts click in his ear. Binharic hymns ring with insistent thunder. He ignores them. His soul is primed for the murder-make.

All machines can be destroyed. All enemies laid low. All it takes is defiance. It demands iron in the soul. He will not be found wanting. Not in the sight of the Omnissiah.

Brynjar stalks alone through the ailing districts of the great ship, tracking the retreating skitarii from the depths. Fatigue aches in his bones, slowing his steps. He passes the ill-gotten gains of the enemy, cogitators and metal stacked like cordwood, waiting to be harvested back into the hungry maw of the forge.

A crimson-fielded stasis reliquary waits, braying corruption as sycophantic magi scuttle and worship about it, as though it were a fane.

Brynjar snarls and leaps forwards, crushing one of them outright like an insect. The corroded iron of its spine snaps, even as he seizes its fellow, pulping its skull in one hand before throwing it aside.

The unclean light washes over him and he kneels down, driving his servo-arm through the panelling, rupturing the debased mechanisms in a rain of sparks and wriggling cables.

The light snaps off with a burst of ozone, and Brynjar rises, reaching in to steady his prize at last.

His hand finds his hammer once more.

Now, he thinks. *Now this can be ended.*

CHAPTER TWENTY-NINE

SUBTLE BLADES

'Defiant little things,' Nyrandvari muses. The Architect of Sorrows postures and preens about Ivar's bound and hanging body.

Ivar feels the new surges of pain, rising and then abating. The light around him has taken on a harsher resonance. It hurts his eyes, searing through the film of blood that blocks his vision. His words come in a slurred rush, unintelligible.

'Ah, but in the end you will break. That is the glory of the machine's true calling. It endures where flesh fails. That is why the galaxy had a skeleton of cold iron, before your Emperor spread his curse of biological aberration across the cosmos. What did it gain him? Of eighteen sons, how many failed at the crucial test?'

'Russ,' Ivar whispers. 'Russ.'

'Your godling is not here, child.' Nyrandvari stalks around the edges of the chamber and then gestures sharply, hand moving in a fluid cutting motion.

The walls fold away. The light grows brighter still. The tremoring of a hundred hammers surrounds him in a wall of noise.

His senses pulse, electric, in absolute overdrive. Stimuli on every level assail him.

Ivar blinks away the blood and looks out at the fires of the infernal foundry.

Fiery matter pours through the core of it, manipulated by immense gravitic engines. Metals and rarer elements are siphoned away, torn from the slurry. Ships have been fed into it, rendered down to nothing more than raw materials. Other stranger things have been sifted from out of the warp. Space hulks broken apart, their components strip-mined. Asteroids composed of meat and teeth. Budding planetoids that scream and bleed.

'Do you like it?' Nyrandvari asks. 'A variant upon the macro-scale harvesting engines of the beings who term themselves *Kin*. With my own alterations, of course. One must never be afraid to glean inspiration from other sources, after all. It is a bountiful galaxy. It would be remiss not to exploit what resources remain to us.'

'Nothing true in you, monster,' Ivar murmurs. He shakes himself again, and the chains rattle. New blood runs down his wrists. He isn't clotting any more, he realises. The *Healer*, the Larraman's organ, no longer works its craft.

Instead, he haemorrhages and withers like stuck meat. Hung like a fresh kill.

'You cannot wound me with words, little wolf,' Nyrandvari chitters. It lets its armatures click once more and another platform rises up to meet them.

His armour hangs, suspended on grav-plates. It has been cleaned and dressed with a skill even Brynjar could not have mustered. Perfect.

Even monsters can craft fine works.

'Even I could not destroy this,' the magos whispers. 'The armour of one of your priesthood. It will make a fine display.'

It stalks across to another bench and lets its mechadendrites coil outwards around…

His crozius.

Ivar looks at the weapon, laid out upon a bed of crimson silk, as though it too were bleeding. All the detritus of war has been scraped from it. Every crevice has been artfully cleaned. Polished. No powdered bone or burnt blood. Nothing stains it. Like the armour, it is pristine. Whole. So very unlike himself.

'Masterful,' Nyrandvari says reverently. 'I have a singular passion for weaponry. I have collected examples of it dating back to the epochs of the Golden Age of Technology. We have lost so much potency, and yet we have gained in brutality.' It turns back to regard Ivar, eyes clicking in its face as it looms closer to him.

Ivar jerks forwards to meet it. His teeth find the grubby flesh of one cheek and *tear*.

Nyrandvari squeals in sudden pain. One unignited armature slaps feebly at Ivar's flesh, beating at his shoulder and neck, trying to force him back. The other comes up a second later, and the stun goads plunge into the centre of Ivar's chest.

Ivar bellows in pain and rage. He yanks his head back and spits. Blood and oil spatter on the floor alongside a pale lump of mutated flesh. 'Now yours is added to the tally, butcher.' Ivar laughs. 'Add your own iron to the forge. Your own life to the bill of slaughter.'

'Ingrate!' it seethes. 'Such bounty I place before you and you *wound me* so! I will pin you out next to your arms and armour. Perfectly vivisected. Portions of you skinned or disarticulated. Displayed like the curiosity you are. A failure. A trophy.'

Every part of the magos coils and trembles. Electoos glow along its flesh, shivering with fresh conductivity. It drives the tendrils back into Ivar's neck, letting them wrap around it. Tightening.

Ivar's eyes are wide, his fangs bared and bloody. He feels the first flaring of the mechadendrites' killing energies, smells his own cooking flesh. Ivar's features contort into a grin.

If I die here I will look death in whatever face it shows me. No fear, just as Russ would want.

All is motion. Immense cogs spin and grind together, propelled by the plasma beat of vast reactors. The machine is a flawed colossus. Guided by a perverse will, fuelled by the power of the warp and the things which dwell within it.

Components turn, wreathed in witchfire and corrupted Motive Force. Arcs of it pass between immense copper spheres, conducted into eldritch pathways. Circuitry nests drink light and vomit it through false logic gates in waves of colour that should not exist.

Lesser minds might find it beautiful. Brynjar can only consider it depraved and unholy. His servo-arm steadies him as he heaves himself up onto another plinth of black stone.

Every part of him recoils from the wrongness of the forge. As one of the Vlka Fenryka he understands the corruption etched into every component of it. As a student of Mars he knows it for the incarnate blasphemy it is.

An immense spider made of blades and wheels, burning with unclean energies. A parasite engine designed to undo the perfection of better machines. Its existence is an affront. Even being within its confines makes his skull thrum. Toxic homilies drift on the air. Servitors hang from their stations, garrotted by interface cables. Lesser adepts, their black robes dangling like funeral shrouds, are nailed to eight-pointed stars.

Suffering fuels this monster.

It is the oil that feeds the machine. Human pain flows within it, defiling every surface with its passage. To even stand within it is to feel sullied. Brynjar hates it. At the very heart of his soul he has always despised the hollow artifice of the Archenemy. Corrupt and corroded, tainted relics or stolen materiel hoarded in places such as this. Made a part of a treachery ten thousand years old. A never-ending war that has split the galaxy in twain. Stability set against ruin. Order amidst Chaos.

He looks around and judges his next leap.

All is motion. There is no true structure or centre to the place. Brynjar's augmetic sight realigns against the blazing heat of the smithing that surrounds him. Ingots hewn from the flanks of ships are being smelted apart, great streamers of liquid metal drawn out and manipulated into shape. Servitors, stripped down to muscle and nerve entwined about the hafts of immense hammers, control the angle of impact, their skulls like tiny pearl adornments upon the implements.

Against the scale of such things he wonders at his chances. Ivar is alone and ensnared by the enemy, reduced to mere prey by the ravages of the Dark Mechanicum. Brynjar is but a single devotee. One weapon against the foundries of the unholy.

Yet he is my equal. My friend. My brother. I will save him. At whatever cost.

Brynjar draws back, hammer held close to his body, and then sprints forward and hurls himself into the flaming abyss.

All that remains to them is battle.

Jolfr feels the savage pleasure sing within him, the ice-joy of combat and blood. Each swing of his axe cleaves apart another foe and leaves it as mere debris upon the ground.

He has never felt more alive. The others must feel it too or they would not fight with such primal desperation. Streaked with rancid oil and fouler blood, scoured by the shrapnel the enemy have become.

They fight as one.

'No masters now, brother!' Ytri calls. 'Only duty!'

Jolfr laughs. It pours from him in ragged bursts as he turns and ducks, pivots and swipes. 'Is that what you call this sport?'

'It is like they do not even try! Look at them! Broken toys from the cradle of unclean gods! Let them try to best me! Let them dare!'

The burns and cuts upon Ytri's plate are still fresh. Jolfr does not have to be a Wolf Priest to know that the other warrior is bleeding within his armour. Trusting to rage as a balm against pain. Drowning any perceived weakness in the slaughter of the enemy. Reinforcing it with his bluster.

'We hold them here!' Jolfr calls. 'You and I! The others can hold the lesser paths into the ship. We draw them in, and we crush them.'

'Where are Ivar and Brynjar?' Ytri spits. He drives his boot into the face of one of the downed skitarii, pushing until its iron skull breaks. Brain matter spurts up his greave. Ytri looks down at it with undisguised loathing. 'Dead? Prisoners?'

'We will find them,' Jolfr insists. 'Once the ship is liberated and the crew safe.'

'Pah!' Ytri turns back towards the other pack leader, kicking another corpse out of his way. The rusted augmetics clatter along the decking, trailing scraps of black fabric. 'From what I see the mortals are giving a good accounting of themselves. We'll help them hold.'

'They're blood to Fenris.'

'Some of them.'

'Many.'

'That's why they're fighting well.' Ytri grins. 'And dying well.'

Jolfr scowls. 'You're too keen to see them suffer.'

Ytri shrugs. 'Builds character. They'll be stronger from the fight or they'll see their friends die and crave for vengeance. Whatever fires the bastards up, I reckon.'

'Thank the Allfather you're not in charge then,' Jolfr says.

'You can't see me in the armour of a Priest? Or a lord?' Ytri grins. 'I'm meant for better ends than this.'

Jolfr nods. 'As you say. Though I'm no judge of such things. I leave that to my betters.'

'Plenty of those about,' Ytri says with a laugh. 'Don't worry, brother. I'll still remember you when I'm raised up on the shoulders of our fellows.'

'Are they bearing you to a throne or your grave?'

'I fear neither!' Ytri declares, throwing his arms wide. Firelight catches upon the ravaged armour. Bloodstains glitter like trails of rubies upon his plate, caught in the notches and gouges. In places, Jolfr cannot tell whether they belong to the warrior or his foes.

'We need bigger guns than this. More than us. More than the mortals.'

'Aye. The ship's guns will have to cut us free from this little trap.' Ytri turns his blade in his hands, pointing it down the central docking umbilical that still binds them to the forge. 'I look forward to watching them all burn.'

CHAPTER THIRTY

DIVINE RETRIBUTION

Pistons larger than main battle tanks slam down before him, hissing with steam, glowing red-hot even against the furnace-crimson.

The works of the enemy intensify about Brynjar. Moulds bubble, filled to the brim with molten run-off, screaming as they are shaped and pressed. Caught between attack and defence, the Hell Forge radiates its choler, alive with focused and living anger. A beast, at last provoked in its place of power.

Brynjar prays he is beneath notice, calibrating his armour systems specifically to run on low power. He can barely feel the energy from the reactor as it sustains him. Even the blue-grey of his armour has been smeared with ashes and soot, rendering him a shadow against the perpetual hellfire that surrounds them.

The fire and smoke assail his senses. Everything reeks of heavy industry, pulverised metal, and burning flesh. Nothing is wasted here. Armour, weapons, flesh and souls are all mere raw materials for the infernal artifice of the Dark Mechanicum.

He creeps forward, hammer readied. His mind ticks in perfect rhythm with his plate and augmetics. Stalking around the pistons, barely even recoiling from the force of their impacts, Brynjar measures his breathing. He pauses. Waits. Watches. Computing the patterns. Judging the timings.

The memories of Mars stir again in his mind. Burning white-hot like the radiance of plasma reactors upon the slopes of Olympus Mons. Old training resurges. The bonds of old pacts between Terra and Mars. Mechanicus and Imperium.

Rise, son of two worlds. Brother of Fenris, acolyte of Mars.

Brynjar Drakefang hurls himself forwards.

He surrenders to gravity, passing underneath the rising piston, ducking as he does. His hammer rises, striking the next in its ascent. The metal deforms. Mechanisms judder as he vaults under the stymied machine.

He feels the tremor passing through the forge. Systems seize. No alarums sound above the howling gale that already assails the interior forge. His helm blocks out all sound. Brynjar pauses in between the banks of alternating pistons, rows of them miles across, their hammering feeding the manufactora below.

The smells of engine oil and weapon coolant rise in pungent waves, channelled up through furrows in the grating around the pistons.

'I am coming, brother,' he whispers to himself. 'I shall be the blade that pierces the heart of the foe. I will be the hammer that breaks the unclean's lair apart.'

The rapid tattoo of the pistons falters as irregularities continue to creep into the rhythm, yet more chaos blighting the near-ceaseless works. Discordant strains echo about him, muted and filtered by his systems.

He is immune to the madness, deaf to the corroding song. He swings his hammer again, igniting it only at the last second, the moment the next piston strikes true. Brynjar slams the lightning-wreathed weapon into the side of the plunging metal and watches the pulse of mutual annihilation.

Metal flies free, a rain of shrapnel that tears into its surrounding supports. Hydraulic fluid gushes out in waves of gold, rendering the hellish light around them momentarily prismatic.

There is no time to admire it. Brynjar is moving again. Spinning through the tumult, weaving amidst the ratcheting insanity of the forge's underbelly. He breaks as he goes, every movement turned to a methodical act of destruction. Wall plates shatter and buckle. Circuits break and capacitors overload in rains of cerulean sparks.

I serve the Machine God as Destroyer. The Master of Ruin. With the solidarity of steel do I commit the works of the enemy to holy dissolution.

Machine spirits cry out around him, a never-ending litany of artificial pain and binharic release. Datagheists and meme-djinns skitter across his consciousness, not to infect but to venerate. A ripple of annihilatory thanks bristles against his dulled armour systems, catching on the cognitive functions of his augmetics.

Part of him wants to weep for the injuries done to such holy machines. Torn from the vessels that once carried them to the stars, that made them arbiters of sacred conquest. Bearing up the Martian need for control out from Sol's glittering light, twinned to the Imperium's own desires for dominance. Instead they have been perverted. Ruined. Broken upon the wheel of the hell-fane that consumes all about them.

Brynjar grits his teeth and raises his hammer again. He brings it down against one of the nearby walls, over and over again. The plate comes apart in a rain of scrap and smouldering machine parts. He does not stop.

By the time Brynjar realises that he is screaming with rage as he hews into the flesh of the forge, he barely recognises it, even as it echoes within the cage of his own helm. He pulls back, trembling, gazing at the clods of ruined metal and machine that litter the ground at his feet. He reaches down to his belt and allows himself a smile.

'They will be dead soon, then we can return to the pressing matters at hand.'

The magos struts and pronounces each word with all the gravitas of a bored trade magnate. The exo-frame contorts, bending as though it were a giant squatting down to survey some tiny life form. Ivar struggles again. He feels like an insect, pinned in place by a curious and sadistic child.

'I will wipe your precious vessel clean of life,' it continues. 'Make slaves of your kinsmen and trophies of your battle-brothers. Locked together in a final tableau. There might be some poetry in that, at the end.' It tilts its entire artificial body just to move the head of the writhing knot of flesh chained within it. 'Your kind enjoy poetic verse, do you not? Sagas from out of your dreary past. Tedious and tiresome next to logic unchained.'

The forge thrums anew with his movements. Nyrandvari is the conductor, and the destruction that coils about them is its symphony, writ upon the universe.

Empyreal taps open in the exterior, forcing the uncontrolled warp through to writhe amidst the liquid metals. Faces and forms push their way up, droplets of hissing metal spitting from their non-flesh, screaming in limitless agony as they thrash in their own hells. The dishonoured dead, wights drawn up into their own torment. Ivar cannot tell if the howling tortured are loyalist or damned.

All are equal in their agony, no matter the gods or spirits they honour.

He shudders in his bonds. Acid claws at the back of his throat, melding with the copper tang of his own blood. Some part of him recognises that he has become a foundry in his own right. Alloying together his pain in the crucible of his own biology.

An irony for a practitioner of the healing arts. No Wolf Priest should be brought so low as this.

'You are too used to easy prey,' Ivar murmurs. He rocks himself in his binds and then spits onto the decking, a sizzling gobbet of blood and saliva. 'When was the last time your soldiers were truly tested?' He laughs weakly. 'Or perhaps it is by design, for a coward and a parasite.'

'Do you so yearn for death, lapdog?' it asks resignedly. 'All you accomplish is wasting your own breath and trying my patience.' A thought passes through it, and the blades extend from the end of an outstretched arm. 'Shall I pare out your multi-lung? Perhaps then we would see how well you breathe, hmm?'

'Unchain me then,' Ivar says. A slurring, rattling sound echoes out of him, near drowned amist the screams. 'Let me down and we'll see how quick your knives break.'

'Such pride,' Nyrandvari says.

'The Allfather gave us plenty.' He laughs again. 'Perhaps he passed over Mars when bastards like you were crawling about on its surface.'

The blades graze his throat, pressing against the dark and blood-streaked flesh. 'Do not tempt me, Sixth Legion. Your death would be a waste of resources, but the joy it would provide could be utterly incomparable.'

The magos pauses, knives clicking and shivering. It draws them back and turns. Nyrandvari's head snaps round and it begins to blurt again in binharic rage.

Something shudders in the great workings. Fuel lines ignite, casting enormous plumes of flame up and into the heart of the foundry. A great support sags, weeping its own rivers of liquid metal from the superstructure. Another explosion follows it. Closer now.

Ivar laughs again as he recognises the telltale detonation of krak grenades. 'Your false Omnissiah cannot protect you now,' Ivar whispers with glee. 'See how the Unmaker God comes for you, as all false works are laid low. Destruction itself.' He breaks down into exhausted joy.

Nyrandvari whirls about, robes flying in a storm of black. It lurches forwards, iron stilts clattering upon the central dais. It snarls like broken servos. 'Blasphemer!' Nyrandvari screams. 'What have you mongrels done?!'

The blades finally bite home, plunging into Ivar's chest. The Wolf Priest screams as his nerves catch fire, burning agony saturating his being. He feels the shock passing through him, grounding itself along the chains. His fingers knot and tighten, opening and closing in futility.

Ivar feels his hearts stop.

Then he feels them surge to life once more.

He screams. Each beat is brilliant, white-hot insanity. It hammers through him. Everything and nothing. Everywhere and nowhere. It fills and fuels him.

Forge and furnace. Burning together. Allfather protect me. Fenris!

His fingers lock tight about the chains and Ivar pulls himself up, swinging himself forwards.

His feet catch the magos squarely in its centre mass, slamming into it with a sickening crunch of birdlike bones. It staggers back, metal feet almost slipping out from under it as it struggles to maintain its balance. It grinds to the edge of the platform and wheels about, binharic rage spewing from it. Mechanisms click and realign, unfolding from beneath the robes and armatures. It fires a beam of crackling unlight.

Ivar drops. His whole weight sags in his restraints, lowering him from where he had hoisted himself up. The blast sears the chains apart, and he hits the decking with a wet and meaty thud.

The magos chitters as it stalks forwards, weapon primed and

aimed directly at Ivar's head. <A fine effort, Space Wolf, but there will be no respite for you. I look forward to seeing what I can make from your flesh.>

The air sizzles between them. Nyrandvari pushes the barrel closer, till it grazes Ivar's blood-slicked hair.

Ivar snarls. Adrenaline burns in his veins as he drives his fists against the floor and pushes himself up, overbalancing the magos and pushing it back. Ivar staggers like a drunkard, flailing from side to side, all grace abandoned. His muscles bunch as he stumbles, almost falls, and then grasps at the waiting crozius.

The weight of it almost breaks his unarmoured form. He hisses with the effort, whirling around and slamming the unpowered weapon towards the magos.

It cannot move fast enough. Tendrils whip out, trying in futility to knock the crozius aside, but the bladed wing tears into its throat. Ivar clings to it, like a drowning man to debris. Pulled along as the magos totters backwards, whining in binharic feedback.

Ivar growls, low in his throat. 'You are nothing. You have no power over me.' He thrusts the weapon forwards and then yanks it back in a spray of hissing ichor.

He watches the magos fall, gurgling, into the fire and the darkness.

CHAPTER THIRTY-ONE

FIRE WITHIN, FIRE WITHOUT

The climb might well destroy him. If so it would be a fitting end. Brynjar does not doubt that. He has resigned himself to the act. There is no greater sacrifice than to die for a brother. In service to the Chapter. For the strength of the pack.

He digs his gauntleted fingers into the mechanisms of the tower, while all around him is reduced to confusion and fire. On instinct his servo-arm reaches out and steadies him, biting into the rock and iron of a ledge.

There is only pain now. The darkness and the smoke closes in around him like a god's fist, as though the forge in its wounded fury could pry him from the walls. Brynjar holds on for dear life.

He looks up, forcing his hands to move. Each new choice propels him a little further. Closer to his goal, to the last flickering location marker that designates his brother.

Are you alive, Ivar? The kraken could not kill you. Neither will this petty monster.

A sudden scream snaps his attention up. Something hurtles past him, a flurry of black cloth, rusting iron and squirming flesh.

Brynjar almost laughs. 'Thus,' he growls, 'are all tyrants and blasphemers rewarded.'

He forces himself up. Over and over. Even the pain dulls as he scrambles higher, never looking back, only pushing himself onwards. Only allowing the summit to command his attention.

Brynjar pulls himself up and over the lip of the great raised dais, panting, soaked with sweat within his armour. He takes a moment to right himself, gaining his footing and his bearings as he looks around at the horror of what the forge truly encompasses.

So captivated by the vistas of hell that he almost misses the prize he has come for.

'Brother,' Brynjar hisses.

Ivar sprawls like some hunting trophy, an animal skinned and prepared for an obscene feast. His body is a tapestry of wounds, new cuts and violations warring over the old. Blood covers his brother's skin. It leaks in sluggish trails from his interface ports, from his eyes and ears. Ivar is a broken testament to woe and suffering, writ at the hands of the insane.

'Wondered...' Ivar slurs. His head rises weakly. 'If you would ever come.'

'Idiot,' Brynjar growls. 'Did you truly think I would leave anyone behind? Least of all you?'

'Help me, brother,' Ivar whispers. 'My armour. Bring me my armour. Please.'

Brynjar nods. He looks around at the pristine display of armour and arms, presented like a museum display with all the childish pride of its curator on show. He reaches out and then stops. Instead of plucking a piece from its mounting, he kneels low and begins to check at the belt.

'You must have something here that will make you hale enough to walk,' he growls.

Ivar murmurs something under his breath as Brynjar checks and rechecks. He undoes a small bottle and opens it. The herbal stink of it fills the air around them, even in the smoke and stench of the forge. He begins to apply it to Ivar's wounds, to the waiting interface ports. He stands again and walks over to the armour.

'Now, brother. Let us make you whole.'

Around them the forge contorts with new anger. All pretence of civility and order evaporates, though there was precious little being maintained. The grubby pretension of its master, enforced upon a construct grown wilful from its time in the hell-bright abyss.

The warp is upon everything, within and without. It burns and coils and curdles, wrapping the station in its infective whim. The intimacy of communion, of baleful and unholy unity, that the pretenders of Mars could only dream of.

<Did you think it would be so easy?> The voice hisses from all around. The forge trembles. Control valves rupture and spit fire, steam rising from every crack and crevice. The Hell Forge speaks and it screams, building to a howling crescendo of frustrated ambition. <Did you think that I was merely flesh and blood? That such a stunted form could contain my majesty? I am multitudes, cousin. I am an eternity which your pretender priests would never understand. I am the forge, and the forge is me. Such is my glory. Behold my wonder. Kneel in the dust of your failings and *understand* me for what I am. All that you have played at. All that you would yearn to emulate through your false fear and disgust.>

<What are you?> Brynjar cants as he works. Ivar suffers beneath his ministrations. Every connection between flesh and armour births new suffering. His hands are a blur as he sanctifies and checks his work. The unguents and balms have calmed the tremoring in Ivar's flesh, soothed the fever that burns within

him. He will live. That is what matters. He slides the other warrior's helm into place.

<I am Nyrandvari,> it says simply. <True son of Mars. Visionary upon the Eightfold Path. Architect of Sorrows.>

The tower drops beneath them.

Suddenly they are in freefall, the entire mechanism retracting through the core of the station, servos screeching as braking mechanisms try and fail to arrest the descent.

'No,' Brynjar growls. He moves quicker. So very close now. He pulls Ivar up against him, bracing the armoured form against his, holding his brother in place as mechadendrites find another interface port.

'Holy machine, know activation,' Brynjar intones.

Ivar's reactor burrs to life. Brynjar steps back, bringing his fingers together in the sacred cog of Mars. The platform shudders, jolting as the brakes finally lock. It seizes in place, and Brynjar mutters a grateful prayer. He reaches down and heaves the other warrior to his feet. 'Can you walk?' he asks.

Ivar's skull helm dips and nods, tilting one way and then the other as he seeks his balance. 'I can,' he growls. 'If it is the last thing I do, I will walk from this place.'

Swooping cherub-things, bat-winged and screeching, flap around them. A chorus of howling servo-skulls, crowned with iron spikes and fingerbones, blare into the air above them. In every perceivable alcove, the slaves of the forge stir. Hands twitch from their grim repose, seeking their weapons. Hatches scrape open with a gasp of dead hydraulics.

'You could have chosen better words,' Brynjar snarls. He raises his hammer. Ivar mirrors him, his movements still sluggish compared to the Iron Priest's fluid and methodical preparations. 'Regardless. We find a way, or we carve one.'

* * *

<We have gunnery control. The work crews are about their business. Praise the Omnissiah for timely restoration. Service as certain as if carved upon doctrinal wafers.>

Albertus-Nu's body is in constant motion. He stands at his lectern, borne aloft upon the backs of countless servitors. He moves with the surety of their iron tread, each of them a component in the great mechanism. All contributors to the opus machina.

<Toil is sacred! Praise the Machine God for the requirement of manual contributions. Flesh is weak and so it must feed the machine until subsumed by holy steel! Embrace this, children of the Omnissiah. Glory in your tasks.>

The ship's bellicose spirit stirs and struggles. This enforced serenity is anathema to a warship, even the least of them. Albertus-Nu can feel the displeasure as it radiates out from the enginarium, coiling in the very air. Noospheric frustration ripples above him, about him. The ship's choler is crimson and it blazes star-hot. Heat ripples surround the aged magos as he conducts the choir electric.

He is fire and light and fury. He is the guiding hand of the ship. All it requires is the second component in the ritual surety of command.

<Do you hear me, Garald Helvintr? Do you heed the readiness of the ship? Let us sail and kill. Permit me the chance to cleanse this abomination with shell and shot.>

Garald does not reply. He cannot.

He weaves and fires, ducking behind overturned supply crates and cogitator banks. He slams his back against the wall, armour and leather scraping and catching on the scarred metal.

Battle has tarnished every part of the ship, but here, towards the bridge, the expended wrath of the enemy seems all the keener. They have taken to vandalism and blasphemy with an enthusiasm that he would not have expected from the augmented and partly lobotomised soldiery of the Dark Mechanicum.

Twisted and perverted or no, they once cleaved to the same creed as the Mechanicus. Held the same beliefs. Could they really have deviated so absolutely, a schism so intense that it defied their ossified expectations?

Perhaps that is how heresy finally claims a man, when he ceases to worry about breaking with law and tradition.

His station gives him leeway, Garald knows. His father had always imparted that as sacred wisdom, that a rogue trader was beholden only to the Emperor. There were things he could do that others across the grand span of the Imperium could not. Entire domains had been carved out by such sanctioned largesse, added to the Emperor's dominions and yet nominally administered or governed by one of the dynasties.

Command. Control. The burden of rule.

Garald reloads his pistol and closes his eyes. He feels every breath he takes, every droplet of sweat that soaks his skin. Battle nerves wrack him and he presses back harder against the wall.

There is no room for weakness here. All there can be is frost and iron. The inheritance of his dynasty and the trust of his allies, settling upon him in a cold mantle. He feels the weight of it pressing down upon him.

Do you crumble, boy? Or do you bear it with grace, even as it burns your flesh with its chill?

Garald pushes off the wall and turns into the hail of fire, adding his own to the fury of the exchange. Bolt rounds detonate around the retreating enemies, the skitarii reduced to firing in random scattershot bursts.

Las fire fills the corridor in a wave of scarlet light, refracting off the raised shields. The Fenrisians laugh as they fight, pausing only to hurl grenades into the midst of their iron foes.

The skitarii's armoured fists snap out, knocking the primed explosives away with methodically casual backhands. The frag grenades hit the wall, barely having bounced before their short fuses detonate.

The first shieldbreakers sprint through the smoke and fire, axes raised, edges blazing as they sweep down through the murk. Heavyset and armoured for void-combat, the men and women of the assault units slam into the skitarii lines. Growling as they attack, over and over. The blades bite deep, gouging into the metal of the monstrous soldiery. One hews down so far that it takes off a skitarius' arm.

The iron monster flinches back, blood and oil pouring from the stump of its elbow. It blurts in alarm and pseudo-pain. The weapon falters in its grip, sagging down enough that the next blow catches it in the neck. The head tumbles free, hitting the ground and rolling to lie beside the severed arm. Both twitch with residual nervous feedback, spasming on the floor, as though seeking fresh victims.

A storm of shot hammers into the gap, reducing the twitching body to shards and shreds, lying in a pool of its own fluids. The other units click and whir, drawing closer together, stepping over their slain as they retreat towards the bridge.

Garald ducks low and rushes forward, gesturing ahead of him with his axe. The others move, war cries upon their lips, their own weapons readied. The stampede motion makes the deck rumble and tremor as though they were burning at full combat speed.

The walls of bodies clash.

Skulls are cracked by swinging maces and swords. Men and women drop only to be trampled underfoot with muted relish. The skitarii's eyes glow red as they fight. Even as they die.

Garald throws himself at the closest of them, taking advantage of its distraction.

'Too many foes, is it?' He laughs as he hits the thing square in its barrel chest. It pushes up at him, cybernetic limbs scrambling for purchase as he cuts and slashes at its metal skin with his powered axe.

Down amongst the dead and the dying, he forces the axe blade through the cyborg's shoulder.

Sparks claw at Garald's face, and he jerks back with a hiss of pain. Other hands reach down, pulling him up even as they pin the enemy and begin to take it apart in a manic frenzy. They scream and cheer as the skitarius finally comes apart. Limbs tear away in a shower of sparks and strange humours, gouting onto the floor, till the metal feels slick and tainted underfoot.

'Down!' a voice booms with its own tectonic fury.

It rings with a command so absolute that Garald's legs go out from under him. He falls to the floor with the others and rolls to one side, pressing himself against the walls of the corridor.

Bolt rounds hurtle through the fray and drive the armoured horrors back. Bursting apart in pinpoint-accurate explosions, tearing the enemy at the joints. An arm spins free amidst a screech of hateful scrapcode.

Iron gods of their own stride amidst the tumult.

The Space Wolves come in a slow, almost glacial advance. Loping through the fray, weapons raised and firing. Ytri is the first of them to break ranks, hurling himself forwards, laughing. Garald has never seen one of them laugh before. It is like watching a sword laugh or hearing the joy of artillery. A façade breaking. No longer simply the Angels of Death, but all the sins and glories of humanity magnified. Men wrought into weapons. Savage implements with the hearts of mortals, touched by the God-Emperor's light.

Ytri raises his great sword and the ragged edges of it crackle with murderous lightning, arcing between the notches in the blade. He heaves it down through one of the cybernetic monsters, parting it from crown to groin in a rush of unclean fluids and already disintegrating flesh.

'You like that, false-man?' he cackles, spinning around to swing for the central warrior. Its weapon jerks up, capacitors whining. The barrel dents as it catches the sword. The alpha's iron limbs twist, yanking it to one side.

Ytri's armoured fist snaps its head back savagely. It staggers and chitters, head tilted. Steam hisses from between plates lacquered in obsidian and crimson. Its entire being shudders apart, yawning open in a hideous maw. Blades and plasma-cutting torches unfold from the spreading plates. A breaking engine. A devourer.

It crunches closed around Ytri's right arm. Knives and fire click and whir over his armour, pinning him in place, etching their rancid patterns into the plate, seeking flesh and blood.

Ytri's blade slams against the thing's back, pommel smashing against it as he tries to dislodge it. The angles are all wrong. He screams in pain and anger. With all the hate and fury of his bloodline, he grabs at the skitarius and pulls hard, slamming it into the wall and then round.

The others understand. Bolter fire tears into it. The alpha bleeds sparks, oil and blood weeping from it, hitting the floor in droplets that sizzle like acid. It convulses around him.

Garald can only watch, seizing his moment, pushing himself onwards towards the bridge. Buoyed up by the presence of the Wolves.

'We sought you, lords!' he cries. 'And now you are the ones to save us!'

Another howling monster bounds through the smoke, body aglow with overworked implants. Molten metal pours from its mouth and eyes, a screaming rictus of machine-agony.

Odr meets it, throwing himself between the advancing thing and

Garald. He raises his bolter, already firing, shots detonating against glowing armour plates, bursting in the heat haze that surrounds it.

Ytri is screaming. The others, mortal and Astartes alike, are pivoting to meet the threat.

It raises immense claws, industrial killing implements, gnashing at the open air. Screaming through iron teeth filed to murderous points. They meet in mutual annihilation, like a sun meeting a singularity. Odr howls with pain and rage, falling back, blood gouting from his armour as the thing bursts apart like a bomb.

The air is filled with shrapnel and flame, with screaming and roared curses.

Garald almost tumbles to the floor. He staggers, guided by the crowd, feeling the impacts and support of their hands as they slap his back or move him forwards. He feels almost drunk. Lost to the thrill of battle, the rush of near-death.

The Wolves are venting their loss and their wrath, creating the space needed between the mortals and the monstrosities.

One of the mortal warriors is at his ear. 'Now you're fighting like a frostborn!'

He looks to her and nods back. 'What is your name?' he asks.

'Kaedra, lord. At your service.' She points ahead, through the gap that the wave of soldiers moves them inexorably towards. The doors of the bridge are wedged open, servos jammed. The once proud murals have been savaged, clawed at and defiled. Burn scars reach up to the heights with yearning and hate. An understanding from their masters that everything that bears honour should be destroyed.

'Spite,' he mutters. Kaedra glances at him as he speaks. He looks back and shakes his head. 'Never mind.'

'You've been too far away from it,' she says, and points. Together they stride through the doorway, under the wolves rampant and rune-etched metal. The silver and gold that once adorned it have begun to run, whether from heat or corruption he cannot tell. Garald's eyes flick down, following her finger.

The command throne.

His command throne.

All his life Garald has struggled to find his place. The weight of a responsibility and duty that he did not fully understand. He understands now.

This is where he belongs.

His fingertips brush the arm of it. He barely realises that he has already crossed the distance between the doors and the throne. He steps around it, looking at the artfully carved steel of it. Every angle perfect.

Garald sits.

The ship's spirit rises around him, anger saturating the air. The distant howl of wolves, building to a crescendo. Garald's hands move in time with it, lost in their own dance. Slaves to a symphony only he can hear.

<Do you hear me?> The voice is a machine-blurt through the ether. Binharic prayers cascade up through the trembling cogitator banks. Vox-horns begin to grind to life, converting the words into discernible Gothic.

'Do you hear me?'

'I hear you. Who speaks?'

'Albertus-Nu, Master of the Enginarium. The core systems have returned to us. We have command of the gun decks, Omnissiah be praised. All that remains is for systems coordination with the bridge. The precise angles are calculated. Inloading now.'

An honour guard forms around him. Warriors, armsmen and bridge crew. Those still living begin to limp and shuffle to their stations. Garald smiles and closes his eyes.

'We are ready.'

* * *

At her heart, the *Swift Spear* has always been a vessel of war.

A spurned and lesser daughter of the forge, fit only for picket duty or escort, it had been given to Garald Helvintr as a tacit insult and as a challenge. A minor position to master, before any true heights would be offered to him.

It is an old thing. Capricious and taciturn as though it can sense its own perceived inferiority. Yet the core of it, the very soul, *yearns* to be recognised for what it is. Not an afterthought.

A ship of war.

A *weapon*.

Caught in the great metal spider of the Dark Mechanicum, it struggles and howls. Tectonic tremors pass through its adamantine skin. Denied communion and vengeance alike.

Voices cut through the clamour. Soothing at first, growing in insistence. Acknowledging her majesty. Directing her wrath.

Even bound, the vessel can respond.

Minor thrusters engage and fire along her length, minute adjustments that slowly and ponderously turn her. An iota, by astronomic standards. But enough.

Albertus-Nu's holy firing solutions saturate her being. The commands of her captain ring true once more. Within her gunnery decks the liberated dedicate themselves once again to service. Chains, their massive links grinding in the darkness, finally lever the macrocannon shells into place.

<In the Omnissiah's name,> the magos' instruction rings out, <deliver your wrath.>

The flesh voice of her captain speaks a simpler prayer.

'Fire.'

CHAPTER THIRTY-TWO

HELLBREAK

The impact is a singular thing.

So close to the enemy's stronghold, enveloped and enfielded, the detonation scours the hull of the *Swift Spear* in fire and debris. The ship's flesh ripples and buckles. Compartments vent. Secondary airlocks snap shut as though by instinct alone. A flood of reactionary compensations as the ship suffers and crew die.

Cold corpses vent from raw apertures in the hull, all breath stolen, even before the forge or the warp alike consume them in their fires.

Yet the shell strikes true.

One of the immense arms that hold them in place explodes. Struck precisely at the joint, it ruptures apart, venting plasma and ignited promethium in great tsunamis of fire. The air itself screams, venting outwards in a mockery of the *Spear*'s own pain.

The forge howls its own agony. Carried on tocsin and alarum. Ringing with the tolling of unclean bells.

Like a nest of vermin stirred by a careless kick, so the maddened voice of Nyrandvari rouses every asset it still possesses to war.

'We must be close by now,' Ivar mutters, frustrated by his own progress.

His every movement feels mismatched, stunted. He might as well be the malformed clone vessel of Nyrandvari's limitless cruelty and black joy. His armour barely feels real, a stolen memory.

Am I still hanging from those chains? Has he corrupted my very mind? Is this real? Am I?

He could be mere meat for the machine. His armour already slag, his weapons repurposed for some vile end. Organs taken to be preserved in jars or added to a bleak display. Till he is just a brain and spasming nerves, locked forever in a fantasy that keeps him from screaming.

'Close enough,' Brynjar says. He turns and fires behind him again, a hand bracing Ivar's shoulder as he does.

Their pursuers are hideously mismatched, spider-legged things piloted by shrunken beings no better than servitors. Weapons platforms that lope and chatter, skulls nailed to their edges whose jaws move in a constant refrain.

Brynjar's first shot blows out the shoulder of one. It turns its head dumbly, looking down at the arm which lies upon the metal base of the platform, its only weapon taken from it.

'Keep moving,' Brynjar growls to Ivar.

Something explodes nearby as structural collapse ricochets through the forge. Next to the unfolding atrocity, Brynjar's grenade trick is a mere campfire flame. Everything sings with binharic hatred, scrapcode invectives clawing at every system, upon every frequency conceivable.

Ivar laughs. 'Think we've upset our host.'

'It'll have to accept our apologies,' Brynjar says with a chuckle. He fires again and then pushes Ivar onwards. 'Keep moving,' he says again. 'The sooner we get to the ship…' He trails off.

'Don't worry, brother,' Ivar grunts. The pain rouses once more. Fresh and terrible, setting his nerves ablaze. His skin burns with fever, crawling until he shivers within his armour. 'I don't plan on burdening you with a corpse.'

'If you died, who would fix the others, eh? Which of us would tend to the dying and take back the legacy of the Chapter? Who would drone on in the dark and the cold?'

'Maybe Vili,' the Wolf Priest muses.

'Enough of this,' Brynjar says. 'No more melancholy, or I will beat you to death here, myself.'

'Decades, waiting for that opportunity.' Ivar laughs. He hunches over, coughing up blood within his helm. 'Skitja,' he mutters. 'The enemy's craft has been fierce.'

'I have never yearned for a chance to humble you, brother,' Brynjar says. He fires again, pausing only to reload. 'We were little more than children then, fresh recruits destined for different moulds within the forge. No more. You have always had my respect, and my brotherhood.'

'Thank you, brother,' Ivar whispers, his head lowered. 'My wounds must be great if you are reduced to this flattery.'

'Oh, shut up, Wolf Priest,' Brynjar snarls, and laughs. 'Look.' He gestures ahead with his hammer. 'Almost at the gates of the ship.'

He lifts Ivar, supporting him under his shoulder, both of them limping along like one of the magos' unhinged servants. The docking spur they hurry down shudders again. Cracks spread throughout the iron and stone, tension ratcheting through the mechanisms. Belts snap and flick free, chains whip. Overworked cogitators finally detonate in riots of daemonic fire.

'One last thing to do,' Ivar mutters.

He reaches down to his belt, nudging aside the chained bottles of unguent and tincture. Fingers drift over blades and needles, before finally settling upon the stocky solidity of a grenade.

Brynjar nods. 'A fine sacrament. A final one'

The ship is sealed when the docking umbilical finally dies.

Whatever pursuers had risked its unstable bulk, crawling and skittering after the two Space Wolves, have as their last thoughts frustration and fear. Not fear of the roaring detonation which claims them, body and soul, but of failure and the wrath that their master will exhort, even after death.

Their final binharic screams echo against the hull, carried out in the wave of the explosion, drowning in the warp, committing themselves to the ringing madness of the forge.

In the heart of it, a struggling mind contorts. Heir to a hundred bodies, but beholden only to one, the Architect of Sorrows reasserts itself. New anger floods the armatures of the forge, the very fabric of it yoked to its singular will. The augmented and enshrined brain of Nyrandvari, the miles of nervous tissue it has cultivated throughout the obscenity of its domain.

Pain. Insanity. Anger. So very *mortal* of it.

Every part of it, flesh and iron, seizes. It clamps tight. Blades and cutting tools as vast as freighters vent their choler in one final act of defiant avarice.

One of them plunges home even as the ship's engines flare and push it off. Lesser boarding tubes snap and splinter away, raining metal and armaglass down upon the lower reaches of the fane.

The blade strikes the *Swift Spear* like the tail of a scorpion, black lightning screaming down its length. Scrapcode wails through it in a toxic tide. The ship snaps free, studded with multiple barbs, like a pinned sea-beast. It turns away, burning hard.

The Geller fields of the *Swift Spear* convulse. In her sanctum Narayis screams, even as her eyes are locked wide, her guidance saturating the ship.

Garald feels the synaptic agony of the ship in his throne, pulsing through the entirety of the command space. Consoles blow out in rains of fragments. The lumens flicker in mad configurations before shattering.

The light strobes from white to crimson, over and over. Somewhere the adepts upon the bridge begin to howl in pain.

Below, Albertus-Nu pulls himself free from the dais in a flurry of cables, quickly folding his secondary arms across his chest into the configuration of the cog.

<Omnissiah, vouchsafe me from corruption. Protect the integrity of circuit and synapse that–>

<IMMATERIAL TRANSLATION IMMINENT. TRUST IN THE MACHINE, THE MACHINE IS LIFE.>

The magos barely has a moment to compensate before reality hits them like a hammer blow.

'ILLUMINATION'

Ritual. Meditation. Dream.

Lesser men would have lost their sanity at such unending routine. Onouris prides himself on his discipline, honed down these long years of struggle and vigilance. Pain is an illusion, as ever it was. He knows himself to be master of his own flesh. Captain of his pernicious soul.

Ritual. Meditation. Dream.

The specifics differ enough to keep it interesting. Sometimes his thoughts soar upon philosophical zephyrs, contemplating all that has befallen them. Desperate to glean some understanding of the great designs that bind the universe. Ancient mysteries and bleak wonders, the works of races long since vanished or changed, before mankind even crawled from the primordial muck.

Other days – insofar as days still have any true meaning – he focuses upon the arts martial. He revisits the old lessons, walking through them as easily as any other memory palace. Old aches crackle through his form, astral and physical, as he remembers the punishments for ill-discipline.

The flat of a curved blade striking the small of his back. A gentle tut of judgement. The sun beating down upon him till his augmented musculature shimmers with sweat and every movement is a heat haze.

His mind exalts. It sings. Even now, distracted and separate from his flesh, he holds one hand out. In the air before him, his bolter hovers, partly deconstructed. His brow furrows as he relives another memory of pain.

Ritual. Meditation. Dream.

He transmutes the base into lustrous perfection. Every tiny gesture of his fingers provokes a new reaction. Components come apart and re-form. He knows each of them intimately. He has lost count of how many times he has put his gifts to this purpose, the act of weapons maintenance so natural now that it is instinctual, muscle memory.

Perfection in mind and body is essential for the works to come. He must honour his father with nothing less. A perpetual quest for knowledge and understanding. To dispel the only true evil.

Onouris remembers an old tale from his studies, etched into the ponderous archives of the Apocrypha Terra. That even the gods, in their labours of creation, rested at least once.

Here, where there is no time, and no true respite, he denies himself that privilege.

It is the domain of gods to indulge themselves. We mere mortals are only able to content ourselves with toil.

He opens his eyes.

Onouris' fingers close into a fist. The components tremble in mid-air and then contract. Tiny motes of lightning drift between them as they reunify. Clicking together, one after another. He sighs and lowers his hand, letting the bolter follow it gently to the table before him. He lays it down upon a length of crimson silk, admiring the contrast between the black and red.

The walls of the chamber are crafted from pure thought. Cold white stone, carved in precise angles by the masons of his mind. Banners hang from some of them, scarlet fabric fluttering lightly in the breeze, woven through with silver and gold threads that catch the beautiful light.

'It is always more glorious than you remember, brother,' Qar says.

Onouris looks around. The other warrior leans against a column, arms folded, watching him with bemused detachment. His helmet rests on the edge of an ornamental balcony. Blue and gold glimmer in the false sun. Even the sight of it brings a swell of pride to Onouris' hearts, accompanied by a faint sadness.

'Aren't all things?' Onouris replies. 'We build these temples to memory, in our minds and souls. The ideal versions of ourselves and all we wished to accomplish.'

'Pretty dreams, but nothing more,' Qar says and steps forwards. He flexes his arms and meanders towards the table. He nods down at the reassembled bolter. 'You are getting better.'

'I was always good at this, brother,' Onouris begins, but Qar interrupts him with a chuckle. He sweeps his arm around.

'Ah, but you are out of practice. Are you not?' He laughs. 'Too busy being lost in your dreams.'

'Dreams can build empires, brother.'

'As easily as lies,' Qar counters. 'There is no greater burden in an empire of deceit than to be a seeker after truth.'

'That is why we are here.'

'Is it?' Qar muses. 'I thought we were simply watchdogs. Guarding eternity. Whichever delusions you must spin for yourself.'

'Unbecoming,' Onouris says. He meets his brother's gaze. 'What we do here has purpose. We play our part.'

'Perhaps,' Qar says. 'Or this is some punishment, taking us away from where we are most needed. All the scrying in the universe cannot save us from irrelevancy.'

Onouris' tanned skin crinkles with distaste. He reaches out with his left hand, sweeping the bolter to one side. His other takes hold of a quill. 'We will be remembered, brother. I can assure you of that.'

'Promises are cheap, brother. We have all clung to oaths for too long. To Emperor and Imperium. Gene-sire and Legion. What has it bought us?'

'It gave us purpose,' he says. 'Even in despair.'

CHAPTER THIRTY-THREE

SHIPDEATH AND DOUBT

All ships can fall to bitter death.
To ice and seas that strangle breath.
He fights, by Russ, in search of fate.
So near, as storms and foes abate.
A journey winds and weaves its route
Yet all can be undone by doubt.

Shipdeath.

It is the great fear of every voidfarer, to have your ship die under you.

The engine decks are silent. Despite the best efforts of his thralls, of the enginseers and tech-adepts, the ship lies quiescent and dead. Mauled by Nyrandvari's final spite.

'May all the spirits of death and vengeance take that monster,' Brynjar growls to himself.

<In cant, if it please the honoured Iron Priest.> Magos Albertus-Nu shuffles forwards, balanced upon the iron spikes which have long since replaced his legs. His red robes would have trailed

upon the decking were it not for the shrunken coterie of servitors that limp and scuttle behind him, holding the fabric up in grubby, oil-stained iron fingers. <In the darkness of system failure, so is the light and radiant speech of the Omnissiah required more than ever.>

<Forgive me, magos,> Brynjar responds. His own binharic is a terse snarl. <What say you? Will the reactor sing once more?>

Two smaller mechanical arms unfurl from the magos' robes, knotting together in contrition while his other arms gesture round to the vast ranks of machines looming like mausoleums in the darkness.

<They are wounded, perhaps critically.> Albertus shakes his head. The vox-grille set where his lower jaw and throat once sat whines with feedback. <The works of the unspeakable schismatics, all hate of the Omnissiah be upon their redacted memory, have grievously assaulted the core infrastructure of the holy machine. I have requisitioned work crews in order to facilitate the work.>

<Analogue methodologies must prevail, I assume.>

<I have dispatched able runners from amongst the serf cadres. Should they survive they will bring all able personnel to us, in order to facilitate repairs.>

<And if they do not survive?>

<Then we shall send more serfs.> He gestures dismissively. <Until the optimum outcome is achieved. Blood spilled in the name of the Omnissiah is but lubrication for the splendour of the machine. Praise be unto the Machine God for this bounty of flesh!>

<As quickly as we are able,> Brynjar cants. <We should spread lesser adepts throughout the deck to adhere a noospheric communion net, once our resources are consolidated.>

<Wise. Very wise. You are not as much a savage as others might

believe. Fenris and Mars would be proud of the wisdom they have hammered into your bones.>

<Let us worry more about the bones of the ship, magos.>

<You make a reasonable hypothesis. Bless the Omnissiah for granting you such logic.>

'I seek the Priest Brynjar!' a flesh voice calls from above. A Naval ensign, undershirt soaked with sweat, his jacket discarded. He practically bowls over the railing on one of the high gantries. A handheld stab-lumen flashes wildly in his right hand. A data-slate is held awkwardly under his left.

The boy is young. Not Fenris-born. The frost and fire have not marked him. He pants like a grox, slumping at the iron railings, clinging to them as though he might collapse.

<One of yours?> Brynjar cants to the magos.

Albertus-Nu chirrups in binharic amusement. <Oh no. Not one of ours at all.>

'State your business!' Brynjar calls up. 'There is much work to be done.'

'Word from the bridge, lord. The lord captain demands a status report.'

<Demands!> Albertus-Nu chirrups, his hands clapping together in a rattle of bemusement. <He remains an amusing aberration, so very bold!>

'Enough,' Brynjar grumbles, before he turns his attention back to the runner. The boy stares up at him with undisguised awe, jaw moving as he struggles to form words. Brynjar laughs and steps forward. 'Return to your master. Tell him that the servants of the Omnissiah are well aware of our plight. The ship will be readied. Our course will be righted.'

CHAPTER THIRTY-FOUR

THE WYRMS OF DOUBT

There is nothing more caustic than doubt, yet now we drown in it.

The thought burns bright in Ivar's mind, refusing to flee as he pushes himself up from the berth within the apothecarion, hissing with every movement.

'Healer, tend to your own wounds,' he mutters. An old tribal aphorism. 'You cannot save others if you are broken yourself.'

What would the Slayer think of me now? Lost and alone. Broken and bloodied. And for what? For pride? Glory?

He finds his feet unsteadily, milling around the apothecarion like an invalid. Ivar reaches out and lets his fingertips trace along the smooth metal and plastek of the work tables. Still stained with his blood. Nerves still spasm with phantom pain, bone-deep. Soul-deep. Etched into his very being by the timeless malice of Nyrandvari.

The ship is dark and silent around him.

Perhaps this is death? Perhaps I have passed beyond Morkai's gate and this is some shadow of the world. A phantom of the Underverse. That would be fitting, I think.

He feels entombed. A sepulchral pressure crowds in about him. Ivar feels, in that moment, how he imagines the honoured dead within the Dreadnoughts must feel. A living death bound to cold iron and darkness, forever separated from the light and warmth beyond. Condemned to the deep shadows of the Aett, just as the Fell-Handed is.

Darkness and dreams are forever the reward of service, it seems.

'Where are the others?' he whispers to himself. 'Where are my brothers?' Ivar almost laughs. 'The warriors of my wyrd. Victims of my pride.' The thought brings a spasm of pain through his ruined flesh. Still bonded to his armour, enshrined in his agony.

There is no vox. No light. His sight has compensated, flesh and machine both, and yet the absence weighs heavily upon him. He winces again as he moves to the door.

No response.

The old stories resurface in his mind, riven through with white-hot pain. The ships of the dead that haunt the Underverse, piloted by blind and screaming wights. Chained to the mechanisms, jaws rattling impotently in their worm-eaten skulls.

Beyond the door such horrors could await him. Ivar is not even sure that his own flesh persists within the armour. He too could be pallid and crab-eaten. Less than nothing. Just a phantom bound to old routines.

'I am not a ghost,' Ivar growls. 'I am Ivar Krakenblood.'

The door grinds. Ivar steps back, hands reaching for a weapon. His crozius remains absent. Fingers close around a scalpel, plucking it up from one of the benches, clenching it in a ceramite grasp. Ivar can feel the metal of the handle deform under his grip. He realises he is trembling.

He looks to another of the benches and sees what remains of Odr. His brother died uglily, and well. So little remains of him, barely half of his torso. Enough that there is still hope of recovering his legacy for the Chapter.

Ivar hears the grinding again.

Fingers hook themselves around the gap in the doorframe, pulling the door open by force. Struggling against the recalcitrant locking system. A final heave of effort and it slides open.

Vili leans into the chamber.

'Wolf Priest,' he says with a nod. Jolfr crowds in beside him, face marred with concern. He has allowed Vili the honour of the liberation, even though the trials have blunted his youthful exuberance. Vili bows his head, his awe yet unbowed. 'It is good to see you hale.'

'Brothers,' Ivar says. He hisses as he moves. 'What news?'

Jolfr laughs. 'Ever hunting, aren't you? We came here to make sure you weren't dead.'

'I never thought you would be,' Vili puts in quickly. Jolfr looks at him and scoffs. 'You are hard to kill, brother.'

'Enough,' Ivar growls, wincing. Pain wars with frustration within his veins. 'What news?'

'We're dead in realspace,' Jolfr says at last. 'Whatever last spite the Dark Mechanicum hurled at us, it left us floundering. Near enough a blind jump along your ancestor's path.'

'Throne damn them all,' Ivar says. 'The path is the path. Brynjar will–'

'We shall see if the Iron Priest can solve these miseries,' Jolfr says. He puts a steadying hand on Ivar's shoulder. 'The sooner we can move the ship the better.'

'Where are the others? Bloodiron Wrath?'

'Licking their wounds, no doubt.' Vili scowls. 'The vox is silent.'

'We will find them,' Ivar says. 'We are all sons of Fenris. Alive or dead, no ship is a mystery to us.'

* * *

Work crews trudge the corridors in uneasy silence, guided by hand gestures and the hissed binharic of the tech-priests. Days are spent in desperate toil as the Iron Priest and the Magos of the Enginarium work to restore primary systems.

Time passes like a fitful nightmare, weighing relentlessly on the psyche of all.

The ship remains a corpse. Perhaps nothing will change that and no amount of struggle or toil will restore wholeness to what has been shattered.

Garald shakes aside the thoughts and wipes sweat from his brow. He grunts and pulls at the burned-out cogitator bank, trying to lever it onto the waiting cart. He no longer wears the hunting leathers of the Helvintr. He has stripped down to his undershirt, the jacket discarded. He stops, rubbing the dirt from his hands onto his trousers.

We all have our parts to play. Those were the Wolf Priest's words after he had finally found his way to the bridge. Wounded but not broken. Just as Garald prayed the ship was.

'Let me help with that,' a voice calls.

Velaq hurries over, joining him at the end of the cogitator. They heave it across together, letting it clatter into place, the cart straining beneath the weight.

'You shouldn't try to do so much alone, lord,' she says, rubbing at the back of her neck. 'We need our leaders hale more than ever now.'

He laughs. 'We need all the hands we can muster if we're to get the ship moving once more.'

'And set what course?' she asks. He looks at her, at the tan brow narrowed in frustration. The nervous sheen of sweat, not born from effort but from worry. 'Even if we don't die here... will we make it back to safe harbour?'

Garald sighs. 'That... remains to be seen.' He leans against the cogitator, soot staining his bare arms. He pats at it, trying to clear the marks from his pale skin. He only seems able to spread it, like a creeping taint. 'The Wolves will set our course.'

'If they can find an accord,' she whispers.

'Mind yourself,' Garald hisses. 'We cannot give them cause for injury or alarm. They serve the Imperium, the same as we do. They will not steer us wrong.'

'As you say, lord,' Velaq replies. She pats the cogitator. 'The sooner we are in motion the better.'

'Truest thing I've heard in some time,' Garald says, allowing himself to laugh.

'We have been made madmen by this,' Brynjar growls. 'The All-father has damned this quest! Root and branch! Woe after woe has chased us down. Made sport of us.'

'We have weathered worse, brother,' Ivar grunts. Every movement hurts, low pulses of agony saturating his being. He can feel the ache in his organs, radiating through his bones and muscles. 'Hold your nerve. Glory awaits.'

'Glory!' Brynjar slams his hand against the dead projection table between them. 'Still you persist with this! This pursuit almost killed you. It almost killed all who follow you! And for what? Your damned need to be a legend!'

They have met alone in one of the ship's many briefing chambers, as dead and abandoned as any other part of the ailing vessel. No honour guards. No representatives of the crew.

Ivar laughs coldly. 'And yet here we stand.'

'Do we, brother? You seem barely able to manage it.' Brynjar scowls. 'This is how we die, Ivar. For your pride and your failings. You have done this to us.' His finger jabs at Ivar's armoured chest, pushing him back with each accusing thrust.

'Enough!' Ivar snaps, seizing Brynjar's wrist. He forces the other warrior back with a single shove. 'I will do what is expected of me. Now tell me, what news of the repairs?'

Brynjar snarls with frustration as he drums his fingers against the console, balling his hand into a fist. 'Slow. Methodical. The magos has taken charge of it. He understands the gravity of the situation. He will kindle its heart anew, or we will all freeze to death. Assuming the oxygen does not bleed away first.'

'That is no end for a warrior, brother. It will not be our end.'

'Is that your vow, Ivar? Just as we would pursue this path to Gorm and no further? That we would return to Fenris in honour? In triumph?'

'I have done what is necessary.'

Brynjar laughs bitterly as he turns his back upon Ivar. 'Necessary for who, Krakenblood?'

'Brynjar–'

'There is work to be done, brother. I have your mess to contend with.' He pauses in the doorway and growls, low in his throat, before he passes into the deeper darkness.

CHAPTER THIRTY-FIVE

BASE MATERIALS

Kaedra coughs and spits to one side, wincing when she catches sight of the red-and-black streaked spittle. She is lying on her back, half hanging out of a maintenance grating while a red-robed tech-adept hovers about her, clucking instructions through a vox-grille that covers his entire lower face. Bellows wheeze in his chestplate, rising and falling in a faltering cadence.

'Carefully extricate the cogitation node,' he warbles.

'What?' Her left foot lashes out, the boot catching the adept in one of his metal legs. He squawks in some cogboy curse and then leans closer. 'Speak Gothic, damn you!'

'Remove the round machine component from its crevice. It should lie just before your ocular range. Even you could not miss the component in question.'

'Hot as a fire mountain in here and twice as cramped. If you're trying to cut me up for parts, there are easier ways, cogboy.'

'In an ideal universe we would work with far more suitable tools towards a perfect end. Alas, we do not occupy that faultless state. We must make do with what the Omnissiah has provided.'

'If I could be anywhere else, Allfather knows I would,' she grumbles. Her hair has tumbled loose. Days have passed with no opportunities for bathing. Barely any time for rest. Kaedra can't even remember the last time she pissed.

Dehydration hasn't helped with that. She feels as stripped down as any one of the Mechanicus adepts. Even servitors have their chances to recharge.

Only suffering feeds and only the dead have seen an end to woe.

'What I wouldn't give for a song of cunning escape and triumph,' Lyf grumbles. The big man hefts a bundle of cables upon his shoulder, tight enough that they cut into his neck. 'Know any like that, skjald?'

'I might know one or two. A lover fleeing across the ice from a jealous husband, before the righteous vengeance finds him. The drake's dance from out of the dread pit Alaxxes. Wheels of fire within the sea of stars. Many and more I know. None entirely fit for here and now, mind.'

'Pity,' he grunts as he lowers the bundle. 'Could have used some inspiration. That's what you trade in, aye?'

'Has been known,' she mutters and slides out from under the grating. She smears oil onto her knees and wipes grease from her forehead. 'Any word on if we're making any differ-ence here?' She looks at the tech-adept quizzically, even as he descends into a flurry of binharic somewhere between prayer and admonishment.

'No word's come down yet,' Lyf says.

The only light comes from hand-lumens, from scavenged lumen-globes or servo-skulls, or from the magi themselves. The Mechanicus are ubiquitous throughout the ship, an intercon-nected web of communication, illumination, and expertise.

Kaedra has never spent so much time around the Martians

or any of their ilk. Even servitors were a revelation to her when she finally came to the Uppland. Thralls, broken in spirit and strengthened in body. Offered up on the altar of the Allfather, the better to serve His will.

When she first saw one, all dead grey skin and poorly maintained implants, she had thought it an Underverse horror from the old stories. A wight finally digging itself from its shipwreck grave to drag her from her home and devour her amidst the snowy wastes.

Now she recognises the honour it represents. A sacrament, serving as either reward or punishment. A creed she can respect for its brutal and direct simplicity.

The lights flicker.

Kaedra's jaw drops. She looks up, starting forward. All the others begin to clamour and point. The adept blurts aloud and then folds his hands upon his chest in the mark of the cog.

'Is this it?' Kaedra asks. She nudges the crimson-clothed shoulder of the adept. 'Have we done it?'

He caterwauls in binharic, like an animal sensing an oncoming disaster. Barely half a minute has passed since the ship's systems breathed life into its bones once more. Half a minute until the light dies, mourned only by their howls of frustration.

'Well, skitja,' she curses.

Ivar finds little joy in reflection.

He walks the ship alone, devoid of brother or guide. Every step is haunted by Brynjar's words just as every new revelation is a barb against his soul. Dead systems greet him at every turn. The ship bears scars, wounds upon its form and spirit that might never heal. A full accounting of the damage would take months, he has no doubt. An interminable amount of time wasted in dry dock, restoring it to former glory. Resupplying it with arms and manpower.

So many dead.

Brynjar and Albertus work with scraps, struggling to effect repairs to the best of their ability. Bending every resource at their disposal to a task that is not simple survival for them but a matter of faith.

Has that certainty been pared away by Nyrandvari's works? Am I still Ivar Krakenblood, son of Fenris? Warrior of the Rout? Or did he die within the forge of hell, his mind and soul stolen away to live a half-life in service to false gods? Cold and screaming beneath the Underverse's tides?

Fear is anathema to him. Doubt should not touch him, yet even now its claws savage his soul. Ivar girds himself. Each step is a triumph. Every moment is another breath stolen from the hands of the shrunken magos.

I live. I endure. Not a figment. Not a memory. No ghost nor wight. I am Ivar Krakenblood.

The surety quickens his step. New strength surges through his maimed nerves and tormented muscles. The pain flickers within his flesh, leaching into his armour. The plates tremor unbidden, exaggerated by the reactions of the artificial muscle fibres.

Were he laid out upon his own slab, at the mercy of his own knives, he could make a swift accounting of his ailments. A Wolf Priest should be capable of that, at the very least. To judge a brother's flesh and spirit. Tend to their soul and their body. Break them. Remake them. Shape them into the proud warriors they ought to be.

Just as he has been shaped. Moulded for some great purpose by the hands of the Allfather, or Russ, or any number of capricious and contrary gods and spirits. Perhaps even Mother Fenris herself reached down to make him who he was, weaving the cold fire of home into his bones.

Perhaps that is enough. It could be. No great destiny or glorious last stand. No wyrd worthy of the sagas. Just service. Duty. Honour. Knowing when to turn back…

Frost crunches beneath his boots. Heat bleeds from his armour, the hot, acrid exhalations of a weary predator upon the plain. Ready to slump down in the snow and die, bones returning to the soil, or to be gnawed at by scavengers.

Just as the ship is dying, embracing its own fate.

Soon the slow poison of oxygen deprivation will creep in. For the base humans melancholy will fade into mania, even a kind of euphoria, before death swallows them down. That is one of the faces that death has chosen to wear as it comes for them.

'There will be no cowards' deaths for us,' he says. 'Blade to blade we will meet our fate. Whatever it shall be.'

He looks up. He looks *out*. His meandering course has brought him here, to one of the ship's observation bays. Gilded monsters surround the great aperture like pinned trophies, all the horrors of the void tamed and slain by Helvintr hands, rendered dull beneath the dead lumens and starlight. Another time, another place, it might have been impressive, but all past joy has fled.

We may as well be displayed. Trapped, mocked. The fates have damned us all. I have…

Ivar growls to himself. He reaches out, bracing the flat of his palm against the statuary. He looks down and drums his knuckles against it. 'How has it come to this?' he whispers.

'The Allfather must hate us,' Ytri growls, and then looks at Vili. 'Some of us, at the very least.'

Jolfr laughs and steps up beside his brother. Their gallows humour rattles from the walls of the meeting hall, and the hanging banners stir with it. They need no light to see, their eyes shining in the darkness.

'We have been helping where we can,' Vili says. His body

trembles with constrained energy, all his youth bleeding away into the cold of the ship. 'The Iron Priest and the Mechanicus are working to restore the *Swift Spear*'s soul to its bones.'

'A foul thing to have the two be separated,' Ytri says with a nod. 'Still, any work that gets us moving once more is good work. The sooner we are away from this cold and dead place the better.'

'Afraid?' Jolfr laughs. 'Thought you were tough as iron and twice as stubborn.'

'Not enough to make me an idiot,' Ytri grunts. 'We have all lost too much for that.'

Again the mood sours. 'Indeed we have,' Vili says at last. 'Odr died as a hero. Glorious to the end. No son of Russ could ask for better.'

'Better than defending a coddled lordling who has never known the ice?' Ytri says.

'Than dying in service to the Allfather.'

'Aye, that I can accept,' Ytri says at last. 'He will dine at the Allfather's right hand. Drinking, feasting, and fighting for all time.'

'Would that we should all be so blessed,' a voice cuts in.

Ivar limps into the chamber through one of the many forced doors. He winces with every movement, wounds weighing heavy upon him.

'I had not thought to see you, Wolf Priest,' Ytri says with a nod. 'I half thought you ready for a sarcophagus.'

'No interment for me,' Ivar grumbles. 'Not yet.' He looks around. 'You have all done well. Despite everything. We endure no matter what the universe throws at us. You are heroes, worthy of the sagas. Fenris will remember our names, until the very Wolftime.'

'Pretty words.' Ytri laughs. 'If only I could trust them.'

'Doubt them all you like, brother, but do not doubt my sincerity,' Ivar says simply. 'We move forward together or we die, unremembered, in the dark.'

'He is right,' Brynjar says.

The Iron Priest stands in the doorway, arms folded across his chest, looking at the gathered warriors before he walks to stand beside Ivar.

'Brother,' Ivar says cautiously.

'I came to tell you that the repairs are almost completed. Albertus-Nu expects complete ignition within a matter of hours. Then we can be under way.'

'Thank you, brother,' Ivar says.

'We have all suffered,' Brynjar says. 'We continue to suffer. If we succumb to our doubt and despair, we will never return to the hearth.' He pauses. 'I cannot condone all you have done, Ivar, but there is no malice in your heart. Pride, hubris, arrogance… But you would never put your brothers at risk for glory alone. You serve the Chapter's will.'

'All I can do is try to do so,' Ivar says, nodding.

'Then let us see where this road leads.'

<Kindle the fire of the Machine God!>

Albertus-Nu strides along the quiescent walkways of the enginarium, flanked by censer-swinging servitors. He reaches up with all four of his arms, stirring at the air like a mad conductor. All around him there is motion. Work crews dart from station to station, serfs heave coal into furnaces, servitors click and rattle in their berths.

<Defy the enemies of man! Thwart the alien with the purity of technology! For the void belongs to mankind, and the sacred union of Terra and Mars!>

He pulls a series of levers and breakers, alternating each one in holy rhythm. Light flickers around him, rising from the great plasma conduits, drawing up and then retreating like the waves of an ocean.

<He has set fire in the firmament and given us the tools to tame it! He speaks with the voice of the electromagnetic spectrum! He resonates in the very flesh of creation! Praise the Omnissiah, who has given such bounty unto us!>

He pulls the last levers and his fingers hammer at runic keys. The whir around him builds to a crescendo.

<Let there be illumination!>

'THE LOST CHILD'

'Brother?'

Onouris has grown to hate the quiet and the dark. When the light fades and the silence falls, when the work stalls and he must linger in his own memories. It tastes like dust and ashes here. The silence only ends when he can hear the screams of the dying and the wounded.

Everything becomes a smear of firelight and the shadows of falling bodies.

Wolves begin to howl, somewhere distant. Carried on the carrion winds of artillery detonations, ringing like the sounding of a horn. He stiffens, body recoiling at the sound. Anger and sorrow surge within his hearts. He tries to steady himself, as though he might fall to the ground and weep.

'We are so close,' Onouris whispers. 'Brother? Can you see it?'

There is no answer.

Onouris reaches out and takes hold of his staff, using it to lever himself up from where he has been reclining. Distant thunder and orbital bombardment light the chamber he finds himself in.

Outside the trees are burning, withering in the kindling winds. The white stone is stained with soot, gummed with powdered human remains. Here and there only shadows linger, burned into the stonework.

It is an end, of sorts. A final act of punctuation upon their golden epoch. Driven home by a spiteful culture that had never truly welcomed them.

'We thought we served the only good,' Onouris sighs. 'Yet we were so ignorant, even to the end. Weren't we, brother?'

Qar does not answer. He lingers in the shadows. Onouris lets his eyes close, lets the tears trace their way down his cheeks. To stand here in the utter collapse of their achievements hurts too much to give voice to. He understands that.

There would be other, later, pains. Wounds that would never heal. Losses beyond count. All passion and intent torn away and cast to the wind, hidden and nurtured down the long centuries, metastasising into millennia. Slumbering in a warp-spun chrysalis until the appointed hour of return. To reign again, free from the confines of their own hell.

To build an empire of substance. Of purpose. One that will nurture the true potential of the human species. That was our goal, was it not?

He can barely remember.

'I understand now. I know the realm as it was, father,' he says at last. 'Our realm. Worlds of learning. Vaults of knowledge. Do you remember it too, my brother?'

Qar holds his peace, haunting the ruin as a spectre in a tale might. He waits in contemplative silence.

'Has your patience run out at last, my brother?' Onouris laughs, if only so he will not weep. 'Bitter monologues screamed into the dark do not quite match up to philosophical musings.' He looks around. 'Even these quaint surroundings, hardly the most refined of salons, have now fallen to ruin.'

Scrolls lie half-burned across the broken desk. Sheaves of parchment have caught on the splintered edges. Leaves of vellum blow along the floor. There are human bones alongside them. Shattered and burned, the detritus of attendants or scholars.

'We are not what we were.'

The words hang in the air, near lost amidst the smoke and conflagration. The darkness crowds in around him, borne down upon the storm clouds that foul the sky. A city of glass and white marble drowning in fire and blood.

Everything is sullied and stained. With ash and gore. With shame and old failings. He cannot bear to relive it. Not again. Yet memory is fickle. It ebbs and flows like the tides. Sometimes he dreams of transcendent undertakings. Past glories writ large upon the canvas of his dreams.

'It is upon us at last,' he whispers. 'The hour of judgement once again.' Onouris shakes his head. 'We cannot escape the echoes of our own fall.'

The shadows wheel above, black even against the smoke of the burning city. Carrion birds scream and the ships that scar the sky howl with them.

'I wish you were here, brother. Truly. I wish you could understand what I am trying to achieve. What we are shaping here.'

I do not wish to be here. I do not want this fate. I wish, with all my heart, that I could set it right once more. Why does it never change?

Onouris raises his hands and psychic fire kindles around his fists. Where the flaring unlight touches, the ruin begins to fade away. Drifting like smoke, unmaking the stone as though it were burning paper. A child's fabrication. A dream that must die, as all dreams do.

'It's time, brother.' Onouris turns and looks at his brother, the eye-lenses of his helm glowing low in the darkness. He looks down again and realises that he too is armoured. Prepared for the war that was always inevitable. 'Once more into the fray, as wolves descend upon us.'

CHAPTER THIRTY-SIX

FALSEHOOD'S SONS

She sees the light. Throne of Terra, she sees it.

Not the true and beautiful radiance of the Astronomican. She seeks it, her warp eye yearns to see it once again, but it evades her. Instead there is the false light. A lie that draws her in like some nocturnal insect.

Captivating. Brief. Exquisite. Whoever has crafted this beacon has artistry in their soul, Narayis has no doubt of that. It burns so brightly. Forged from the warp and old shame. There is such *longing* within the core of it. A dream within a dream. The potential for beautiful and glorious unity turned to ashes.

She sees…

A king crowned in fire. A throne of weeping gold. Chains of cold iron binding him upon his knees. The looming shadow made of howls and screams, blood and nightmare. The crack of a snapping spine and a dying future.

She snaps back in her throne, panting. Smearing the blood from her eyes, leaving trails along her pale cheeks. Her breath pounds in her chest, her entire body aflame with psychic pain.

It hurts to dwell upon this lonely light, drawing its power into herself. That is what it wants, she realises.

It is a lure. Dangled before the hopeless to entrap them, down amidst the deeper darkness.

'We have stopped,' Narayis whispers, thumbing the vox-link upon her throne's arm. 'We are stopped but we are not safe. You have found your destination, my lords. The enemy is here at last.'

She lets her head droop, her eyes closed. The ship's pain is in her bones now, infecting her with its slow death.

'This might be my final flight,' she muses to herself as her fingers slip away from the rune, silencing her voice for the rest of the ship. 'One last act of duty, before the end. They will etch me in the annals. I hope it is as one who fought, not who was lost. Defying the void, not merely given to it.'

She wonders which of her siblings, her cousins, any of the myriad successors waiting in the wings, will be burdened with a vessel next. To share in her family's triumphs or to drown in loss and void-madness as she has.

'When next you sail the stars, my kin, think of me. Light a candle and commend my soul to the Cartomancer, who guides all ships and those who see.'

There are none to answer. All servants and lesser kinsmen have been dismissed to their own chambers, to reaffirm her strength with their own silent contemplation of the universe.

All that remains is the silence and the light. She moderates her breathing, feeling the tremor in her chest, the fluttering of her heart. Fear and confusion war within her, like fighting dogs.

Like wolves.

She swallows back her laughter and takes another heaving breath.

Control is everything. Embrace control. Hold fast to what you can control, everything else be damned. You are the light. You are the ship.

'I can do this. I am strong. They have faith in me, and I have faith in myself.'

The light hurts. It burns, brighter and brighter, dancing before her eyes in a riot of false flares, rising up from the core of it like incandescent steam.

An unnatural thing, shaped by unclean hands.

'Break it,' she whispers to herself. 'Shatter it. End it. God-Emperor, please.'

CHAPTER THIRTY-SEVEN

FALSE DAWN

The system has no sun, and yet it burns. Light fills it, carried on spectra tamed from long-dead stars. Aglow with the radiance of a flame-crowned king. Golden and crimson war for supremacy, woven around the centrepiece of the hollowed-out system.

The worlds have been reaved clean, worn smooth by the action of a god's hand. They hold in place, spheres without music, not even turning. Not moving. They sit amidst the tableau, silent implements in some vast mechanism. Caught in the light of a single burning point of space and time.

It too is a world.

If the dead orb which entombed the *Spinebreaker* was the prototype, or some failed iteration, Garald could well believe it. This place, the *False Sun* spoken of upon the map, blazes in the fullness of its power.

Sigils rise from its surface, mutating as they ascend, breaking apart and re-forming. A web of patterns and ritual etchings, warping the reality around it. Soul-light flickers from rune to rune, shifting over and over. Knowledge begetting power. Spiralling into liberating madness.

It glimmers like the holy fire of the Astronomican, but Narayis' Navigator's sight cannot regard it for long. Something infernal moves within it, swimming through tides of inchoate ambition and white-hot *yearning*. It resonates.

'*Unclean light. Unclean. Unclean!*' Narayis' voice echoes from the vox-transmitters, a shrill and pleading refrain. It hurts for her to look at. It is painful even for her to vocalise.

Garald winces away from it, muttering under his breath. Old litanies of peace. Protection. Voidfarers' oaths and promises. 'Vouchsafe the stalwart Navigator against the warp's tides. Let her sight be true and her defiance fierce.'

'Old songs,' Bodil mutters. 'Fine omens, even here. At the edge of madness and damnation.'

'Always so full of positivity, aren't you, gothi? I can see why the lady of the dynasty keeps you around.' He laughs, then pauses.

They stand upon the bridge, gazing out at the ruinous devastation. Destruction warped into ritual, set burning against the very skin of the universe. The light captivates. Cajoles. *Look too long,* Garald thinks, *and you could almost understand it.*

'Such things are not for us,' Bodil says, as though sensing his wandering thoughts.

'For the best, I am sure,' Garald sighs. 'The God-Emperor has set these things in the heavens to test us, no doubt.'

The old woman laughs, rattling and birdlike. 'It is not the Allfather's work here. It is the old blight that Russ himself once faced down. The old enemy come again.'

'You were not there when Fenris burned, were you?'

'To my eternal shame, I was not,' she allows. 'Out amidst the sea of stars, serving my queen.'

'She is lucky, to have such an advisor,' he says quietly. 'Just as I am lucky to have you with me.'

'You flatter an old woman, my lord,' she says.

'No, I tell the truth. If anything I have not been honest or earnest before, in telling you how much I have come to rely upon your guidance.'

'Ah, we have come a long way from the times when I was simply an old storm crow, set against you. A reminder of higher judgement.'

'Her judgement.' He almost laughs. 'Our distant queen.'

'She is not your blood, I know this. She is not *my* blood, either. A house, a dynasty, a family… It is always more than simple blood.' She shakes her head. 'Do all the tribes of the ice charge to the same war-drum? Of course not. Even when Russ bound them together, they were still possessed of the old grudges and enmities. That is how they remained strong. Yet they were born of Mother Fenris, and ran in her savage pack.'

'And that is enough?'

'It is all we have, lord.'

'All we have…' he muses.

Garald reaches over and enters a code into the keypad by the viewing aperture. Slowly the shutter begins to grind down, sparks flickering from the edges. 'I've seen enough,' he says. 'Any more would be heretical, I've no doubt.'

'True wisdom, lord, is found in knowing the limits of what must be known. Perhaps that is why we trust in skjalds and stories. You cannot burn a memory, unless you also burn the people who hold it.' She pauses and sighs. 'Just as the Allfather's watchers once tried to.'

'Then what remains to us?'

'Only that we uphold His truth and fight to the last drop of our blood.'

The preparations began almost as soon as they dropped into the system.

The Space Wolves dominate the hangar decks, driving out the mortal elements, be they technicians or soldiery. Only the armoured warriors have the freedom of these levels as they ready their gunship, and gaze out through secondary viewing apertures.

It is the cruel mirror of the dead world that so tormented them. Set to burning, alive with old fire and new hate. Its very existence baffles the auspex. False returns flood the ship's sensoria. It is and it is not. It cannot and should not be. Chronos click over, run too fast or count backwards. Time and space are unglued beneath the enemy's attentions.

Past and future, bound together by pitiless malice.

'This is the lair of the enemy,' Ivar says. 'Their final redoubt. The end of our hunt.'

'And all it cost us was nearly all we have. Ship, crew, and brethren,' Ytri mutters. He glowers at Ivar. 'Right into their trap, with less than a dozen swords. If this were a battle upon Fenris, then your warriors would drown you or dash your brains out before you killed them all.'

'You are welcome to try, brother,' Ivar replies coolly. The skull helm turns and fixes Ytri in its sights. 'I hope at least one of you retains the skill to return my essence to the Chapter.'

'There will be no killing here today,' Brynjar says. He stands away from them, checking and rechecking the weapons of the packs. Each is laid out upon an arming bench, slowly being taken apart and reassembled by the Iron Priest.

There is a soothing beauty in the action. Even if it only calms Brynjar.

'Not amongst brothers, at the least,' he finishes.

'It is sorcery, no doubt,' Jolfr says. He has his back to the burning world, silhouetted against its bleak beauty. 'A false star in a dead system. A work of woe. Maleficarum.'

'Baubles can be broken,' Ytri growls. 'We shattered their last unholy work. This will be no different.'

'Do not be a fool,' Brynjar says. 'Whatever keeps it burning, it is potent. Be it the will of their gods or the works of their sorcerers. Such things do not break easy. Remember the sagas sung of Prospero. The old verses of the skjalds who walked that cursed world. Maleficarum in the very air. The domain of daemons and the damned.'

'Fear will not unman me,' Ytri boasts. 'Let us be a dagger to their hearts.'

'You will have your chance,' Ivar says. 'We all will.'

'If you insist upon this folly,' Brynjar calls from the arming benches, 'then we shall face it together. One will.'

'One will,' Ivar says, and nods. He moves from them, turning his crozius over and over in his hand. Weighing its worth as thoroughly as he has the souls of his brothers. His gaze does not reach the burning world beyond the viewports, captivated instead by the squat power of the waiting Thunderhawk.

'You have come far at my side, my brothers. Through trials and tests. You have followed me this far and together we have faced odds that would have broken lesser warriors a thousand times over. I am as proud of you as of any tribesman who would have sailed to war with me before my first death.' He pauses and glances back to them.

Jolfr looks at him with pride. Ytri's arms are folded across his chest in silent judgement. Brynjar has only just stopped his labours, turning to regard Ivar with his cold scrutiny. The other brothers of the pack gather by their leaders. Vili crowds in at Jolfr's side, practically frothing at the mouth with battle-eagerness.

He will make a fine Wolf Guard, one day. Or ascend to some other high position.

Ivar nods to Vili and then looks elsewhere. Orwandil and Hrungnir watch and wait. By contrast Akaz and Gillingr mill with barely contained frustration. Guided by Ytri's potent choler, they bear it into everything they do. Even their grudging support.

'The enemy have shaped these woes for us. Set our path and carved it into our wyrd. They think we will falter at these final barricades. Slink back into the sea of stars to lick our wounds. No, brothers.'

His crozius ignites in a snap of disruptor field activation. He sweeps it before him, leaving an after-image scar upon even their augmented vision. 'I will not let these weaklings craft our fate for us! We are more than their petty sorceries! We are the Vlka Fenryka, the Wolves of Fenris. We are the Allfather's hunters. We tread where others would dare not! We leave red snow in our wake!'

Fists drum against armour in a steady tempo. Each impact resonates through the great hangar space. Brynjar's cybernetic hand joins the beat, adding to the rhythm.

'We will avenge the slights done against us! We shall drown the enemy in their own blood! And if they dare to rise against the Imperium once more, then we shall bury them beneath their monuments!'

'*Fenrys hjolda!*' they cry. With one will. With one voice.

'*You are sure, lord?*'

Garald's voice has been rendered tinny by the vox, half-drowned by the roaring of the Thunderhawk's engines. Ivar parses it regardless.

'I am sure. Our descent alone may be enough to evade notice, and if not... then we will fight the bastards to the death. Hurt them, if we are able. Break their works and retrieve what is ours. Failing that... We go to an end worthy of the sagas.'

'*What are your instructions?*'

'Provide what aid you can, captain. If we call upon you, answer. If not, then you must bear our brothers' legacies back to the Chapter. To Fenris. Carry our saga back to the hearth.'

Silence reigns for one long moment. Drawn out into an eternity.

'*Understood, my lord. It has…*' Garald pauses. '*It has been an honour to serve you.*'

'It has been an honour to know you, rogue trader.'

The link dies.

Ivar gazes up the ramp at his waiting packs. Locked in place, their weapons readied. Each one a killer. A warrior. A brother. Bloodied and battered. Yet still, they stand ready.

'One last plunge of the spear,' Ivar says as he ascends. The ramp begins to rise behind him. 'Into the enemy's heart.'

'JUDGEMENT'

He is armed and armoured now.

Onouris feels complete for the first time in a geologic age. No longer yoked to visions and caged by patterns. He walks free, abroad and unfettered. Knowledge flows from him in tangles of white light, woven into fabric, tamed into the form of great honour rolls of dangling scripture. Even now, invisible hands pin it in place, their fingers working over the surface to etch and burn and ink.

Oaths of moment. Promises of pain and glory. Old songs and new ideas. All the preserved and conjured memory of mankind's pre-eminence, and the echoes of what is to come.

He is his father's son, once more. Scholar and warrior, garbed in cold azure instead of the rich red of their glory days. He reaches out and his staff snaps into his grasp, light coiling about its haft.

Memory no longer terrifies him. The past is a discarded shroud. Only the present remains, and it is his to tame. To shape.

He strikes the base of his staff against the ground and it

shatters beneath his feet. Each shard becomes a stair, glimmering like pearl in sunlight. He ascends, step by step, trailing the corposant of unbridled wisdom.

As he goes, he brings the staff around. Tapping at the sealed chambers one after another. Watching as the black cracks spiral through them. Piteous moans echo from within some, where his fellow scryers kneel, hands pressed to plinths or locked around the relics they hold. Others open to dusty sighs and silence.

Azure flames split the darkness. Blazing in the hollow pits of eye-lenses, flaring suddenly into being in sconces, or even hovering as orbs of ghost light. He smiles to see it. Roused at last.

'We have struggled too long against our natures, my brothers,' Onouris calls. 'To be seers and scholars is our calling, true, yet we were made to be weapons. Held in the hands of an ungrateful master but weapons nonetheless. Now, as before, the barbarians return to our gates.'

Glittering sand flows up the steps in his wake, milling about his feet like the motion of a tide. Lapping at his armoured ankles, creeping up to form new patterns upon his armour. Rattling their way across the blue plate, dancing upon the golden trim.

'Can you feel it, brothers?' Onouris asks. 'The world changes about us. What can this be if not the gift of the Architect of Fate?'

He looks around. The others are rising from their sanctums now, their motions slow and measured, like the dead slinking from some low barrow. Onouris smiles beneath his crested helm when he sights Qar, bowing his head to his brother. Honouring him.

'Let them come, brother. Let them test their savagery against our learning. This is the test. The eldest game played out once more.'

CHAPTER THIRTY-EIGHT

SWIFT SPEARS

The Thunderhawk descends upon wings of fire, plunging through the darkness and into the light.

There is no heat. It blazes with false flame, a clinging aurora that shifts and flickers. Spelling out new configurations and patterns. The dead world was a failed experiment, its rhythms out of sync with their maker's designs. This has no such flaw.

The sigils that weave about the Thunderhawk are as perfect as they are toxic.

Monstrous eddies and zephyrs rise up from the gleaming surface, immense ley lines aglow, carved by geologic effort and tectonic will into the flesh of the falsehood. Shapes resolve as they descend, the bright avenues of an enormous city, sprawling out like a craftsman's schematic. Flawless and peopled only by ghosts.

The auspex resounds with phantom signals and false positives. Within the confines of the gunship they hear the pilot's frantic reports. A haunted expanse of vitrified stone, ablaze with sunfire and echoing with old battle.

Statues rise from the surface, as immense as the legendary Titanoliths upon Terra itself. Not made in the images of the Allfather's favoured sons, but in the likeness of heathen gods. Bird-headed scribes hide their faces between hands which still grip quill and chisel. Jackals regard the mortuary quadrants with avaricious longing.

Slowly the monstrous effigies begin to turn. The scribes uncover their faces, each new visage a study in horror. Distended maws rimmed with needle teeth scream in silence as they rotate in their bizarre marionette's dance.

Plasma glimmers in the depths of their throats as the defences finally rouse themselves to speak with fire.

It bursts around them in a wave of miniature supernovas, staining the air with flame. Each detonation ignites another ring of sigils, accelerating their relentless permutations. Ivar hears them drumming against the hull like rain. Each impact rings with meaning. Whispers caress the Thunderhawk, insinuating their way inwards, carried upon the roar of wind and engine.

Somewhere, something begins to laugh. A low, rattling sound that coughs its way through the vents and echoes over the vox.

'No hope. No hope. No hope.'

'The works of the enemy are deceit,' Ivar intones. 'Despair. We are immune to it. As we always have been. We are the claws that tear their lies apart. Ten thousand years we have hounded them. Never once letting them rest.'

'That is why they cannot shoot straight,' Ytri says with a laugh. 'Ten thousand years ago Russ broke them as warriors. They failed then, and upon Fenris, and they falter once again now. How else can we stab at their hearts with such fury, eh?'

'We do not underestimate any foe,' Ivar chastises. 'What they were, what they have become, it does not matter. They are lethal now, for all their tricks.'

'Let them come,' Ytri growls. 'We owe them a tally of the dead. They can throw whatever they like at us.'

The air trembles around them and the Thunderhawk shudders. It stops, held tight, as though in some great hand.

The sigils drumming at the gunship's iron skin tighten like a noose, seizing around them with sudden and tremendous force. The walls bend but do not buckle. Faces press themselves against the metal, tongues lolling impossibly from between the distended plates, lapping at the air as they laugh.

The ship rolls, tumbling hard to the right, tearing them free of the arcane grasp. It drops suddenly, plunging towards the gleaming surface of the false world. The engines kick and stabiliser jets pulse, driving them upwards once more.

The Thunderhawk finally answers flame with flame. Missiles hurtle from under the wings of the ship, striking one of the rotating statues at its centre. Explosions ripple up its span, cracking the blue and gold, revealing the many-hued fire that vomits up from within. The sky blazes, bubbling and rippling as the unholy ignition claws at the heavens. The web of crackling symbols breaks apart, tumbling away in rains of glittering dust.

'Anything can be broken,' Ytri affirms. He drums his fist against the wall behind him. 'Strong as the foundations of the Aett.'

'Careful,' Brynjar says. 'Or perhaps it will be us who are broken.'

The light burns around them, inconstant and shifting. Bleeding through from the world's profaned heart, drawn up like water from reservoirs. The Thunderhawk fires as it weaves between obelisks and pyramids, tracing the strongest of the lines of fire cut into the surface.

'Bring us down where the enemy's light is strongest,' Ivar growls.

The Thunderhawk banks, then hovers, before the thrusters finally begin to fire, stabilising it as it descends. Iron treads impact the gleaming surface of the world, casting a momentary shadow upon the trapped auroric patterns.

The ramp slams down, casting up a pall of glittering dust. They move out, led by their priests into the crucible of battle once more.

Black and blue-grey, the Wolf Priest and the Iron Priest stand, weapons raised and waiting. Their brothers fan out behind them, bolters prepared.

'You see?' Ytri laughs. 'Cowards. They bring nothing to bear. No strength. No show of force. They hide in their blazing nest.'

'No,' Ivar says. He raises his hand. 'There is something here.'

CHAPTER THIRTY-NINE

GHOSTS OF THE PAST

To honour the past is a good and noble thing.

To become trapped in it is a curse.

Ivar looks around the plaza that they stand in and finally understands what it means to be bound by such a past. Perhaps he has fixated so long on the future that he has lost sight of that. Now it returns with a wave of vertigo. Absolute understanding floods him as he looks at it, in the burning shadow of the largest pyramid, where ghosts make war.

It is a frozen tableau made of light and trickery. Warriors clash upon the false marble of the plaza, halted mid-rampage like a pict taken at the height of battle.

There are warriors in high-crested helms, bolters raised to fire, curved blades held aloft in brazen defiance. Uniformed human soldiery, marked with esoteric unit designations, man positions along elevated walkways. One, an officer, is pointing down, past the Thunderhawk and the gathered warriors. Ivar turns, following the phantom's gesture.

Wolves stand behind him, locked in place, charging forever.

They wear the patterns and colours of the old Legion, visible even through the all-consuming light. Brothers, ten thousand years distant, preserved eternally like hololiths, trapped like insects in amber.

Darkness shudders within them. Scrabbling against the edges of the warriors, imperfections bound to their hearts. Sins worn within their souls.

How much is this a reaction to our presence, a tacit insult? And how much is simply how they have always viewed this moment?

Prospero.

This is not that benighted world. Not a place of reckoning, dust and ashes. This is a simulacrum. Crafted from memory, maintained almost as a museum to their shame. A prison for doubt and weakness.

'Caution,' Ivar says quietly. 'They are here.'

The false Wolves break apart, shattering like crystal. For a moment the darkness within them holds their form, great lupine shapes made of shadow and smoke. Eyes flare crimson in elongated skulls, before the façade shatters further. The impression of fur peels away, darkness abandoned, light surging from within, becoming scales and feathers.

Ivar fires. The others are mere seconds behind him. The daemon-things shudder and laugh as the shells hammer into them, blowing away rains of luminous plumage and clouds of pseudopod matter.

Judgement!

The words impress themselves upon the world. Not spoken, simply rendered into being. Reality rings with them, clamouring through the false world's flesh.

Judgement!

'Behind!' Brynjar calls. Ivar whirls about, firing almost without thinking.

The ghost-images of the Thousand Sons stand, limbs trembling, weapons held idle at their sides as runic symbols bleed from them, drifting up and into the air, resonant with meaning. The mortal infantry dissolve into screaming soul-light, hurtling upwards into the heavens. Around the plaza the obelisks burn like beacons, casting their own great spotlights into the heavens.

They widen. Cerulean cuts etch themselves into the sky, light and souls pouring from them like blood from a severed artery. Winding their way upwards, surrounding the world in a howling ring of immaterial agony. Things swim their way free of the tide, driving themselves off on great fins like deep-sea creatures.

The world cackles around them. Enervated by the raw expenditure of power, ringing like an unholy bell. Shaking existence merely by its presence.

'We have to move,' Ivar snarls. He gestures with his crozius. 'We need cover!'

'I can't raise the ship,' Brynjar growls. 'I cannot warn them.'

'Look at that, brother. Do you truly think they need to be warned?'

'What in the Emperor's name is that?' Garald rises from his throne, stopping halfway across the central dais of the bridge. 'Someone, tell me what that is?'

'Maleficarum,' Bodil whispers. 'The sorcery of the Archenemy.'

The world is burning, its hateful radiance transmuting, transforming. Lights blossom from it like comets, a writhing tide of unreality swarming towards them. He can see things squirming and flailing within it, forcing their shape into being.

Undulating bodies swim outwards from the sea of fire, mouths yawning, too many eyes blazing with inhuman colours. Despite the void between them, despite the adamantine and armaglass, Garald can still hear them screaming.

'Evasive manoeuvres!' he calls, already aware that it is too late.

A torrent of soulfire and daemon-matter slams itself against the active voids with a static shriek, white-hot and blinding. The entire ship shakes, tilting. The horizontal suddenly becomes near vertical, dislodging Garald from his feet. He hits the deck, cursing.

'Damage report!' he shouts.

No one answers.

No one, except the screaming.

The lumens flicker crimson again, and Kaedra laughs.

'Never a dull moment, eh?'

'I'd kill for a dull moment,' Lyf grumbles.

They have remained at battle readiness since the shipdeath and rebirth. Every last warrior prepared for the eventuality of enemy action. Now it seems they were wise to do so. Blades have been prepared, firearms checked and rechecked.

The lights hold their bloody glow and then fade. Darkness returns, not the reassuring purity of the lumens. The ship begins to tremble. It begins to howl.

Metal deforms, peeling away in great sheets of mutilated decking, thrown aside in rains of molten steel. The open air ripples and flickers as shapes begin to intrude, pushing themselves through the skin of the universe. Needle teeth gnash at the air as fire blossoms around them.

'Oh Throne, oh holy and sainted Throne of Earth,' Lyf hisses. He begins to fire. Kaedra staggers back and does the same. The others join them. As much fury as they can muster, hurled back into the face of hell.

The daemon's smile widens as it lunges forward to feast.

CHAPTER FORTY

SHRINES TO MEMORY

The tunnels wind beneath the skin of the world, more grown than carved. Ivar leads from the front, his crozius raised, casting its sacred light into the undying darkness.

Above ground it had seemed like the entrance to some librarium or mausoleum, but the moment they passed below it transmuted. A maze, a nest, a lair for the enemy to skulk in.

All pretence. Show. Above, it is memories of high ideals; below, it is the same as ever. The enemy are beasts, nothing more. Every insult they could throw at the Vlka Fenryka, they inhabit. Ten thousand years of rank hypocrisy and degeneration. No better than the corrupted trolls which dug their way into Fenris' skin, or their beastmen slaves.

Just monsters from the old sagas.

Ivar glances about. Ytri and his warriors hold the rearguard, weapons raised with practised determination. Jolfr and Vili follow close behind Ivar and Brynjar. Orwandil and Hrungnir come after them, checking and rechecking their weapons.

'I expected better from the bastards out of legend,' Ytri says.

'They put on a pretty show above ground, but down here? Nothing.'

Ivar grunts. 'Appearances can deceive.'

They pass through chambers of brilliant, glistening crystal, burning sapphire and emerald threaded through like veins. The passages open up beneath the earth, forming plunging pits of resonant growths that make Ivar's teeth ache, channelling fire up from what passes for the enemy's core.

'Maleficarum,' Brynjar curses.

'Aye. Some foulness writ on the scale of giants,' Ivar says.

The light carries through the tunnels, buoyed along by whispers and echoed chanting. Laughter drifts upon the sorcerous winds, drawn up from the depths. From out of memory.

'They cannot let go of their past,' Ivar says. 'This whole thing is a monument to their failings. A wound they cannot escape from.'

'And a trap, more than likely,' Jolfr says. He pats his axe. 'We will make them remember what the sons of Russ have wrought.'

'Do not be so eager to find battle,' Vili says. The others look at him. 'So I have been taught by my mentors.'

Jolfr laughs. 'You've got teeth now, pup,' he says. 'Even here in the lair of daemons.'

The chanting grows louder.

'Listen,' Ytri says. He gestures with his blade. 'From below.'

Civility reasserts itself. The rough-hewn crystal and stone fades away, replaced by resurgent architecture. White marble stairs wind down before them. The Wolves descend, checking each turn.

They exit into a wide gallery, a vast sprawling semicircle. Black pillars face outwards, while the inner walls are ringed with exhibits. Floating orbs of witch-light drift along the edges, pausing to illuminate each alcove.

There are complete sets of armour, some of them pre-Imperial.

Xenos relics glisten with strange gems and eldritch psycho-plastics. Weapons hang in suspensor fields, their edges still trailing blood drops. Everything is carved from white marble and cohesive thought, a psychoscape shaped and maintained by raw will. Aching with pain.

'Spread out,' Ivar orders. He gestures with his crozius, directing them to the inner edge of the gallery. He looks down into the centre of the enemy's works. Blinding light circles around the interior of the figmented space, great wheels of directed psychic ephemera reshaping and rotating.

'Allfather...' Ivar whispers.

Nine figures stand around a central plinth, eight with their heads bowed. The ninth stands at the head of a lectern, arms raised, holding a staff aloft. He conducts the light with yearning alone, letting the fire of it coil down the black wood of the ritual implement.

The staff moves, leaning forward, turning over the plinth, till the flames surround it, embrace it. Against the blue-white light, Ivar can see what sits upon the black stone of the central pedestal.

The Vargrtiðhorn.

Gorm's folly. The object of his doomed quest. The focal point of all their woes. Now it makes sense; how the sorcerers could have addled their course and polluted their wyrd. Ivar's destiny, suborned by the old foe. It is almost enough to make him laugh.

He gestures to the others. They spread out along the edge of the chamber, each taking position behind one of the pillars of black obsidian. Ivar closes his eyes and braces himself.

'Come, cousins, there is no need to hide. We can speak as reasonable souls, can we not?'

'There can be no peace made between oathbreakers,' Ivar shouts down.

The lead figure laughs. His hands continue to move to the ritual's rhythm. 'Oh, I wholeheartedly agree. There is no time for peace any more. Yet that does not mean that an accord cannot be reached. You have come so far, after all. Suffered much.' He laughs again. The sound is oddly lyrical, coming from the ornate blue-and-gold armour. 'Ten thousand years is a long time to wait for a reckoning, yet in the end it was worth every moment.'

'I will not waste words with you, sorcerer!'

'Must we be reduced to such petty insults? I am a man, just as you are. I have a lineage. A name.'

'Speak it, then. Let me know who I will be killing.'

The sorcerer cuts across the air with the staff. The other eight chanting figures go to their knees as one. Behind him, nine figures lurch from the darkness like automata.

'I am Onouris. Born of Prospero. Most grievously betrayed. Fatespinner. Keeper of histories. And worry not, I will keep your memory when this is done.'

The void shields buckle and break, washed away by the warp's relentless tides.

Unholy fire wreathes the ship, swaddling it in suffering. Within its halls madness walks. All the crew can do is flee before it.

Lyf and Kaedra have long since cast aside their guns. They do not even have the will left to draw blades. Instead, they run through the corridors of the ship, intent upon the bridge.

'This is death,' Lyf hisses. 'The Underverse's last gulp. Swallowing us all down. Nothing left but death.'

'No,' she gasps. They stop, braced against the walls of a minor service corridor.

The ship groans around them, shaking with fresh impacts and new violations. Caught between life and death, ailing as surely as its crew. The plex-glass of lumen-globes and lumen-strips crunches beneath their feet.

The only light comes from the lines of hellish fire spreading like cancer through the walls.

Maybe we are already holed through, she thinks. *We could already be dead and not even know it.*

'We need to keep moving,' she says at last, swallowing down the taste of bile at the back of her throat. 'Get to the bridge. Link up with other survivors. *Something.*'

'Something,' Lyf repeats numbly.

She draws her hand back and slaps him hard. 'Focus!' she snaps.

'Sorry. Sorry!' He shakes himself, looking down as though ashamed. 'Those things...'

'Cannot and will not stop us.'

Somewhere, far too close, something else explodes. She spits to one side, clearing the acid from her mouth. She lets her hands find the access wheel of the waiting door, fingers tight around the metal as she begins to pull.

'Too late.'

The voice is suddenly at their ears.

Kaedra turns, too slow, barely aware. Lyf is closer. Faster. He pushes her through the opening door and slams it shut. She hits the ground hard, barely able to roll. She feels something snap in her wrist.

The pain dies mere seconds later, swallowed by the fear and the sound of Lyf's final, terrified screams.

It seems like forever. It feels like no time at all.

The runes upon the doors of the bridge have burned away, flowing in trickles of molten iron and silver. They have done their work, though. Where other parts of the ship have suffered and burned, the bridge holds. Less of the capricious madness dances from mind to mind. Fewer of the crew are dead by their own hands or by the talons of something else.

The old gothi staggers from one bridge station to another, offering blessings and casting bones. Garald has been following her course, desperately seeking communion with the surface, or the other parts of the ship.

'Anything?' he asks again.

'Nothing, lord,' Velaq says. She has more duties now than just auspex. Everyone is filling gaps, struggling to hold the command decks together.

Let us in.

The voices are becoming more insistent. Drifting through the ether in place of vox, clawing at the warded doors of the bridge. Louder and harder to ignore. Already he has had to shoot at least one crew member who tried to open the doors, fumbling blindly at the controls while they wept blood.

A messy mercy. Even after he had shot them three times, they still tried to drag themselves up to the console.

It will be so much easier. Let us in.

'Try again,' he says to Velaq. 'Raise Albertus-Nu, or Narayis. They know what needs to be done.'

Too late. Too late.

The bridge doors begin to glow. Subtly at first, a spreading warmth blossoming into an inferno. The metal glows, red-hot, then white-hot. Flames start to lick their way through the door, a riot of impossible colours.

He draws his pistol. The others follow suit. Every last sidearm is brought to hand as the first distended head forces its way through the growing wound, wriggling like a parasite.

They fire as one.

The daemon laughs as the bullets find it, gouging at its flowing, shifting flesh. Each wound becomes another mouth, another eye. Vomiting fire, spitting madness.

'Go back to whence you came!' The reedy voice rises, riven through with pain, breaking under the physical and spiritual strain. The old woman limps between the monster and her master. The bag of runes and bones at her hip burns so bright he worries it might catch fire.

That is the least of her worries. The lowest of her agonies. Bodil stands in the eye of the storm, before the yawning mouth of the unholy, and she does not falter.

She knows no fear.

Her weathered hands cross over her chest, forcing themselves together in the sign of the aquila.

The bullets continue to hit the monster in a rain of glittering blood and wet, crawling flesh. A tendril hits the deck and slithers forwards, leaking liquid flame. It coils around the old woman's leg and then jerks back, pulling her screaming into the rent in the bridge doors.

'Lord! Can anyone hear me?'

'Narayis! Whatever access or authority you need, it is yours. Activate the Geller fields! Void shields be damned!'

CHAPTER FORTY-ONE

BROKEN WYRD

'You knew we would come here,' Ivar growls down at the coterie of abominations.

Onouris' shoulders move in a slow shrug, exaggerated by his armour. 'You? No. If you must lie to yourself and think yourself special then that is your failing. Perhaps one day you will even correct it.' He laughs. That damnable lyrical sound again. 'I speak for this conclave. We are of one mind and purpose, as we have ever been.'

'You set this trap for me. For those of my blood.'

'The Wolves of Fenris? Of course. We baited a trap and prayed it would bear fruit. All such deceits are the Changer's sweet reward. You are no one and nothing to us. It mattered not who would come here, seeking after their lost treasure. Only that someone would. Did you truly believe that our works were devoted to the least of Fenris' bastards?'

'Mind your tongue, sorcerer, before I feed it to you,' he snarls. 'Know that your death comes swift at the hands of Ivar Kraken-blood, Wolf Priest of Fenris, expected or not.'

'Ah, there is that barbarian spirit. Unbroken these last millennia. No matter how often you are chastened, or your wretched rock burns, still you endure with that swagger.'

The sorcerer's fingers tremble around the length of the stave, lowering it to gently touch the entwined fields of fire around the Vargrtiðhorn. Reality ripples around it, shuddering as though struck. Light stretches out from it like a heat haze. Shimmering through false futures.

A great tree burning against the hell-sky of the warp. The howling of distant wolves. The thousandfold dead, chewing at the roots of the world.

A thousand ends. A million deaths. Woven together into a tapestry of apocalypse and pain.

'We sift the future for the ideal path. All you see here are mere loci of potentiality. The ideal food and drink for such as we.'

'I have heard enough.'

'Of course you have, Ivar Krakenblood. What is the alternative? To face down your own weakness? Your seething desperation for relevance?'

'Be silent!'

'This does not end with you returning home in glory. It ends in death and fire and dishonour.'

The figures behind him continue to lumber forwards, forming an honour guard of silent ceramite. Their eyes burn with blue flame, weapons raised at last for the murder-make.

'Kill them all!' Ivar snarls. 'End them!'

They leap from the high tiers of the gallery and hit the ground almost in the same moment, dislodging dunes of glittering dust.

The wages of sorcery, Ivar does not doubt. *How many years have they striven here in the darkness? Working their bleak wonders and worming into the Imperium's flesh in search of revelation.*

Around the nine sorcerers, the warp congeals, a crackling

pillar of psychic force more potent than any void shield, orbed in lightning and howling winds. The silent warriors advance, unbothered, through the tumult. They open fire. Each bullet burns with unholy flame, bursting apart in micro-warp explosions. Tiny infernos burn about the Fenrisians as they weave through the unfolding madness. Each shot from the advancing Thousand Sons is precise, as though plotted by cogitator.

They clash.

Blade meets blade, powered weapons locked together in a glowing riot of competing fields. The packs fight with their own unity, unbowed by their wounds and their losses. They howl and roar, laughing as they engage their foes.

This is the oldest struggle. Man against monster. Brother against brother.

Ivar's crozius takes the first of them apart. He swings it round, shattering the Traitor Space Marine's weak guard, battering the curved blade away and crashing through the breastplate. Screaming light and burning dust pours from the wound. The helm turns, slowly, almost confused, before he brings the weapon down again and shatters the visage. No flesh stares back. Only dust.

The others fight together. Jolfr and his brothers form one ragged knot of defiance. Brynjar rallies Bloodiron Wrath to his side. A final bulwark against the unholy. Ivar has never been more proud.

True Fenrisian defiance sings in their every action. Warriors of the Rout, every one.

Vili weaves around one of the silent automata. The youngblood slashes and hacks, even as Jolfr and the others rain their own blows. The thing turns, pulled in too many directions, its armour aglow with storm-light beneath the domed sky. Constellations from another time burn there, immortalised forever.

Vili drives in hard, his sword's teeth tearing at the foe. Splinters of gleaming metal fly away in a rain of sparks. Still it makes no noise. No utterance of pain. They are beyond it. Removed from the great game of warriors.

That, Ivar thinks, is their weakness as much as it might be their strength.

Vili's blade comes round again and scores across the chestplate. He kicks it back and smashes the pommel into its face again and again. Till the light bleeds out of its eyes and it collapses to the ground. The only thing left to mark its passing is the etchings upon its breastplate.

Qar.

Ivar wonders if it is a name or some forgotten oath.

It matters not, as it dies.

+ENOUGH!+

The voice cuts through the howl of false winds, tearing at them all.

Onouris rises upon a disc of writhing metal and bone, staff raised. The storm is one with him now. Burning through him. Lightning is caged in his marrow. His armour pulses, so bright that Ivar can see the bones within.

The other eight falter. Forced to their knees, moaning and screaming as the conflagration grows around them. Diminishing them even as Onouris' power surges.

Ivar feels the other warrior's hate, incandescent. It swamps him. It earths itself around them, drawn towards a singular focus.

Fire envelops Vili in a crushing vice. Armour cracks, even as the youngblood struggles. He manages to take a few halting steps, weapon raised. An oath upon his lips. 'Fenrys hj–'

Then it is gone. Lost to the storm.

Ivar screams. He forces himself forwards, step by bloody step through the roaring hell-light. Feels it dancing across his plate. The others are firing, but no bolt round can touch the sorcerer. Fire rimes him, a shield of withering insanity.

Ivar pushes himself forwards, his own hate wielded like a weapon, held before him as surely as his crozius. His black armour is silhouetted against the absolute fire of the inferno. He feels it lap against his plate, stinging the skin beneath.

'Do you really think,' Onouris hisses, 'that you can stop me? I have endured millennia without your mongrel breed ever coming close!' He laughs. Each time he does, it is another hammer blow of light and power. Forcing the lesser sorcerers down and onto the ground, their helmed faces against the sigil-etched floors.

Their power leeched to feed his, all brotherhood forgotten.

More of the silent warriors lurch through the fire. Their bolters pan with machine-like precision, firing their screaming rounds of witchfire and spite.

The others are fighting, shadows against the flame, only the runes and wards upon their armour aglow within the darkness. Ivar's senses parse each image. Jolfr with his axe raised high, swinging it through the crested helm of one of their automata, the Rubricae. Ytri's hulking form is shoulder-charging a sorcerer into a pillar, driving him into the stonework so hard that armour and masonry crack.

Brynjar… The Iron Priest is a rock in the storm. His hammer sweeps across the maelstrom, trailing lightning, shattering the webs of sigils that try to ensnare him.

He is utterly material, even as the immaterium coils about him as though it were a kraken made of dark flame. Ancient enmity drawn up from the depths, one-eyed and bellowing.

Ivar sees them all. Loyal and traitor. Living and dead. He sees the defiance of his brothers and the pitiless hate of the foe. He tastes screams ten thousand years cold. The dust and ashes of atrocities long buried. The skjalds sing their songs into the infinite ether only for them to be parroted back. Repeated. Mocked.

The storm laughs at him. It roars like the howl of long-ago wolves. Screaming from the air like orbital bombardment.

Ivar ignores it. Ignores all of them. He advances through the cloying power. He has endured worse in his time. Storm and tumult, kraken and tempest.

'I shall weather all storms,' he mutters. 'I will endure all trials!'

Another of the Rubricae warriors staggers closer, struggling against the currents and tides, blue plate rippling in the heat, drifting from colour to colour. Flitting between potential states. The gold blazes and cracks, runs and resets.

It lurches forwards, swinging at him with a curved blade of brass and iron. He barely blocks it, his crozius shuddering as it absorbs the blow. He drives it back, raising his absolvor bolt pistol and firing. Over and over, unloading the pistol into its visor until the helm bursts apart in a rush of screaming soul-matter and glittering dust.

Time stops.

Onouris looks down at him as a god might regard a supplicant. 'Do you truly think you can harm me, pup?'

'I don't have to.' Ivar laughs. 'You are too focused on your works. Too bound to your little heresies.'

He raises his crozius. He defies the foe.

He makes his own fate.

It falls, dancing with lightning and fire as it splits the air. Purity hews through the unholy.

'*No!*' Onouris calls, realising too late his true objective. Just as Ivar realises that it was never about this moment. Nor this prize. His wyrd was more and less than that.

'I renounce you, and all your works. All your traps and lures. You have no power over me!'

The crozius strikes the horn and all the world trembles, resounding with the howl of it. With the anger of wolves.

The flawless, rune-carved surface shatters. Bands of iron tumble away in a rain of metal and scrimshawed beauty.

'You shall never know your wretched home world again! You shall suffer in the shadows until your name is forgotten! Only your crimes shall be your monument!'

The sorcerer screams the words, howling them as the final conflagration erupts around them, and all becomes fire.

The ascent is always harder than the fall.

The poison fire flows through the tunnels as though they were veins, a final calamity wrought upon the works of the enemy.

They carry Vili's body up through the flowing madness, onwards towards the surface, even as fire and atrocity bleeds from the walls. Daemons, their integrity robbed, push themselves into existence only to die. Torn apart by bolter and blade, reduced to smears of black blood and ashes.

Onouris' screams haunt their steps. Dead, alive, Ivar knows and cares not, nor whether this breaking bauble is prison or tomb. Agony. Loss. It sounds the same from the lips of puling heretics and unclean heathens.

'Bear him up,' Ivar says. They carry him, the three of them. Ivar, Ytri, and Jolfr. All bear the pain within their helms. The others form his honour guard, killing the daemons who would dare to stop the final march of a brother. Of a hero.

Upon the surface, the great ley configurations have blackened and shattered. Tectonic agony convulses the whole world with fire. The pyramids lie broken, their precious contents buried and forgotten.

It begins to rain ashes.

Ivar looks up, past them, as the Thunderhawk finally swings in, low over the horizon.

CHAPTER FORTY-TWO

REFLECTIONS

'Is she voidworthy?'

Ivar asks the question to the almost empty room and basks in the silence that follows it. There is something primal in that moment that reminds him of home.

And then there is the ache that comes with such thoughts. Potent and soul-deep.

You shall never know your wretched home world again! You shall suffer in the shadows until your name is forgotten! Only your crimes shall be your monument!

Onouris' words are poison, still flowing through him. Everything is tainted. Duller, somehow, as though standing in the cursed light of that place has made the universe lesser. A tarnished shadow of all that has been lost.

'The ship,' Ivar repeats. 'Is she voidworthy?'

'Ah, the repairs have continued apace,' Garald murmurs. Here in the briefing chamber the rogue trader too seems diminished. Shrunken by the trials and the darkness. He sinks down into a waiting chair, fingers caressing the upholstery with nervous enthusiasm. 'Albertus-Nu thinks we should be ready for prolonged travel within a week.'

'And Brynjar?'

Garald is silent.

'What of my brother?'

'He maintains his vigil below, lord. Keeping his own company. Even those who remain of Bloodiron Wrath do not walk his path.'

'That…' Ivar sighs. 'That pains me.'

'We have all suffered, lord. All lost.'

'We all must mourn in our own ways,' Ivar muses.

'How do you mourn?' Garald asks.

The question hangs in the air. Ivar steps backwards, leaning against an iron pillar. 'I hold in my heart the memory of all who have fallen. I return their legacy to the Chapter.' He pauses. 'Or keep it safe until such time as it can be. That may be… some time.'

'I understand, lord,' Garald says.

'Perhaps you even do, captain.' He laughs. 'The universe has grown strange. I am used to simpler tasks.'

'In my limited experience, lord, your kind are nothing if not complex.'

'Do you believe in curses, captain?'

'I believe we live in a very complicated galaxy, my lord. One that my gothi was always pushing me to understand.'

'She will be missed.' Ivar pauses. 'She was brave at the end, as I have heard it.'

'She died a hero, lord. A hero of Fenris.'

Ivar is silent for a long moment. 'I remember,' he says at last, 'what that was like.'

'We have lost too many heroes,' Kaedra says. She sits with the other crew, soldiers, armsmen and officers, in one of the barrack halls of the ship. 'Too many taken from us too soon.'

There are nods and shouts of agreement. She pushes herself up and walks around the tables, surveying every man and woman.

'We have all known loss. So many who must be remembered. In time I will ask you for their stories. For now, I have one of my own.'

She takes one deep and halting breath. 'One who saved my life. Who was friend and comrade. I made him a promise and I intend to keep it. Let me tell you of Lyf, who fought and died for his ship.'

'Brother?'

'I do not wish to be disturbed.' Brynjar does not look back. He does not have to.

Ivar walks into the arming chamber. It is perhaps the deepest part of the vessel that Brynjar could have chosen to hide in. 'I know, brother.'

'We are cursed, Ivar. You heard the sorcerer, clear as I did.'

'I did.'

'And yet you risked it all. Damned all our wyrds. And for what?'

'For justice,' he says at last.

'Justice.' Brynjar laughs. 'Is that what you think?'

'It is what I know, brother.' He sighs. 'The horn was a poisoned chalice. It was taken to damn us. Perhaps it is better that it doom me for my pride.'

'That was not your decision to make.'

'And yet, here we are.' Ivar is silent. 'We cannot return to Fenris. Not with this dark wyrd hanging over us. We must find our way, until the omens are cleared.'

'A fine trick, with no gothi,' Brynjar says.

'I know.' Ivar pauses. 'Brother–'

'Go.' Brynjar scowls. 'There is work still to be done.' He growls and turns from Ivar. 'Had I known you would bring this doom upon us, brother, I would have left you to rot at the magos' talons.'

Ivar waits, silently staring at his brother's armoured form, hunched over the arming bench, hands moving at their work. He hesitates for a moment, his plate trembling. He considers reaching out, in reassurance and fealty. In brotherhood…

When Brynjar finally looks back, he is gone.

Gingerly, Ivar pries away the armour. The wounds done by the enemy were hateful and insidious. A thousand tiny haemorrhages and cuts criss-cross the young warrior's skin. A web of malice, etched forever into a brother's flesh and spirit.

Ivar is silent as he undertakes the final duty. His free hand finds the back of the Fang of Morkai, petting it almost indulgently. Reverently.

'You were never the least of us, my brother. If anything, you were the very best of us. You were the promise of a future we have yet to seize. You were my brother, and my friend. I wish, dearly, that you had gained the fate you sought.'

Fate.

Ivar laughs bitterly. He reaches down and begins, slowly, to cut.

'Be at peace, brother, and know that your legacy returns to the Chapter. To be kept and preserved until such time as I am worthy enough to deliver you home. That your strength may live again in the blood of another.' He pauses.

'For that is the glory of the sons of Russ, and the wyrd of the children of Fenris.'

EPILOGUE

They come to him, one by one. Brothers, all. Some are fresh-forged and newly blooded. Others have given their blood and sweat to the Chapter down decades of service. All are worthy. All are born of the flesh of Fenris.

He stands upon an outcrop of rock as the winter snows crowd in around them. The others kneel before him, down amidst the cold, their eyes downcast. He watches them, measuring their potential. Judgement finds them, one by one. It is as though he can sniff out their weakness by sight alone. He knows their records, of course. Those who have proven themselves. Others who bear such wondrous potential.

He nurtures them. Fenris is a harsh world and few things grow there that are not hardy. Warriors are just another crop. A resource that must be tended to. A pack that must be led.

'You come here today as brothers,' he says. His voice resounds with vox-amplification. A raw growl of emotion. 'All of you are equals. Even I stand before you as a brother. Without rank. Look at me.'

They all look up. None of them wear helms. He sees fresh faces, some pale and young, devoid of scars or tattoos. Others are worn like old granite. They are drawn from every region of Fenris, from tribes without number. All the names are known to him. It is simply that, here and now, they no longer matter.

'I have brought you here for one purpose,' he says. 'That you might learn from me. There is always wisdom to be imparted. Lessons to be learned. Sometimes those lessons are writ in blood.' He laughs bitterly.

Silence reigns. Only Fenris speaks. The wind rises with the storm's anger, drumming at flesh and armour. None move or react. They will not show weakness beneath his scrutiny.

'There are brothers who labour still in the Uppland. They have passed beyond the sight of seers and auspex. They fight on, so we choose to believe. Somewhere that the light of the Wolf's Eye might never find them.' He kneels and scoops up a handful of snow and soil, levering it from where it clings to the rock.

'We will keep the hearth until they return or we shall remember them as fallen brothers. We honour their sacrifice and keep their names alive in the sagas.' He pauses and turns from them, looking back through the snowfall.

Above them all the Aett looms, as unmoving and indomitable as the legacy of Russ himself.

Ulrik the Slayer returns his gaze to the gathered warriors, letting the sodden earth fall from his fingers. Returning it to Fenris as though it were a brother's due to the Chapter.

'Let me tell you, brothers, of the Saga of Ivar Krakenblood. Wolf Priest of Fenris and seeker after wyrd.'

ACKNOWLEDGEMENTS

This saga owes its existence to many different individuals.

I would like to thank Kate, Will, Paul and John for all contributing to Ivar's journey at one point or another. Each of you has left your mark upon his tale, at its beginning or its end, and I owe you all everything for the opportunity and the feedback.

As ever I would like to thank my family, loved ones, and friends, who offered their boundless support as I wrestled with the trials upon the page. I would especially like to thank my parents, who have never faltered in their support of my work. My wife, Anne-Sophie, and our cats – Whiskey and Cosmo – for all the emotional support while I ran with the packs. Thanks also to my hobby circle, for always being there for me when I didn't believe in myself, with a special mention for Mark-Anthony, the best novelist I've never read.

Like the Wolves of Fenris, there is a proud and strong lineage with their fiction. This novel truly stands on the shoulders of giants. Dan Abnett, Chris Wraight, William King and others all contributed to my reading and research pile. I hope I have done them proud.

ABOUT THE AUTHOR

Marc Collins is a speculative fiction author living and working in Glasgow, Scotland. His first works for Black Library were the Warhammer Crime novel *Grim Repast*, and the short story 'Cold Cases'. Since then he has written the Warhammer 40,000 novels *Void King, Helbrecht: Knight of the Throne, Krakenblood*, the Dawn of Fire title *The Martyr's Tomb*, and the Horus Heresy novel *Eidolon: The Auric Hammer*. When not dreaming of the far future he works in Pathology with the NHS.

MORE FROM
BLACK LIBRARY

MASTER OF RITES
by Rob Young

The Khorsari Reach has been lost to the Imperium for over a decade, locked behind the warp storms that cling to the edges of the Great Rift. Its worlds have been claimed by the Death Guard, its people slaughtered by the servants of the Plague God. But these are the worlds of Ultramar, and they are protected.